THE
ILLUMINATI

Larry Burkett

A
JANET
THOMA
BOOK

THOMAS NELSON PUBLISHERS
Nashville

Published in Nashville, Tennessee, by Thomas Nelson, Inc., and distributed in Canada by Lawson Falle, Ltd., Cambridge, Ontario.

All scripture quotations are paraphrased.

Library of Congress Cataloging-in-Publication Data

Burkett, Larry.
    The illuminati / Larry Burkett.
      p.   cm.
    "A Janet Thoma book."
    ISBN 0-8407-7685-3 (pbk.)
    I. Title.
PS3552.U7243I45   1991
813'.54—dc20

                                    91-24026
                                    CIP

Printed in the United States of America

7 — 96 95 94 93

CONTENTS

ACKNOWLEDGMENTS

Obviously this is a book unlike any I have ever written before. Prior to *The Illuminati* I had written nonfiction only. It is my sincere desire, as a fiction reader myself, that good, non-offensive fiction be made available to the public. I trust this is the first of many novels that I will write. I would like to say thanks to my editor at Thomas Nelson, Janet Thoma, for all the help and encouragement she provided. Also, thanks to Adeline Griffith for her editing and typing skills, and, very importantly, to my wife, Judy, for her tolerance while I was working on this book (and two nonfiction books).

My biggest concern in writing a novel is that someone may read too much into it. Obviously, I tried to use as realistic a scenario as possible in this story. But it is purely fictional, including the characters, events, and timing. It should not be assumed that it is prophetic in any regard. As best I know, I have a gift for teaching, a talent for writing, and no prophetic abilities beyond that of any other Christian.

Most of all, I trust that you will enjoy reading this book as much as I have enjoyed writing it.

In Christ,
Larry Burkett

P R O L O G U E

THE COLLAPSE
OF AMERICA

On February 16, 2001, the President of the United States scheduled an emergency press conference at the White House to discuss his executive order to suspend the Congress. In normal fashion, half of the media staff were assembled at the White House, while the other half were focused on the Senate.

The hastily assembled media room in the Senate building was packed with news people. The last eight years had been a media dream. First the depression of 1996 had sent millions of Americans into the streets to protest as they saw their homes repossessed and businesses ruined. Then the 2000 election of liberal Senator Mark Hunt to the presidency was a clear mandate to government: Restore the economy and stop the rampant crime wave sweeping the nation.

Hunt's reforms pitted him against the Congress, as funding for essential services was drastically reduced. Now, in an unprecedented move, President Hunt had suspended Congress.

"Ten seconds. Stand by. Rolling."

"Good evening, America. This is the World News Network, coming to you from the floor of the Congress, where for only the second time in the last one hundred years the House has decided to take up the gauntlet and actively seek to impeach a president. It did so once before, in 1974, but then-president Richard Nixon resigned the office before he could be impeached. There is no evidence that President Hunt is considering resigning. In fact, he has all but dared the Congress to try to impeach him.

"Here with me now is Senator John Grant, the senate minority leader and the strongest opponent of President Hunt.

"Senator Grant, what is your reaction to the president's move, and is it constitutional?"

"The president invoked the Balanced Budget Amendment and virtually shut down the Congress. This is an unconscionable decision."

"Explain the Balanced Budget Amendment, Senator."

"It is the constitutional amendment passed during the previous administration, which gives the president line-item veto power to control the flow of funds through the government. It was first used to freeze the United Arabs' assets after they invaded Israel in 1997."

"How has President Hunt used this bill?"

"Just today he announced that all funding for operating the Congress will be suspended for the duration of the fiscal year."

"What exactly does that mean?"

"It means that we can't operate for the next five months. It also means that the president holds the reins of this government, since Congress can't pay its bills."

"Kind of the old 'golden rule,' isn't it, Senator?"

"What?"

"'He who holds the gold makes the rules.'"

"Well, the president may think so, but I'm about to show him he's dead wrong. I believe there are enough votes in the Congress to bring him to trial. His actions are clearly unconstitutional."

In his earpiece the commentator heard his director comment, "Keep it up. This is the best stuff since the Nixon investigation. Our Insta-pol shows that we have over 70 percent of Americans watching us right now. Hold it a minute. We have a news bulletin coming in now from the White House. Stand by, we're going to the White House now. . . ."

"Senator Grant, we have just received an urgent message from the White House. Please stand by while we get this latest update."

The life-sized monitors in the newsroom sprang to life. The familiar face of Linda Lipsey, WNN White House correspondent, appeared on the screen. "I'm standing in the press room of the White House now, where the president will be addressing the nation in just a moment," she reported. Even as she spoke, the door adjoining the press room and the Oval Office opened, and President Hunt strode through, flanked by secret service agents. The room, which had housed so many past briefings with other presidents, seemed to take on a life of its own with news people and their crews pushing and shoving each other for the best positions.

President Mark Hunt was dressed in his usual, gray pin-striped Shap Brothers suit. His black hair, with only the hint of gray around the temples, gave him the appearance of a Hollywood-cast politician.

A hush came over the room as the president stepped to the podium with the familiar presidential seal emblazoned on it.

Cal Rutland, the president's ever-present aide, took his place behind and a little to the left side of the podium. And, as he did, Linda involuntarily shuddered. She had covered three presidents for the network and had always worked well with their press contacts, but Rutland was somehow different. His cold, dead eyes were shadows of evil with no sign of life in them. *Or, maybe, no soul,* she thought.

The normal fanfare surrounding a presidential press conference was totally absent. Clearly each member of the attending press sensed the sobriety of the occasion. There was tension in the room.

A solemn President Hunt began, "Ladies and gentlemen, I have something to say that is of the most critical importance to our nation. I wanted the American people to hear this announcement directly. That is why I called this briefing.

"As you well know, fellow citizens, our nation is struggling for its very economic survival. As your president, I am empowered to invoke the Balanced Budget Amendment to reestablish the stability of our monetary system. I have chosen to do this by two methods: First, I have authorized the national budget director's office to freeze all government spending until a new budget can be drafted that will match our income and expenses. Second, I have authorized the implementation of a new electronic monetary system known as 'Data-Net' that will restabilize our currency. Without this, my advisers tell me, the entire economy might collapse. But even with these changes, the crisis is not past. With the escalation of tensions in the Middle East and the disastrous increase in petroleum prices, we face the possibility of a worldwide depression.

"Clearly the Congress lacks the will or the courage to deal with this crisis, despite my consistent warnings that action must be taken quickly."

Senator Grant nearly leaped out of his chair when he heard the president's last statement. "Lies! Lies!" Grant muttered through clenched teeth. Common sense told Grant it was useless to rail at a monitor. *I'll wait my time,* he thought, trying to control his anger. *As minority leader, the networks will want my rebuttal.* Shifting his attention back to the screen, he heard:

"Congress has recently attempted to usurp my authority and return control of the economy to the greedy self-interest groups whose policies got us into this disaster. I simply cannot allow that to happen. I feel too great a compassion for the millions of jobless, whose families will suffer through no fault of their own.

"Reluctantly, I have suspended the funding for this session of Congress," the handsome president stated in an apologetic tone. "Until this crisis is passed, I am declaring a national emergency and assuming total responsibility for the nation's welfare. Earlier this morning I instructed the Justice Department to initiate the necessary petition to the Supreme Court. At two o'clock this afternoon, by a margin of five to four, the justices confirmed my actions. I am therefore reallocating $800 million, appropriated to the Congressional operating budget, to the government Jobs Services Program.

"Remember, fellow Americans, we are all in this together. You have elected me as your leader to make these very difficult decisions. We cannot allow those who would use your grief for their own benefit to destroy what we have worked so hard to build. Thank you, and good evening."

With that the president walked off the platform and through the open door that led to his office, leaving the stunned press crews behind.

JEFF WELLS

The events leading up to the congressional showdown in February, 2001, had actually begun two years earlier under the most unlikely circumstances. With the presidential elections coming up the next year, three probable candidates were vying for the position. Senate Majority Leader Mark Hunt was running under the banner of progressive leadership to stop the nation's economic slide into a major depression. Considered a radical liberal by many within his own party, he was finding it difficult to garner the support he needed to replace the incumbent president, Andrew Kilborne. Even with the economic problems, Kilborne was considered to be the Democratic party's best hope.

The wild card was the ultra-liberal Governor Jerry Crow of California. His main appeal was to the fanatics that made up the National Civil Liberties Union, the Gay Power Society, and the National Organization for Women's Rights.

In one of those strange turn of events, an incident at the California Institute of Technology would change the whole complexion of the presidential race and the country.

For decades, an enormous earthquake had been predicted for the California coast. Recent minor tremors had been interpreted as forerunners of the "big one." In a coordinated effort, designed to more accurately predict the location and intensity of the quake, a study group had been established at Cal Tech which brought together some of the best talent available. After several weeks of exhaustive research, the group was preparing to consolidate its findings and issue a statement to the government's office of geological study at the Livermore Laboratory in California.

Most of the research group reached the same conclusions; the earthquake would hit the San Francisco Bay area with a force of approximately 6 on the Richter scale. However, one of the group, a doctoral candidate by the name of Jeff Wells, had reached a radically different conclusion. Working from a uniquely different perspective, Wells predicted that the big quake, with a magnitude of at least 8.2, would occur beneath the islands of Japan between January and May of 1999.

As Dr. Jack Rhinehart, the project leader, handed Jeff's paper back, his sarcasm was evident as he addressed his assembled team. "Well, it seems that young Mr. Wells is fallible after all. According to his calculations, or his miscalculations I should say, he has the earthquake occurring next year, and about four thousand miles west of here. Thankfully for us, that will not happen, especially since he shows the epicenter to be in Tokyo, rather than San Francisco, as the correct equations show."

Jeff blushed when the entire group laughed, but he took the teasing good naturedly. Then, looking down at his calculations, he said courageously, "I'm sorry, sir, but I am correct. The other calculations are wrong."

Professor Rhinehart wheeled around, his eyes flashing with anger. "Just who do you think you are, young man? These equations came from the computer center at Livermore Laboratory. Do you actually think your program is right and theirs is wrong?"

To Rhinehart's utter amazement Jeff answered, "Yes, sir, I do. You see, I built in variables to compensate for some additional geological indicators. I believe there are signs in previous test data pointing to a major build-up in the primary plate area under Japan."

"How could you possibly know that?" the professor questioned. No sooner had the words left his lips than he regretted saying them. Suddenly he sounded like the student and Jeff the instructor.

Jeff responded quietly but confidently, "It's just that in setting up the equation I noticed there might be an additional factor that had not been taken into consideration. My equation indicates that the next major quake will be much stronger than expected and centered over the plate convergence in the Pacific. Basically that's right under the population center of Tokyo. Maybe you could have Livermore check it out."

With that, the whole group roared. The idea of having one of the premier computer centers in the world, noted for its physics in tracking and predicting earthquakes, recheck its program equation because a junior instructor said they were wrong, was laughable. Only Professor Rhinehart didn't share in the humor.

His eyes still flashing with anger, Rhinehart challenged Jeff, hoping to belittle him. "I'll make you a deal, Mr. Master Programmer. I'll have Livermore recheck your equations. When they are proven wrong, you will apologize to this group."

After a brief pause, Jeff asked cautiously, "And, what if I'm right?"

"What did you say?" Rhinehart growled as he slammed the papers down on the desk in front of him.

"What if my analysis is correct, sir? Will you notify the proper authorities so preparations can be made? An earthquake of this magnitude in Japan will generate a fairly significant tidal wave."

Rhinehart snapped back, "I will personally call the news media and notify them of your electrifying revelation. I worked on the program in question myself; that's how I know it cannot be wrong. We had nearly thirty mathematicians working with us, checking every possible iteration."

"I don't see how they missed this, then," Jeff said. "I found a paper written by Dr. Landill of the JPL space division on the influence of gravitational forces on satellite orbits. From his calculations, it seems clear that changes in the earth's gravitational forces cause variations in low earth satellites. So I factored in the variations in the orbits of these satellites over the western Pacific. I believe the results are fairly conclusive."

The meeting ended with Professor Rhinehart furiously cramming the papers into his battered briefcase. He was tired of all the talk about the genius Jeff Wells, whose IQ topped out well above the maximum 180 registered by conventional tests. Faculty gossip just added to the boy-genius myth. It was rumored that Wells had developed a complete, computerized star chart by the time he was twelve.

When one of the physics professors said he had seen a program written by Jeff that computed the orbits of all the man-made satellites, Professor Rhinehart had retorted, "So what? So has the group at the Jet Propulsion Lab." The other professor had countered with, "Yes, but Wells did his at age fifteen from information supplied by magazines and on a PC!"

Much of Rhinehart's negative attitude was because he had been the rising star as a student at Cal Tech and then later as a research faculty member. He was not about to share the limelight with anyone. So when Wells was recruited to do his graduate work at Cal Tech, the "green-eyed monster" reared its head.

"He had better breaks than I did early on," Rhinehart said defensively whenever he heard anyone lauding Wells' abilities in the faculty lounge. "His mother was a research scientist and adviser to Presidents Kennedy and Johnson. With her as a tutor, he couldn't help but succeed."

The more he was around Jeff Wells, the more miserable Rhinehart felt because inside he knew Wells was a whole level above his own intellect. Wells had a singular gift of being able to take very complex equations and reduce them to simplified programs that would run on just about any computer system to which he had access.

Rhinehart had done everything in his power to keep Wells off the geological research project. But in the end the final selection had been made by the faculty team, and Jeff Wells was the first student selected to assist the senior staff. He was resigned to the fact that he could not block Wells' appointment to the project, so the professor shifted his energy to making Jeff's life as miserable as possible—a task for which Jack Rhinehart was well suited.

I've got him now, Rhinehart thought gleefully as he hastened to maximize on Wells' single error thus far. He called his counterpart at Livermore, Dr. William Eison. "Bill, this is Jack Rhinehart. I need your help."

"Good to hear from you, Jack," the burly mathematician on the other end said, but he was thinking *I wonder what this jerk wants. I was hoping I was rid of him when he went up to Cal Tech.*

"One of our research students ran our seismology equations through the university's computers and came out with some different results. Obviously he's made an error and my equations are correct, but I'd like to have you run them through your system."

Yeah, in other words, there's a new star on the horizon and you want to extinguish his light real quick, the Livermore scientist added silently. "Okay, Jack, I'll run your numbers through Gerta, but we cooked that program three ways from Sunday already. If there was a flaw, I think we would have caught it. What does your whiz kid think he's found anyway? Have we missed the blow off of Mount Saint Helens again?" Eison asked.

"No, but listen to this! He says his equations show the big quake will hit Japan some time early next year, and it will be about an eight."

"You're kidding! I'll be sure to run his numbers twice. If he's right, I'll move to Arizona and buy some beach-front property."

"You don't mean to say that you think his figures could be right, do you?" Rhinehart asked incredulously.

"Most probably not," the overweight scientist said as he shifted his sagging paunch under his belt. *I've got to get on that diet one of these days,* he thought. *Too much cafeteria food.* "But who knows when it comes to computers? I still don't really trust 'em. One of these days we'll all be taking orders from one of 'em if we're not real careful."

"Probably so," Rhinehart agreed. "Idiot," he said aloud after he hung up the phone.

Two days later Jack Rhinehart was roused out of a sound sleep by the electronic beeping of his telephone. "Yes, who is it?" he growled into the receiver.

"Rhinehart, it's Eison. That kid who ran these numbers . . . who is he?"

"He's a doctoral candidate by the name of Jeff Wells. Why? Why are you calling at six in the morning anyway?"

"We've been at these numbers for the last twenty hours and we can't find a flaw in his logic. It looks like your whiz kid has hit upon the greatest discovery in seismology since the seismograph was invented."

"You mean to say you believe his calculations?" Rhinehart shouted as he bolted upright up in bed. "But that's nonsense. He doesn't know beans about earthquakes."

"Maybe not, but I can tell you this, his insight is like none I've ever seen in my sixty-two years. We need him here as quickly as possible. Some of our boys don't fully grasp how his equation works. It would appear that he has created a three-dimensional relationship."

"A three-dimensional equation? That's impossible," Rhinehart sputtered.

"Never say 'impossible,' " Eison said with an air of contempt in his tone. "Einstein was working on three-dimensional equations in his last days, but he coded everything so nobody has been able to crack it since. Maybe your boy is the one. Whatever . . . we're sending the jet down to John Wayne Airport to pick him up in an hour. Have him there."

Depression swept over the scrawny instructor as he heard this news. *A dumb kid is going to get the recognition I should have,* he thought as he slipped his heavy glasses on. "I'll come up with him, Bill."

"Sorry, we don't need more hands right now, and we're gonna be overrun with reporters and politicians when this news breaks."

After hanging up the phone, Rhinehart sat in numbed silence. Then he called one of his lab assistants and told him to notify Wells of the waiting plane. He was fuming when he slammed the phone down. "There's no justice," he moaned. "No justice at all."

That plane ride to the Livermore Laboratory would change Jeff Wells' life forever. For the next three days he was bombarded with questions about how he had devised the quantum equations used to integrate all the billions of bits of data used in his calculations.

Jeff spent hours sitting around the big conference table in the "think tank" room at Livermore, trying to explain his equations to the ten top physicists at the research facility. Often in frustration they would throw up their hands and demand that Jeff diagram his concept on the chalkboard. More often than not, all this accomplished was more frustration.

One day as he was being questioned, Jeff stood and leaned over the table, his big frame giving him more the appearance of a linebacker than a scientist. "I can't explain what I don't understand myself," he said politely. "Somehow I just see problems in more than one dimension. I don't have to think about it. Usually the equations just come to mind."

"But I don't understand, Dr. Wells," one of the obviously frustrated mathematicians said gruffly as he leaned forward in his chair in a manner meant to impress his colleagues. "Who taught you to do this?"

"No one taught me, I guess," Jeff responded as he sat back down in his chair. "And it's not 'Doctor.' It's just plain Jeff."

The red-faced scientist sat back in his chair, careful not to notice the smirks on the faces of several of the less-stuffy scientists.

The focus of the conference shifted from questioning Jeff on his formula to why he predicted the earthquake to be imminent and centered in the Tokyo area. He explained his computations to the small group of scientists, who were transfixed at not only what they heard but what they saw.

Jeff pushed a button recessed into the table top, swinging a hidden computer keyboard into position. As he began to type in the commands that initialized his program, the only sound that could be heard in the room was the slight mechanical ring of the plastic keys as he punched the data in. As if in unison with his actions, the wall on the opposite end of the room divided and began to retract into a hidden cavity, revealing a wall-sized computer screen.

Dr. Eison, along with Jeff, had labored several days to convert Jeff's program to operate on the massive Cray computer system nicknamed "Gerta."

The display screen, covering nearly the entire wall, sprang to life. A computer-generated model of the earth was displayed in full color: The oceans were painted a light shade of blue and the land masses reflected variations of green and brown. The known geological faults were displayed as red dashed lines, and small glistening satellites circled the globe at all heights and directions.

Jeff began to demonstrate his program while Dr. Eison discussed the concept of using variations in the satellites' orbits to monitor changes in the earth's magma. By the end of the thirty-minute session, those in attendance were believers.

Later that day, Jeff was asked to repeat the demonstration for the benefit of the entire Livermore scientific team and the reporters who had been invited.

"No one can be absolutely certain of the timing of a major earthquake," Jeff said as he sat down at the computer console and began initiating his program once again. "The difficulty is that the forces are released as the earth's plates slide past each other. Friction can cause the force to build up and suddenly release or skip, much the same as when you press chalk against a chalkboard. Sometimes it slides along; other times it grates and skips."

When he heard Dr. Eison clear his throat and noticed the frowns from some of the attending seismologists, Jeff realized he had committed a *faux pas;* he had taken a complex technical subject and reduced it to laymen's terms. That made a big hit with the press, but it rankled those who made their living by keeping things complicated.

"Anyway," he continued, "Dr. Landill of JPL Labs documented minute changes in the orbits of several satellites throughout the last two decades, which were unaccountable except for changes in the earth's gravitational field. These were thought to be random changes and largely ignored, except by the satellite trackers. I felt they might be related to earthquakes on the surface so I programmed an equation to factor in these changes with the known epicenters of recent quakes."

"Impossible," argued one of the scientists who had missed the earlier session. "We have been trying for years to accumulate and process that kind of data. We can't do it even on the Cray 1612, and it has thirty billion bytes of RAM."

"I believe you can now," Jeff responded confidently as he pressed the "enter" key on the big console. Instantly the full-sized screen on the wall blossomed into a scaled replica of the earth in three dimensions, just as it had in the earlier demonstration. With each stroke of the keys, more detail came into focus. Suddenly satellites began spinning around the globe, each in its own unique orbit.

As Jeff manipulated his program, the red lines began to appear once more on the earth's surface. "These represent active known faults," he explained for the benefit of the reporters and scientists who had missed the earlier session. "Notice how the orbits of the satellites crossing over the fault lines cause them to shift."

The shift in the orbits of the low-altitude satellites was the most dramatic; the high-altitude satellites had the least reaction.

Jeff explained, "I have exaggerated the orbital variations to make them more measurable. The satellite orbits you see on the screen are amplified by a factor of ten to the fourth power." Even the most stoic scientists stared in awe as they watched the computer-enhanced graphics display the orbits of several hundred satellites superimposed over fault lines in the earth's surface. Each knew that what he was seeing was as revolutionary to the field of geology as the splitting of the atom was to physics.

"How can we be sure that your program is accurately depicting these changes and not creating them?" someone in the group asked.

"I thought that might be a possibility too," Jeff replied patiently, "so I applied the equation to some past seismic activity to verify the results."

Swiftly moving his fingers across the keys, Jeff initiated another sub-routine. The screen shifted from a total earth view to the continent of Asia. A dark red line dominated the landscape.

"This was the site of the 1996 earthquake in Beijing, China," he said, still typing in commands. "It measured 6.7 and resulted in the loss of approximately 1.5 million lives. As you can see, the actual date and magnitude are displayed on the screen. Thus far, this is historical data gathered from seismographic devices in the area. Now we'll roll the program back and use only the data known before November 16, 1996—the actual date of the disaster."

As Jeff typed in the commands, an observer in the back of the room was drafting a memo to his boss. It read: "Senator Mark Hunt. Believe I have found the man to analyze computer capabilities. He is Jeff Wells, a student at California Institute of Technology. You'll read about his work shortly. Cal." He made a mental note to fax the memo as soon as possible.

Jeff demonstrated his program, using only the information available before the actual earthquake in China. The results were inconclusive. Then he punched up another overlay that included the satellites passing over the area. "This is data from Dr. Landill's observations," he noted. Suddenly, the program came alive. A warning indicator flashed on the screen with an arrow pointing directly at the city of Beijing. The program then showed a steadily increasing probability of a major earthquake, predictable as much as two years in advance. As time progressed, the calculations became more and more precise until one month before the disaster the warning sign shifted to an alarm predicting an earthquake on the order of 6.5 to 6.8 on the Richter scale. The orbit of a low-orbit U.S. spy satellite developed what looked like a wobble on the expanded scale of the computer-enhanced program.

Finally, using data from several other lesser quakes, Jeff demonstrated the capabilities of his program. "It is not as accurate with smaller quakes," he apologized. Some of the less stuffy scientists chuckled.

"That's like apologizing for the brush strokes in the Mona Lisa," one of them muttered, setting the entire room into laughter—with a few exceptions.

"With some more refinement, I believe we will be able to predict major earthquakes accurately, both in time and magnitude," Dr. Eison added from his position next to Jeff. "We'll take this prototype program and work out the details. Show them the real thing, Jeff," he said somberly.

As his fingers flashed across the keyboard, Jeff progressed to the last stroke necessary and then halted.

Dr. Eison announced, "Ladies and gentlemen, what you are about to see has already been screened and verified by members of my staff. For the immediate future, it cannot be made public. That is the responsibility of President Kilborne and his national security adviser. You will be advised when the information can be announced."

"Okay, Jeff. Proceed," Dr. Eison said as he sat back down.

The screen shifted back to the global picture of the earth. Then, as it rotated slowly, the image first zoomed in on the North American continent. Then the United States. Finally, the state of California filled the entire twenty-foot screen.

Jeff stroked more keys and small red lines began to appear on the outline of the state.

"These are fault centers," Dr. Eison explained. "At present, they have not been given an intensity value."

As Jeff tapped more keys, the red images shifted to bright and dark shades. The brightest appeared in the lower third of the state's image, very near Los Angeles. A second lighter red image appeared in the upper third of the screen, near San Francisco.

Dr. Eison explained, "The image at the top is the San Francisco fault. Conventional wisdom has been telling us the Pacific Plate will rift here. And we have been concentrating our evacuation training here. If you will, please, Jeff."

Jeff changed the image so that the state of California was superimposed over that of the entire globe. Suddenly, satellites appeared, crossing in nearly every conceivable angle.

"These satellites have been provided courtesy of the Russians, the Chinese, the Libyans, and the Japanese," Dr. Eison said in a sarcastic tone. The room erupted with laughter.

As the orbits passed over California, each satellite dipped and wobbled. It looked as if some mighty magnet was trying to dissuade them from passing that way. Homing in on the northern fault, the program began to spit out calculations. Earthquake Predicted: 1999; Location: San Francisco fault; Magnitude: 5.6 to 5.8; Estimated Damage: Minimal.

A hushed sigh went out from those in the room who had family and friends in the Bay area. A major quake had been predicted there for so long that everyone thought the end might come any day, but a 5.8 earthquake was like a popgun to that area; it might rattle a few buildings, but little more.

Without speaking, Dr. Eison motioned to Jeff to continue. The program now zoomed in on the other side of the Pacific rim, namely the southern part of Japan, where another bright red line appeared. Once more the calculations began: Earthquake Predicted: 1999; Location: Tokyo; Magnitude: 8.2 to 8.4; Estimated Damage: 2.3 to 2.5 million deaths.

The gasps made in the room by the non-scientists sounded like a scene from a horror movie, but even as they were trying to comprehend what they had just seen, the image was zooming in even closer. The display showed the city of Tokyo in computer imagery just after the quake struck. Virtually no buildings were left intact in the downtown area. For forty miles around, the program displayed massive fires and destruction.

The next insert read: Residual Tremors Predicted: 6.5, 6.3, 6.0, 5.4, 4.9, 3.5 over the next seventy-two hours. Predict Tokyo uninhabitable for at least twelve months.

Even as the roomful of scientists and reporters was trying to absorb the enormity of it all, the screen shifted again.

Tsunami expected in Pacific basin. Amplitude: 300 feet. Rate of Travel: 300 to 400 mph. Expected Target: Philippine Islands and U.S. West Coast. Inland wave in California predicted at 16 feet.

"The earthquake will create a tidal wave—called a tsunami—that will travel across the Pacific at a rate of three to four hundred miles per hour," Dr. Eison explained. "It will hit the Philippines and California with the force of a multi-megaton bomb. The backwash from the wave will hit the coast of California and will sweep inland, virtually wiping out the Southern coast for at least one mile inland."

"Doctor, do you realize what you're saying?" shouted one of the reporters. "Thirty million people live in the area you describe."

"I realize that all too clearly," Dr. Eison answered solemnly. "I hope we're wrong, but I don't think so."

"What are you planning to do?" asked another reporter. "I live in L.A. and so do several million of our readers."

"That's really not up to me. That is a decision for the governor and the president."

This is our chance to take Governor Crow out of the race, thought Cal Rutland, aide to presidential candidate Mark Hunt. *All we need is a disinformation campaign. . . .*

THE ILLUMINATI

When the news about the predicted California tidal wave hit the media, the public reacted predictably—with panic and outrage. The press demanded that Governor Crow do something. However, there was nothing that Governor Jerry Crow could do to prevent the natural disaster, and his popularity rating dropped dramatically; it was exactly what Mark Hunt's election committee was hoping for.

An avid and vocal gay rights activist, Crow had hopes of being the first gay to run for the presidency under the banner of a major political party. His successful moves to revoke the tax-exempt status of most of California's religious institutions had won him national acclaim. And his petition to the FCC to revoke the licenses of all religious broadcasters in California had launched him on the path to the White House. When the FCC granted his petition, most of the stations were turned over to the gay power groups. This same strategy was used across the country to unseat the several thousand religious broadcasters then in place. With most of those stations under the control of gay power groups, Crow had a national forum.

Although it had been only three weeks since the information from Jeff's program had been made public, to Crow it seemed like a lifetime. Everywhere he went the media were there, asking what he was going to do about the crisis. The pressure drove him back to his old escape mechanism: cocaine.

What do those idiots think I can do about an earthquake? Crow thought angrily as he woke in the aftermath of a severe cocaine crash. He had agreed to kick the habit when he made the run for the presidency; his advisers had told him the country wasn't ready for a president who used drugs. *I'll change that*, he decided as he snorted another line of the white powder. *I'll get drugs legalized and use the tax revenues to build more shelters for the homeless. In fact,* he thought with a stroke of genius, *we'll use those useless church buildings for homeless shelters.* "I'll teach those pious hypocrites," he said aloud. "They're against anything progressive."

Later that morning as the governor was discussing the earthquake with an aide, he quipped, "It might not be so bad to get rid of half the people in Southern California." The aide winced and said, "Don't repeat that in public, Governor. A lot of voters in Southern California wouldn't agree with you."

"They're all a bunch of crazies," he shouted. "What do they expect me to do? Do they think we can just tell an earthquake to go away? I think Hunt's using this thing to make me look bad. Why couldn't a tidal wave hit Virginia?"

The aide looked away from the drug-laced governor with contempt. He knew Rutland was right when he argued that Hunt would be the better candidate. The governor was a disgusting representative for gay power. Maybe the next election. . . .

As with most crises in America, interest began to fade within a few weeks after the initial furor. Several well-known scientists came out against the predictions given by Jeff's program, citing flaws in the logic, particularly the part about the effects on satellite orbits. Governor Crow immediately focused on these, complaining to all who would listen that the whole idea was a plot to discredit him personally.

"We will not be diverted in our efforts to save lives in the area where the earthquake is expected," he announced. "But we simply cannot spend countless millions of dollars on the word of a slightly neurotic college student."

Then on May 12, 1999, an earthquake with a magnitude of 5.4 struck the California coast just north of San Francisco. Since hundreds of thousands of citizens had been evacuated from the area, there was virtually no loss of life, except for the few derelicts sleeping inside abandoned buildings. In fact, there was very little damage to existing structures since new building codes had been initiated after the '96 quake, in which hundreds of lives were lost as several office buildings collapsed.

Immediately Governor Crow issued a statement on public radio and television vindicating the position he had taken on the supposed earthquake in Japan: "As you can see, our plans were right on target. Our evacuation saved hundreds of lives, and the earthquake struck exactly where our experts said it would. Californians can rest easy tonight under the leadership of Jerry Crow."

At the Executive Office Building in Washington, D.C., the phone in Dr. Lowe's office started ringing as soon as the news of the quake in

California was known. Dr. Lowe, the senior technical adviser on President Kilborne's staff, picked up the receiver and heard, "Doctor, this is Cal Rutland. I assume you have seen the news report on the earthquake in California?"

"Yes I have," the tuxedo-clad scientist replied. He was about to attend a formal banquet at the White House for the Japanese ambassador.

"Are you still certain about the other event?" Rutland asked, referring to a conversation they had had the day after the Livermore press conference.

"Yes. As a matter of fact, I was just preparing a report for the president on the need to evacuate the Southern California coast. I can find no flaw in Wells' prediction of a Pacific tidal wave."

"We don't think that will be in the best interest of our candidate, Dr. Lowe. We would like for you to advise the president that you disagree with Wells' conclusions."

"But this report is conclusive," Lowe argued. "When that quake hits the Japanese islands, we'll have a wave on the West Coast that will rival the destruction of Pompeii."

"Doctor, sometimes the few must be sacrificed for the good of the many. Remember the group to which you have sworn allegiance. Ours is the responsibility for building a better, more secure world for future generations. With the governor refusing to act and the president taking no action, the support for Senator Hunt will increase."

"But I will be finished in the scientific community when it gets out that I ignored this data," Lowe contended as he slumped back in his old leather chair.

"We'll make sure that when the facts are known, Doctor, they will show that you recommended immediate action by the president but he chose to ignore your advice. You will be exonerated totally. Just say nothing—other than sending a memo directed to President Kilborne's eyes only."

"You can do that?" the startled scientist asked.

"There is very little we cannot do, Doctor. We have been preparing for this election for a very long time. Longer than anyone outside can imagine."

Lowe shuddered involuntarily as he listened to Rutland's plan. The destruction that a tsunami of that magnitude would cause was almost incalculable. "Are you absolutely certain about this earthquake?" Rutland asked coldly.

"No one can be entirely sure of something like an earthquake," Lowe replied cautiously. His hedging was conditioned by years of political maneuvering. "But I have reviewed the data from Wells' program very carefully and I believe it is accurate—even brilliant."

"You had better be right, Doctor. We cannot afford to make Governor Crow into a viable candidate at this time. We're too close to our goal now," Rutland said sharply.

"I understand," Lowe assured him. "I want this just as much as you do."

"Just remember that the Society makes no allowances for failure!" Rutland said coldly.

Rutland represented a group that had actually been formed nearly three hundred years earlier in Europe, and the group from which they sprang had been formed centuries before that—when the Roman Empire was little more than a few loosely knit tribes.

The original group had been known as Druids. They were the titled gentry of Middle East traders who had developed from tribes of roving bandits. The Druids became a vicious, secret society dedicated to the preservation of their members at all costs. Nothing was beyond their order of "ethics," including murder, kidnapping, and slavery.

Later the Druids took on a nearly supernatural aura in the minds of the simple people they dominated. Their wealth and power made it possible for them to operate outside the confines of the law. Those who opposed them would simply disappear, never to be seen or heard from again. Thus, rumors circulated that the Druids had the power to make people vanish. As the stories were told from generation to generation, they were elaborated and exaggerated. Eventually the Druids were equated with demons and various gods.

So similar were the men who inherited leadership in each successive generation, they seemed to be the reincarnate images of their predecessors. Thus also began the legend of eternal life within the Druids: reincarnation. In truth, it was the intense dedication to a single organization and centuries of exacting training that kept the group so uniform and seemingly reincarnate. However, these legends served the purposes of the men who served the organization and were therefore preserved and promoted.

As Europe developed into the dominant economic center of the civilized world, the Druids saw their influence waning because few Europeans were interested in or impressed by the superstitions of the Middle East. To extend their influence in Europe, the Druids changed their name to the Freemasons and adopted many of the same rituals and religious traditions practiced within the Christian churches. These rituals, mixed with Eastern mysticism, resulted in almost instant acceptance.

Immediately many of the leaders of society were wooed into the order of the Freemasons, and they in turn brought in many of the second social level who were anxious to associate with the elite. From the Freemasons, a small group of world leaders emerged, dedicated to the establishment of a worldwide order, known as the "Illuminati," or "the enlightened"; later they would be known only as the "Society." Each member of this group was carefully chosen from the larger group of Freemasons. Each represented the highest level of authority within his particular discipline. Thus the group contained not only political figures, but also religious, economic, academic, and military leaders.

The group flourished from just after the time of Christ until the fifteenth century in Europe. When the New World was discovered and the pathways to America opened up, leading members of the Freemasons were sent with the earliest pilgrims to ensure their foothold on the new continent.

By the time of the Revolutionary War in America, most prominent American leaders were counted among the Freemasons. As centuries passed countries came and went, along with their rulers, but the Masons continued to flourish. Eventually the movement in America spread to the common man and millions of working class people were recruited to the order of Freemasons, thus ensuring their acceptance in a democratic society.

But always at the top, unknown to all but the very few, was the ruling body known as the Society. This group made decisions determining which wars were to be fought and how they were to be funded. By the time of the First World War, their economic power was so great that governments could be toppled simply by the movement of money and support as directed by this group. Generations passed and the old line died off, but still the Society persisted.

Now, nearly two hundred and fifty years after America had become a nation, the Society was stronger than ever, and its original purpose was becoming a reality: a one-world economic system, controlled and directed by this shadowy group of the most influential men (and now women) in the world.

For hundreds of years the Society had been taught that a chosen one, or "Leader," would rise to bind the world into a single economic unit. Several times in history men had risen to positions of power from the inner circle of the Society to grasp the reins of power. Notable among them in the twentieth century were Lenin, Hitler, and Mao Tse-tung. But the time was not right for the one-world system, and each in his own time had been subverted and ultimately defeated.

Little known to the rest of the world at the time was that the purges executed by Stalin in Russia were to eliminate the order of Freemasons that threatened his power base. His attempt to demolish the

Society doomed communism to oblivion as the Society directed an economic attack against the party. By the late 1980s, when another Russian leader was appointed to the inner circle, the economies of both
Russia and China were virtually destroyed. The Russian economy was
steered back to prosperity under the control of the Society.

The Society in America progressed on a parallel track to that of
Europe. Because of the enormous economic wealth of the United
States, it was necessary for the Society to organize yet another group of
influential leaders who would serve as advisers to the inner circle. This
group became known as the Council on Foreign Relations. Comprised
of some of the best-trained minds in America, the Council eventually
took on a semi-official government position as advisers, not only to the
Society, but to presidents as well.

Thus, a system of governments within governments developed
worldwide, the ultimate purpose being a base of power from which
the "Leader" could control the entire world.

In the computer room at Andrews Air Force Base, Jeff Wells was
developing a program to calculate the effects of the tsunami on the
California coast. What he read in the printouts made him wish he
hadn't looked. He checked and rechecked his equations because it
seemed no one was taking his prediction seriously.

"The coasts of Southern California and Mexico should be evacuated," he had told Dr. Eison. He was sure that Eison agreed with his
conclusions, yet even he had failed to do anything about it.

Jeff thought, *Here I am—hidden away in a government facility,
isolated from the press and their questions. It is almost as if someone
wants the disaster to occur.* His thoughts were interrupted when he
heard, "Mr. Wells?"

"Yes," Jeff answered, as he was startled back to reality.

"Come with me," Rutland said. It was more a command than a
request.

"Where are we going? I have a lot of work to do," Jeff replied
defensively, even while he was getting to his feet. The look in Rutland's
eyes had put him in motion. And without any further word, Rutland
held the door, clearly indicating he expected to exit immediately.

"I'd like some answers," Jeff said with as much gusto as he could
muster. "Why am I being detained?"

"You'll get all the answers you want," Rutland said with a sem-
blance of courtesy. But his eyes revealed what his lips didn't; he had no
intention of discussing the matter.

Jeff followed Rutland to another part of the building, to an office
where Senator Mark Hunt was waiting, seated in a leather chair be-

hind a large desk. As they entered, the senator spoke. "Ah, young Mr. Wells, I presume."

"Yes," Jeff replied, recognizing the senator immediately. He had read much about Senator Hunt in the newspapers over the last several months, as had everyone in the country. Most of the media proclaimed him to be the answer to the nation's troubles.

With the economy in its thirtieth month of recession and more than twenty million Americans unemployed, a change of administration was certain, and the front-runners were Senator Hunt and Governor Crow. According to the papers President Kilborne still had a chance, but only if the economy took an unexpected turnaround. Personally, Jeff liked Kilborne. He had a lot of good ideas, but he was saddled with an economy so weighted down with debt that many predicted another five years of recession before it would begin to recover.

Jeff was greeted with a warm smile as Senator Hunt motioned for him to sit down in the chair nearest his desk. Cal Rutland took a chair across the room, as if to become a spectator.

"I assume you know who I am, Jeff?"

"Yes, sir," Jeff said honestly, relaxing a bit as he felt the personal warmth of Hunt's smile and courtesy.

"I won't try to snow you, Jeff . . . uh, may I call you Jeff?"

"Yes, of course," the young scientist replied.

"Good! I understand you're some kind of computer whiz. Is that right, Jeff?"

"Well, I don't know about that, Senator Hunt," Jeff said hesitantly.

"Please. Call me Mark. And don't be so humble. I like men who are the best at what they do. If I'm going to lead this country out of the mess it's in, I'm going to need men who are confident of their own abilities." He glanced across the room at his aide as he added, "Cal here thinks you're the best at what you do. Or you're going to be." Cal twisted a bit in his chair but remained silent.

"I need your help, Jeff," Hunt continued. "When I'm elected president, we're going to need to bring this nation's economic system out of the dark ages, and it will take all of us working together to do it. We can no longer hide our heads in the sand."

"But Sena . . . uh Mark, I don't know anything about economics. Surely you have advisers who . . ."

Hunt didn't let him finish. "I have plenty of people who understand how economics used to work, Jeff. We don't need those old-fashioned ideas anymore. We must either become innovators or become a third-rate power. My administration will have the best minds working on the economic models. What I will need most is that computer brain of yours. Cal tells me you stumped the boys at Livermore."

"Well, I don't know, sir. They didn't want to believe what my program predicted."

"Idiots, Jeff. You remember that. They are idiots! It's the same mentality that is trying to hold this country back. I want you to learn all there is to know about how the world banking system operates. Then I want you to design a computer system that will connect every computer in the world to each other."

Jeff wasn't sure he had heard correctly. "Link all the computers to a common data network? Why that would take a computer larger than . . ."

Hunt interrupted to say, "I don't care what it takes, Jeff. We have the same kind of idiots working at the World Bank that you saw at Livermore. Dr. Eison and a few enlightened souls will cooperate. Your job will be to galvanize them into a working team, and Cal will handle the others," he said as he glanced across the room at Rutland.

"You see, Jeff, everyone we have contacted so far says that it would take a computer that doesn't exist yet to do what I want. But let's not worry about that now. I want you to design a program that will make the 'Data-Net' work now."

"The 'Data-Net'?" Jeff queried.

"Yes, that's what we're going to call the system. I want the McDonald's in Moscow to be able to talk to the McDonald's in Paducah, just like I can with my bank. And I want every transaction to go through one central location here in America. We will become the clearinghouse for every transaction in the world. Can you do it?"

"I don't know, Senator Hunt," Jeff replied, reverting to the formality he felt most comfortable with. It was hard for Jeff to call someone of the senator's stature by his first name. "But I would like to see some data to evaluate. Maybe some from the Federal Reserve."

"We'll do better than that, Jeff," the senator said excitedly as he got to his feet and started around the desk. He leaned against the edge of the desk near Jeff. "We already have you cleared to review the existing World Bank System in Brussels that was started by the Kennedy administration back in the sixties. You'll have full access to all records."

"You can do that?" Jeff was clearly impressed.

"You'll discover that we can do a lot, Jeff. There are many people in the world who think it's time to link it all together. You just get that brain of yours to perking on the problem."

"One thing, though," Cal Rutland interjected suddenly from his spectator position across the room. "Don't mention to anyone that you're working with the senator. If the press finds out, they will make an issue out of it."

Hunt straightened to his feet, walked back around to his chair, and, looking at Cal with some disdain, he said, "If you had let me finish, I was going to talk to Jeff about that."

A quick glance at the senator's aide revealed to Jeff what he thought was a glimmer of hatred in those dark eyes. Jeff was getting a bit nervous and involuntarily rubbed his hands together. He recalled what he had heard his father say often when he was a child. "In the real world the big fish eat the little fish . . ." and then he would add, "unless the little fish is a piranha." Jeff suspected that Cal Rutland was one of the piranhas.

Just then, Jeff thought of something else. "I've got a problem, Senator. I've still got classes that will start soon at Cal Tech."

"Jeff, when your predicted earthquake hits, I think I can guarantee you a Ph.D., based on your work. That is, if there is anything left of Cal Tech."

Even as he spoke, Mark Hunt knew he had said too much. A glance at the expression on his aide's face told him that the Society would not take his offhand remarks well. Stiffening a little at Rutland's frown he thought, *So what! I'm the only viable candidate they have.*

"Then you actually believe the wave will hit California?" Jeff asked cautiously.

"I told you I believe in you, Jeff. So if you say it will, I believe it." Even as he spoke, he remembered an earlier meeting with Kilborne in which he had assured the president that Jeff's prediction was not credible. At the press meeting tonight with the Japanese he would dump the whole load on Kilborne.

"Why don't you tell President Kilborne then?" Jeff blurted out with an unexpected surge of courage and emotion.

"Whoa! Just a minute, Jeff," Hunt quickly replied as he looked over at Rutland, who by now was looking away. "I did tell the president, but no one wants to believe it."

"But a million or more people may die," insisted Jeff as his mind reviewed the computerized scenes of the tsunami sweeping inland. "And what about the Japanese?"

"We'll warn them again, Jeff, but right now everyone wants to believe the San Francisco quake was the 'big one.'"

"That's ridiculous," Jeff said defensively. "My program clearly predicted a smaller quake approximately twelve days before the shift in the plates below Japan."

"Twelve days!" Hunt snapped. "Did you tell anyone else about this?"

"Yes, of course I did. I told Dr. Eison at Livermore."

"Well, then, I'm sure the president knows too," the senator said, trying to appear calm. "Maybe they just don't want to believe you, Jeff." Inside, the senator's heart had done a flip. If that quake had hit before the press meeting with the Japanese, he would have lost the edge. Then he realized that the meeting had been scheduled exactly ten days after the California quake. Somewhere inside he felt a tinge of uncertainty. He thought, *They knew, but they didn't tell me. They must have set the time for this evening's meeting. They control Kilborne's schedule too!*

Cal Rutland was perceptive enough to know what was going through the senator's mind, so he stood quickly and said to Jeff, "Well, we should get you back to your work." *Let Hunt wonder why he wasn't told about the timing of the second earthquake*, Rutland decided wordlessly. *The Society has a few more surprises for this pompous idiot.* After a hurried good-bye, Jeff was ushered out of the senator's office, while the senator was slipping on his dinner jacket for Kilborne's reception.

In the next morning's newspaper, the press conference reported how the president's science adviser, Dr. Robert Lowe, had publicly resigned after stating that he had warned President Kilborne that the west coast of California should be evacuated. The article also noted that Senator Mark Hunt had personally urged the president to act while there was still time to warn the people of California and also the Japanese.

The president denied that either his science adviser or Hunt had suggested that the program, created by Cal Tech student Jeff Wells, was believable. However, the reporters present were given documents bearing the president's own initials, proving that Dr. Lowe had notified the president at least twice of the impending danger.

The report in one newspaper read: "President Kilborne was seen storming out of the meeting and has been unavailable for comment. Some members of Congress have suggested that if the predicted wave does strike the California coast, the president should resign. The latest polls show that approximately 70 percent of American voters now believe the potential disaster is imminent. Both President Kilborne and Governor Crow now trail Senator Hunt by at least 20 percentage points."

3

DISASTER STRIKES

I t always amused Haru Ashimo, lead engineer at Nippon Industries in Tokyo, to observe foreigners visiting Japan for the first time when one of the many tremors hit. Tremors that nearly gave most Americans heart failure scarcely fazed the Japanese in multi-story buildings. Western visitors would turn white with fear as the buildings swayed and would often gasp, "What's happening?" Usually the Japanese would simply sit rigidly in their seats waiting for the tremor to subside. A few of the more Westernized might joke by quipping, "I don't know. It might be an earthquake." Then they would pretend to duck under their desks for protection, only to reappear immediately while their Western counterparts cowered beneath desks and tables. Far too polite to laugh, the smiles of the Japanese nonetheless betrayed their amusement at the sight. When the tremors subsided, the Western businessmen would crawl out from under tables red-faced, as they observed the Japanese going quietly about their work.

When the tremor began on May 25th, most of the stoic Japanese just sat placidly, while others gathered the loose items on their desks to keep them from crashing to the floor. They had ridden out many tremors before and accepted them as a common occurrence. Usually the tremors would last only a few seconds at most. The "earthquake-proof" buildings would sway on their huge roller foundations and then settle back into their normal positions.

On this particular Thursday morning, the building at the Nippon Industrial Complex seemed to sway more than usual. Instead of a normal five-second tremor that quickly subsided, this one began to build. The Nippon building, one of the safest in Tokyo, had been constructed to the highest earthquake standards only two years earlier, so the workers felt entirely safe.

Within ten seconds, the building was rocking and lurching like a wild bronco, and for the first time an expression of fear was evident on the Japanese workers' faces.

"My God, the building is going over!" Kimo Sarusso, one of the engineers, shouted over the rumble of the quake.

"Be quiet!" snapped Ashimo from his position at the lead engineer's desk. "This building is designed to withstand earthquakes. It will not fail."

The tremors were now coming with such intensity that the whole building felt as if it was being launched into space. Suddenly a crack appeared in the outer wall where the windows and support structures came together. Ten seconds later the twenty-story building became a massive heap of rubble and broken bodies.

Outside in the streets, people were trying desperately to escape the falling debris from the collapsing structures. Unfortunately, there was no place to hide. Huge chunks of concrete came rocketing down among thousands of people who instinctively threw up their hands to cover their heads.

Upper story windows shattered, showering those below with razor sharp shards of glass. Entire streets were lifted stories high and dashed to the ground, flinging cars and trucks as if they were children's toys. At Tokyo International Airport, jumbo jets on the runway were tossed high into the air, as if thrown by some invisible hand. The giant 797s crashed back onto the tarmac like birds crumpled by a hunter's shotgun blast.

Delta Flight 44 was approaching Tokyo Airport when the first big shock wave hit. The flight controller, Mira Akai, seeing the scope she was watching go blank, had the presence of mind to key her mike and shout, "Delta 44, abort approach and turn to a heading of 213 immediately!"

John Grey, the captain of the 797 Boeing fan jet, immediately applied power to go around. It seemed like an eternity as the big engines spooled up to takeoff power. Out of his window, he saw the runway buckle and bulge toward his aircraft. It all seemed to move in slow motion as a mountain of asphalt rose to meet the floundering aircraft.

"Roger, retract the gear!" Captain Grey shouted to his copilot. The many hours in the simulator now paid off as the copilot reacted instantly to the captain's command and pushed the landing gear control all the way in. The plane rose in response to the reduced drag and began to climb slowly.

"Max power!" Captain Grey ordered. "Firewall it!"

Again the copilot responded as directed and shoved the engine controls full forward to the emergency position.

The big turbo fan engines providing power to the descending aircraft had now spooled to 70 percent of their power curve and the plane wobbled skyward.

"Now if she'll just hang together," Grey shouted over the whine of the engines as he rolled the aircraft to the right in an effort to escape the rising mountain of runway.

The plane just cleared the edge of the runway when the ground erupted into a shower of dirt and debris. The mammoth jet plane vibrated as it was struck by the erupting ground, but it continued to rise above the turmoil.

"Thank God we weren't hit by the pavement," the captain said as the perspiration dripped off his forehead. "It would have been like flying through shrapnel." He eased back on the wheel as the plane continued to climb, now well above the chaos below.

"Man, that's as close as I ever want to see an earthquake," his copilot said as he flexed his hands. He had been gripping the controls so tightly that he had a difficult time moving his fingers.

"Yeah," agreed Gray, "but think about those poor devils down there." He pointed out the window to the ground below. It looked as if a huge plow had cut its path right through the center of the world's busiest airport.

Flying west over the city of Tokyo, the passengers and crew of Delta Flight 44 were witnesses to one of nature's most savage displays of raw power. Every structure in downtown Tokyo was swaying, and hundreds of older buildings had crumbled into piles of debris, surrounded by plumes of dust that obscured the skyline in some areas. Bridges connecting Tokyo with its lifeline of highways had collapsed, throwing hundreds of vehicles into the sea. The tunnel connecting the main island to the outer islands, built at a cost of nearly $12 billion, had broken open, creating a huge siphon as the sea water rushed in.

"Poor devils," Captain Grey said again, despondently. "What an awful way to die—trapped in an undersea tunnel!"

The quake lasted seven minutes, reaching a peak at the epicenter of 8.6. In that seven minutes, three million people were killed in and around Tokyo, and several million more were injured. Virtually all power and communications were cut off from the world's financial center, causing chaos on the world's markets.

Aftershocks would continue to strike the island for the next five days, causing more damage and complicating the rescue process. But in that first seven minutes, nearly $4 trillion worth of property had been destroyed. Many of the world's largest and most sophisticated manufacturing plants dissolved into rubble.

Unknown at that time, an even greater disaster was developing under the Pacific Ocean. There had been earthquake-born waves before in history but never on the scale generated by the Tokyo quake. Historians reported a tsunami hitting the Philippine Islands in 1792 after the eruption of an underwater volcano in the Pacific Basin, north of the Philippine Trench. The wave was estimated to be three hundred feet high in the shallows of the China Sea, and traveled at approximately two to three hundred miles an hour. Several ships at sea were lost and never heard from again, obviously victims of the huge wave. Only the sparse population in the Philippine Islands kept the death toll down to twenty thousand.

Two characteristics of the quake in Japan now combined to create disaster on the far side of the Pacific. First, the plate shift was so massive and violent that the underwater land mass displacement was estimated at six trillion cubic yards, or approximately equal to the size of the state of Georgia. That much mass shifting position pushed an incalculable amount of water ahead of it. Second, the land mass moved in exactly the plane Jeff's program predicted: an easterly direction from the Japanese islands, toward the western United States.

As the volume of water pushed its way beneath the ocean only a slight swell appeared on the surface, but beneath the surface a rip tide some two thousand feet deep and four hundred miles wide was sweeping across the Pacific at a speed of several hundred miles an hour. Even though media services picked up the accounts of the earthquake in Tokyo from airborne observers, such as Flight 44, no hint of the impending disaster approaching the U.S. mainland was reported. An Enterprise-class nuclear submarine traveling four hundred feet below the surface on maneuvers reported the underwater shock wave, but the transmission lasted only twelve seconds before the sub broke into pieces. Underwater sonar detectors used to track Pacific traffic recorded the sounds of the crumpled hulk sinking to the ocean bottom. They also picked up the sounds of two other nearby subs splitting apart like model toys.

Once the underwater wave hit the shelf near the west coast of California, the water backed up and began to force its way to the surface. Billions of tons of water, propelled at more than four hundred miles an hour, became a full-fledged tsunami by the time the wave was three hundred miles from the coast.

In the weather radar tower at Point Magoo, California, Frances Akins was taking her hourly check of the Pacific weather conditions, prior to transmitting the marine report. The sky showed no appreciable accumulation of cumulonimbus, or thunder boomers, as Bill Frank, the local TV weather man, insisted on calling them. *I wonder why they always seem to pick the buffoon types to do the weather on*

TV, Frances thought to herself as she checked weather scopes. *I'm sure he flunked the third grade twice.* Then, as she viewed the radar sweep one more time, something began to appear on her scope.

"What the . . . ?" she exclaimed as the image on the screen began to develop into what looked like a mountain to the west.

"What's the trouble, Frances?" Andy Maury, the station supervisor, asked. Andy had taken over operation of the Magoo weather station after the Navy decided to shut the facility down as part of an economy move during the Kilborne administration. He had thirty years of forecasting experience, including his twenty-three-year stint with the Navy, mostly aboard the big carriers. Not only was he the director, but he was also part owner of the now-private forecasting station, which sold information to the local television stations as well as various marine groups.

"You'd better look at this, Andy," Frances said as she thumped the screen in a characteristic reaction left over from the days when CRTs were run by vacuum tubes. In the environment of integrated circuits and crystal displays, thumping did little but serve to relieve frustrations. Refraining from a second thump, Frances said, "I think the Doppler must be conking out. It shows the ocean is growing a mountain." Even as she spoke the image grew larger; it looked like Mount Rushmore had been transplanted to the Pacific and was headed toward the California coast.

"Well, I'll be . . ." Andy Maury said. "What do we have here?" Even as he spoke his mind signaled an alarm. He had seen a similar image somewhere in his past. "Have you recalibrated the scope lately?" he asked, knowing that Frances would have done so earlier.

"Of course!" she answered indignantly. "I do it before every scan."

"I knew you had, Frances, but I still had to ask," Andy said apologetically. He knew she was a competent meteorologist and was more than slightly sensitive about being the only woman in a crew of ten men.

"I know, Andy," she said in a more contrite tone. "But everything was fine when I started the noon sweep."

In addition to the normal array of meteorological radar gear, the Magoo station had the newest laser equipment, dubbed the Weather Wizard. Although still relatively new equipment, a trained operator, which Frances was, could track a Pacific storm to within a few feet as it approached the mainland. It was this equipment to which they now turned.

"Crank up the laser and point it at your mountain," Maury suggested. "It's probably just a false echo, but I'd like to be sure."

Inside, the station director wasn't nearly as calm as he appeared outside. *I know I've seen this before*, he thought as his mind raced, seeking the answer. *Come on, bring it up*, he chastened his struggling memory. *I know this pattern from somewhere.* . . . Secretly he was praying it was just a simple equipment failure, but deep inside he felt an uneasiness.

Frances quickly cycled the laser "Weather Wizard" through its self-tests. The system was designed to verify squalls and other weather conditions containing solid or liquid particles, such as rain and hail. Its use in tracking rain storms, thunder clouds, tornadoes, and the like was unparalleled in meteorology.

"It's calibrated and ready to go," Frances announced as she flipped the scan indicator to long range.

Suddenly the display screen was filled with the same image that was showing on the Doppler. The automatic alarm on the laser system screeched out its warbling sound, indicating a major obstruction in a scanning field that should have been clear.

"It's a tsunami!" Maury shouted as his mind clicked with the image that was now being displayed on both screens. "I saw one like this in the Navy when an earthquake struck mainland China. Look at the size of that thing! It must be nearly three hundred feet high."

"A tsunami!" Frances repeated as she tried to decipher what that meant. "How could a tsunami just appear from nowhere?"

"It's from the earthquake in Japan," Maury shouted as he reached for the phone. "I'll call Los Angeles International and see what they have." Even as he spoke, he punched the auto dialer to ring the National Weather Service station at the L.A. airport.

The calm greeting from the L.A. tower told Maury they were oblivious to the potential disaster.

"L.A. Weather. Robert Atkins here."

"Bob, this is Andy at Point Magoo. Do you guys have anything on your long-range radar at about 210?"

"Yeah we do, Andy. But we thought we were having an echo blip on the system so we dropped back to the seventy-five mile range. Why do you ask?"

"Because what you saw is not an echo!" Maury literally screamed into the phone. "It's a tsunami heading toward the mainland."

"A tsunami? That's impossible," the head of the National Weather Bureau for the Los Angeles area replied. "This thing just popped up on our screen a few minutes ago. It's got to be an echo."

"I'm telling you it's for real, Bob. It's from that quake in Japan, I think. Probably surged underwater until it hit the shallows. That thing is going to hit your area in less than an hour. You need to get all the planes you can in the air!"

Atkins sat at his desk without responding for several seconds. Was Maury kidding him? He had never heard him say or do anything that was non professional. But a tsunami? "Look, Andy, I appreciate the call, but you must be wrong. How could a tsunami make it across the Pacific without us knowing it? Besides, we would have been warned well in advance."

"Bob, you've got to believe me! It's a tsunami! The biggest I've ever heard of, and it's going to hit your area in forty-seven minutes at its present speed. Remember the stories in the papers about the possibility of a wave from the Japanese earthquake? Well, they must have been true and this thing is the result."

"That was just some wild theory by a college kid, Andy. Our guys in Washington said to forget it."

"Just cycle your radar over to long range and start tracking this thing and you'll believe it! You need to get every plane in the air and then try to get your people out of there!"

"Yeah, well, thanks a lot for the tip, Andy. I'll see what I can do," Atkins said as he leaned back in his chair. *I can just see the inquisition in Washington if I empty L.A. International on a tip that a tidal wave might hit,* he thought as he sipped his coffee. *No way I'm going to do that with three years left to retirement.* His thoughts drifted to the home he and his wife, Sara, had just bought down in San Diego. *Not on the beach,* he reflected, *but close enough to walk on it anytime we want to.*

"Wait, Bob!" Maury shouted as the phone went dead. He knew his counterpart at the airport weather station was not going to listen. He hung up the phone and tried to decide what to do.

The next twenty minutes were pure frustration as Andy Maury attempted to call everyone he knew at the Weather Bureau in Washington. All he got was a lot of "I'll tell him you called when he returns, Mr. Maury." No amount of pleading or cursing could get even one of the secretaries to alter her normal routine. His shouting about a tsunami might just as well have been a casual warning about an impending rain storm. Nothing he said had impressed them. *Naturally not,* he thought sarcastically. *They live three thousand miles from the Pacific.*

Maury was not the only person trying to alert the nation. At the office of the president in Washington, D.C., the phone rang. Clarence Barrett, the president's appointment secretary, answered it: "President Kilborne's office."

"Clarence, this is Andrew. I need to talk to him right now!" Secretary of Defense Andrew Singer, a no-nonsense ex-chairman of the joint chiefs, had been chosen by Kilborne to restore some discipline in the demoralized ranks of the military, which had been decimated by budget cuts. Recently he had been trying to ferret out what appeared to be a secret society among some of his most influential military leaders. General Gorman, chairman of the joint chiefs, had reported that several top ranking officers were engaged in secret meetings outside the normal service protocol. If he didn't know it was the top brass of the United States military, he might have thought it was the beginnings of a military coup, he had told the president earlier. But that was not the subject of this call. He had just gotten word that one of his boomers had gone down in the Pacific. And even more frightening was the report of missile subs lost by the Russians and Chinese, who had probably been shadowing his sub.

"What's it about, Andrew? He's in conference with some Senate group."

"You need to get him out! One of our boomers is down and so are two other subs—one Russian and one Chinese."

"I'll get him!" Barrett said immediately. *What now?* he puzzled. *The president's had about all the bad news he can stand to have dumped on him, except the start of World War III.* He trembled even as he considered it. World tensions were at an all-time high since the depression hit. Clarence Barrett punched the interrupt code reserved for messages of the highest priority.

President Kilborne leaned over to his interoffice phone, glad to get a short respite from the verbal lashing he had been receiving from the Senate leaders because he had ignored Bob Lowe's earthquake warnings. It still hurt as he remembered how Lowe had shafted him. "Yes, Clarence, what is it?" he whispered into the receiver. Then he realized he didn't have to whisper since only he could hear his secretary.

"Mr. President, Andrew Singer is on the hot line. I think you need to talk with him. It's urgent." The tone in Barrett's voice transmitted the alarm he had picked up from the secretary of defense.

The president pressed the mute switch as he turned back to the senators, "I'm sorry, gentlemen, you'll have to excuse me for a few minutes." Even as he spoke, Barrett, who had opened the office door, was directing the irritated senators out of the Oval Office.

"I'll be back, Mr. President," the senator from Ohio said very curtly. "You still have some explaining to do if you want my support."

Kilborne sighed as he punched the talk button. *Maybe I don't want your support,* he thought. *Maybe I don't want this job anymore.*

"What's up, Andrew?" the president asked as he mentally braced himself for more bad news. *Maybe I won't have to worry about the next elections,* he contemplated. *One more disaster like that press conference, and the Democrats will probably lynch me.*

"We've lost a missile sub in the Pacific, Mr. President. And the Russians and Chinese have lost the attack subs that were trailing her."

Suddenly Kilborne was totally alert. "Did we have an exchange?" An exchange of warship hostilities was another way of saying nuclear battle.

"No, sir. None that we know of, and the monitors on the radiation satellites show no signs of nuclear detonation."

"Thank God," Kilborne said with obvious relief. "Then what happened?"

"We don't know, sir," the ex-general, nearly twice the age of the president, replied.

"As well as I can determine, we had a distress call from our boomer saying they were caught in a sub-surface current of some kind. The next thing we heard was the sub breaking up. The Russians reported much the same thing. The Chinese aren't saying anything at present, as is normal. They just lost one-third of their total attack sub force so they'll be hot. We've already sent them assurances, through channels, that we didn't sink their sub."

Thank God, it wasn't an exchange, Kilborne thought as he tried to piece together what this might mean. Just then his secretary broke in over the intercom again.

"Mr. President, Dr. Patrick Holmes is on line two. He says it's most urgent. I told him you were talking with General Singer and he says it's related."

Dr. Holmes, head of the U.S. Oceanographic Committee which coordinated all the industrial nations to manage the oceans, was the most knowledgeable government official on international use of oceans. His office managed hundreds of surveillance satellites and underwater pollution detectors to see who was dumping their wastes in the oceans and harvesting more fish than allocated. The committee operated much like an ocean cartel, controlling the use of the common seas. He also had the best communications with the various scientific groups from each country. He had just received an urgent message from the monitoring station outside the west coast of the United States.

"This is the president," Kilborne said slowly and deliberately as he transferred over to line two of his private phone.

"Mr. President, I have just received word from our monitoring station in the Eastern Pacific that a three-hundred-foot tsunami is headed toward the California coast. It will hit in less than thirty minutes."

"What! Are you sure, Patrick?" the president shouted in spite of himself.

"Very sure, Mr. President," the young oceanographer said. "The wave traveled across the Pacific in the trenches until it hit the shallows. Now it's bunching up. The surface wave is traveling at over three hundred miles an hour."

"Just what Wells' program predicted!" Kilborne shouted in anger. "No wonder Lowe stabbed me in the back. He must have been working for Hunt. What do you suggest, Patrick?"

"Nothing. There's nothing we can do now."

4

PANIC

I want every radio and television station in Southern California to go to emergency broadcast," President Kilborne instructed his civil defense director, Craig Newball, over the phone.

"Why, Mr. President?" the startled Newball questioned as his feet fell off the desk top and hit the floor below.

"A tsunami will strike the California coast just above Los Angeles in less than twenty minutes," Kilborne snapped impatiently. "Notify everyone who can do so to head inland. And Craig . . ."

"Yes, Mr. President," the elder member of the civil defense team replied breathlessly.

"I want a full contingent of civil defense people mobilized in California immediately. Call Crow and have the National Guard brought out. If he gives you any static, tell him I'll nationalize them if I have to."

They really did a job on Crow, too, Kilborne thought. *Whoever they are. . . .*

For ten minutes some radio and television stations in Southern California blared out an emergency alarm, but nearly three-fourths of the stations wouldn't interrupt normal programming to carry the message. A few disc jockeys assumed it was some elaborate practical joke and simply ignored it, and many of the listeners thought it was just another test of the emergency broadcast system. It didn't really matter because the Californians who did believe the broadcasts were scarcely into their cars when the gigantic wave struck.

The unbelievable force of the wave as it hit the shore, bringing with it tons of debris from the sea, shook mountains as far inland as San Bernardino. The Queen Mary and Queen Elizabeth II, anchored at the Los Angeles harbor as floating casinos, were swept up in the wave and flung miles inland, along with thousands of other vessels.

The sound of the wave was bone chilling. Everything in its path was swept before it. Buildings and houses alike collapsed under billions of tons of water crashing inland at nearly three hundred miles an hour.

The wave penetrated nearly three miles inland before the fury of the tide beat itself out on the hills and valleys surrounding the greater Los Angeles area. Further to the south, in the less-populated communities along the coast, scarcely a person survived the roaring torrent of salt water. As the water rushed back to the ocean it carried with it homes, cars, and people; few would ever be recovered from the depths of the Pacific.

Even as far north as San Francisco, the ocean rose nearly twelve feet, causing massive damage to sensitive ecological systems. Buildings collapsed as their foundations were undercut by the rushing water. The bay area suffered an estimated $3 billion in damage. Some three thousand lives were lost, but with the enormity of deaths in Southern California, these went almost unnoticed except by friends and family.

Disaster relief teams were flown in from every part of the country, as well as from Canada and Europe. In an effort to control the marauding bands of looters drawn to the disaster area, civil defense armies were formed out of National Guard units from around the country. The fighting between civil defense troops and heavily armed gangs became so intense that units of the U.S. Army had to be flown in to reinforce the National Guard troops. The scene in Southern California took on the appearance of a war zone. President Kilborne authorized the troops to shoot on sight anyone found looting or molesting another citizen. Civil rights groups, led by the National Civil Liberties Union, screamed that such action was a violation of basic human rights. In the wake of devastation, few Americans lent a sympathetic ear.

As the marauders expanded their territory to neighboring states, it appeared that a civil war might break out for control of the area. Automatic weapons were in such demand by frightened citizens that they became the currency of the day. An M-19 automatic assault rifle sold for as much as ten thousand dollars on the black market.

Viewed from the air the coast of California, from just north of Los Angeles to south of San Luis Obispo, looked as if a nuclear blast had hit the area. All the structures that once had housed businesses and residences were swept into the sea or deposited along the coast for several hundred miles, creating navigational hazards to ships that were bringing in relief materials. Pirates, both American and Mexican, terrorized the coastline in power boats modified for use as assault craft. Ships approaching the California coast were in constant danger of being boarded and pirated. The U.S. Navy had to provide heavily armed cutters to patrol the shoreline in support of the relief ships. Even so, small-scale naval battles were fought as the pirate boats often matched a cutter's firepower. Even the redirection of several larger naval vessels did not deter the pirates. Their smaller crafts were no match for the Navy's bigger ships, but their speed and maneuverability made them difficult targets.

Full-time television coverage saturated American viewers with scenes of the ravaged west coast. The blame for the disaster was placed clearly upon President Kilborne and Governor Crow. The nightly news carried interviews with leading government officials who were demanding Kilborne's resignation. It was fruitless for Kilborne to even attempt to appear in public. Friends and families of the victims in California, gathered outside the White House, shouted and screamed obscenities at him whenever he was seen. The media refused to provide any time for the president; for all intents, he was a man without a country.

Seeing what had happened to Kilborne, Crow attempted to shift all the blame onto the president, even going so far as to insinuate that California officials had plotted to keep the disaster from the public at the president's orders. Both men's ratings plummeted in the polls.

Senator Mark Hunt addressed the nation regularly on the need for a strong president to lead the nation out of the economic crises caused by this natural disaster. In an interview on "The Nation's Leaders," a program that achieved an unprecedented first place in the prime time ratings, he said: "Fellow Americans, we face a time of the gravest dangers. The man who will lead this country in the coming years will either be a savior or a devil. As of today, the government has run out of funds to operate. Years, and even decades, of misusing public money has bankrupted the wealthiest country on earth. I would like to say here and now that I don't believe that President Kilborne, a long-time Democratic ally, purposely deceived the people of this nation. He simply lacks the leadership ability to handle the situation. His earlier indecision cost more than a million lives; further indecision may cost our freedoms.

"I have offered a bill in the Senate banning the possession of firearms. I acknowledge that the Constitution gives Americans the right to own and bear arms, but our founding fathers could not have foreseen armed gangs of criminals looting and raping their neighbors under the protection of our Constitution. I also realize that there are special-interest groups within this country that oppose my bill. To them I would say, 'Go to California, and then tell me about your right to bear arms. What about the rights of the honest citizens being terrorized by armed criminals?'

"As president I will authorize the Army to arrest and confine any-one found carrying a weapon that can be used against another person. I will restore law and order to this grand nation."

Following Hunt's address on television, the media provided scenes of the new battle lines in California where armed bandits were assaulting a town. Women and children were being gunned down; horrifying scenes filled the screens of American homes. Skillfully sprinkled in between the graphic scenes were on-the-spot interviews with hysterical mothers carrying dead and wounded children. Screaming mothers cried, "Help us! We need to get rid of *all* guns!"

In another segment, Mark Hunt interviewed a well-known psychiatrist about the proposal to ban all firearms. "I believe the psychological advantage will swing to the public. The criminals will know that carrying firearms will result in their arrest and conviction. I would say it would be a definite plus for all Americans."

The nightly Insta-pol showed an overwhelming 88 percent of all American viewers approved the senator's bill. Calls flooded the Senate and House, demanding its immediate passage. Within two weeks, the bill banning possession of all firearms became law. Kilborne vetoed the bill, stating that he believed it to be unconstitutional.

When the new poll results came in, they showed that Senator Hunt's commanding lead virtually eliminated all other candidates from the upcoming presidential primaries. Clearly Mark Hunt was to become the next Democratic candidate for president of the United States. The more tightly the depression gripped the nation and the more violent the criminal element became, the more Americans were convinced the country needed a strong, dynamic leader who could restore order.

The only issue left to be answered in the Hunt campaign was that of his vice-presidential running mate. Cal Rutland had advised Hunt to delay selecting his running mate. He didn't need a strong candidate since he was miles ahead in all the polls, and a weak candidate might hurt him before Kilborne and Crow were eliminated in the primaries.

This issue was the subject of a meeting between Hunt, Rutland, and two members of a group of investors that had backed Hunt's political career for the past three years. Cal Rutland called them the "Society." The meeting was held at Hunt's expansive summer home in Boone, North Carolina.

"Senator, we're very pleased with the way you have handled yourself in the media. You will have the full confidence of the American public when you take over the White House," commented industrialist Jason Franklin.

"Thank you," Hunt said as he surveyed the older man, whom he knew by reputation only. He was chairman of the Franklin Foundation, which held assets of over $2 trillion in companies all over the globe. It had been rumored that Franklin himself was dead because so few people had actually seen him over the past ten years. In spite of himself, Hunt was awed. He knew that one word from this man could plunge nations into ruin, not to mention better-than-average politicians. Now he knew where his campaign funds had been coming from the past three years. Franklin was his benefactor.

"I have to say that I am both honored and somewhat amazed to see you, sir. I've heard it said that you had died."

"As you can see, Senator, the reports of my death have been greatly exaggerated, to quote a famous writer."

Hunt laughed with a gusto that betrayed his uneasiness in the presence of his newly discovered mentor.

"I would like to introduce you to someone who is a real fan of yours, Senator. In fact, she was the one who elicited my support for your campaign."

Hunt looked up. He could barely restrain a gasp as the light illuminated the woman's beautiful features. She was obviously older than Hunt, but her skin was unwrinkled and her features still sharp and unblemished. He knew her immediately, but the pictures he had seen scarcely did her justice.

"Mrs. Alton, what a great pleasure to meet you," Hunt said with his most charming smile. *Kathy Alton!* he thought pensively. Even though her astronaut husband, Colonel Lee Alton, had died leading the joint U.S., Soviet, and Japanese expedition to Mars in 1995, it was Kathy Alton who had actually saved the space program. Her open pleas to the world television public not to allow her husband's death to eliminate space exploration had turned the tide. In the last moments, as the Mars astronauts' air supply ran out, Kathy Alton was on television declaring that her husband's death was an acceptable sacrifice if future generations could explore the stars.

But that was before the Great Depression struck the world. Now money was so tight in the U.S. and Russia that all space exploration had been canceled. It was all the U.S. could do to keep the wheels of government running on one-third less income and ever-compounding debts.

Even so, Americans had adopted Colonel Lee Alton's wife as a symbol of courage and character. In a generation that had little to cheer about, great crowds had come out to see her as she toured the country. Without question, Kathy Alton was the best-known and most-admired woman in America.

Hunt was snapped out of his reverie as he heard Jason Franklin say, "Senator, Mrs. Alton is here at my request to discuss an important issue. As you realize, we have invested a great deal of time and funding into your campaign."

"I do appreciate all you have done, Mr. Franklin. I knew there was a supporter behind the campaign, but I didn't know who it was."

"When I say 'we,' I refer to the Society, not myself."

Suddenly Hunt was struck with a new realization. "The Society! Are you a part of the Society?"

"Let's just say that I agree with their goals, Senator. But more importantly, I want to know if you do."

"I'm not sure what you mean," Hunt said, now cautiously choosing his words. He had always assumed the Society was a group of philanthropists bent on having their influence felt in government, but Franklin needed no group through which to operate. He was the single most influential man in the world.

"The Society's goals include establishing a worldwide monetary system and a total world market."

"I certainly do agree with that goal," Hunt declared, perhaps too enthusiastically. "We need to re-establish the United States as a global economic power."

"The days for this nation or any other nation to rule the world economically are over, Senator Hunt!" Franklin said flatly. "It is time for the U.S. to accept the fact that we are a one-world system, not a self-first nation."

"But I don't see how that will be possible," Hunt argued. "Americans will never accept a minor role in . . ."

"They will accept it because they will have no choice!" Franklin snapped. "You will sell them on the idea, and we will provide the motivation."

Hunt just stood there, stinging from the reproach in Franklin's voice. It had been a long time since he had been scolded like a school boy. Even if he had wanted to say something, he couldn't think of anything at that moment. And the look on Franklin's face was clear; he neither wanted, nor expected, any response.

"What I wanted to talk about, Senator, is your running mate—the vice-presidential candidate. I have a suggestion to make."

Suddenly on his guard, Hunt realized that Franklin was not a man to make a casual suggestion about anything. He was accustomed to his suggestions becoming actions.

"I would like for Mrs. Alton to be considered as your running mate."

"Mrs. Alton!" Hunt blurted out. "But she has no political experience."

"That is a point in your favor in these times," Cal Rutland commented. "She has no political baggage to carry."

Hunt stopped for a moment to think. It was obvious that Cal knew about Kathy Alton before this meeting. But he hadn't shared his information. Mark Hunt then realized his aide carried a lot more weight than he had realized. He also knew he was backed into a corner.

"I'll need to give this some thought, Mr. Franklin," Mark Hunt responded with his long-practiced political smile.

"Do that, Senator," Franklin replied with only slightly veiled irritation. "But I will expect to hear from you on this matter within two days. In the meantime, I would suggest that Mrs. Alton and you spend a little time getting better acquainted. She can be a valuable asset to you."

Hunt realized that, as far as Franklin was concerned, the issue was settled. He had the sinking feeling that a trap had been sprung, and he was in it. He wasn't sure what Kathy Alton had to do with the Society, but he knew she must be a part of a larger scheme, which he had yet to learn.

As the senator and his aide flew back to Washington later that day, Rutland tried to strengthen Franklin's suggestion as he commented, "Think of it this way, Senator. Kathy Alton is bound to be a big asset to you. First, she is a well-known woman who is not associated with politics. Second, she has the ear of the most powerful man in America."

"Tell me something, Cal. Did you know Franklin wanted her as my running mate?"

"I knew," Rutland acknowledged matter-of-factly.

"Why didn't you tell me before the meeting, so I wouldn't walk in blindly?"

"I couldn't, Senator. I was instructed to keep my mouth shut."

After a slight pause, Hunt asked slowly and deliberately, "Who do you work for Cal? Them or me?"

"Both, Senator," he countered. "I'm on your team, but we're both on their team."

"Well, you inform the Society that I'm not some lackey to be told what to do. I won't take Alton," Hunt declared.

"You'd better think that over carefully," Rutland said coldly, his eyes riveted on Hunt's. There was a look of urgency in Rutland's piercing eyes. "That would not be a wise decision at all. Your campaign has been financed at great expense to the Society, and they would not take a 'no' lightly."

"What can they do at this late date?" Hunt asked, trying to bluff his way as he had all during his political career. "I'm their candidate. Kilborne and Crow have been beaten by this earthquake thing."

"Senator, the goals of the Society are greater than any one man, including you or me. John Kennedy thought he could overrule the Society and learned better—the hard way!"

Hunt felt his bravado crumble as he heard Rutland's last comment. The aide knew his boss patterned his entire political career after his boyhood idol. The shock of his matter-of-fact announcement had its desired effect. *Could Jack Kennedy have been eliminated by the Society? Was that even possible?* Hunt asked himself. *Yes*, he decided, *it was. That would explain the misinformation surrounding the assassination and why so many witnesses died mysteriously.*

"Think of it as a positive step, Senator," Rutland continued without waiting for a response from Hunt. "Kathy Alton will represent no threat to your power in the White House. She will simply bring in a new dimension to your administration—the women of America. Her influence will rally the working women to your programs. You'll need their help to make changes."

"I guess you're right, Cal," Hunt heard himself say. He knew he was beaten. Then, in an attempt to salvage some of his pride, he added, "Besides, I suppose having the first woman vice president on my team won't look bad in the papers, will it?"

In the sleeping compartment of the big jet, Kathy Alton smiled as she listened to the conversation over the monitor. *He's a true politician*, she thought to herself. *His convictions last just as long as they encounter no opposition. He'll be an insufferable chauvinist, I'm sure. Lee would be amazed to see how far his sacrifice has brought me and how much further there is to go.* For a moment she was drawn back into her grief over Lee's death. Then, with a resolve steeled by years of indoctrination, she decided it was a necessary casualty of progress.

Three days later Kathy Alton was announced as Mark Hunt's running mate.

5

THE ELECTION

With the unprecedented move of announcing Kathy Alton as his running mate before the Democratic primaries, Senator Hunt nailed the coffin shut on President Kilborne's renomination. Even the president's staunchest allies began jumping ship, trying to strike a deal with the Hunt team.

The American voters, fed up with hard times and frightened by the growing violence nationwide, were looking for new leadership. Daily they were bombarded with scenes of looting and widespread civil disobedience, and daily Mark Hunt flooded the airwaves with promises of better times and an end to violence in America—just what the American people wanted to hear. As the economy continued to slow and revenues declined, Washington was forced to make more budget cuts. And with each new budget cut by the Kilborne administration, Hunt's position strengthened.

To most Americans, the nomination of Mark Hunt on the Democratic party ticket was the long-awaited answer to their many problems. The effects of the depression on those who were less than fifty years old were especially devastating since most of them had never experienced any really difficult economic times. The depression of 1929 was nothing more than a chapter in their Economics 101 textbooks. And the recession of 1994 had been tempered by massive government spending. To them it was an accepted fact that the government would hire the unemployed during a recession. That had worked fine as long as the money continued to flow in from the Japanese and from the European Community.

Few American workers grasped the fact that as the money poured in, ownership in many American industries shifted to Europe and Japan, especially Japan. By the year 1995, nearly half of all businesses in America were owned by the Japanese. "So what?" the politicians had said. "After all, they still employ American workers and feed the American economy more money."

The day of reckoning began in January of 1996, when the Saudis announced that they were running out of oil and would be raising their base price by fifty dollars a barrel. With half the available oil reserves contaminated from the nuclear fallout of the Israeli bombs that had rained on Iraq and Iran during the 1994 war, the Saudis controlled 80 percent of the available Middle East oil reserves. The European Community had access to the north shore oil of England and France, but other countries scrambled to bid for the oil supply they needed.

Japan outbid the United States, winning by a wide margin. The U.S. economy received a double-barreled blast as a result. First, the available oil supply was reduced by 40 percent and immediate rationing took effect. Non-business vehicles were limited to ten gallons of gasoline per month, and prices shot up to nearly five dollars per gallon. This triggered an inflation rate of 30 percent per year, effectively wiping out many businesses, retirement savings, and Social Security. The elderly went back into the work force *en masse*. The competition for jobs between the young and old became a political issue.

Next, the Japanese began a systematic shutdown of competitive industries in the U.S., saving the jobs for their Japanese workers by shifting manufacturing back to their factories at home. By the time the public was aware of their strategy, most of the major industries were gone, and the only jobs available were in lower-paying service industries. The result was a devastating slowdown of the U.S. economy that dragged virtually every nation outside of the European Community and the Asian Triangle down with it. The Japanese began systematic price slashing to siphon business away from both the U.S. and Europe. In one year, they virtually captured the world market for automobiles, heavy equipment, aircraft, and defense armament. The result was an unemployment rate of nearly 25 percent in the U.S.

The next blow to the economy came as the Japanese gradually withdrew their loans to the U.S. government, citing their need to develop business within the Asian Triangle. Without this money to feed its ever-growing deficits, the government was forced to begin massive cutbacks. There was talk of a new constitutional amendment to rescind the Balanced Budget Amendment, but somehow Congress could never develop the momentum to push it through.

The desperate need for finances led the Kilborne administration to sponsor a bill to rescind the tax exempt status of all non-profit groups, including all religious organizations—a move proposed and supported by the National Civil Liberties Union and most other liberal factions. The bill was passed into law despite vigorous lobbying by church leaders. The result was immediate economic trouble for all churches.

Christian leaders railed at the government's actions and promised picketing and mass demonstrations. Meetings were held in churches throughout the nation to discuss the growing trend toward disenfranchisement of Christians. The recognized leader of the protest movement was Pastor John Elder of Atlanta, Georgia. As the pastor of a ten-thousand-member Baptist Church and as a worldwide television minister, Elder was the principal spokesman for the evangelical community.

Elder was no stranger to controversy. He had organized and led three of the largest anti-abortion rallies in Washington. He had also organized a very effective grass roots organization, the Constitutional Rights Committee (CRC), to oppose politicians who were recognized as anti-Christian. At least six liberal senators and ten congressmen had been voted out of office through his efforts.

The *coup de grace* for the U.S. economy was delivered by the Japanese when they announced they were calling due nearly $3 trillion loaned to the United States. They publicly stated that when the U.S. treasury bills they held came due they would expect prompt payment, because the money was needed to rebuild Tokyo after the earthquake. This announcement sent the U.S. stock market into its steepest decline since the collapse of 1996. Financial markets around the world reacted with panic as they feared the U.S. would default on its debt.

In a specially prepared message, Senator Mark Hunt announced that he had a plan for handling this latest demand by the Japanese and was sure he could work out a settlement satisfactory to both sides. Given the air of animosity that had built up between the two countries since the U.S. had imposed trade restrictions on most Japanese products, the majority of analysts scoffed at the idea. Two days later, the Japanese Minister of France, Isochi Yamore, announced that some mutual compromise might be arranged. They decided to delay any decision until after the elections in America. The announcement came two days before the primaries. No one outside the inner circle of the shadowy group known only as the Society knew that Yamore's actions had been the result of a personal visit by Jason Franklin.

Senator Hunt obliterated Kilborne in the primaries. The mandate by the public was so great that not a single delegate dared to support the president at the convention. With the November elections coming up, Hunt had only to defeat a weak Republican candidate to win the highest office in the country.

The presidential election was not just a mandate by the voters; it was an ultimatum to the Congress. Hunt received 96 percent of all votes cast. Never had a president been elected by so great a margin. The American voters were saying insistently, "Do something!" In an unprecedented move, Kilborne resigned his presidency, paving the way for Hunt to move his administration into Washington. Kilborne's vice president was sworn in to head a caretaker government until January, but in reality, the reins of power had already shifted to Hunt.

Mark Hunt was sworn in as the forty-fourth president of the United States in January, with some two million cheering admirers filling the capital. The inauguration of Kathy Alton as the first woman vice president was hailed by women throughout the world. Even Hunt had to admit the wisdom in Alton's selection. She followed his campaign platform exactly, always deferring to his judgment when a new issue arose. The one thing that irked Hunt was the way the reporters catered to her. When the two of them were interviewed together, it was as if he didn't exist. His solution to this problem had been to send her to obscure locations—where he didn't want to go anyway. And, surprisingly, she had never objected to any assignment.

Hunt had soon settled into a routine of allowing Alton enough publicity to keep her current in the minds of the public, but behind the scenes otherwise. *Besides*, he mused as he glanced over at her on the platform—a picture of poise and beauty—*she's beginning to warm up to me.*

Had he been able to read Kathy Alton's mind, he might have reconsidered his attitude toward her. *A real show hound*, she thought as he strutted around the platform at a Washington press conference. *He's in his glory.* She chuckled silently as he strutted back and forth, obviously for her benefit. *He will learn, though.*

The failing economy provided the catalyst the liberals needed to step up the assault on Christians. In the first six months of the Hunt administration, Elder witnessed an alarming trend toward anti-Christian hostility in the media. All pretext of objectivity was gone, particularly at the biggest and most influential network, the World News Network.

What had been a "situation" became a crisis when the FCC confirmed the ban of all Christian broadcasts on radio and television. The last straw came when the administration pushed a bill through Congress taxing all church property and income. Elder pulled out the stops and rallied his followers to organize demonstrations protesting this blatantly unconstitutional action.

Without access to any public media, John Elder fell back to his only option: organizing "grass roots" committees to keep Christians informed. He and his group began printing weekly newsletters announcing protest rally dates and locations. Condensed versions were distributed through church bulletins in thousands of churches throughout the country.

Elder decided that a mass rally should be organized to confront the Washington politicians. As a forerunner, smaller planning meetings were scheduled in churches by the thousands.

Tony Moran was one of the group leaders whose function was to coordinate his church's participation. He received an urgent call from John Elder's headquarters instructing him to schedule a planning meeting for that evening. Some of Elder's contacts in Washington had notified him that President Hunt had decided to sign an executive order authorizing the so-called "Crack Babies Bill," abolishing the babies' civil rights.

"Notify your group that we're going to march on Washington next Saturday," Randy Cross, a leader in John Elder's Constitutional Rights Committee (CRC), told Moran.

"I don't know if we can get our group together that soon," Moran said. Inside he had a sinking feeling that once they made their move publicly there would be no turning back. He wasn't at all sure he was ready or willing to take that step.

"If we don't act now, it will be too late," Cross warned him. "If the 'Crack' bill becomes law, they'll begin processing the kids. John says we need to act now!"

Tony Moran put the phone down. His hand shook from the fear he felt welling up inside.

"What's wrong, Tony?" Susan Moran asked her husband when she saw his ashen face.

"The committee wants us to call an emergency meeting to plan a march on Washington Saturday."

"We knew we'd have to take a stand sometime," his wife said as she put her arms around him.

Susan spent the next three hours calling every member of their church's CRC group. The meeting was set for seven o'clock that evening.

"I don't think we should go tonight," Tony said as his wife completed her last call. "We're taking an awful risk."

"We have to take a stand sometime, Tony," she replied as they sat down to eat. "First it was the ban on Christian radio, then television. Then the tax on church property, and now this terrible Crack Babies Bill. Who knows what may be next? Maybe they'll declare it unconstitutional to witness."

"You don't understand," Tony said grimly. "Remember Robert

Barnes? Well, he got fired from his job this week because he insisted on reading his Bible at lunch. It's tough enough for us to make it now. What will happen if I lose my job?"

"I don't think a job is as important as a life, Tony. Besides, we're not plotting anarchy. We're just trying to protect those who can't defend themselves."

Susan Moran sounded a lot more confident than she felt. She had seen the trend, even in their own neighborhood, toward religious intolerance. The more the government legitimized it, the more overt it became.

I wonder if this is the way persecution came to the Jews in Germany? she thought. *Were they just eased out of society until nobody really noticed they were missing?*

Even as the Morans were preparing to meet with their group, a meeting was taking place in the White House that would have a profound effect on their future.

"I simply can't believe this report, Cal," President Mark Hunt remarked as he reviewed the document before him.

"Believe it, Mr. President. The FBI has firm evidence that the religious right is planning government assassinations as a part of their opposition to your Crack Bill."

"But they've never been violent in any of their past protests. They shout and scream a lot, but in the end they adjust," the president said as he re-read the document about members of a religious group, calling themselves the Constitutional Rights Committee, who were planning to assassinate several Senate leaders and federal judges. It went on to say that the FBI had also uncovered a plot to assassinate President Hunt if he signed the so-called "Crack Babies Bill."

The Humanitarian Action Legislation, dubbed the "Crack Babies Bill" by the religious right, was legislation Hunt had first sponsored while in the Senate. Nearly twelve million babies born of crack and cocaine addicts over the last decade were wards of the government; over $48 billion a year of taxpayers' money was required to care for them. Hunt had been genuinely surprised that there had been such an outcry in the Christian community when he first introduced legislation to utilize the crack babies for the good of otherwise hopeless people. His researchers had irrefutable evidence that these crack babies had less learning ability than a chimpanzee. And other than a few animal rights radicals, nobody minded using the chimps for the good of mankind. Not only would using the crack babies' organs help many terminally ill people, but it would also bring more than $6 billion a year into the government and eliminate the drain of nearly $50 billion to support and sustain them.

Virtually the entire country supported the bill, except the Christians. They had succeeded in getting the bill delayed in Congress, but one of his campaign promises had been to get the bill passed into law, which he planned to do by executive order immediately. The procedure on the crack babies would be done humanely. Those who were diagnosed as mentally deficient would be sent to government hospitals where they would be injected with coma-inducing drugs. From there they would be transported to organ banks throughout the world where their organs would be used to help productive people live useful lives.

Hunt slammed the report down on the Jeffersonian desk that had been used by so many previous presidents. "I want this made public, Cal. Get it leaked to the press so that it doesn't look like we did it. But get it done!"

"I'll do it, Mr. President," Rutland promised as he picked up the report. *Perfect*, he thought as he returned the report to the pouch labeled "Top Secret." *I knew how he'd react to that part about his bill.* Rutland smiled as he visualized the reaction to the article in the press. *The religious right can protest all they want, but the more they protest, the more they will appear guilty. As long as we control the media, the public will accept what we say as truth.*

THE ARRESTS

J ohn! You're not going to believe this! Come here! Hurry!"

Pastor John Elder knew his wife was watching the morning news. For her the latest news, along with the current weather forecast, was a daily routine before starting breakfast. Julia Elder was a typical Baptist minister's wife most of the time, but lately her life was being reshaped. As a pastor's wife, she was accustomed to life in a "fishbowl" within the confines of their church membership, but as her husband was being thrust even more into the public eye in the protests against the government, she was being placed in a much larger "fishbowl."

In response to his wife's shout, he asked, "What's wrong, honey? Is the weather girl topless again?"

The comment was meant to be amusing but Julia was not in a humorous mood. Inside, the bile of fear was rising in her throat. "You'd better get in here, John. You're on television."

Elder hurried into the living room. As he entered, he heard the announcer from WNN say, "The FBI report states that an underground religious group known as the Constitutional Rights Committee, or the CRC, led by the Reverend John Elder, a Baptist preacher from Atlanta, Georgia, has made several threats on politicians who oppose the group's teachings. Elder, who heads a ten-thousand-member organization, has led many protests in the past, including the notorious 'midnight run' on Congress."

"That's a lie!" Julia Elder shouted. "We had nothing to do with breaking into the congressional building. Those were not our marchers."

"Of course, they weren't," Elder said, trying to calm her down. "Don't worry about it, dear." It wasn't surprising that his group was getting the blame. He had irritated both the politicians and the press when he led several thousand peaceful demonstrators in a march on Washington to protest the government's blatant assault on religious freedoms.

The misinformation was created when the vandals who had been arrested claimed to be members of the CRC. Later he learned that they had done so in exchange for representation by the National Civil Liberties Union. All of those arrested received small fines and suspended sentences. Yet when some members of the Constitutional Rights Committee struggled with the D.C. police along the parade route, they had been arrested, cited for assault, and sentenced to three years in prison. In addition, CRC's demonstration permit had been permanently revoked, and as group organizer, Elder had received ninety days in jail for contempt of court. All the public saw were the short clips of his CRC members shoving the police. What the media didn't show was that the marchers had just been struck by night-stick-wielding police officers.

Elder's attention became riveted to the television. A reporter was asking the deputy attorney general from the Department of Justice what the government's response would be.

John Elder saw his own face appear in one corner of the screen as the young deputy answered, "We will watch this Constitutional Rights Committee very closely. At this point I cannot comment on our plans, but we certainly do take their threats seriously. Plots to assassinate members of government have been authenticated. This group has demonstrated that they will resort to violence if necessary to achieve their goals. We have evidence that they are teaching their members guerrilla tactics."

The scene shifted to a heavily wooded area where armed men and women were engaging in what was obviously combat training.

"Lies, lies! Those are not our people," Julia protested.

"Easy, Julia. We knew this wouldn't be easy. Just remember what I keep telling the members of our group. The politicians are not our enemies, even if they are against us. Our enemy is the master deceiver."

As tears welled up in Julia's eyes, her voice broke and she struggled to maintain her composure. "Maybe so, John, but you're going to be the one who will bear the brunt."

"A lot of God's people will bear the brunt, Julia. I just happen to be the spokesman right now. Remember that Peter and John rejoiced at being found worthy to suffer for the Lord."

"Yes, but I also remember that Peter was crucified and John was banished," Julia retorted, with just the slightest hint of her usual humor returning.

"I wish that we could be found as worthy," John said to no one in particular as he sank into his favorite chair and turned his attention back to the news program. "Sometimes I think it would be easier to be martyred than to fight the politicians."

"This is Nathan Mather in Detroit; I'm outside the Government Service Center," the onsite reporter said. "With only three hundred new service jobs available for this city of one hundred thousand unemployed workers, nearly ten thousand people applied for the positions. The service center director tells me that according to the new job preference bill, only workers over sixty-five will be considered for these positions."

Stepping up to one of the younger men in line, Mather asked, "Sir, are you aware that the available jobs will be filled only with over-sixty-five workers?"

"Yeah, I heard that, but I'm goin' to stay in line anyway. I have a wife and four kids to feed."

"What do you think about the jobs bill since the Japanese car companies left Detroit?"

"I think it stinks. Hunt promised he would do somethin' to help us. I listened to his promises and voted for him; now I expect him to keep his word."

"Well, as you know, the older generation holds the majority vote in our country now. Don't you think it will be difficult to get support for any new jobs legislation favoring younger workers?"

After a moment's hesitation from the young man, he stood straight and spoke with conviction, "Maybe so, but I'll tell you this: these so-called older workers caused this mess we're in, an' now they want us to pay the price. There's nothin' right about that! They may have the vote, but we have the power. We need Hunt to act." Looking away from the reporter and into the camera, he continued, "You hear me, President Hunt? Do somethin' now!"

A troubled John Elder turned away from the television. "It seems that every group is being pitted against the other. The young against the old, blacks against Hispanics, Christians against non-Christians. If anything else happens, this country could be in real trouble. Everything I see around us now reminds me of what I've read about pre-World War II Germany. Inflation was running 1000 percent per month, and unemployment was nearly 40 percent. The people were ripe for a political savior."

"But our economy isn't that bad, is it?" Julia asked. She wasn't sure if she was trying to convince herself or her husband. She knew John had a better grasp of history than most men of his generation.

"Our economy is in a depression and it's getting worse. Americans have always believed that the government had some magic genie that could be called forth to save them from any economic trials. Now they know better. When President Kilborne announced that the FDIC could no longer insure bank accounts, depositors rushed to get their money, only to discover that there wasn't any money. So a lot of older people saw their life's savings evaporate, and they had to look for work. All this jobs bill has done is to alienate the younger people who are already strapped with tax upon tax. It's just a matter of time until our government runs out of money totally. Then they'll either print it or scrap it altogether."

"But the Balanced Budget Amendment is supposed to keep that from happening, isn't it?" Julia asked.

"Theoretically yes, but most Americans don't understand what it actually means to run out of money. It would cost millions more jobs and ignite riots in the cities. I don't know just what can be done, but I'll guarantee you the government is looking for a 'rabbit in the hat' right now."

"I don't understand," Julia said. "The government can't just ignore the Constitution. The Supreme Court won't allow it, will they?"

"Julia, we don't know how far politicians like Hunt will go to make themselves look good. Even the Supreme Court may not be able to stop him now. It's possible he is part of an effort to take over the government."

"What do you mean? You've hinted at that before."

"The attacks on Christians are accelerating since Hunt's landslide election. Our people in Washington believe there is a secret society within the government that is behind both the attacks and Hunt's election."

"What kind of society? Does it have anything to do with you being accused of heading a subversive group?"

"I don't know, but their strategy seems to be to stir up hatred of Christianity."

Raw emotion caused Julia's voice to waver as she said, "I can't believe we're in the middle of all this. This is America, not China."

Before her husband could reply, the sound of screeching tires was heard in front of the house. Julia looked out between the blinds and saw several men in dark suits emerging from two plain black cars. A mobile van from Channel Six TV pulled into the driveway behind them; several people jumped out and began to set up remote camera equipment. One of the dark-suited men yelled at the TV crew and the camera was quickly relocated at the edge of the Elders' driveway.

Two of the men approached the front door while another went around to the back yard. Julia's heart almost stopped as she realized they were probably surrounding the house.

"John, you'd better come look at this," she whispered as her knees began to weaken.

"What, honey?" he asked as he saw her pale. "What's wrong?"

Before Julia could answer, the front door burst open and two men pointing automatic weapons called out, "John Elder? FBI! You're under arrest!"

The last thing Julia remembered seeing was her husband's shocked expression—then darkness. She slumped to the floor, and as John attempted to reach for his wife, one of the men blocked his way and shoved him against the wall. In one swift motion he was handcuffed and a choke collar attached to his neck and wrists. John knew not to struggle against the collar. He had experienced the same apparatus when he had been arrested while leading demonstrations against abortion clinics.

Within minutes the news networks were showing footage of "suspected terrorist" John Elder, being taken to police headquarters by FBI agents who "had been tracking his whereabouts for several days."

After the news report, several hundred members of the Atlanta-based CRC gathered in the church sanctuary. The mood was one of shock and disbelief. There was a buzz of conversation until Bill Frost, area director of the CRC, stood to speak. "I know you're all worried about Pastor Elder. These are troubled times. If this can happen to a man of God, it can happen to any of us."

"Where's the pastor now?" someone asked.

"We don't know. All we know is that he was moved from the city jail to another location after the judge refused to set bail."

"How can he do that? I thought everyone was entitled to bail."

"They charged him with heading a terrorist organization, so the judge can deny bail."

"Terrorist organization!" someone yelled from the back. "You mean those accusations on television?"

"It would appear so," Frost said. The anger in his voice was evident. "We have attorneys working on it now. We don't know what the next step will be. When the pastor is arraigned, we'll know more."

"What about Julia?" one of the women asked. "Where is she?"

"They haven't charged her with anything, as far as we know. She fainted during the raid on their home. She's okay, but I understand she's under sedation. It was a traumatic experience for her."

It would be several days before anyone from the CRC heard anything about their leader. And then the news would change all of their lives forever.

SELLING THE NATION ON DATA-NET

Three days after Elder's arrest, President Hunt announced to the nation that the Japanese were again demanding repayment of the nearly $3 trillion the United States owed them. In a special message from the White House, he agreed to hold a live press conference, but without any question-and-answer session.

As the reporters and photographers filed into the press room, the president entered from the Oval Office access door. This time his appearance was without the normal fanfare of "Hail to the Chief." The president's usual contingent of secret service and the ever-watchful Cal Rutland accompanied him as he took his position behind the plexiglass podium in the press room of the White House.

"Ladies and gentlemen, fellow Americans, we face the gravest financial crisis yet in our nation. Even as I was working to resolve the economic chaos facing our country, others have been working to undermine my efforts and make the plight of working Americans more severe.

"The earthquake that struck the islands of Japan and wreaked such havoc there also destroyed much of our productive capacity, and cost many lives. As you know, previously the Japanese demanded immediate repayment of all loans, then agreed to negotiate with my administration. Now, once again, the Japanese are demanding that we immediately repay the loans made to us over the last thirty years. To do this would require that we mortgage every asset in our country. It would plunge this nation into economic ruin and prolong the depression by at least ten years. We would become virtual slaves to the very nation we helped to rebuild after World War II.

"As your president, I cannot allow this. I have been elected with a mandate to restore law and order, as well as economic stability to our country. We have taken the first step toward restoring law and order by way of a crackdown on organized terrorism. Now the immediate need is to restore economic stability. As many of you are aware, the Japanese have chosen to shut down their largest U.S. industries to preserve jobs for their people. They have consistently demonstrated a lack of concern or empathy for the workers of this nation who sacrificed to help them when they were down. Therefore, I have decided, with the counsel of several leading members of Congress, to invoke the Omnibus Banking Act of 1983 and suspend all repayment of foreign debt.

"Let me emphasize that this in no way jeopardizes the deposits of Americans. In fact I have instructed the Treasury to stand behind all deposits of American citizens one hundred percent. Those who lost their savings in the recent bank collapse will be repaid in full. Withdrawals will be limited until the economy recovers, but no American will lose a dime. You have my word on that. This may result in some temporary inconveniences to large depositors, but remember, it is for the good of the whole nation. Dr. Russell Siever, former secretary of the Treasury, has been appointed to head a task force to oversee this effort. I'll let Dr. Siever explain how the Banking Act will be put into operation."

As the president stepped down from the platform, someone started to clap. Then the entire group, including the secret service, joined in thunderous applause.

In the press secretary's office, the Insta-pol rating showed that 83 percent of the polling group supported the president's decision. "We did it!" Ross Newton, the press secretary, shouted. "The public bought it. Hunt could sell day-old fish for deodorant."

Russell Siever began the thirty-minute presentation exactly as he had rehearsed it. "Let me say that I totally support the president's decision. It is the responsibility of the government to protect the interests of its own people first. For too long we have allowed private interests to shift money and jobs out of our country. Without the generosity of the American people, these other countries would still be living in the Dark Ages." Again, spontaneous applause interrupted the speech.

"For the average American worker, there will be no noticeable changes. You will still be able to pay your bills and transact normal business, but any large transfer of money will be prohibited unless it is an internal transaction, such as buying a home or a car, or ordering business-related materials.

"All transfers of ten thousand dollars or more will require the approval of the Federal Reserve Board or its appointed representatives. In order to stop the black-market practices of special interest groups, all transactions from this date forward must be made by check or credit card. By Friday of this week all citizens will be required to turn in their cash and will receive an equivalent credit in their checking accounts. In a few weeks all depositors will receive a debit card that will allow them to transact business without the use of checks.

"Implementation of this system will not only stop the flow of assets from our country, it will curtail armed robberies, the sale of illegal drugs, and money laundering by the criminal element. As an additional safeguard, the debit cards will carry a personalized number and, eventually, a fingerprint image of the owner that can be traced, in the event it is lost or stolen. Remember, this is for your protection.

"We are determined to solve the economic problems of our nation. This is but the first of many steps the president has proposed to reemploy Americans and once again make this nation the most prosperous in the world."

The tally board in the press secretary's office flashed off and then back on as the final Insta-pol survey was taken. "The score is 65 percent," he said over the intercom to the president's office. "That's enough to call it a mandate, sir. Only 22 percent opposed, and 13 percent still undecided. Three to one. It's a go!"

Later that day Jeff Wells met with President Hunt, Cal Rutland, and Russ Siever in the Oval Office to go over the final procedures for the Data-Net System. Jeff handed a stack of papers to the president before sitting down. "Is the system ready to go, Jeff?" the president asked as he looked through the papers.

"Yes, sir. We've tested the program several times. It really turned out to be a lot simpler than we had thought, Mr. President. With a little help from some of the IBM engineers, we were able to link several of their new 1520s together."

In one of his rare compliments, Cal Rutland added, "Jeff's being modest, Mr. President. The people at IBM said his program is the most innovative approach to networking they have ever seen. It is impossible to break into the codes, and it can handle millions of inputs simultaneously."

"Actually the key was using the laser input and output channels," Jeff said humbly. "That, and the new bubble memory from ICAN, gives the 1520 the ability to store almost limitless data. It even has the ability to correct its own errors and repair flawed circuits by patching around them. It's like . . ."

"Okay, okay. I get the picture." It irritated Hunt that he never could grasp the rudiments of computers. *So what,* he thought. *I control the guys who make them run. That's better.*

"When will we be able to connect to the Federal Reserve System?" Russell Siever snapped as he looked at Jeff. "I want to begin as soon as possible."

"It's already in process," Jeff replied, a little brusquely. He didn't like Siever much, though he didn't know just why. Maybe it was the way he treated the others around him—like they were inferior to him. With the exception of Rutland, that is, whom everyone seemed to fear. *Maybe that's it,* Jeff thought. *Maybe he hurts my pride.* But inside he knew it was something else.

He allowed his thoughts to drift back, nearly a year, to when he had first begun to piece together Data-Net.

The program required linking tens of thousands of different systems together so that any computer in the world on the system could communicate with any other computer. For the first several months the task seemed impossible, at least with the current technology.

One evening he and his assistant, Karen Eison, Dr. William Eison's daughter, had been discussing the problem. Karen was a real asset to his work. She was one of the few people, outside of Dr. Eison himself, who seemed to grasp his logic. They had met when he was working with the staff at Livermore and she had quickly earned his respect. When Dr. Eison had suggested Karen as Jeff's lab assistant, after he had been tapped by Hunt to build the Data-Net system, he had readily agreed. *Perhaps too readily,* he later thought. He didn't have room for any emotional entanglements at this time in his life. But the relationship had developed into a thoroughly professional one. She was as competent a programmer as he had ever worked with, even if she didn't always understand his system. Actually, few people did.

Karen's plans for the relationship were quite different from Jeff's. She had been hopelessly in love with him almost from the moment they had met. She knew he was brilliant. He had to be to command the respect of her father, who was head and shoulders above most of the other scientists in the field of computer physics. She had once heard her father say to an associate, "This young man makes me look like a computer hack. He has a gift for computers like Mozart had for music. His kind only comes along every few hundred years or so."

But what had immediately attracted her was who Jeff really was. He was shy and sensitive, but he would stand up to anyone who challenged his work, including her father. Best of all, he accepted her for her abilities, not because of who her father was. Most of the men who had courted her were awed by the renowned Dr. Eison and were seeking his approval through her. As a result, she totally rejected them.

For the first time she was the pursuer, but Jeff seemed oblivious to her real feelings. No matter how many times she maneuvered the situation so they could be alone together, he never discussed anything but work.

He was gifted; there was no doubt about that. Even though she had a master's degree in mathematics, she could barely understand some of his equations. His solution to the networking problem was nothing less than genius. She had believed from the beginning that what he was trying to do was impossible. Without telling Jeff, she had discussed the concept with her father who said, "We are probably a decade away from the technology that would make this feasible, Karen. And thank God for that. I'm not at all sure we have the wisdom to handle such potential power. The ability to number and monitor every person in the world is the ability to place the power to rule the world in the wrong hands."

Although she never said so, she was also secretly thankful that Data-Net seemed beyond their technology. The events of the past several years had shaken her confidence in man's basic good nature, including those in the country she loved.

The breakthrough had come as she and Jeff sat discussing the problem. "To monitor and process input data from every section of the world requires millions, if not billions, of input channels," Jeff said for the tenth time that evening. "Even if there were a computer capable of processing the data internally, the input and output [IO] would bog down hopelessly. It would take an IO processor working at the speed of light, and then a CPU operating even faster."

"Faster than the speed of light? That's impossible," she replied.

"Not so—well at least theoretically," Jeff corrected as he picked up his drawing pen. "The one thing in the universe that travels faster than the speed of light, that we know of, is magnetic flux."

"Like in a magnet?" she responded.

"Exactly. Remember the principle of magnetic flux? In order for a magnet to exist, the lines of flux must extend from one pole to the other, simultaneously. In theory that means that the lines extend across the universe and back, instantaneously." Jeff sketched a magnet on the chalkboard as he spoke, carefully drawing ever-extending lines from pole to pole. "If these lines are varied," he said as he rubbed out a few with his hand, "say by the close proximity of another magnet passing through the field, the change would be reflected instantaneously across the universe."

"I understand the theory," Karen answered as she puzzled over his reasoning. "What are you getting at?"

Jeff's mind was now operating at full speed. "If we use a modulated laser IO, the input signals will be available at the speed of light. We can simply encode the light pulses to identify the source. Same thing for the output. Then what if we process all the data in a magnetic bubble memory?

"The input/output capabilities would be adequate, and the storage and processing unlimited. IBM has been experimenting with flux memory for more than a decade, so in theory it might work. If I write my program to run on a Cray 1520, it should take less than a hundred or so linked together."

"A hundred!" Karen blurted out. "Computers? That would make it the biggest system in the world—by a factor of twenty!"

"Probably more like a factor of fifty," Jeff corrected. "It will take some engineering, but it might just work."

The next few months were filled with long days and even longer evenings as Jeff outlined his needs to bedazzled engineers. At first they also said it was impossible. "Even the equipment to handle the laser input/output would need to be designed," the IBM engineers said, shaking their heads. But Jeff had already determined that the laser communications system used by AT&T International could be adapted perfectly for his use.

With the full force and power of the government behind him, Jeff was able to get teams of IBM and Cray engineers working together on the project. Within four months they had a working model and within six months Jeff's program was being debugged.

Although there were still some rough edges to be worked out, in little more than one year the largest, fastest computer system in the world was on-line and processing data from several thousand businesses through the central banks. Soon, virtually all the stores, fast food restaurants, banks, and businesses in the country would be routed through a single point: Data-Net. Literally every transaction in America could be monitored and recorded. All that was missing was the elimination of all cash transactions, which President Hunt had accomplished skillfully. In a move approved by the vast majority of Americans, a new, cash-less economy was ushered in.

Jeff snapped back to the present as Russell Siever was asking for the second time, "Well, is the system ready or not?"

"It's ready," Jeff replied, still feeling uneasy inside. "Or it will be in the next week or so."

"Good, it won't be long now before we put the system on-line," the president said. "Jeff, I want you to stay on top of the problems. We have been in contact with members of the European Community and they have agreed to use the system. Are you sure we can handle it?"

"Yes, sir," Jeff responded. His mind was still preoccupied by something that kept nagging in his subconscious. *What is it?* he wondered. To bring the president up to date, he said, "I have worked closely with Dr. Thornton on the E.C. data processing system. He's really excited about being able to operate on a common currency exchange. It will greatly facilitate business between the U.S. and Europe."

"What about the Asian market group, Russ?" the president asked his economic advisor.

"The Japanese are still fuming about your announcement. They say they'll fight the system as long as the U.S. holds their assets."

"They'll come around," Cal Rutland stated coldly. "It just takes the right motivation."

Jeff glanced at the presidential aide and saw just the slightest curl of his lip. Whether it was the beginning of a smile or a snarl, he couldn't really tell. Based on past behavior, he suspected it was a snarl. Before he could say anything, the president stood up, indicating the meeting was at an end.

CHAPTER

8

ASSASSINATION

Two days after the meeting with Jeff Wells on the implementation of Data-Net, Russell Siever was meeting with Cal Rutland to discuss what appeared to be a shift in the Supreme Court's decision on Siever's pet project: the Fair Tax Bill. Siever had personally drafted the bill for the administration. It was his contribution to the anti-Christian campaign. He was livid when he stormed into Rutland's office.

"I heard from our contact on Justice Bowman's staff that he may oppose the Fair Tax Bill. Have you heard anything?" Siever asked with clenched teeth.

"It looks certain," Rutland said in a calm voice. "But only if he is still on the Court."

Siever stopped for a moment, then replied, "Bowman's not about to quit. And he looks like he could live to be a hundred."

"Perhaps his health is not as good as it appears. In fact, he may already have a terminal condition."

Siever paled measurably. "We can't just take out a Supreme Court Justice. The public outcry would bring us all down!"

"We can do anything that is required. Remember that!" Rutland responded coldly. "This is not a game. We will need control of the Court to implement Phase Two."

Over the next several days, items began to appear in the media indicating that Justice Bowman was siding with Justices Hartman and Kinney to uphold the so-called "Fair Tax Bill." Nothing could have been further from the truth. Justice Bowman had already decided that taxing church income violated the very principle of separation of church and state. But in his normal manner, he refused to be interviewed or to discuss the pending issue. "With Bowman's vote, it will be five to four against the bill," Marcia Harms, aide to Justice Bowman, reported to Cal Rutland. "They plan to hear argument tomorrow."

"You're sure he's going to veto the bill?" Rutland asked matter-of-factly.

"Positive," she replied. "He's had us go all the way back to Marshall's argument against Virginia's tax on church property. He'll use this case to reverse the property tax bill, too."

Rutland hung up the phone and dialed Jason Franklin's private number. Franklin had been waiting for the call.

"You were right," Rutland said when he heard the scrambler connect.

"Is it set?" the aged industrialist asked without further response.

"Tomorrow," Rutland replied. Then he filled Franklin in on the details of his plan. He heard the line disconnect and replaced the receiver.

In a routine established through years of habit, the Supreme Court Justices arrived at their offices by seven o'clock in the morning. They spent an hour or so going over the court docket and receiving briefings from their assistants on applicable laws and previous Court rulings. This morning three justices—Hartman, Bowman, and Kinney—all arrived at almost the same time. Their chauffeurs dropped them off at the justices' entrance and proceeded to the Court parking lot to await their call to return home.

Justice Bowman was the elder statesman of the Supreme Court; he had been appointed by President Kilborne three years earlier. Then seventy, he was the oldest Supreme Court nominee in history. But his staunch adherence to the Constitution had won over the Senate and assured his confirmation. Along with Kinney and Hartman, the three became the guiding force behind the Court's direction, bowing to neither liberals nor conservatives. Their positions were "liberal" as often as "conservative" on any issue, and seldom did they all three take the same side on a case. The one issue they seemed united on was the potential invasion of privacy created by the new cash-less system proposed by the Hunt administration. It was no secret that Bowman eagerly awaited the first case to make its way through the lower court system.

Recently, Kinney and Hartman had inflamed the Christian lobby by voting on the side of the government in regard to taxing church property. In their majority ruling they stated that the Constitution did not specifically prohibit taxing church property, provided the same standard of measure was applied to all taxed properties within the community. It seemed probable that Hartman and Kinney would apply the same reasoning to the taxing of church income. Bowman would be the swing vote. Information was leaked to the media that made it appear he was siding with the more liberal element on the court. This infuriated many church and quasi-Christian groups, including the outspoken Constitutional Rights Committee. Recent interviews with supposed members of the group demonstrated a growing demand for action. The arrest of John Elder was reportedly met with threats of retaliation.

The last to arrive, Justice Bowman stepped out of his vehicle unaware of the two armed, masked men that stepped out from either side of the building and opened fire with automatic machine guns. The three justices were cut down where they stood. They died almost instantly.

As soon as the firing began, security police emerged from the building. Several were cut down by the gunmen, but the odds were in favor of the policemen. As more armed guards appeared, the masked men bolted away to a waiting car. The car was roaring down Pennsylvania Avenue when several heavily armed security guards—part of the elite force recruited for protection of Washington officials—stepped out into the street. They poured a fusillade into the accelerating car, killing the driver instantly; the vehicle went out of control and burst into flames as it crashed into a parked car. Within seconds, the gunmen's car was an inferno.

In the White House press office, the phone rang a few minutes later. As the wail of sirens sounded in the background, Cal Rutland heard the voice on the other end say, "It's done. The car burned with the bodies inside."

Rutland hung up the phone. *It's time for Phase Two*, he said to himself quietly.

The news media carried countless scenes of the justices lying on the sidewalk in front of the Supreme Court building. Then the scene would shift to the burned-out vehicle where the two gunmen and their driver were cremated.

The TV anchorman from WNN was questioning one of the many Washington police officials on the scene: "Is it true that the gunmen have been linked to the CRC—the militant religious group that has been making threats on government officials?"

"I can't comment on the case at this point," the deputy commissioner replied.

"Do you expect any arrests?" the newsman asked in typical reporter fashion. "Is the arrest of John Elder in any way linked to this assassination?"

"I can't comment. Mr. Elder was released yesterday by order of the district judge. We will be questioning members of his group about his present whereabouts."

John Elder had indeed been released on his own recognizance the previous day. At the time, he assumed that the government had decided they had no case against him. He would soon learn the true motive.

Before the news interview was over, the Insta-pol showed that 78 percent of all those polled believed Elder and the CRC were responsible.

Later that day at Elder's church in Atlanta, a hastily called meeting took place. "John, what's going on?" Bill Frost asked. "It looks like the whole U.S. government is coming down on us. Why?"

"I don't really know, Bill. But remember, we talked about coming under persecution. We've taken some unpopular stands on some issues, and when a country gets into trouble, politicians begin to look for scapegoats."

"I guess I really never understood the true meaning of that term before," Ann Boatman said through her tears. "How can people allow this to happen? We're Americans too and we are just trying to do what is right."

"I suppose that's the same thing the Jews asked in Germany," Elder said. "There seems to be a mass mentality that takes over during times like these. People just want to blame someone for their troubles."

"What about the assassinations, John? This is serious. They think we're some kind of terrorist group. It's just as likely they'll shoot first and worry about the facts later."

"It's hard to believe this is happening, all right. As soon as the meeting is over I'm going to surrender to the local authorities."

"But John, you're already under suspicion. I don't know if they will even set bail this time," Archie Warner, the attorney representing the CRC, said. "I couldn't believe it when they shipped you off to D.C. after the last arrest. You should have been arraigned in Atlanta."

"That was peculiar," Elder agreed. "I'll tell you, I was a little frightened there for awhile. They treated me like I was John Dillinger."

"Who?" Ann asked.

"Never mind," Elder said with a grin. "I guess you're too young to remember him."

"You know, John, I think you were set up by someone in the government. They wanted you in Washington when this assassination took place. What better way than to arrest you, ship you off to D.C., and then release you just before the assassination," Warner said as he paced around the table.

"I've been thinking about that too, Arch. As unbelievable as it seems, I have to agree."

Just then the telephone in the outer office rang.

"I'll get it," Frost said. "I asked a friend in Washington to call if he heard anything."

Picking up the receiver he answered, "This is Frost."

"Bill, this is Sam. You're in real danger. The Justice Department just got warrants for Elder and all the district leaders of the CRC, including you. You're all being charged with terrorist activities and are to be held without bail—indefinitely. Listen to this, though: Justice also got a court order to shut down the CRC and confiscate all CRC's property as evidence. Bill, I'm afraid this thing is rotten at the highest levels here. I wouldn't doubt if they planted evidence."

"What do you suggest, Sam?"

"Have your people surrender to the local police there in Atlanta. Things are so hot here, an accident might happen when the Feds make the arrests. A special anti-terrorist force is being dispersed. The whole scene here in Washington is chaos. It looks like something out of the Middle East. My God, three justices gunned down right in front of the Supreme Court!"

Bill Frost was visibly shaken as he hung up the phone. He had been a practicing attorney for more than thirty years and couldn't believe what he had just heard. *The United States government was involved in framing a religious leader*—it was almost too incredible to believe. Then it struck him: It was too incredible *not* to believe. Most Americans would accept the government's case as fact, given the current atmosphere about religion in the country. Christians had taken on some unpopular causes and had made some powerful enemies, especially in the media.

A web was being woven by their enemies. The more they struggled, the more they would be entrapped. "At the highest levels," Sam had said. *I wonder just how high the level really goes*, he wondered silently.

He could see the fear on the faces of most of the others in the group. They were the leaders of the CRC that had started the nationwide organizations to link churches together. *It's no longer an academic exercise in free speech*, he thought. *Reality has come home to this group. I wonder how many will be able to stick it out?*

After Frost hastily relayed the latest news, John Elder stood up.

"Christian friends, this is what we all feared most, and yet what we all really expected. Perhaps the persecution has come a little sooner than I had predicted, but here it is. Now each of you must decide Whom you will follow this day. Things look bad, but the Lord is still with us. Just remember, our enemy is not the people who seek our destruction; it is the enemy of Christ. This battle has been planned from the beginning of time. We're just the foot soldiers. Take heart and don't deny what you know to be the truth. God will prevail, even if we fail. Let's pray. . . ."

The pastor led his accused leaders in prayer for more than an hour. After the others left, Elder, Frost, and Warner sat in the pastor's study for nearly another hour waiting for a reply to Archie's call to a friend in the Atlanta police department. He had asked his friend to ensure that the local police place them in custody before the federal officials could serve their warrants.

"I need to share something with you that I never shared with anyone except Julia," Elder told his friends. "I was always concerned that people would think me some kind of kook, or worse.

"For years, when I was a child, my mother said I would sit up in my bed with my eyes wide open, as if I was in trance. She said my eyes would be moving just like I was watching a scene in front of me. But when I woke up, I couldn't remember anything about it.

"This continued for quite some time—until I was thirteen years old. Then, she said I sat up one night and began describing what I was seeing. She had been waiting for that moment, so she was able to record everything I said. I'd like for you to hear it."

Elder opened his desk drawer and took out a cassette. "I made a copy from the original reel-to-reel," he explained as he dropped the tape into the player on his desk. "Remember, this took place nearly forty years ago." The men listened to the voice of a young boy as he told of thousands of Christians being arrested and imprisoned because of their faith and tens of thousands of others hiding from the police. Trials were held, with religious leaders from around the world testifying to the guilt of those accused, especially one—a pastor, known to be their leader.

Elder stopped the tape momentarily and explained, "The pastor in my dream was accused of treason against the government and sentenced to be executed. He was brought before a man of great power who had become the leader of the United States, although he was not the president. This man was heralded as a great peacemaker who had been able to save the world from destruction, but he was the enemy of God's people and intent on seeing them imprisoned or destroyed." Then he started the tape again.

The voice on the tape began a two-sided dialogue:

"I have the power to set you free," the man said to the pastor. "All I require is your pledge of allegiance to me."

"Never," responded the pastor. "You are the enemy of my God and, therefore, my enemy."

"Then I will destroy you and all that are yours," the leader threatened. "You are entirely in my control, and I alone have the power over life and death."

Again the pastor repeated: "Never!"

The tape ended there with the young boy waking from his dream and his mother telling him what she had heard.

"I never had the dream again," Elder said. "I often wondered if it really was the imagination of a young boy, or if perhaps it was a premonition from God."

"Maybe it was your imagination, combined with Bible stories your mother had told you," suggested the matter-of-fact attorney, Warner.

"Perhaps," Elder responded. "But you see, my parents weren't believers, and I had never read the Bible at that point. It was listening to this tape that made me start to seek some answers in my life. I became a Christian because of it, and later a pastor—maybe the pastor in my dream!"

The phone ringing interrupted their conversation. Warner picked up the receiver. "Warner here," he said.

"Listen, Arch, this thing is really big. The Feds have a warrant out on your pastor that reads like a Mafia contract—it's 'dead or alive.' The others are wanted for conspiracy. By the way, you're not listed on the warrants but Frost is."

"What should we do?"

"I talked with a detective friend of mine who is willing to take Elder and Frost into custody on my assurance that Elder is not dangerous. He's not, is he?"

"Absolutely not. I'm sitting with him right now. He's about the meekest terrorist you'll ever find," Warner said with a weak smile.

"You need to get him out of there and down to the station as soon as possible. The Feds are having a little trouble convincing the local judge that all these people are involved in a plot to overthrow the government, but they'll find a district judge who will accept their D.C. warrants if he won't."

"Meet us outside the police station. We'll be there in thirty minutes," Warner said as he hung up the phone.

"Come on, John, we need to get out of here," Warner said anxiously. "Once the government realizes that a lot of other people know you're in custody, they'll walk a lot softer."

Within an hour Elder, Frost, and six other CRC members on the federal warrant were being held in the Atlanta city jail in protective custody. It took less than twelve hours for the federal marshals to get a federal judge to give them custody. Elder was whisked away in a waiting car. Frost and the others were herded out to a waiting van.

9

CONTROLLING THE ECONOMY

Events were moving so fast that most Americans could scarcely keep up with them. The nightly news programs were expanded to a full hour on all the networks and carried the highest prime time ratings. Each network was vying for the latest details on the economy, the assassinations, and the crackdown on the religious "terrorists."

Americans flocked to their banks to surrender their currency in exchange for bank credits. To encourage the process and to reduce any potential opposition, Russell Siever came up with an ingenious idea: The exchange would yield a dividend for the public. For each dollar surrendered, a depositor would receive a 50 percent bonus in exchange credits. This quieted all opposition to the new system.

Drug dealers, accustomed to carrying large amounts of cash, had a problem: how to exchange their currency without tipping off the IRS to their illicit business. Siever quickly found a solution to that problem also. He worked out an amnesty program whereby they could make a one-time exchange, no questions asked. The dealers with savvy could read the handwriting on the wall and grabbed the opportunity to cash in their profits. With the removal of all currency, the sale of illegal drugs would be very difficult.

Media interviews with reformed drug dealers helped to sell the no-currency system to the public. Shortly after a WNN news interview with ten reformed dealers, public acceptance of Data-Net shot up to over 90 percent. Had the Insta-pol survey included the Christian community in their statistics, which they purposely did not, it would have shown overwhelming opposition to the idea. Christians feared the control that such a system could yield to the government, but since they were ignored by the media, their voices went unheard.

The subject of the cash-less economy was debated on the WNN

evening news by members of the National Civil Liberties Union (NCLU), who expressed concern over the potential invasion of privacy. Russell Siever represented the government's position.

"Dr. Siever, how can we be sure that the government won't use this system to control its citizens? After all, the control of someone's ability to buy or sell carries an awesome power, doesn't it?" challenged Fred Lively, the head of the NCLU.

"Certainly, Fred, and we're acutely aware of that. But remember that we are a democracy and the people of this country rule by the way they vote. Any politician who attempts to control the freedom of the American people will quickly find himself on the outside looking in."

"But what about the rights of the minorities?"

"Well, if you mean the drug pushers, criminals, and anarchists, they will have a difficult time of it because we will be able to shut them down. For us to do that, the honest people of this country have to give us a little flexibility. But I can promise you this, Fred, and you know me well enough to know I do what I say: If you, or any other member of the NCLU, see any abuses of this authority, I'll help you bring it to the attention of the president. But, also think of the positive side. Criminals will no longer be able to rob honest merchants who work for their money. With no cash in the registers, all a thief can get is a computer tape, or maybe a refrigerator, if he can run with one on his back."

Lively laughed heartily. He had been well coached in what to ask of the nation's budget manager. His instructions from the Society's inner circle had been clear: "Ask the questions, then support the program."

The Insta-pol showed that nearly 100 percent of the viewers supported Dr. Siever and the new monetary control system.

Within one month, all currency had been converted and the Data-Net system was up and operating, with only a few glitches in the start-up. Sometimes, due to an overload on the telephone lines, the computer-operated cash registers would hang up while trying to access the central processor. Once new lines were added, however, the system improved greatly.

Merchants loved the new system because they were able to receive their funds transfers immediately. However, those without computerized registers had to fill out debit vouchers to get paid. This delay in converting sales into profits ensured they would change over quickly. One huge advantage of the new system was the ability to determine immediately whether or not customers had the funds available. If not, the transaction would halt while the customer arranged a credit loan from the central bank. These loans were closely monitored and payments deducted from the customer's account automatically each month. It truly looked like a win-win situation for all involved.

The transfer to a total electronic system was extraordinarily simple. Most people perceived any change as better than the status quo. With nearly 30 percent of the working population unemployed, the emotional strain was taking a fearsome toll. Crime was up several hundred percent in most cities from the previous decade. Suicides, especially among the young, were epidemic. What most of the public didn't realize was that while the transfer over to electronic money had slowed the drug traffic, it had not lessened the demand for drugs in the inner cities. The result was a new crime wave with gangs of youths stealing everything from television sets to automobiles and bartering them for drugs. The media was quick to blame the Hunt administration for not doing enough to stop the crime and put people back to work.

"I don't know what they expect of me!" President Hunt said angrily as he slammed the paper down on the breakfast table. "How am I supposed to put people back to work? The government's dead broke."

Cal Rutland's deadpan expression revealed no sign of emotion, but inside he was smiling because he knew it was almost time for the next phase. "Mr. President," he began in his normal, condescending tone.

Hunt glanced over at his aide. *Just the way he uses the title is disrespectful,* Hunt thought. *He acts like he's the president and I'm his lackey.* Mark Hunt had been trying to decide how to divest himself of "the shadow," a name he had overheard other staff members call Rutland. He knew he would have to be careful. Rutland was a direct link to the Society and it wouldn't be wise to oppose them yet. *But I'll dump him as soon as possible,* he promised himself resolutely.

"Yes, Cal, what is it?" he asked in controlled annoyance.

Appearing not to notice Hunt's irritation, Rutland replied, "Dr. Siever has an idea that may be of merit. He asked to see you later this week."

"Schedule an appointment immediately," the president commanded. *Siever's a good man,* Hunt thought to himself. *He knows his place.*

"Yes, sir," Rutland replied with mock submission.

Since John Elder's arrest, he had been shifted from one detention center to another. After being held by the local police, the FBI had assumed control and transferred him to the Federal Penitentiary in Atlanta. There he was strip-searched, told to shower, and refitted with drab prison clothing.

When the agent in charge entered the cell, Elder asked, "When will I be able to see my attorney?"

"Shut up!" the agent commanded. "You'll get to see an attorney when we say."

"This is still America, isn't' it?" Elder replied sharply.

Grabbing Elder by the choke collar, which had been designed for maximum control over unruly prisoners, the agent jerked him to his feet. The pain was almost unbearable. The slightest upward pressure on the collar pulled the confined man's arms backward while forcing his neck into a near-breaking position.

"Mister, it's creeps like you who use the system to cry for help after murdering innocent people. If it were up to me, I'd break your neck right now!" the agent threatened as he released his grip on the bar.

Elder fell to the floor gasping for breath. He had been through this during the abortion protests. As his mind cleared, he silently prayed, *God give me the strength to bear the suffering and the grace to forgive.*

For the next three hours, Elder was intensely interrogated by three FBI agents about the assassinations of the three justices. He steadfastly denied any involvement or knowledge of what had happened. Often his refusals were met with outbursts of threats from the agent in charge. Elder had no doubt that he meant what he said. It was only the presence of other agents that spared him any more abuse during the interrogation.

In an adjacent room, Robert Jenkins, the Atlanta director of the FBI, asked the Washington director, "How do you expect to get a conviction with this kind of interrogation? You guys have violated every civil rights statute in the book."

"Look, as far as you're concerned Elder doesn't exist," the other man said. "You don't seem to understand. His organization killed three Supreme Court justices. If they get away with this, there will be anarchy in this country."

"I'm not sure the way he is being treated is not anarchy," Jenkins suggested. "If we're not a nation of laws, we're nothing."

"Don't give me any sob stories. Come up to Washington and see what's going on. Then tell me about your civil rights. We're on the brink of revolution in this country, and groups like this CRC want to push us over the edge."

"Then move him out of Atlanta. I won't tolerate any more brutality to a prisoner in my district. I don't care what he's accused of."

"We'll move him, but not until I get word from the Bureau."

Elder's attorney, Archie Warner, had filed the necessary forms to declare a habeas corpus in Federal Court for the release of John Elder and the other six men who had been arrested. After reviewing the petition, the judge asked the FBI's attorney to present cause why the men should not be released.

The attorney presented the executive order signed by President Hunt declaring the seven men to be terrorists and ordering the federal officers to hold them without bond. They were to be held in isolation until such time as the president ordered otherwise. In effect, Hunt had signed an order disallowing their civil rights under an 1862 law drafted to control the abolitionists during the Civil War. President Lincoln had used it to arrest and confine the government of Virginia at the outbreak of hostilities.

"This case has been removed from my jurisdiction," the judge declared angrily, slamming his gavel down on the desk.

"Wait!" Warner said. "These men have not been formally charged with any crime or arraigned in any court."

"Take it up with the Supreme Court," the FBI attorney said callously, as he closed his briefcase and walked away.

"This is unbelievable," Warner shouted after him. "This can't be happening."

That afternoon Archie Warner began the process of contacting as many of the CRC in Atlanta as possible. He was impressed with the efficient system of communication that had been set up to contact other members. Within five hours, over eight thousand contacts had been made and a meeting organized. What none of the group knew was that hundreds of their phone lines had been tapped and monitored. Word of the meeting was immediately sent to a special White House line: Cal Rutland's private number.

Rutland received the news of the meeting with uncharacteristic excitement. *Perfect*, he thought. *Now it's time to play the trump card.* Picking up the phone, he dialed the number he had committed to memory.

The telephone rang in the study of Jason Franklin. He picked up the receiver but said nothing.

"The meeting is on for seven this evening. Ask the leader if I should activate Judas."

Franklin turned to another man in the room and relayed the message. Amir Hussein, known to those in the Society as the Leader, replied, "Do so immediately."

After Franklin relayed the command to Rutland, Hussein stood to leave. "So it has begun, after all these years," he said to Franklin. "Our position will be secured soon.

"Make no mistakes," Hussein warned. "The enemy we fight will not give up easily. We must totally discourage and destroy his followers. They are weak, timid people who will desert when things go against them. But the leadership must be scattered and discredited. Anarchy must reign before the new order can be established."

Amir Hussein was born in Israel of an Israeli mother and Iraqi father. His mother was barely fifteen when she was captured by an Iraqi border assault team making skirmishes into Israel. After six months in captivity, she was released—when it was discovered that she was pregnant. The father of the unborn child was Achmed Hussein, the camp commander where she had been held captive.

Amir's mother, Saulif, found herself an outcast among her own people, shunned even by her own family. As a child, Amir, then known by his mother's family name, Flome, was persecuted mercilessly by other Jewish children.

His mother died when he was twelve, and Amir became a street beggar. It was apparent to all who knew him that Amir was no ordinary child. He had the cunning of a mongoose and the temperament of a cobra. By the age of sixteen, he was the recognized leader of the street gangs in the Palestinian occupied territories and supplied illegal weapons to the Arabs there. By the time he was twenty, he had amassed a considerable fortune by trafficking arms and explosives from Syria and Iraq into Israel.

He was arrested by the Israeli Mossad after a massive crackdown on Arabs in the occupied territory. Only the fact that he was half Jewish saved him from immediate execution. He was ordered out of the country and warned that if he was found in Israeli territory again, he would immediately be executed.

Amir migrated to America, where most of his fortune had been invested, and took the name of his father, Hussein. He continued to deal in arms from the United States. In fact, his contracts were so valuable that often the CIA would use him to supply clandestine operations in the Middle East and Africa. By the time he was thirty-five, Amir Hussein was considered to be one of the world's wealthiest and most influential men.

Within the Society, Hussein was known by reputation only. But the greatest portion of his wealth was spent promoting the interests of the Society and the concept of a one-world government, which he proclaimed he was destined to head.

Hussein had but two passions in life: a deep hatred of Christians and Jews, and a total commitment to establishing Satan's kingdom on earth. He determined that it was best to remain in the background of the Society, using Jason Franklin as his spokesman—for the time being.

"It is time to implement Phase Two," Hussein told Franklin.

"I will see to it," Franklin answered obediently.

Later that evening, in another part of Atlanta, Archie Warner addressed an assembled group of Constitutional Rights Committee members. "We need to organize a nationwide demonstration to protest the illegal arrest of John Elder and six of our district leaders. They have been falsely accused of anarchy and the Federal courts refuse to allow anyone to see them. The only way we're going to get help is by public awareness."

"Wait!" one of the members protested. "Remember what John told us after they arrested him the first time. We can't give them any provocation. The government is spoiling for a fight, and we can't win in the streets."

"So what are we to do?" another of the group called out. "Leave them to rot in jail?"

Soon the whole group was shouting at each other.

"Wait!" Warner bellowed from the podium. "The only way we're going to get the word out is by organizing protests all across the country. This can't just be a local thing, or the media will ignore it and more of our group will be arrested. Is there a way to contact other churches and groups in the country?"

Several people raised their hands and told about specific contacts they had in other cities. Amelia Frost, who had once worked as John Elder's secretary, rose to her feet and spoke. "Pastor Elder told me how to contact all the other groups around the country in case something like this happened."

Warner took the floor again and said, "Amelia, why don't you and the others who have contacts come forward." Soon more than fifty people had gathered and had begun to share information about how to contact CRC groups across the U.S. They were quickly organized into contact teams, and volunteers were recruited to call the names that had been assembled. Each group had a list of nearly one hundred people to call, and each person called would be instructed to respond in kind.

After the meeting ended, Warner was talking with some of the groups' leaders. "I'm impressed with how well John has these groups organized. It's as if he expected to get arrested."

"He did," one of the men said. "He was expecting persecution to come. Praise God that the pastor believed in organization and discipleship. We're ready to act."

The telephone calls went out across the country to Christian leaders in every community. It had been decided in advance that the first protest rallies would be held the following week. The organizers estimated that three million Christians would rally across the nation. A massive rally was scheduled for Washington, D.C., with at least two hundred thousand people from the area marching on the capitol.

Unknown to the leaders, word of the rallies was immediately relayed to the FBI in Washington. Law enforcement authorities across the nation were notified that the protesters planned to disrupt cities with violence if necessary. In virtually every city, including Washington, the protesters were denied demonstration permits. When this information made its way back to the Atlanta headquarters, meetings were held to decide what course to take.

"We have no choice but to go ahead with the demonstrations," Archie Warner said to the assembled leaders. "There is still no word of what's happened to John and the others. If we don't do something, the government will think they can get away with this."

"You're right," several others agreed. "We can't just wait and do nothing."

"If we protest without permits, we'll play right into their hands," argued Bob Bierson, one of the organizers. "John warned us not to take the law into our own hands but to leave it to God."

"That's all well and good," said Warner, "but I can tell you that politicians understand nothing except numbers. If you don't protest, they won't listen. The next time it may be one of you. John wouldn't leave one of us in prison without doing all he could to help, would he?"

"No, he wouldn't," the group agreed. The vote was overwhelmingly in favor of continuing the protest marches. At Warner's suggestion, the protests were delayed for another week to give the groups more time to organize, and the word went out across the nation once more.

The phone rang in the Washington, D.C., office of Cal Rutland later that afternoon.

"Rutland," the aide said as he answered the call.

"It's under way, just as you asked."

"Good. You're sure they will go through with the protests?"

"Yes. The group is committed to the demonstrations, permits or not," Warner said trembling.

"Excellent," Rutland said as he hung up. "Excellent."

Rutland rang the private number of Jason Franklin.

This time the phone was answered by a voice he knew well. It was the Leader, Amir Hussein. "Good evening, Cal," the heavily accented voice said. "Are we ready?"

"Phase Two is in place. The protests are scheduled for next Friday," Rutland assured him.

"Very good. Execute the Judas Plan immediately."

With that, the line went dead. As Rutland hung up he thought, *I'll be glad to . . . immediately.*

Later that day, President Hunt was meeting with his top advisers. The discussion centered around the recommendation the president had just been handed by Russell Siever.

"I can't do this, Russ," Hunt insisted. "If I try to cut off funds for operating the Congress, I'll be impeached."

"Not so, Mr. President," Siever responded. "The budget amendment gives you the ability to line-item veto any spending necessary to balance the budget."

"But it was never intended to shut down the Congress," Hunt said, a little less emphatically. "What do you think, Pat?"

Attorney General Patrick McMillan sat silently for a few moments before he responded. "It's probably legal, Mr. President, but it'll raise the biggest stink in Congress you ever saw."

"But it will send a clear message to the Congress that you can play hardball when it comes to appropriations," Siever said confidently as he glanced up at Hunt. He wondered if Hunt was smart enough to see through the smoke screen they were laying down. Probably not, he concluded. What they had planned was so radical, nobody would ever guess it.

"I don't know, Russ," Hunt said, for the fourth time. "To suspend Congress . . . it's never been done before."

"These are difficult times, Mr. President. It will take some imagination to make the changes needed."

"I can see Grant's face now," Hunt mused, warming to the idea. "He'll have a stroke over this."

Siever and Rutland knew they had won. The president was a politician through and through. He would never pass up an opportunity to stick it to the Congress.

"After all, a sabbatical won't do any of them any harm, will it?" Hunt laughed as he thought about Senator John Grant's reaction. His old nemesis would croak.

"When are we talking about doing this?" Hunt asked, enthusiastically now.

"Well, first you will need to get your Supreme Court nominees approved," the attorney general said as he considered the proposal. "Since only the Senate can do that, we need them in session. Then, with the three new members you appoint, the Court will affirm your actions."

"I love it!" Hunt said, slapping McMillan on the back. "The Senate passes on the men who will approve their furloughs—I love it. Grant will get an ulcer over this."

"What are the chances the Senate will pass all three?" Hunt asked his attorney general.

"I think Billings and Stroud are certain. We should have approval by early next week. Cummings probably won't make it. But that's okay, we've got Anderson as a substitute."

"Won't that cause a problem? What if he votes against this congressional appropriations thing?"

"It's Ms. Anderson, sir. She's the district judge from Mississippi. I doubt she'll side with Congress. But, even if she does, we still have the votes."

The president stuttered a bit over his mistake. "I have no objection . . . if we still have the majority in the court."

"We will," Siever assured him. McMillan confirmed it with a nod.

"What's happening with the terrorist thing?" Hunt asked as he glanced at the FBI's report.

"We have the leaders of the group from Atlanta," McMillan replied guardedly. He had told Rutland that Hunt didn't totally buy the FBI report.

"Have they been arraigned yet?" Hunt demanded.

"No, sir. We felt it would be better to hold them until we have rounded up the other leaders around the country. In the current climate this thing could get real nasty." The attorney general began to sweat. He knew they were on dangerous ground legally. He had been instructed by Rutland to transfer Elder to D.C. and hold him in solitary until notified.

"Listen, this is not Russia, Pat," the president said angrily. "I want those people to have the right of counsel and the courts. My detention order didn't mean you could hold them indefinitely."

"No, sir, we just want to be sure that the FBI doesn't find itself confronted with a terrorist army when it rounds them up."

"You keep me informed on this thing, Pat!" Hunt said emphatically. "I don't mind pulling the Congress' chain a little. They're big boys. But I don't want this country to become a police state."

"Yes, sir, we'll keep you up to date. It shouldn't be too long now."

"See to it!" Hunt ordered. His mind was trying to focus on something, but he just couldn't bring it together. This paranoia in the press about terrorists had him concerned. Other than the threats and the killings of the justices, he couldn't see any evidence of a terrorist organization at work. The FBI reports were vague and, he suspected, contrived. *I wonder if Randall is a part of the Society?* he thought. The very thought of his FBI director being in the Society alarmed him. *If that's so, I can't trust anything I read!*

At a meeting held at Jason Franklin's home later that day, Cal Rutland said, "We're going to have to move a little faster than we had planned. It would seem our president isn't quite the idiot we thought."

"We're close to putting it all together. We can't move too fast or we'll draw attention to ourselves," Franklin said as he paced nervously back and forth. "What does Siever think?"

"He says most of what we need is in place. The Europeans say Wells' program is remarkable. They think the system can be implemented worldwide in weeks instead of months," Rutland commented with just the slightest touch of respect in his voice.

"Does Wells know how the system is to be used?" Hussein asked.

"He's a bright kid," Rutland answered. "I'm sure he's smart enough to figure it out. But he's totally engrossed in the nuts and bolts. He won't give us any problems. After the system is up and running, we'll have several people capable of managing it."

"That's our one weak point right now," said Hussein as he stood looking out the window at the rain. "Tell Siever to keep a close watch on Wells."

"What about the demonstrations?" Fred Lively of the NCLU asked. "Are we sure they will start this week?"

"Judas tells me that everything is progressing normally," Rutland said coldly. He had no respect for the skinny lawyer, who looked oddly like a cadaver. *The NCLU has a real surprise coming too*, he thought. *It's funny, really. They're destroying the only system that will tolerate them.*

"Are you sure Judas will be able to deliver?" Lively asked in a commanding tone. He had great ambitions when this whole thing came together. He would be part of a new system, a founding father, so to speak. Plus, he would be in a position to teach his archenemies, the Christians, a real lesson. *God, how I hate them. No wait,* he thought, *not God . . .* he didn't believe in God. *Anyway, I hate them,* he concluded.

"Judas will deliver. This has been in planning for a long time," Rutland said in a condescending tone.

"Is everything ready?" Archie Warner asked the rally organizers. They had chosen the term "rally" because they didn't want their groups to be thought of as demonstrators.

"It would seem so," Bob Bierson replied. "I just wish we could talk to Pastor Elder. I'm still not certain this is what he would want."

"Well, we can't just leave him and the others to rot in jail and not do anything, can we?" Warner sometimes wished he had never gotten involved in this mess. He thought back to the time when he had first been approached by Elder, asking for his help. John was an up-and-coming pastor with a nationwide television program. He was beginning his campaign against the government and needed some legal help in filing briefs. Warner had welcomed the work then. He had practiced law in Atlanta for nearly twenty-five years and didn't really have anything to show for it. He had invested in the Atlanta real estate market before the depression and had been wiped out long before the rest of the country.

Right after he did the work for Elder, his fortunes picked up. Unbelievably, he was contacted by Jason Franklin's real estate firm about handling some transactions for him. Jason Franklin had been almost a mythological figure to Warner up until that time. He could afford to hire the best legal help available, and Warner had no illusion that it was him. The two-hundred-dollar-an-hour fees Franklin paid helped Warner to survive financially.

When Franklin's accountant approached him about handling an offshore deal involving several millions of dollars he was skeptical at first. Why would they want him and not someone adept at international law? Then he was told that the transaction was to involve some Colombian banks and he knew it probably involved drug money. At first he refused, but when Franklin withdrew his other business he was right back where he started—broke. So he took the work. The fee for the very first project was nearly two hundred thousand dollars, more than twice what he had ever made in his best year. He quickly salved his conscience about the source of the money, and adjusted to the lifestyle he had always wanted.

Then, two years later, Franklin had called him to a meeting at Jekyll Island to discuss a new position. What he heard there had visibly shaken him. It was believed that a group of terrorists calling themselves the Constitutional Rights Committee was operating under the guise of a Christian organization. Their leader was reported to be a well-known television evangelist, John Elder.

Warner was told that the FBI wanted to force the group out in the open, to make them openly violate the law. To accomplish this, pressure would be put on the CRC and their leader, John Elder. Since Warner had done work for Elder previously, he would volunteer to handle the legal work the group would need.

Soon Warner was being provided with tens of thousands of dollars to feed the CRC. Elder believed that Warner was tapping his rich friends for the funds they so desperately needed. But then the battle with the government, including the IRS over the group's tax exemption, was on and the funds were thought to be a godsend.

Periodically Warner would be given the names of individuals to be recruited by Elder as contributors in each district. Warner would suggest these people as sympathetic to the Christians' cause. Their level of giving quickly helped them to gain positions of leadership in each group. When the tax-exempt status of churches was threatened, they were the first to contribute several hundred thousand dollars to a defense fund. Warner's firm was the leader in each defense effort, always careful to defend, but not win.

Each of these leaders became established in the churches and other elements of the Elder organization; then they recruited other men and women to work at lower levels in the organization. Within two years they had infiltrated every level of the CRC and participated in virtually every phase of planning. Their code name was "Judas."

It was this internal substructure that would be essential during the planned demonstrations. Warner realized that what they were about to do might result in the imprisonment or even death of hundreds, perhaps thousands, of innocent people. His conscience bothered him, but he knew he was caught in a very carefully spun web. If he wanted to stay out of prison, he had to continue. He also knew what Franklin was capable of doing if crossed.

CHAPTER

10

THE RIOTS

Friday, the 12th of October, was the date chosen to hold the nationwide rallies. The idea was to focus attention on the plight of Christians in general and John Elder and the other arrested leaders in particular. A few groups had been successful in obtaining permits, but in most cities the authorities refused to grant them. With little or no sympathy in the media, the complaints by the groups went unnoticed. There were a few articles stating that a neo-Nazi organization or a religious protest group had been denied parade permits. Usually this was accompanied by a statement that the group sought to demonstrate against Jews, blacks, or other ethnic groups. With the depression deepening and more people out of work every day, there were few sympathizers among the general public. The nation was rapidly developing a disdain for anything to do with Christianity.

At 3:00 P.M., Eastern time, the rallies began to organize. By 3:30, there were groups assembled in sixty cities across the country and nearly three million participants. In each city the marchers, with arms linked together, were confronted by hundreds of baton-wielding, helmeted police, as well as recruits from the National Guard who had been warned that the demonstrators intended to ransack the cities.

In Atlanta, the group marched down Peachtree Street carrying banners saying, "Where is John Elder?" and "Religious Freedom." The Atlanta group started their march singing the "Battle Hymn of the Republic," but they had scarcely moved twenty feet when the police began warning them to disperse or be arrested. The demonstrators, nearly one hundred thousand strong, ignored the warnings and moved forward, *en masse*. As the group advanced, the police fired nausea gas into the crowds, which included women and children. Those in the front dropped to the pavement, retching and vomiting, as the gas surrounded them. Someone in the group yelled that the police were using poison gas and the marchers panicked. From somewhere inside the group, guns were produced and the sounds of gunfire filled the concrete canyons of Atlanta.

Several police officers were hit and fell to the pavement. The marchers who had drawn the guns continued to fire. The rally leaders were stunned! At first they thought the initial gunfire was aimed at their group, but, as several of the police officers fell, they realized the shots were coming from within their group.

"Oh God! Stop firing!" Bob Bierson shouted as he saw the police scatter, take defensive positions, and draw their weapons. Several of the leaders rushed to stop those in their group who were shooting at the police. Others rushed toward the police, frantically shouting for them not to shoot.

But it was already too late. The police fired as quickly as they drew their weapons. The marchers were scattering, but bullets are faster than legs and people were cut down as they ran.

Anne Bierson saw her husband cut down by a fusillade of bullets from the police. She knew he was dead from the way he fell. She grabbed her three-year-old son, Jackie, in her arms as she ran for cover behind the cars parked along the street. As she ran, she felt what seemed like bee stings in her side. Ducking down behind a car, she noticed a red stain covering her right side and realized she had been shot. Jackie, terrified, was screaming and trying to pull away from his mother, but Anne would not let go. Her hold on him was all that saved his life. A hail of bullets continued to ricochet off the buildings and vehicles. As Anne cried out, "Oh, God, don't let them kill my boy," she was struck twice more by the advancing police. With her last breath, she rolled over on top of her son, her body becoming a shield against the bullets.

When it became obvious that women and children were being cut down by their crossfire, some of the police officers began to shout to the others to cease firing. Even though the whole episode was over in less than four minutes, when the casualties were counted there were two dead and ten wounded police officers. And among the marchers, there were forty-three dead and sixty wounded—thirty seriously. Twelve women and eight children were among the dead.

The same drama, with only slightly different statistics, was replayed all over the country. The media rushed in to film the bloody aftermath and reported that the terrorist groups had viciously attacked police and other officials, just as they had threatened.

By evening, curfews had been declared in several cities, and massive police raids were organized to capture the scattered rioters. Video tapes of the shootings were seized as evidence, and the FBI assigned all available agents to review the tapes for suspects. The most extensive manhunts in recent history were organized to locate and arrest the remaining leaders of the group known as the Constitutional Rights Committee (CRC). The FBI produced long lists of suspects, carefully prepared in advance, based on informants' testimonies. The movement to eliminate Christianity in America had begun in earnest.

After the networks aired scenes of the riots, angry mobs stormed churches across the nation, wrecking and burning, without opposition from most law enforcement groups. Pastors, priests, and parishioners alike were dragged from their homes and beaten by mobs of youths, ready to vent their anger, spurred by their economic circumstances, on anyone. It didn't matter that most of those accosted had nothing to do with the actual riots. Their guilt was only that others pronounced them to be Christians, thus conspirators.

Randy and Harriet Cross were two of those fleeing for their lives in Atlanta. When the shooting began, Randy grabbed Harriet and their son Matthew, and ran for cover. In the confusion, they were able to make their way back to their car and then home.

"Randy, what's happening?" Harriet cried in a shaky voice. "Who started the shooting?"

"I think some of our group did," Randy replied in a rasp, his heart still racing from the adrenalin. "I couldn't see who it was, but I saw two police officers fall when the shots were fired."

"But the members of CRC have never been violent, even when the police provoked them. Why now?" Harriet sobbed. "Oh Randy, I saw Christine Wise and her little girl lying in the street. I think they were both dead."

"There's no telling how many people were injured, or killed— probably a hundred or more," Randy speculated as he held his wife and son close to him. "I'm just so grateful that you and Matthew are okay. But Harriet, we need to get some things together and leave here immediately."

"But why, Randy? This is our home. We haven't done anything wrong."

"I don't think that's going to matter much. This riot was no accident. I think someone planned it carefully, and if I'm right we're in real trouble."

"Planned it? But why?" Harriet asked as her mind raced in terror.

"I don't know, but it follows the pattern we've seen over the last few years. I should have known something was wrong." Even as he thought about it, he realized that those he had seen shooting from his group were new members. *Plants!* he suddenly realized. *They were put there just for this time. That's what I had been sensing. They were always the first to volunteer for anything, but I never saw any real commitment to the Lord in them.*

"Hurry, Harriet," he said forcefully. "If I'm right, we don't have much time."

"But where will we go, Randy?" she sobbed. "What are you afraid of?"

"Our neighbors! We don't know who we can trust any more," he said grimly. Inside he knew that the whole country could explode with violence at any time, and someone had done a very thorough job of ensuring it would be directed at Christians.

Randy said, "I just remembered an almost forgotten passage in the book of Matthew: 'Then let those who are in the cities flee to the mountains; let him who is on the housetop not go down to get the things out that are in his house; and let him who is in the field not turn back to get his cloak. But woe to those who are with child and to those who nurse babes in those days!' John Elder quoted that reference often in our meetings, but I never really understood its significance—until now!"

President Hunt spent much of the day viewing the news about the riots and the violent reaction against Christians across the country. There were scenes of mobs, made up mostly of youths, stoning and beating people who were trying to protect their churches. The media equated being a Christian with being a part of the terrorist movement.

After reviewing the FBI file on the Constitutional Rights Committee "terrorists," as the media so fondly referred to them, Hunt could find no previous acts of violence attributed to any except a small group from Oregon. This group had actually evolved from a band of fanatical tax protesters. Their religion seemed to be related to tax exemption only.

"This whole thing is a gigantic setup," the president said, slamming the report down on his desk. He punched the intercom button: "Cal!" he shouted, "Get Randall and McMillan, and come in here. You tell them I want them here in fifteen minutes! And tell Russ Siever I want him here, too!"

On the other end of the intercom, Cal Rutland knew that Hunt had been reviewing the FBI report thoroughly. *He saw through it,* Rutland thought silently as he dialed the FBI director. *Too bad for him.*

"Ben, this is Cal. The president wants you and the attorney general over here right away."

"What's up?" the sixty-year-old Randall said. He had been a statistician for the FBI for nearly thirty years until tapped by Hunt to become the director. He knew that the assignment had actually been maneuvered by Jason Franklin. Several years earlier he had been assigned to investigate Franklin. At the time it was thought that Franklin was involved with organized crime through some of his legitimate businesses.

Randall's investigation showed that there was definitely a link between some of Franklin's companies and large transfers of cash, disguised as foreign sales. Still, he had no connection to Franklin himself since each of the corporations used figureheads as shields for the parent company. He was preparing his report for the director when he received a call from someone claiming to have information on Franklin that would be of great interest to him. He agreed to meet with the informant.

His first encounter with Cal Rutland had been the start of a new career for Randall. Rutland, brandishing CIA credentials, shared a file on Franklin that included details about his involvement with the CIA as an undercover link with the drug dealers. The file, signed by the CIA director, clearly exonerated Franklin from any liabilities associated with his role.

Rutland had informed Randall that not even the president was privy to the information presented in the file. He said that to reveal any of the details would jeopardize not only Franklin, but hundreds of other operatives working on the drug connection. He appealed to Randall to clear Franklin of any suspected involvement in the drug trafficking in the interest of national security.

At first Randall insisted on taking the issue directly to the FBI director and letting him make the decision. But, two quick calls by Rutland to the secretary of defense and the vice president, who was himself a former head of the CIA, convinced Randall that the information was too sensitive to risk, even to the files of the FBI. Eventually Randall agreed to close the file on Franklin, listing the inquiry as unsubstantiated rumors.

Little did Randall know that his response had saved his career. Already in place was a well-documented connection between Randall and the drug lords, including several millions of dollars deposited into foreign accounts in his name. The Society was taking no chances on having Franklin compromised, even by unprovable allegations.

When Mark Hunt had become president, one of his first actions was to appoint Randall director of the FBI. Randall guessed correctly that it was Jason Franklin who had initiated his promotion. Although he had no knowledge of the Society, except by rumor, Randall became a supporter of Jason Franklin, believing him to be a strong patriot.

Once he became the FBI director, Randall was provided with well-prepared secret documents that detailed a plot within the Constitutional Rights Committee organization to assassinate several government leaders in Washington who had taken positions against religious groups. He had been unsuccessful in tracking down any specific facts on the group, and most of the details had come from informers highly placed within the organization. Randall didn't know that the informers had been recruited and paid by a private organization, one of Franklin's companies.

Rutland, responding to Randall's earlier question about the president's summons, said, "He's read your report on the terrorists and wants more confirmation."

"Can we show him the Franklin documents?" Randall asked. He had been told that Rutland had access to the documents if necessary.

"No!" Rutland said emphatically. "There are too many lives at risk. He's just likely to spill the information to the press." Rutland knew that the FBI director was a typical weak-kneed bureaucrat. If Hunt put pressure on him, he would collapse like a punctured balloon. *Well, I'll just have to see that that doesn't happen,* he decided as he dropped the receiver into its cradle.

President Hunt's management style was that of a loner. He wanted to make his own decisions, and even his cabinet members were little more than window dressing to placate Congress. Now that Congress was suspended for the lack of operating capital, Hunt was even more isolated. He had virtually no need for regular press conferences, since his opponents were denied media coverage. That fit well into the Society's plans, and Rutland had been able to convince the president that the CRC terrorists represented a valid threat to his own safety. This further isolated him, so he was rarely seen outside the White House and only then with a multitude of bodyguards. *That may change now,* Rutland decided. *He'll get a lot bolder if he thinks the crisis was contrived. That may work out very well,* he mused, his face twisted into an evil smirk.

The attorney general and FBI director arrived in less than twenty minutes. Hunt was sitting behind his desk, still reading the police reports on the violence caused by the demonstrations when Rutland ushered them in. The report read like something out of the early sixties: Three hundred demonstrators dead, seven hundred wounded, many seriously, including women and children. Against that were sixteen police killed and another sixty-five wounded. Many of the witnesses had similar reports from widely separated areas. The gunfire started in the ranks of the demonstrators, but was always from those well back in the crowd, and apparently only by three to five people at most.

Seems strange, Hunt thought, *that only three people would pack weapons if the design was to wipe out the opposition. It seems more likely that they were planted to start a riot.*

Siever was the last to arrive, taking his customary place opposite the president's desk.

"Gentlemen, I think we have a problem," Hunt said sharply, slamming the report down on the desk. "Ben, I want to know why the FBI is making a case against a group of citizens who appear to have done little more than protest some valid discriminations against them—including unlawful arrest and detention."

"If you're referring to the Constitutional Rights Committee, Mr. President, you signed the executive order yourself," Randall said nervously.

"You know perfectly well that I did that based on evidence the FBI supplied, linking the leaders of this so-called terrorist group with the assassinations here in Washington."

"Yes, sir, that's true," the sweating FBI director acknowledged. "Our evidence . . ."

"Do you mean this garbage?" the president shouted as he threw the reports into the director's lap. "That's trash! There is nothing in that report that would get any one of them convicted for a traffic violation. It's all testimony from a few FBI plants in their groups. There is not one shred of real evidence. Any third-year law student could get this thrown out as hearsay."

"The riots, Mr. President . . ." Randall started weakly, as he glanced at Cal Rutland.

"The riots," Hunt shouted again, flinging the other report at the director. "The riots are a lot of garbage. This report reads like the Kent State killings during the protests of the sixties. The only people who brought guns seemed to have been the police."

"The rioters fired on the police . . ."

"Yes, and according to the police reports they must have been suicidal, since only three or four in each group brought guns, and all the police brought theirs. Don't you think it a little strange that the scenario was identical throughout the country? Especially when the rioters took all the punishment. They were either incredibly stupid, or they were set up."

"Set up?" Randall said more to himself than to the president. "But why?"

Cal Rutland interrupted, "Mr. President, this group has been under surveillance for several months now. Our informers . . ."

"Shut up, Cal!" the president snapped. "I suspect you're more involved with this than anyone else. It was you who convinced me to sign the executive order. Come to think of it, it was also you and Siever who suggested the furlough for the Congress. Just what are you and your Society up to?"

"I'm just trying to serve your best interests, Mr. President," Rutland said calmly. But his eyes betrayed the hatred boiling up inside.

"I think you'll be able to serve my best interests somewhere else!" the president said with unconcealed anger, his face reddening even as he spoke. "I want you and Siever to pack up and clear out by tomorrow morning. Ben, you may be an innocent victim in this whole thing, but I can't take that chance. I want you to resign effective tomorrow too."

Rutland said nothing. From the look on his face it was impossible to tell if he had even heard the president. If Mark Hunt could have read Rutland's mind, he would have seen a black hole developing. Rutland was a man possessed by but one thought: Promote the Society. Now Hunt represented a stumbling block to his plans.

"Pat," the president said to the attorney general, "I want Elder and his people released immediately . . . and that means immediately! If you can't do it, I'll get someone who can. Where are they being held?"

"I'm not really sure, Mr. President," the shaken attorney general said. "The FBI has them."

"Well, you find out this morning!" Hunt ordered. "In fact, I'm appointing you temporary director of the Bureau—effective right now. Get those people released!

"And Pat, I want this witch hunt for the demonstrators called off."

The attorney general looked over to Rutland, who showed no visible signs of reaction. He sat motionless, like a cobra poised to strike.

"Cal, your last official act is to call a press conference for two o'clock today. I want representatives from all the media there. I'm going to lay this deception out for all America to see. Oh, yes, I'm also going to restore the Congress' funds and shut down this electronic funds thing before it goes any further. I know where Data-Net is headed now, and I plan to nip it in the bud. You can tell Franklin, and anyone else involved with the Society's plans, that I'm the president and the American public is my boss."

With that, Hunt dismissed the group like so many school children held over for detention. Randall left looking like a whipped puppy. He knew his career was over once the word got out; he would be lucky if he weren't brought up on charges of civil rights violations when the Congress got wind of what he had allowed.

Patrick McMillan had a thousand questions going through his

mind. Had they really railroaded an innocent group of citizens? He realized that he had relied heavily on the reports from the FBI in making decisions. He was determined to find the facts for himself.

Only Rutland left the meeting with a full grasp of what Hunt had discovered: that a secret organization had manipulated the top echelons of the government to accomplish their hidden agenda, and that Jason Franklin was part of it.

As soon as the meeting with the president was over, Rutland called Franklin and told him what had happened, "It means we'll have to move the schedule up," he said. "Siever says that the new file is ready at Data-Net. He activated it immediately after the riots. Our next move is to deal with Hunt."

"Right," Franklin agreed. "Maybe this is better. Can you get a look at his notes before the conference?"

"I can do better than that," Rutland said as his eyes narrowed. "Leave it to me. Our beloved leader is going to present the best speech of his life."

Rutland spent the next hour calling the various press organizations announcing the unscheduled conference. The reporters were measurably shocked that the recluse president was scheduling another press conference.

Randall White, manager of WNN's Atlanta office, asked, "Does this have anything to do with the suspension of Congress and the recent riots?"

Rutland, in very untypical fashion, responded, "The president has decided to take direct action to resolve the crisis facing our nation. That's really all I can tell you. The conference is scheduled for two o'clock." *It should be quite a show*, Rutland added silently. *I personally wouldn't miss it for anything.*

Within an hour after the riots, Randy Cross had loaded his family into their car and headed away from Atlanta, toward his parents' home in Jacksonville. Even as he was preparing to leave, the FBI had issued an alert to local authorities to apprehend the organizers of the demonstration-turned-riot. The Atlanta police received a bulletin with Randy Cross' name at the top. The fax from the FBI office in Washington was carried to the local magistrate's office and warrants were issued for the arrests of those involved.

The local television stations carried the pictures and names of the suspects, supplied by the FBI. In a matter of less than two hours from the time the warrants were issued, calls flooded into the police with information on the whereabouts of Christian leaders under suspicion.

This same scene was being repeated all over the country as ex-friends and neighbors turned against church leaders.

Randy had driven less than fifty miles when he told Harriet, "We're low on gas. I'm going to stop at the next exit. Do you and Matthew want anything?"

"I just need to use the rest room," she replied, still upset over the riots and having to flee her home.

Randy exited the interstate, pulled up at the pumps at a large Texaco station, and filled the gas tank while Harriet and Matthew used the rest rooms. After checking the oil and tires, he handed the attendant his credit card.

The attendant ran the card through the Data-Net verifier twice, then he said, "Sorry, mister, the machine won't take your card."

"What do you mean?" Randy said as his heart skipped a beat. Inside he had a terrifying feeling that he knew exactly what it meant.

"It just won't go through. Sometimes it does that when you've charged too much on your card."

"I pay my cards off every month," Randy said in a defensive tone.

"Listen, mister, I don't make the rules. If your card won't go through, it won't go through. You got any other credit cards?"

"Yes, I have my bank debit card," Randy replied, his hand shaking as he reached for his wallet again. He handed the bank card to the attendant as Harriet walked up.

"What's wrong?" she asked. "You look pale."

"The card won't go through," he whispered under his breath so the attendant couldn't hear. "He's trying the debit card now."

"What does it mean, Randy?" Harriet asked as she felt the chill of fear creeping over her.

"This one don't work either, mister," the attendant said. "I ain't never seen anything like it. It don't say 'rejected.' It just don't do nothin'."

Fear swept over Randy as he realized that somehow access to his bank account and credit had been stopped. *No cash and no credit!* he reasoned. *They've cut off our means of support!* "Is the station owner here?" he asked with confidence he wasn't feeling.

"Yeah, he's in the bay workin' on a car."

"I'll go see him," Randy called back over his shoulder as he went through the door to the shop area. As he entered the bay, he saw a large man working under a car on the grease rack.

"Are you the owner?" he asked as politely as his fear would allow. He had thought about just driving away, but he knew the attendant would call the police and they would catch up with them before they had gone much more than a few miles.

"Yes, I'm Bill Parks. What can I do for you?" the man answered agreeably.

Thank God, he sounds like a nice guy, Randy thought. "We have some kind of mix-up with the verifying system. It won't take either of my cards. It just stops and does nothing."

"Stupid system!" Parks snapped. "I don't know why anyone agreed to do away with cash anyway. Worked pretty good until the government spent it like drunken sailors."

"I totally agree," Randy said as they made their way into the store area.

Wiping his hands on the rag he had retrieved from his back pocket, the owner asked the attendant, "What's happening?"

"I don't know, boss," the attendant replied as he lit his cigarette. "It just don't work."

Taking the debit card, the owner placed it in the system verifier and punched in the access codes for Randy's number. The machine whirred as the scanner passed over the card. But instead of flashing either the green light signaling acceptance or the red light signaling rejection, the process simply stopped. The system printer, which would normally print out the automated receipt or a message defining why it was rejected, sat silent.

"That's the strangest thing I've seen since this stupid system was installed," Parks said, whacking the scanner with the palm of his hand. "I'll have to call the 800 number for Data-Net, mister . . . Cross," he read from the card.

In one swift motion, he punched the access button on the terminal that would have automatically connected him to the 800 number. Instead, all he heard was a constant busy tone.

"The whole system must be screwed up," Parks said angrily as he stuffed the rag into his back pocket. "You'll just have to wait here until they clear it, mister."

Randy's heart nearly leaped out of his chest. "I'm in a big hurry," he said as calmly as possible. "We have an emergency in our family. Listen, I live in Atlanta. We'll be coming back this way. Suppose I leave the card with you and give you some collateral to guarantee payment. Could I just stop back by tomorrow?" He hated to lie but knew that each minute he spent at the station placed them in greater danger.

"What kind of collateral?" the owner asked.

"You hold these rings," Randy said, lifting Harriet's finger in front of his face.

"My wedding rings!" Harriet protested. Then she saw the look on Randy's face and hastened to agree. "Well, I guess it's okay, if you're sure you'll hold them." She could hardly hold back the tears as she slipped off the rings.

"I can't take your wife's rings, mister," Parks said reluctantly as he eyed the two-carat diamond.

"It's okay," Randy assured him. "I'm an attorney in Atlanta. We'll be back."

"Well, okay then," the owner said. "But if you aren't back in a week, the rings are mine. Okay?"

"That's fine," Randy agreed as he hurried out the door.

He started the car and shifted into gear, heading back onto the interstate again.

"Randy, those rings cost nearly four thousand dollars," Harriet said as she let the restrained tears flow.

"It was definitely the most expensive tank of gas we ever bought," he tried to say lightheartedly. "But someone has put a stop on our accounts. Hopefully it's too soon for them to have a tracer. But it's only a matter of time until they get the computer program working on it. We need to get away as quickly as possible."

Harriet felt the panic grow inside as she held Matthew close. "How can they do this to us?"

"I don't know, but they're doing it," Randy replied as he made some mental calculations. "We don't have enough gas to make it all the way to Jacksonville, but we can make it to Dad's cabin at the lake. He always keeps it stocked for when he and Mom come up. We'll stay there while we try to come up with a plan."

"But what about our home and your practice?"

"I don't know yet, honey. But the three of us are still together, and we're still free. I have to believe the Lord will help."

"It's like the country has gone mad," Harriet cried. "We haven't done anything wrong."

"Somebody is behind this. It's too well-planned to be circumstantial. We need to pray for our friends. Some won't be as fortunate as we are."

11

KILL THE PRESIDENT

There have been some changes made to my program," Jeff Wells complained to Dr. Siever as he scanned the Data-Net files. "Someone has modified the search routine used to screen users."

"I know, Jeff," Siever said as patiently as his present frame of mind would allow. *That stupid Rhinehart,* Siever thought angrily. *He said he could modify the program to screen the names we gave him without interrupting the system. We would have been able to track the movements of every Christian in the country. Rounding them up would have been simple. Instead, he's probably warned the leaders that we're on to them now.*

Russell Siever had been groomed by the Society for the position he held in the Hunt administration. Orphaned at thirteen, he was sent to live with his aunt. With an inheritance of some three hundred million dollars, to be turned over to him in varying stages, he had few material needs.

Under the tutelage of his aunt, he studied international finance at Princeton, and was then recruited by a member of the Society whose job it was to seek out new, young talent. While in graduate school, he was selected to be a part of a group traveling to Europe to study the development of the European community. By this time an avowed socialist and atheist, Sievers was attracted to a young English woman traveling with the group. Their mutual interests included an elitist view of themselves, a disdain of religion, and a desire to establish a new world order.

It was during his studies in Europe that Siever was exposed to the one-world concept of economics. At first he dismissed it as idealistic and impractical. But, as his new friend Elisa pointed out, the European Community was the first real step in that direction. Elisa had been well trained in her home on the assets of a one-world system by her father, a British financier and member of the Society.

By the time Siever had completed his doctoral work, he was an established member of the Council of Advisers for the Society. He was easily worked into Washington society and later served as adviser for several presidents. His vast wealth and international contacts, provided by the Society, made him a coveted ally to many political leaders.

Now, as secretary of the Treasury, he was overseer of the Data-Net system. The cash-less economy, long predicted by Bible scholars, was fast becoming a reality—or nightmare, depending on which side of the system you were facing.

Several days earlier Jason Franklin had instructed that Phase Three be implemented immediately. Initially the Data-Net system would be used to locate the Christians. Later the system would be used to choke off their resources.

Siever had hired Dr. Jack Rhinehart to make the necessary changes to the system after Rhinehart had assured him there would be no difficulties. Rhinehart had been trying to work his way into the system ever since his colleague, Dr. Eison, had mentioned that Wells had been selected to design it. Siever knew they would eventually need to replace Wells, and Rhinehart had sold him on the idea that he could re-program the system.

That stupid Rhinehart screwed up the system, he thought again angrily. When he told Franklin, the warning had been clear.

"Don't slip up again," Franklin warned. "We can't afford mistakes at this point. Use Wells to fix the program."

Siever was trying to think of just how to do that when Wells called him. He was trying his best to placate the young scientist. "Jeff, we tried something that didn't work very well. It's extremely important that we get the program operable again immediately. I'll send the details up to your office, but this information is top-secret for now, so don't discuss it with anyone."

Jeff Wells was clearly puzzled, and a little disturbed.

"Why would Dr. Siever have someone else modify my work?" he asked Karen.

"Really, Mr. Wells, do you think you're the only programmer in the world?" she teased.

"No, but you can't just patch into a system as complicated as Data-Net," Jeff said defensively. "Whoever wrote the subroutine didn't understand the use of virtual memory. It slowed the system down by reassigning priorities. Eventually the whole system just ground to a halt."

"I was just kidding," Karen replied, seeing his reaction to her remark. "You're the only programmer I ever met who can make this system work. I have been helping since the start, and I still can't do more than work inside your subroutines."

"It's really not all that complicated," Wells said for what seemed like the hundredth time. "It's all a matter of allowing the machine to work on multiple projects and then schedule them out in priority."

"Okay," Karen replied, "I know. I know. I understand what you're saying. I just don't understand why it works."

Jeff was about to launch into his theory of simultaneous processing using magnetic bubble memory when the courier knocked on his door. He handed Jeff a sealed pouch and asked that he sign the receipt. After the courier left, Jeff opened the pouch. It contained a laser disc and a letter from Russell Siever.

"What does it say, Jeff?" Karen asked when she saw him frown.

"Dr. Siever wants me to modify the Data-Net so it will screen a group of users from the system. He also wants the names and locations forwarded to the nearest local law enforcement when they try to use their cards."

"Can you do it?"

"Yes. It's not much different from the file we set up to monitor how much credit a user has. But that's not what's bothering me."

"What is it, Jeff?" Karen asked. She had never seen him so grim.

"The data file he wants created must be able to handle up to twenty million names initially."

"Twenty million!"

"Think about it, Karen. We would be building a file of twenty million people who could potentially be barred from using the Data-Net. Essentially that means they would not be able to buy or sell anything."

"But Jeff, the whole purpose of Data-Net is to allow people to buy and sell without currency anywhere in the world. Why would anyone want to stop twenty million people from using it?"

"Control!" Jeff exclaimed as he finally realized what they were after. "Control! There is a group—a very large group—that someone wants to be able to control. What better way than to cut off their use of Data-Net. They would have no way to buy anything—not even food."

"They couldn't do that," Karen argued, unable to accept what Jeff was saying. "It would be illegal."

"Not if you had the ability to change the law," Jeff's mind was now racing in an effort to piece the puzzle together. "Why else would Dr. Siever also want their locations sent to the police? They want to be able to stop a large group of people from buying and to know where they are."

"What can we do?" The realization of what Jeff was suggesting seemed too incredible. Total control over someone's life? This is America, not China! But since the depression, and then the disaster in Japan and California, it seemed the whole country was changing. Maybe even the government is looking for someone to blame for its troubles. "Who are they looking for, Jeff?"

"What do you mean?"

"I mean who are the people they want to bar from using the system?"

"I don't know," Jeff said as he looked at the disk in his hand. "But somewhere in this file is the answer, and I'll find it. But, Karen, don't say anything to anyone about it just yet. We don't know who else is involved.

"In the meantime, I'm going to stop what they're doing in Data-Net by removing the patch. I'll tell Dr. Siever I needed to do it to restore the system's integrity."

A few minutes later, the terminal at the Texaco station outside Atlanta, as well as thousands of other Data-Net terminals that had been hung up, suddenly came to life.

"Request approved," the printer spewed out as the green light winked on.

"Stupid system," Bill Parks, the station owner, said as the terminal came alive. "It cost me twenty sales because I couldn't handle anyone's card." His calls to the Data-Net 800 number had never gotten through. Thousands of other merchants across the nation also had their terminals hung up as they processed cards of the Christians in Rhinehart's file. They had totally jammed the Data-Net's 800 lines, trying to get the system to work.

I hope those folks don't come back after the rings, Parks thought guiltily. *Nancy sure would love to have it. But I guess it probably isn't real anyway. Nobody would be crazy enough to trade a diamond that big for a tank of gas.*

In his study, Mark Hunt was working on his news announcement. First he would tell the American people he had personal evidence that the group called the Constitutional Rights Committee were not terrorists and that the assassinations were not associated with mainline Christianity in any way. Next he would tell what he knew about the riots: that the organizers were not the ones who started the shooting, but some other group that had infiltratred their organization. He knew he didn't have all the proof to back up his statements, but it would defuse the tensions around the country. Intuitively, he knew that he was right. Somehow Rutland and Siever were behind the whole thing. McMillan was a good man basically. He'd have the FBI track this thing to its origins as soon as Randall was gone.

He had decided to reinstate the furloughed session of Congress immediately. He might not agree with Grant and his crowd, but he trusted them more than he did Rutland and Siever. Jason Franklin was another matter. He would expose Franklin and his Society. It might mean his impeachment since he had violated campaign contribution rules, but that was a chance he would just have to take.

The president had just finished drafting the news announcement on his office computer. In another office, Cal Rutland was scanning the files, searching for the president's personal note pad. He found it under "Hunt news," with the current date. He typed in: "Review Hunt news, 08/12/01."

"Access denied," the terminal replied. "Please provide access code."

"So he put an access code on his note pad. He's getting smarter," Rutland said under his breath. He began a search for the necessary access code. He had tried at least a dozen codes, none of which would work. For the first time in a long time Rutland began to feel the pangs of panic. He needed access to that file or the whole plan could fail.

Then he tried "HUNT" as his access code.

"File available," the terminal responded.

Another stroke of the keys and the message that President Hunt had prepared for the news gathering appeared on the screen.

"Stupid, real stupid, Mr. President," Rutland gloated. "You almost had me there. But now I've got you."

Scanning the file, Rutland saw that it had been routed to the printer in the president's office and the file closed. The White House computer system had been designed so that once a message had been closed, it could not be erased without a permanent copy being made for the archives. However, it could be moved around as long as the typist knew the access code. This was a feature that allowed secretaries to move rough drafts from the files of staff workers and correct them as necessary. The same system applied to the president's files.

Rutland had already prepared an alternate draft of the president's planned news conference, one that was much more to his liking. He simply typed in, "Change: Hunt news, 08/12/01, to: Rutland, 08/12/01, move to: Rutland's file." In the wink of an eye, the computer responded and the notes typed by President Hunt disappeared. The terminal responded, "Changed: Hunt news, 08/12/01, to: Rutland, 08/12/01, moved to: Rutland file."

Then he typed: "Change: Rutland memo, 08/12/01, to: Hunt news, 08/12/01, move to: Hunt file." Again the computer responded and the screen showed: "Changed: Rutland memo, 08/12/01, to: Hunt news, 08/12/01, moved to: Hunt file."

Cal Rutland had taken his notes and substituted them for the president's original notes. If anyone were to bother to check, they would see only what he wanted them to see.

Ten minutes before two, Rutland noted. *He'll be in make-up by now. He wouldn't have a press conference on World War III without his make-up,* Rutland thought with disgust. He stroked the keyboard again and the printer in the president's office came to life, spewing out the information Rutland had just fed into it. In the outer office, Margaret Miller, the president's typist, heard the printer, but thought nothing about it. It was part of President Hunt's normal routine to have staff members forward memos to his private office. She'd pick it up later and file it for him.

A few seconds later Rutland walked in and said, "I need something from his office."

"I don't know, Cal," she said hesitantly. "He doesn't allow anyone in his office when he's out."

Rutland's eyes flashed with anger. "He sent me to get something. Do you want to call him in make-up to ask him!"

Margaret cringed. She secretly feared Cal Rutland. There was something evil about him. "No, I guess it's okay," she said weakly. "If he sent you."

Rutland strode past her before she could say anything else, slamming the office door behind him. He went directly to the printer and retrieved the notes that had been printed.

"Off of his own machine—what irony," Rutland muttered under his breath. He folded the notes in exactly the same fashion he had seen Hunt do many times before, and slipped them into his coat pocket.

The press was gathered for the conference; every network had sent their people, and there was great anticipation. No one had the vaguest idea what President Hunt was going to announce, but speculation ranged from declaring martial law (because of the attacks stemming from the riots) to permanently abolishing the Congress. In their wildest imaginations they could not have anticipated what his real intentions were: to expose a hidden organization within the government.

The sound level in the room made it almost impossible to hear, requiring everyone to talk even louder, further compounding the problem. Camera crews were constantly shouting at reporters who forced their way to the front, often blocking an angle to the podium that a cameraman had fought hard to clear. Security men were everywhere, but the overcrowded conditions made their jobs almost impossible. Most had to be content with standing in back of the room where few of the news people wanted to be. Each person entering the room had to pass through a metal detector, but the sheer volume of carrying cases and suitcase-like containers housing cameras and recorders made a search almost impossible. Tension among the security guards was high since they had so little actual control over the group. "This is really strange," one of them had commented earlier. "Rutland is always so cautious about crowds. I wonder why he allowed so many people in this time?"

"I don't know," his companion responded. "Maybe it's something really big and they wanted all the media here."

"Yeah, well, I don't like it. You could sneak a rocket launcher in here in some of those boxes."

Earlier that day one of the demonstrators from the CRC group in Washington had received a call from Rutland. After he hung up the phone, he had made his way to a drop box at the bus station. There he retrieved a small package containing a plastic cylinder and a vial of deadly nerve poison—developed from the venom of the black mamba snake in Africa. Also in the box was a press pass that would get him through White House security.

As a long-time member of the Society's infiltration group, he knew the risks well. Rutland had told him that once it was done he would be on his own. *That's okay,* he thought grimly. *This is what I joined for.* He pocketed the items and headed back to his car, his curled lip revealing the only sign of his inner mood. *The Christians will sure get tagged with this one,* he mused darkly.

When he arrived at the White House his press pass cleared him through security with no difficulty. He tensed slightly as he passed through the metal detector, but he had been careful to remove his keys, change, and even his metal belt buckle so he wouldn't get stopped by a random alarm. The plastic tube, now armed with its lethal projectile, passed without detection.

Once inside the room, he worked his way as close to the podium as he dared. Several of the cameramen swore at him when he obstructed their line of sight, but he apologized and moved slightly to one side. He kept his right hand in his pants pocket, firmly gripping the slender tube.

The room suddenly hushed as the door to the president's entrance opened. Two security men entered first, followed by President Hunt.

He approached the Plexiglas podium with the air of a man with a mission. His normal press smile was absent and the grim look on his face told everyone in the room this was to be no normal press conference. He reached into his inside coat pocket and removed several sheets of notes, obviously his message for the public.

Just as he laid the notes on the podium and looked up to speak, a slight pop, like the discharge of a pellet gun, sounded. A small projectile, no larger than an upholstery tack, struck the president in the neck, just above his collar. Instantly he fell to the floor, motionless.

The whole thing occurred so swiftly that no one really knew what had happened. Pandemonium broke out. Some of the reporters in the front thought that the president had fainted and moved forward to help. They were pushed back roughly by the secret service men who had drawn their weapons.

A woman reporter, who had been standing near the right side of the podium when the 'pop' sounded, saw the man next to her drop something to the floor. "He shot the president!" she screamed and pointed to the man standing beside her.

The assassin pushed her aside and rushed for the door through which the president had entered. But the large crowd made a quick escape impossible, and the security police had the better position from the perimeter of the room. They moved to cut off all the exits immediately.

Just as the assassin was pushing his way to the outside of the crowd, one of the president's security men leveled his weapon and fired several shots at nearly point blank range. He was dead before hitting the floor. The shots sparked panic in the room full of news people. *En masse*, they pushed and shoved toward the exits, overwhelming the security guards who were hopelessly trapped against the outer walls.

In the melee, Cal Rutland picked up the notes Hunt had brought with him. They had fallen to the floor when the president fell, pulling the podium over with him. Swiftly he exchanged the notes from his pocket with those on the floor, sticking the president's notes in his coat pocket.

In the meantime, several of the secret service men had made their way to the president. Pressing his fingers against the president's neck, one of them said, "He's dead. There's no pulse."

"Quick, call the emergency team!" one of his associates called out to the others in the room. "Begin CPR," he commanded the agent kneeling over the president.

"It won't do any good," the man said as he loosened the president's shirt collar. "Look!"

He was pointing to a small dart sticking in the president's neck.

"He's been shot with a poisoned dart," the agent exclaimed as his eyes settled on the downed assassin.

The room was clearing quickly as the reporters and news people were brought under control. Several of the seasoned war correspondents had stayed at their positions, cameras running to record the events. The entire nation was treated to the scene of the most popular president in history being assassinated on live television.

One of the reporters snatched up the papers it appeared the president had been carrying. As he began reading them, he suddenly shouted, "Hunt had proof that the Constitutional Rights Committee was planning mass assassinations! He was going to declare martial law!"

Suddenly the fear that had gripped the media evaporated and they rushed back to see the notes for themselves. The reporter who had first picked up the papers suddenly realized he had a bonanza of news information in his hands and attempted to confiscate them for his network's use. Instead he was confronted by the imposing figure of Cal Rutland, who simply reached out and took the papers while two secret service men held the shocked reporter's arms.

"I will make copies of the president's notes available to all media representatives," he announced calmly, as he held the papers up for all to see. "You may have two representatives from the media go with one of our agents to copy the notes."

"What happened to President Hunt?" one of the women reporters asked. "Is he alive?"

"I regret to announce that President Hunt is dead," Rutland said with as much emotion as he could muster. "We don't know all the details yet, but it would appear that he was shot with a poison dart fired from a plastic weapon of some kind. We will know more when the FBI concludes their investigation."

"Who was the assassin?" asked a CBS reporter.

"All we know at this time is that he was using a phony press ID," Rutland responded, carefully concealing the elation he was feeling.

"Was he a part of the CRC?" another reporter shouted from the back.

"We don't know that at this time," Rutland said icily. "But if it turns out that he was, the American people have a right to be very angry."

"Can we quote you on that?" asked a reporter from the "Post."

"You can!" Rutland said emphatically. "We will not allow this nation to be intimidated by anyone, including religious fanatics."

The melee that ensued as reporters rushed to call in their stories was reminiscent of a riot scene. Fist fights broke out over the use of available telephones.

Immediately the broadcast media carried repeats of the assassination, with endless rhetoric from those who were on the scene when it happened. Each report focused on the idea that President Hunt was assassinated by a member of the religious right because he was about to bring the full power of the government against them.

When the notes were made public, they contained a step-by-step description of how the president had thoroughly investigated the movements and intentions of the Constitutional Rights Committee and had concluded that virtually all of the fundamentalist churches in America were linked to the group.

The goal of the group, according to the report, was the assassination of leaders who opposed their philosophy, including Jews, Muslims, atheists, judges, and elected politicians, with President Hunt right at the top of the list. Their intent, the papers said, was to establish a government that would return to the fundamentals of the Bible. This message, followed by footage of the earlier riots, portrayed Christians as fanatical terrorists.

The reaction among the American people was, at first, stunned disbelief, then anger as more and more information from the notes supposedly written by the president was made public. Their anger was directed at those whom they knew to be outspoken Christians in their communities. Sometimes it was physical violence; more often it was resentment and an air of hostility. There was a witch-hunt mentality building that was gripping the nation, only it wasn't a witch-hunt. It was a Christian-hunt.

With his family safely tucked away in his father's cabin, south of Atlanta, Randy Cross decided it was time to check on some of the other members of his group. He left Harriet and Matthew and, over Harriet's objection, drove to the local gas station to use the telephone. He was afraid to use the phone at the cabin, since his calls could easily be traced by the technology of the digital telephone system.

He first tried to call his pastor; the phone rang several times, but there was no answer. Then he tried several of the church deacons, with the same results.

After calling a dozen other members of his church and support group, he finally got an answer.

"This is Paula," a small voice said as she answered the phone.

"Paula, this is Randy Cross. Is your dad there?"

"Oh, Mr. Cross," Paula cried. "They've taken Mommy and Daddy." Even as she spoke, she began to get hysterical. Paula had been hiding in the closet in her parent's room for more than three hours, just as her father had instructed her when the men had come to their home. She had not come out until she heard the phone ringing. "Help us, please, Mr. Cross, help us! They have Mommy and Daddy!"

"Calm down, Paula," Randy told her as gently as his racing heart would allow. "Tell me what happened."

"Some men came to our house and beat up my mommy and daddy," she cried as the sobs shook her small body. "Then they took them away."

Randy realized that she was not able to give him any more coherent information about her parents, so he asked, "Is there anyone there with you, Paula?"

"No, sir," she replied, sobbing. "They've taken my mommy and daddy. Daddy hid me in the closet and told me to stay there. But that was a long time ago."

"You do what your daddy said," Randy told her in a calm soft tone. "They will be all right. I'll be coming to get you Paula. Do you think you can pack some clothes?"

"Yes, sir," she replied a little more calmly. "Will you help my mommy and daddy?"

"I'll do everything I can, honey. But right now you need to be a big girl. Put some warm clothes in a suitcase. Do you have one?"

"Yes, sir." Her sobs were subsiding as she realized that help was coming. "I got one for Christmas last year."

"Good girl. Now you pack some clothes like you were going to Grandma's house, and I'll be there in a little while. And Paula, don't answer the phone anymore, okay?"

"Okay," she said. "Daddy told me not to answer it, but they have been gone so long. I thought it might be him."

"I know, sweetheart, but you'll be okay now. You get packed and I'll be there soon."

As he hung up the phone, Randy was visibly shaken. *So it's begun for real*, he thought.

Randy drove back to the cabin with his mind almost numb from what he was hearing on the radio. Reports were coming in from all over Atlanta of armed mobs attacking people accused of being Christians. Salvation Army staff who had fed the poor and homeless in the downtown area were attacked and beaten by angry mobs of young people calling themselves vigilantes. The Atlanta police were attempting to restore order but the sheer number in the mobs made their jobs hopeless. Often the most they could do was call for ambulances to pick up those who were attacked. "The death toll is estimated at more than thirty, and the injured may number in the hundreds," the newscaster said. What was missing was any mention of an organized resistance to the violence. It was as if the civil authorities were allowing the mobs to vent their anger on the Christian groups.

As Randy entered the cabin, Harriet met him at the door. "Oh, Randy, thank God you're all right. You should see the awful things they're showing on television. It's on every channel—mobs of people running around the city attacking anyone reported to be a Christian. They've burned down several churches. It's gotten worse since the announcement about President Hunt."

"What about Hunt?" Randy asked. He had turned off the car radio earlier and had missed the news bulletin.

"He's been assassinated in Washington—shot with a poisoned dart and he died instantly. Security officers killed the assassin. The newscasters say the president was about to deliver a message declaring martial law because of the riots started by Christians."

"I can't believe Hunt would do that," Randy said as he sat down. His knees seemed too weak to support him anymore.

No wonder the authorities are turning their backs on the mobs. They want them to vent their anger on someone, he thought. He was feeling both fear and resentment about what was happening. "We're not behind any of this," he told himself as much as Harriet.

"I've got to go into Atlanta. I want you and Matthew to stay here."

"Into Atlanta!" she cried out. "You can't go into the city. They'll kill you, Randy. I've seen your picture on television twice today. They say you're one of the organizers of the riots." Harriet was on the verge of hysteria. She felt her mind slipping into uncontrollable fear. "I won't let you go!" she screamed. "We need you here!"

"I don't have any choice, Harriet. I called Brent Olford's home and little Paula answered the phone. She's there alone, and she's scared. Apparently a mob attacked their home, and Brent and Betty have been taken away somewhere. I've got to go get Paula."

"Let someone else go," Harriet sobbed. "We need you here. We're your family."

"I can't do that . . . and you know it, Harriet. There's a seven-year-old girl frightened and alone in that house. It's my responsibility to help her."

"What about us, Randy? What will happen to us if you get killed or arrested?"

"You're not thinking straight, Harriet," Randy scolded her. "We're Christians and these are our friends. Now's the time when we need each other the most. What if Matt was all alone and scared in our home? Wouldn't you want Brent to help him?"

The thought of her son frightened and alone at home with both of them gone snapped Harriet back to reality. "Of course, you're right, Randy. You have to help Paula. We'll go with you."

"No!" he said emphatically. "That won't do her or me any good. If I don't come back, you and Matt will be okay here. Dad's old truck is out back. I started it, and it runs fine. He left a full tank of gas in it. Use it to get out of here if someone finds you."

"I will," she promised trying to control the waves of fear that swept over her.

"And Harriet, Dad's shotgun is in the closet. It's loaded with bird shot, but whoever you point it at won't know that. Use it if you have to."

"I can't shoot a gun. You know that," she said, her brow crinkling at just the thought of pointing a gun at another person. "You take it, Randy. You might need it."

"No," he said. "If I need a gun, that old shotgun wouldn't help. Besides, I couldn't shoot anyone either. I guess we're a pathetic pair of desperadoes, aren't we?" They both laughed, in spite of the anxiety they were feeling.

"Yes, I guess we are," she agreed, wiping away the tears. "And the media says you're the organizer of a murderous mob, a real mad dog."

"Someone is directing this campaign against God's people, and doing a very good job of it. But ultimately the decision will be in God's hands. We just need to trust Him."

"Oh, Randy, do you think we'll survive this?" Harriet asked as she hugged her husband.

"Nero was the first politician who tried to exterminate Christianity, and he didn't succeed with all the Roman might at his disposal. We'll survive," Randy said soberly. "It will be tough for a while, and some of us will fall. But we'll survive."

SURVIVING

As Randy was driving back into Atlanta to pick up Paula, he saw the station where he and Harriet had stopped the day before. Almost by impulse, he found himself turning off the highway and into the station. *Now why did I do that?* he asked himself. But something inside kept nudging him to stop. He had to fight off the urge to gun the car and head down the freeway again. *This is really stupid*, he told himself. *What if the police have contacted the station owner and told him to be on the lookout for me?*

He sat in the car, struggling with his decision until he noticed the attendant staring at him. So he turned off the engine and got out of the car. As he did so, the attendant ducked back inside and yelled, "Hey, boss, that guy's here again!"

Randy's first impulse was to jump back in his car and take off, but again something inside told him to wait.

The station owner came out, wiping his hands. "I thought you'd be back," he said in a growl that Randy immediately took for an accusation.

"Say, I'm sorry about the other day," Randy offered apologetically. "I hope I didn't get you into any trouble."

"Trouble?" the burly owner replied. "The only trouble was that stupid system. It finally cleared your card after you left. I guess you want your wife's rings back. I'll go get 'em." He disappeared into an office but reappeared within a couple of minutes. He reached into his pocket and retrieved the rings—a little greasy, but none the worse for wear.

As Randy took the rings, he was still trying to comprehend what the station owner had said. "My card cleared?" Randy asked.

"Yep, a few hours after you left."

Now he really was confused. *How did the card clear?* he wondered. He had been sure that someone had ordered his account frozen. "Can I still use it?" Randy asked, his heart pounding.

"Sure you can," the owner replied, "if you have money in your account."

Randy hurriedly pocketed the rings and asked the owner to process the card again.

"What'll it be this time?" the owner asked.

"One of everything," Randy replied. "Do you have any gas cans?"

"Yeah, I've got some five-gallon cans in the back. Why?"

"I'll take five of them," Randy replied, trying to restrain his sense of urgency. He wasn't sure how long his account would be active again. "Fill them up with regular."

"You think the Arabs are going to cut off the oil again?" the attendant inquired in a sarcastic tone.

"No, I just need the gas for some friends," Randy replied.

He set about collecting all the foodstuffs the service station offered, including several unopened boxes of candy bars. *Not real nutritional*, he thought, *but edible*. When he had the station wagon loaded as far as he dared without looking like a rolling warehouse, he asked, "How much do I owe you?"

"Three hundred thirty-three dollars," the wide-eyed attendant replied. "You gonna eat all that stuff, mister?" he asked in amazement.

"Not by myself," Randy replied. "I have some friends who will help, I hope."

The purchase cleared without further difficulty. Randy would have bought more, but he knew that a station wagon loaded with foodstuffs might attract too much attention. He wasn't sure if the police were looking for his wagon yet. *That's a chance I'll just have to take*, he told himself. He thanked the station owner again, waved to the young attendant, and headed out toward Atlanta and Brent Olford's home.

In Washington, D.C., Russell Siever had just hung up the phone after talking with Dr. Rhinehart. He was enraged as he rung Jeff Wells' office.

Jeff's secretary, Linda, answered the call. "Data-Net director's office."

"I need to speak with Wells!" Siever demanded.

Linda recognized his voice immediately. "I'm sorry, Mr. Siever, he's not in his office right now."

"Well, where is he?" Siever demanded. "I need to talk with him right now!"

"I don't know, sir. He left several hours ago without leaving a forwarding number." She had thought that strange, since Jeff always told her where he would be, but with the chaos surrounding the president's assassination, she hadn't thought to ask him. Even more strange was the fact that he took his personal terminal with him. He had ordered the terminal with a direct satellite hookup when he had gone to Europe to work with the World Bank, but since then he had worked almost exclusively in his office.

Siever slammed the receiver down hard. Rhinehart had told him the access codes to Data-Net had been changed from Wells' central control terminal. Also, the computer patch that the idiot Rhinehart had put in to track the Christians had been removed, so he knew Wells had control of the system. But the screening program had not been reinstated. He had no way of tracking the Christians. He was furious.

Is Wells trying to sabotage the system, or is he really trying to fix it? he wondered. There was no way to know until he talked with Wells. But he had a nagging feeling that Jeff Wells was no longer a team player. He dreaded the call he had to make to Franklin.

Kathy Alton sat silently as the two men discussed her future administration's policies.

"The riots continue to grow across the nation," the slightly built man next to Jason Franklin said without emotion. "There will be no difficulty in declaring martial law. With the Congress in suspension, you will be in total control of the country for at least two months. That will be enough time. What about Data-Net, Franklin?"

Jason Franklin was a man who had had presidents at his beck and call but, in the presence of this man, he felt weak and helpless. The power he sensed in Amir Hussein was overwhelming. It was as if he channeled the energies of the entire world where he wanted them to go. He had twice seen demonstrations of a power he could scarcely believe. One concentrated stare from Hussein could break the strongest man's will. He had no desire to test the man's dark powers.

He himself had been at death's door when Hussein had found him. Franklin recalled the meeting vividly. It was then he had become a true believer. Even after a lifetime of dedication to the Society, he had never really believed in the chosen one—the Leader. To him, the Society had been a means to an end—money and power, both of which he had possessed abundantly. But when cancer struck, neither his money nor his influence could help.

The pain in his stomach had become so acute that no amount of drugs could ease it, even for a short time. His body, once robust, had wasted away to a mere skeleton of ninety pounds. He had become so weak he could scarcely raise his head and had to be fed through a tube in his stomach. His physicians had diagnosed his condition as terminal, and no further treatment would help.

Then one night his old friend, Rabbi Flom, a member of the Society's inner council for thirty years, brought a man by to see him. Rabbi Flom's ties to the Israeli government had been invaluable in securing weapons contracts for some of Franklin's industries. In return, Franklin had covertly donated or raised more than ten billion dollars for Israel.

Jason Franklin, multi-billionaire, had been close to death that evening when Rabbi Flom said, "Jason, my old friend, I have brought someone to help you."

Franklin could not raise his head enough to see who was there, but he answered, "Unless it is God Himself, Rabbi, I don't think he can help me."

"Perhaps it is God," the withered man replied. "At least the god we have awaited so long."

Franklin's body was wracked with pain from the effort of talking. "Fairy tales are for the young, Rabbi. Leave me to die in peace."

"Are you really in peace?" asked the man he hadn't seen yet. "Would you rather die than believe?"

Something in the voice startled Franklin. It penetrated his mind. He knew he had not heard the words; he had felt them!

"I am the one you have heard about from your brothers. The Society was formed for me. It is my time."

In the shadows of his bedroom, Franklin could not see the man standing right in front of him, but he could sense his presence clearly. It was as if a force extended from the man through Franklin.

"Do you want to be healed?" the voice asked. Franklin wasn't sure if the words were audible or coming from within his mind. "Are you willing to serve?"

Franklin spoke in a rasping cough, "I am willing. If you will heal me, I will serve you."

The stranger then spoke audibly, "Leave him!"

A moaning sound filled the room, and a chill that penetrated to Jason Franklin's bones swept over him. But suddenly he felt renewed. He was stronger. "I can move!" he shouted as he sat up in bed.

"Your strength will return in a few days," the stranger told him. "You will live. But don't ever forget that you owe me your allegiance."

"I won't forget, my lord," Franklin swore. From that day on, his life had been dedicated to the tasks assigned him by Hussein. He had been made a key part of a plan so immense that he could scarcely believe it possible. But the events of the last three years had convinced him that it was possible. The world was theirs for the taking. And his benefactor would rule it all one day.

Now he was fearful of facing the wrath of this man who seemingly held the power over life and death, health and illness.

Franklin said nervously, "We have a problem with the network. Dr. Rhinehart made some changes to the system that didn't work. I have instructed Siever to have Wells make the corrections."

"And?" The tone of voice was clearly malevolent.

"The system has been restored and is fully operational."

"What about the ability to monitor the Christians?"

"I'm not sure at this point, sir," Franklin said contritely. "We have not been able to contact Wells."

"I want that network in place!" the small dark man roared in anger. "I want those Christians found and imprisoned. Do you hear me?"

Franklin was taken back by the outburst. It was the first time he had seen Hussein lose his self-control, and he was frightened as he never had been before in his life. Even when facing death, he had not felt the dread that came over him now.

"Make no mistake, Franklin," Hussein said as he regained his composure, "I can return you to the condition you were in when I found you. The control of these Christians is vital to our plans. Once we have those in America under my control, the others will follow. See to it immediately!"

Franklin said nothing. He felt an overwhelming dread. He had already seen evidence of powers that were beyond human understanding. Franklin was a man with no religious beliefs at all. He had always assumed the Christians were to be the scapegoats for the nation's problems, but he had never understood that they played some larger role. Suddenly, in his stomach, he felt an onslaught of the intense pain that had been removed three years earlier. He gasped, and as waves of nausea swept over him, he cried out, "Help me!"

Hussein waited for what seemed like an eternity to Franklin before he commanded, "Leave him!"

As suddenly as the attack began, it ended. Franklin stumbled over to his chair where he collapsed in exhaustion.

"That was just a reminder," the dark man said softly. "Now, where is the man, Elder?" he demanded.

"He's being held in Washington under close guard, as you instructed," Franklin gasped. He was still weak from the attack.

"Good, I want him kept out of sight. Be sure he has no contact with anyone. Have you located his wife?"

"No sir, she has disappeared. The violence has scattered the Christian groups across the country."

"I want her found! And I want that program working. We must know where they are and crush them! Report back to me as soon as you have located Wells."

Franklin sighed with relief as Hussein left the room. For all of his wealth and influence, Jason Franklin knew he was little more than a lackey now. He felt his strength returning, but knew he was living on borrowed time.

Randy Cross was just driving into Atlanta when he saw the first group, or more correctly, the first mob. They were mostly young, rough-looking men, as well as a smaller group of kids—some who looked to be about eight or ten. They were moving toward the intersection where he was headed, shouting something he couldn't understand at first.

He thought about turning around and finding another way into the city, but he noticed a police car parked at the intersection. So he decided to keep going, rather than take a chance on getting stopped for making a U-turn.

As he eased up to the intersection, he heard what the crowd was chanting: "God is dead, God is dead. . . ." Then he saw that the placards they were carrying were inverted crosses—the traditional sign of the Gay Rights Movement. The mob saw him just as he stopped at the intersection. They were still a good forty feet from where he was, but several in the group started throwing rocks and bottles at his car. He knew this was a mob that would attack first and ask questions later.

He gunned the car and turned the corner where it appeared the group was the thinnest. Three of the men ran into the street to stop his car, but he jammed the gas pedal to the floor and accelerated. They jumped out of the way at the last moment, crashing bottles and rocks against his car. His last image of the mob was the three who had tried to intercept him, throwing debris in a futile attempt to hit his car. The police car was still sitting where he had first seen it; the policeman made no attempt to stop him or the mob. *Apparently the Atlanta police have become observers, not enforcers,* he thought. He was shaking from the encounter. If he had any doubts before, he didn't now. His life was on the line. Anarchy was ruling his city.

He was praying silently as he drove on past burned-out homes and hulks of once-great churches that had been destroyed by the roving mobs. The sounds of fire engines and ambulance sirens told him that the violence was far from over. He was tempted to drive by his home, but resisted the urge for fear that someone might recognize him.

It made him sick to see what was happening to Atlanta. The stores that had not boarded up their windows were scenes of broken glass and merchandise strewn all over—inside and out.

Once he was past the inner-city, he realized there was much less damage and more police. Obviously the law enforcement officers were letting the mobs destroy their own neighborhoods and were concentrating their efforts in the more affluent areas to protect what they could. The radio news commentators made it sound like the mobs were offshoots from the Constitutional Rights Committee, destroying property in retaliation for the attacks on their group.

If it's this bad in a city like Atlanta, what must it be like in New York and Los Angeles? he wondered.

He heard on the news that the police had a list of suspected terrorists and were tracking them down. *Well, I know my name is probably on that list.*

The news programs also carried comments about the inauguration of the first woman president, Katherine Alton. The commentators said the new president would hold her first official press conference as soon as possible after President Hunt's funeral. She announced that her administration would support the efforts of President Hunt's administration to re-establish law and order in America.

"Which probably means more of the same," Randy commented cynically.

He turned onto Lenox Avenue, where Brent Olford lived, and let out an involuntary gasp. "It looks like a war zone." And indeed it did. The homes weren't burned, but windows were smashed and doors shattered. The personal possessions of those who lived in the neighborhood were strewn across the lawns. The ravaging mobs had carried off anything of value: televisions, stereos, cameras, and the like. The other items that were only of sentimental value were either scattered or smashed. The dead animals littering the lawns—household pets that had attempted to protect their owner's property—attested to the violence that had taken place. If there were human casualties, and Randy knew there had to be, they were not in sight. He assumed they had either been removed by the police and medics still protecting the city or by friends and relatives.

He drove slowly and carefully, looking for any signs of those who had wreaked such destruction on innocent people. He had no doubt that some in the mobs were neighbors, angry over their circumstances and quick to vent their anger on others.

Seeing no sign of life on the street, he drove into the driveway of the Olford home. He decided it would be less obvious if he went in the back door. The whole area was a mess. Water had flooded the lower level of the split-level home and was running out the back entrance. The destruction outside was bad enough, but it gave no hint as to the total demolition inside the house. The refrigerator and cabinet doors hung open with the contents spilling onto the floor. Walls were kicked in and splashes of blood were smeared on the living room walls. Some- one had spray painted the sign of an inverted cross in every room of the house.

Looking around one more time to be sure no one had followed him in, Randy called out, "Paula, are you here?" There was no an- swer, and he felt a knot in the pit of his stomach. To think of a fright- ened seven-year-old girl in the hands of that mob he had seen made him shudder.

He called again, "Paula, it's Randy Cross. I'm the one who called you. Come on out, honey."

Still no response. The hallway leading to the bedrooms was splat- tered with blood. It looked as if something bloody had been dragged down the hall. He followed the red smear to what appeared to be a child's room. There, against one wall, lay a bloody, blanket-clad bun- dle. His heart stopped.

With his heart pounding, he approached what he knew must be the body of his friend's child. "Paula." His voice broke as he spoke her name. In the poor light of the darkened room he hadn't noticed the shadow of someone crouched just inside the closet. As he bent down over the torn little body, he was suddenly attacked from behind.

"You leave my dog alone!" the shrill voice cried out as she plum- meted him with her small fists.

A relieved Randy grabbed her hands and said, "Wait, Paula. It's Mr. Cross. I'm here to help you." He held her at arm's length as she continued to swing her little arms wildly. Pulling her to him he said more sternly, "Stop it, Paula. I'm here to help. You're safe now."

Suddenly she collapsed into his arms sobbing, "Oh, it's you. I was so scared. My dog, Scruffy, is hurt. He doesn't move when I call him."

"I'm afraid he's dead, Paula." He expected her to break into tears, but she seemed to be in a daze, so he hastened to say, "We need to leave right away. Did you pack some clothes like I asked?"

"Yes, sir. They're right here in my bag." She pointed to the small overnight bag beside the closet door.

"Good, sweetheart. Let's go."

Carrying Paula's bag, he cautiously looked out the back door be- fore opening it. There was a man dressed in old army fatigues standing in the alley behind the house. He appeared to be talking into a hand- held radio. Randy quickly went to the living room and looked out the window, where he saw two more men standing in the driveway of a looted house down the block.

He turned to Paula, "Where is the door to your garage, honey?"

"In the utility room," she said, pointing in that direction. Randy took her hand and went to the utility room. As he opened the door into the garage, he breathed a sigh of relief as he saw the family van. He rushed to open the van door and looked inside, praying the keys would be there. A first sweep failed to turn up the keys, but when he pulled the ashtray open, there they were. *Just where Harriet would leave them, too,* Randy briefly reminisced. He told her a thousand times not to leave them in the car. He bet Brent had told his wife the same thing. *Praise God she didn't listen,* he thought.

Randy knew that his car was probably on the police's wanted list, so it would be best to take the van. But how to get all the things he bought at the service station out of his wagon and into the van? He didn't want to leave that behind, especially the gas. Putting the garage door opener in his pocket, he put Paula and her bag into the van and told her that he would be right back. She started to protest, but his tone of voice convinced her to do as she was told. He went back into the kitchen, looked out of the back door, and to his great relief, he saw that the fatigue-clad man had disappeared. He didn't have time to figure that out; he just made a dash for the station wagon, where he'd left it in the driveway. Jumping inside, he fired up the engine, punched the control to open the garage door, and pulled into the vacant garage space next to the van. Working frantically, he threw everything from his car into the van, while Paula watched in fascination. Taking one last look at the station wagon that held so many memories for him, he jumped into the van. As he was backing down the driveway, he punched the garage door button again. *That should give us a little time,* he thought. *I doubt that anyone will check the garage for awhile.*

As he pulled out of the driveway, he caught a glimpse of the men he had seen watching the house from their parked car. They were going into a neighbor's house. *Are they friends of Paula's family? If so, why didn't they help her before I got here? Are they FBI? Vigilantes?* He didn't have time to ponder the questions. He just dropped the gear lever into drive and sped away. Luckily for Randy and Paula, the men were part of a hastily formed neighborhood watch team that had been set up to watch for looters. The man out front, seeing Paula clinging to Randy, had informed the others to let them pass.

Randy was weaving his way through the city, using back streets as much as possible. He knew the danger from looters was greater on the back streets, but he feared being picked up by the police even more. He passed cars stalled on the sides of the roads, totally stripped. Many of them had been set on fire and gutted.

Paula sat huddled up against the door on her side of the van. No amount of coaxing from Randy could get her to sit next to him. His heart went out to her. He knew there was no way he could explain what was happening, even if he knew himself. *The world's gone mad,* he thought for the thousandth time. *Now I know what the Lord meant when He said, "Let him who is in the field not turn back to get his coat . . ." I wish I were out of this city and back at the cabin. But what about all of our friends? And what must be happening to Christians who live in places like Chicago and New York City? I wish we had a way to communicate. Maybe we could help.*

Just then a car pulled up behind him. He looked in the mirror and saw six or seven teenagers in an ancient Oldsmobile, with the stereo blaring loud enough for him to hear it inside the van. Suddenly, the battered Olds sped up.

Randy guessed the hoodlums were looking to replace their old car with the van, so he floored the gas pedal. In its prime, the Olds would have kept up with the van easily, but its prime was long past. In a couple of blocks, Randy was well ahead of the car loaded with angry teens. But as he looked ahead, the traffic light was just turning red. He knew if he stopped they would easily catch up with him. So instead, he kept the accelerator floored and rushed to beat the light. It turned red at least fifty feet before he reached the intersection, but he never even thought about slowing down. As he sped through the light, two cars approaching from the cross street started through. Seeing that he was sure to hit one of them broadside, Randy twisted the wheel of the van and attempted to slide past the cars and onto the street to his right. He almost made it, too, but the rear of the van skidded into the front car. The van spun around in the street and came to a halt on the sidewalk.

Meanwhile the car full of teens had no chance of stopping since the brakes of the old junker were worn thin. The brake pedal dropped to the floor as the driver smashed down on it. His eyes wide with alarm, he pumped the pedal frantically and the hydraulic system responded by providing minimal braking—just enough to slow the hurtling car to controllable speed. The battered Olds smashed into the parked cars and careened onto the opposite sidewalk. As it hit the curb, the Olds flipped over and rolled three times.

The whole event took less than twenty seconds, but to Randy it seemed more like an hour. The Olds came to rest upside down. Immediately teenagers came crawling out of it from every opening and scattered in all directions. Randy glanced over at the other drivers whose vehicles had been hit either by his van or the Olds. They looked frightened, but otherwise unhurt. Then he heard the sound of a police siren headed toward the scene of the accident.

I'd like to stay, he thought, but Paula's screaming reminded him of a greater danger, so he shoved the van into gear and sped off, past the oncoming police car.

The officer, unable to give pursuit because of the chaos in the intersection, noted the license number and called it in to his dispatcher. But he also noted the pile of stereos and VCRs that had dumped out of the trunk of the Olds when it came to rest upside down. The occupants had made quick exits.

Randy continued through the city without further incident. Once he reached the perimeter, he headed directly for Interstate I-75 South.

I know that policeman got my license number, Randy worried silently. *God, let us make it back to the cabin.*

In fact, the patrol car driver had called the van tags in to the dispatcher who looked it up on the stolen vehicle sheet. "Nothing on the van," she relayed to the patrol car. "Probably just some frightened citizen trying to get away."

"Can't say that I blame them," the policeman quipped. "This place is like a zoo." He put the van out of his mind and concentrated on working out the mess in the intersection.

It was nearly six before Randy pulled up in front of the cabin. Harriet rushed out to meet him. "Thank God, you're okay!" she said as tears streamed down her cheeks. "You were gone so long, and I was so frightened." Then she saw Paula huddled against the passenger door and her motherly instincts took over. She rushed around the van, opened the door, and cradled the frightened girl in her arms.

THE NEW PRESIDENT

Cal Rutland was working in his office when the call came from Siever. He was busy tying the ends together to make the transfer of power go smoothly. Most of the Cabinet positions would stay the same, as would most of the advisory positions. The attorney general, Patrick McMillan, would resign, paving the way for Fred Lively's nomination to that position. There was sure to be a howl from the conservatives in Congress, but by the time the Congress reconvened, the transfer would be several months old, and it would be difficult to remove him then. Rutland despised the slimy little man. *But I know he will prosecute the Christians with zeal—perhaps even persecute them*, he mused.

"Rutland here," he said as he picked up the receiver.

"This is Siever. Have you heard from Wells?"

"No, I haven't," Rutland replied briskly. "Is something wrong?" He thought silently, *Siever, you are an idiot! Bringing Rhinehart in from Cal Tech was stupid. Wells is light years ahead of him*.

"I just got a call from Franklin," Siever said. "He had a meeting with Hussein. He wants the screening program activated immediately, but Wells is missing."

Rutland was surprised that Franklin would mention Hussein to Siever. He was so secretive that only the top three men in the Society knew who Hussein was. Rutland had first met him when he was recruited for the Society in Washington, but at that time he hadn't known who he was. The next time was when the plans for the takeover of the U.S. economy had been laid out. He still had a difficult time believing the meeting had been real.

The man, known only as "Hussein" to Rutland, looked for all the world like Adolf Hitler. Rutland had only seen pictures of the German ruler who nearly conquered Europe, but the resemblance was startling. The mannerisms were the same, and the magnetism was the same.

At first Rutland dismissed the similarities as mere coincidences. After all, it is said that everyone has a double in the world. But this man had the ability to know exactly what someone was thinking and would often answer even before he voiced a question. Then Rutland heard about Jason Franklin's remarkable recovery. Coincidence again? Perhaps, but he didn't doubt the Leader's powers. He had heard rumors from the Society that the Leader was the long-awaited messiah that would rule the world. Having met him, Rutland believed it, and totally dedicated his life to serving him. They had worked together many times since, and Hussein had selected Rutland as his implementor.

"What is the problem with Wells?" Rutland asked, irritated. He could not stand incompetence, and he was convinced that Siever was incompetent. He was dedicated to the cause for sure, but he made too many stupid mistakes.

"He's not in his office," Siever replied coldly, angry because Rutland always acted like his superior. *I'm the one in charge of the Data-Net project, not Rutland,* Siever thought. *After all, Rutland is just a flunky for the president.* "It's not like Wells to leave without notifying anyone."

Rutland sat up abruptly. "Is there a problem with the program?"

"No, not in the main program, but apparently Wells removed Rhinehart's patch, and now the user screen doesn't function."

"Did you ever think that perhaps Wells was going to test the screen before installing it?" Rutland asked, purposely sounding like a school teacher scolding a careless student.

"Naturally, I thought of that," Siever said defensively. *I let him get the edge again,* he thought. "But he apparently assigned a new access code and then took the master terminal with him. We can't get into the system at all now."

That caught Rutland's attention. Wells had always been loyal and obedient in his tasks, but he knew Wells was a genius and would eventually piece the whole thing together. Then he would either have to be recruited into the Society or would have to be eliminated. If Wells had purposely blocked entry into Data-Net, no one else would break his code. Now they had a worldwide system with a single point failure—Jeff Wells.

"What does he know?" Rutland demanded in his normal abrasive manner.

Siever was getting more annoyed by the moment. He knew the thing with Rhinehart had been a mistake, and it was clear that Rutland would not let him forget it. He was caught in the middle of a typical Washington squeeze called "blame the other guy." The next move was obvious; he had used it many times himself.

"I have no idea what Wells knows," Siever replied gruffly. "Remember, he's your man. You chose him personally."

Rutland was not a man to be bullied, no matter what. He responded, "Listen, you idiot, I'm not concerned about whose man Wells is, or was. I want to know where he is now. And I want that system up and running as the Leader directed. If you would like, I'll schedule a meeting with him so he can decide which of us is to die first if the system fails. We're in this to the end, Siever, and it's no game."

Siever realized that Rutland was dead serious. *He's crazy*, Siever thought. *They're all crazy!* Then he remembered that he was in the middle of a plot to overthrow the United States government. He was in it, and there was no way out except to win or die trying. Suddenly the normally pompous statistician-turned-politician was defeated and he knew it. "I'll find Wells," he said meekly.

"Good," Rutland replied firmly. "We're nearly there now, so don't screw it up. If Wells has turned, you call me immediately." With that, Rutland hung up the phone. *He'll have to go when this problem is cleared up*, he told himself resolutely.

From his cell in the stockade at Andrews Air Force Base in Maryland, Pastor John Elder could hear the changing of his guard. He had been kept in isolation for what seemed like weeks now. Any time he was being interrogated, Elder began quoting Scripture verses, infuriating the interrogator. The only thing that saved him from physical abuse was that orders had been given not to harm him. Someone wanted him alive, and relatively healthy—at least for the time being.

During the initial arrest and shuttling around from one location to another, Elder had gotten angry. His rights as an American citizen were clearly being violated. He had demanded to see his attorney and demanded to hear the accusations against him. But then, as time passed, he began to understand more clearly what was happening to him and probably to other Christians. *This is not an issue of individual freedom*, he had told himself. *It is a confrontation between God and Satan; we just happen to be caught in the middle.* Once he stopped thinking about his rights as an American and began thinking about his position as a soldier of Christ, he felt a real peace for the first time in many years.

The only person he was allowed to communicate with was his interrogator from the FBI—a thoroughly abusive man called Morgan. With no outside contact at all, Elder knew nothing about the events that had taken place since his capture. The interrogator had dropped hints about the riots and hunting down the other "terrorists," as he commonly referred to Christians.

At first the interrogations had been long hours in a dull gray room. Blinding lights kept him from getting a clear view of his interrogator. Often the sessions would go on for hours at a time, with Elder staunchly denying any involvement with a terrorist group. Even when he was returned to his cell, the bright lights were kept on constantly. When he slept, it was only for short snatches of fitful rest. Gradually his defenses were being worn down. Elder guessed he was being held at a military installation because of the drab colors on the walls, but he had no hint as to where he might be.

He spent many hours on his knees, asking God to protect other Christians who must certainly be coming under persecution as well. He prayed for Julia most of all. *Sweet Julia,* he thought. *She's never hurt a living thing in her life.*

The sounds outside his cell settled down and Elder knew the guard had been changed. His only way to track time was by the changing of his guard. Even his meals were brought at odd intervals so that his biological clock was confused. He had read in articles written by POWs that much the same technique had been used during the Vietnam War. The purpose was to confuse the prisoner and disorient him.

The single factor that most of the POWs said sustained them and maintained their sanity was their faith in God. Some had started out with faith in their families but had quickly been broken by discouraging letters—both real and faked. But those who had an unshakable faith in God were able to resist discouragement, and even grow stronger. Once he began a regular routine of praying and reciting Scripture, Elder felt his faith and strength returning.

He had often tried to communicate with the guards outside his door but with no success. They might have been deaf for all he knew, since not even one had responded to his questions. He had developed a routine that included witnessing to the unseen guard through the door. He also practiced some of his best sermons on the unseen guards. With the changing of the guard, he began the routine again by asking, "Do you know the Lord as your Savior, Brother?"

To his shock the guard responded, "Yes, I do, Pastor."

"Well, praise God," Elder said in amazement. "Who are you?"

"Let's just say I'm a friend. I heard that you were a prisoner in the solitary cell and I was able to get assigned to the detail."

"Well, it sure is good to hear a friendly voice again. Can you tell me what is happening?"

"It's like the whole country has gone mad, Pastor. Since the president was assassinated, mobs have been roaming the streets looting and raping."

"You said the president was assassinated?" Elder interrupted. "When did that happen? And who did it?"

"I thought you would have known," the guard said in a whisper. "The president was killed three days ago, during a press conference at the White House. The assassin was a man linked to your Constitutional Rights Committee. The press now calls them 'The Terrorists.'"

"Our group has nothing to do with terrorism," Elder said bitterly as he felt himself getting angry again. *Calm down, John,* he told himself. *You've been all through this before.*

"I never thought so, Pastor."

"Call me John, please. We're all Christians in this conflict—not leaders and followers."

"Thanks, John. Anyway, the FBI linked the man to a part of your group in Atlanta. There is a general roundup of all the Christians there and in other parts of the country. But the roving gangs are looting, raping, and killing those known to be Christians, almost with impunity. Like I said, the country's gone mad."

"Is there any word of my wife?" Elder questioned as he held his breath in anticipation. He could take whatever they could do to him, but Julia was another matter. He wasn't sure what she would do if she were imprisoned.

"I don't really know, Pastor, but I would assume she is still free. At least she isn't here. You can bet if they had her you'd be the first to know it."

"I think you're right." Elder relaxed his tense muscles once again. *Thank God, at least Julia is still free,* he thought. "Do you have any idea about the Christian groups across the country? Is anything being done to protect them?"

"Well, Katherine Alton is president now, and she has declared a state of emergency and put the country under martial law."

"What does that mean?" Elder asked as his heart sank a little.

"It means that our new president has suspended the Constitution because of a state of emergency. As the Commander-in-Chief of the Armed Forces, she has absolute authority, at least for now."

"What about the Congress and the Supreme Court?" Elder asked, trying to grasp what he was hearing. *Martial law—in America!*

"Well, the Congress is still in recess, although the president says she will allocate new funding for them shortly. A select group of senators and congressmen are working with her on policy decisions during this crisis."

"A very select group, I would suspect," Elder muttered in a low voice.

"You're right. The group consists of some of the staunch congressional liberals. But it's Lively who's leading the crusade to track down and arrest the Christians."

"Lively? You don't mean Fred Lively of the National Civil Liberties Union?"

"I mean Attorney General Fred Lively now," the guard said with disgust. "He was appointed by President Alton and confirmed by the select committee. He's my boss now."

Dear God, Elder thought. *We really are in the hands of the enemy now.* "Why hasn't the Supreme Court moved to block these illegal arrests?"

"The Court is now controlled by the administration," the guard said bitterly. "The new justices have provided the swing votes. The Court has voted five to four that the president does have the power to invoke martial law in a national emergency.

"One thing about it," the guard said in dead seriousness, "no one can deny we have a national emergency. You can't walk the streets of D.C. unless you're armed to the teeth. And if a civilian is caught with a gun, he's arrested; so only the criminals carry guns."

"You said D.C.," Elder interrupted. "Does that mean I'm being held in Washington?"

"You mean they didn't even tell you where you are?" the guard asked, shaking his head in an unseen gesture. "Actually, you're in Maryland, in the detention center at Andrews Air Force Base."

Elder thought a moment before he ventured, "Can you help me?"

"I don't think so, Pastor. At least not right now. You're under constant watch and all the gates are locked tight. Maybe I can get some word out about where you are. Is there anyone you can trust that I can call?"

"The only person I know of is my attorney, Archie Warner, in Atlanta. If he knows I'm here, maybe he can help."

"I'll try to reach him when my shift is over," the guard promised.

"Thank you," Elder responded. "I know Archie will do all he can."

CONTROL

I n the Oval Office, Kathy Alton was meeting with Cal Rutland and Russell Siever to discuss the Data-Net situation.

"Is there any word on Wells?" the new president asked Siever.

"None," Siever replied nervously. "We have people out everywhere. He must have left Washington."

"What about the girl?" Rutland asked.

"No word on her, either," Siever replied brusquely. The tension between Siever and Rutland was becoming constant now. Siever was determined that Rutland was not going to dominate him or make him the heavy in this Wells thing.

Trying not to show any reaction to Siever's obvious irritation, Rutland asked in a slow and calm voice, "Have you checked with Eison at Livermore to see if he's heard from her?"

"Of course we have!" Siever barked. "If Wells shows up there my men will call immediately. I'll get him. You do your job, and I'll do mine!"

"Easy, Dr. Siever," the president said. "I asked Cal to ride herd on this problem. You will remember he has my full authority. We need to find Wells before something more serious develops. We have too much at stake to allow any problems at this point."

Siever knew he had been outmaneuvered by Rutland again. He felt depressed and deflated. "I'll do what I can," he responded dejectedly.

"You'll do better than that, Siever!" President Alton said sharply. "You will remember what is at stake here. We are talking about the future of the world. This is a battle we cannot afford to lose. We will not allow anyone to stand in the way. Remember that!"

Siever dropped his head. He was defeated. And he knew it. He had hoped President Alton might not rely as much on Rutland, but it seemed she trusted him totally. He was genuinely frightened for the second time in his life. He knew Rutland had directed Hunt's assassination. But even if he wanted to tell someone, who would it be?

Siever laid awake for hours that night, trying to think of an answer for his predicament. When he finally fell asleep, he became immersed in a familiar nightmare—one that had dogged him since one evening when he was eleven years old.

His father had been drinking heavily as usual and began arguing with Russ's seventeen-year-old brother, Ryan, about the loud rock music he had been playing. The elder Siever began destroying Ryan's albums and tapes. The argument quickly dissolved into a minor shoving match and a major swearing match. Finally the father grabbed Ryan's stereo and threatened to smash it on the concrete driveway outside the second-story window.

Russ, who had been hiding outside the door listening to the battle in silent fear, rushed in, pleading with his father not to break the stereo. As he ran toward him, his father swung his free hand and cuffed Russ alongside the head, sending him sprawling across the floor. In a reflex action, Ryan hit his father with a solid blow to his chin; he went down, striking his head on the stereo cabinet.

Russ' mother came running into the bedroom just in time to see her husband hit the floor, blood streaming out of the wound on his head. The scene was chaos with Russ crying and blood covering the carpet.

"Ryan, what happened?" his mother screamed as she knelt down by her husband.

"He hit Russ," a defiant Ryan said angrily. "I just hit him back. I didn't mean to hurt him. But he'd better not hit Russ again."

Just then his father made a moaning sound and started trying to get up. The wound to his scalp was bleeding profusely but was not a serious injury. He looked up at his oldest son. "You get out of my house!" he growled through clenched teeth. "I don't ever want to see you again. You're straight from Hell—you're a demon."

Ryan's mother tried to intercede, "No, Roy, he didn't mean it."

"I want you out of my house, you devil," the father ordered now that he had regained some of his strength.

"I'll go," Ryan responded defiantly. "I don't need any more of your phony religion anyway. You're just a falling-down drunk, looking for somebody to save you from your own stupidity." With that, he picked up his jacket and the keys to his Corvette—a present for his sixteenth birthday.

"Oh, no, you don't!" his father snarled. "I paid for that car. You leave it here."

"It's my car. You gave it to me," Ryan protested.

"Well it's still in my name, and if you take it out of this driveway, I'll have you arrested for car theft. And you know I can do it!" His father spit out the words hatefully.

"Keep your car! I don't need anything you've got!" Ryan shouted as he threw the keys at his father and stormed out of the room.

Russ ran after his brother. "Please don't go, Ryan," he cried. "Dad didn't mean it. He'll cool off."

"I'm sorry kid, but I have to go. It's going to get worse around here with this Holy Joe stuff from him. He won't let up. Just don't let him con you into that junk, okay?"

"Okay, but where are you going? Will you call me?"

"You bet, kid. As soon as I'm settled, I'll give you and Mom a ring. Just remember, I'm your buddy. If anybody bothers you, you give me a call."

With that, his brother left. Russ didn't know it at the time, but he would never see his brother again.

A few weeks after Ryan left, Russ heard the phone ring and picked up the receiver. His father had already answered the call and he listened in when he heard his brother's voice. "Hi, Dad. It's Ryan."

"What do you want?" his father asked gruffly.

"I'd like to come home, Dad. I miss the family. It's been pretty tough these last few weeks."

"Well, we don't want you back," his father snapped. "You made your choice, now you can live with it. We're doing just fine without . . ."

Russ quickly shouted into the phone, "Dad, I want him back. Please let him come home. I love Ryan."

"Get off the line, Russ!" his father ordered. "You don't have anything to say about this. Your brother is possessed by the devil and I don't want him in this house."

Russ heard the other end of the line go dead before he even had a chance to talk to his brother. As he sat there crying, his father came into the room.

"Russ, don't you ever contradict me again," he said with clenched fists. Russ knew he had been drinking and was just likely to hit him again. "If you don't like it here, maybe we can arrange for you to leave, too," his father said as his eyes narrowed. "Do you want to leave?"

"No, sir," Russ said as he felt himself wet his pants. He lived in fear of his father more than ever after Ryan had left. It seemed like he was drunk more than he was sober. But even when he was drunk he insisted on the family accompanying him to church meetings that often turned into little more than witch hunts and hate protests. Virtually no one ever contradicted his father, who was by far the largest single supporter of the small church he attended.

When the call was made for sinners to repent, his father would literally shove Russ and his mother out of their seats and push them up front. His timid, Presbyterian-raised mother lived in constant terror as the group would shout and wail to drive the "devils" away. Even the slightest protest from Russ resulted in a blow to his head that would make his ears ring for several minutes. He usually made his confession of sin, all the while hating the group, especially his father.

When Russ was thirteen, his father died of a brain hemorrhage. He staunchly refused to attend the funeral held by the group of fanatics his father had joined.

Russ and his mother made a concerted effort to find Ryan, who had last been heard from in the Los Angeles area. When calls to the various police departments failed to turn up any news, she hired a detective agency to find him. A few weeks later she received a report that a young man, thought to fit her son's description, had just been killed in a drug-related crime in the Hollywood area. Complete dental records were requested, and upon receiving them, positive verification was made.

The shock of this news, along with the stress of the years with Russ' father, was too much for his mother. One evening she took a bottle of sleeping pills and simply never woke up again. Russ heard a scream somewhere in the distance as the image of his mother lying in her bed flashed before his eyes. He awoke with a start. Once awake, he knew it would be another long sleepless night.

At Data-Net headquarters, in the congressional office building in Washington, Jack Rhinehart was already at work on the problem of locating Jeff Wells. He was still smarting from the tongue lashing he had received from Siever about his screw-up with the earlier program.

"I think I've got it," he said aloud to no one in particular. The staff assigned to assist him knew he was an obnoxious egotist. They did what was required but nothing beyond. They had become experts in allowing Dr. Jack Rhinehart to "shoot himself in the foot." It wasn't that he was incompetent—much the contrary. He was a brilliant mathematician who understood computers well. It was that he looked on everyone else as his subordinates and treated them as such. Collectively his team probably could have matched the abilities of Jeff Wells, but no single person was Wells' peer. Without a total team effort, Rhinehart could accomplish little and they knew it.

Rhinehart was furiously typing instructions into the system console. He had been frustrated at every turn in trying to crack Jeff Wells' access code into the Data-Net. He eventually gave up trying to access the source codes and concentrated on modifying the output menus. Specifically he wanted a total record of Jeff Wells, ID #JDW 100091. He finally accessed the information by instructing the Data-Net operating system that he was a bank official requiring credit information on Wells. The program began to sort out all transactions for Jeff Wells and route them to the printer.

One of the last transactions was the purchase of two coach class airline tickets on Delta. He then called up the Delta file and requested booking information. The tickets had been purchased to Sacramento, California, for Wells and Karen Eison.

"He's on his way to Livermore," Rhinehart exclaimed jubilantly. Rhinehart closed the computer file and dialed Russell Siever's office.

Siever had been sitting at his desk for the better part of an hour just looking out at the city. He was frustrated that he was being blamed for allowing Wells to lock them out of the Data-Net system. *How was I to know Wells would go off the deep end?* he thought morosely. *Wells is an egghead. Who knows what a guy like that will do anyway?*

Even his wife, Elisa, was unsympathetic to his plight. When he had told her about the problem with Wells, she had flared up too, reminding him that Data-Net was the key to controlling the economy. What Russell Siever didn't know was that his wife was a key player in the Society. Her assignment was to monitor and report on her husband's activities.

When the idea of excluding such a large group of citizens from Data-Net was first discussed, Siever had been sure that the Congress or the courts would step in to stop it. He never dreamed the Society was capable of shutting down the Congress and controlling the Supreme Court.

The court, he almost said out loud. *Of course. How could they have known about the assassinations that would allow Hunt to nominate a majority? Nobody could have, unless they also planned the murders. Even Hunt!* Siever felt his blood go cold as he put the facts together. *The Society had the president killed! Rutland was their inside man.* He shuddered with the realization that an organization capable of controlling the United States government would not hesitate to eliminate another person—a problem like him. That's what Elisa had been saying. *She has to be a part of the inner circle too,* his mind screamed.

Just then the phone rang. He was almost too panicked to pick up the receiver. His hand was shaking as he answered, "Yes, this is Siever."

"Dr. Siever, this is Jack Rhinehart. I've got some good news for you."

Siever bolted out of his chair. "Have you cracked Wells' code?"

Rhinehart pulled the receiver away from his ear, "No," he replied, still jubilant. "But I know where Wells is going."

Siever sat back down in his chair, trying to compose himself. It wouldn't do to let a back-stabber like Rhinehart know he was worried. "Where do you think he is going, Doctor, and why?"

"He's on his way to Livermore—probably to see Eison. He's traveling with Eison's daughter. I got a record of all his purchases and saw he bought tickets to Sacramento."

Suddenly Siever felt renewed. Even if Rhinehart couldn't crack the code, Wells could and Wells was almost in his grasp. "Good work, Doctor. But don't tell anyone else. I'll handle it from here. Can you track Wells through Data-Net?"

"No problem," Rhinehart said confidently. "I've already set up a credit tracking routine. If he or the girl use their cards, I'll know instantly."

"Okay," Siever said, breathing a sigh of relief. *Maybe Rhinehart isn't such an idiot after all*, he thought. "Keep on it, and let me know the minute anything else develops."

With that, Siever hung up the phone. He immediately called his long-time friend, Attorney General Fred Lively. It took several frustrating minutes for him to reach Lively, who was in a meeting.

"Yes, Russ? What's up? I was in a meeting discussing the roundup of the terrorists. I understand you have some kind of problem with the tracking system?"

"Yes, but I can't discuss the details right now. It involves the head of the computer department, Jeff Wells. We think he has purposely stopped the search routine."

"So what's the problem?" Lively asked, slightly irritated. He didn't understand computers and didn't really want to. What he did want was an opportunity to teach the Christians a lesson. Without Data-Net, he couldn't do that. He had a lot of grief to lay on those who had caused him so much grief over the years. Christians were against anything progressive, including the new world order, he suspected.

"The problem is Wells has locked up the system and taken off. I need him picked up and brought back to D.C."

"No sweat, Russ. Tell me where he is and I'll have the secret service pick him up."

"Listen, Fred, just picking up Wells is not enough. He's a weird guy and may not want to cooperate. But he's traveling with a young woman—a Karen Eison. She may be the key to getting Wells' cooperation."

"You mean, Dr. William Eison's daughter?"

"Yes, do you know her?"

"Only through her father," Lively said. "He's on our subversive list."

"Dr. Eison is a subversive?" Siever asked.

"He is as far as the Society is concerned. He was approached several years ago about joining, but refused. Said he was not political. And anyone who is not with us, is potentially against us," Lively said matter-of-factly.

How deep does the Society go? Siever wondered as he listened to Lively. "Wells will cooperate if we have the girl. Can you pick her up and keep her isolated for a few days?"

"Like I said, no sweat," responded Lively. "Leave it to me. Where are they headed?"

"Probably Livermore, to see Eison," Siever said as he began to breathe a little easier.

"Just be sure you don't hurt Wells. No one else can get into the system."

"We'll treat him like he's royalty," Lively said flippantly. *Being in charge of my own police force is great,* he thought to himself.

Jeff and Karen had taken an early morning flight to Sacramento and then rented a car for the long drive to Livermore. He still wasn't sure exactly why he had decided to leave Washington and to lock up the system. But he had a bad feeling about how his Data-Net system was being used and wanted to discuss it with Dr. Eison. In the meantime, he needed to make sure that no one else modified Data-Net while he was gone, so he installed his own system code. He had no idea the commotion his actions had stirred up in Washington.

"I still find it hard to believe the government would use the network to discriminate against its citizens," Jeff said as he and Karen drove from Sacramento to Livermore.

"It doesn't seem to make any sense," Karen agreed. "But I noticed the headlines in the newspapers back at the terminal. They all described a massive effort to locate a group called the Constitutional Rights Committee—apparently some kind of terrorist organization run by a religious group."

"I wouldn't doubt anything in our country anymore," Jeff said with disgust. "We're becoming an armed camp, especially out here. Can you imagine the airlines recommending that we fly into Sacramento instead of Oakland or San Francisco? They said the airports there aren't secure and they couldn't guarantee our safety."

"I'm glad you didn't tell me that earlier," Karen sighed, as she slid over next to Jeff. "I probably would have worried about it all the way here."

"I actually heard one of the passengers talking about the planes flying into Los Angeles being equipped with flares in case of a terrorist attack using SAMs."

"SAMs? What are they?" Karen asked.

"Surface-to-air missiles that can be fired by one man. Kind of like a rocket."

"Surely people wouldn't actually do that, would they?" Karen asked as she envisioned the plane they had been on, full of passengers. "Not with children on board too!"

"Apparently there have already been at least two planes shot down over L.A. by either drug runners or terrorists." Jeff realized he probably should never have brought it up. Now Karen, who always saw the best in people, would probably have nightmares about terrorists.

"It's part of the reason why Data-Net was created," Jeff continued. "By going to a cash-less system, the drug trade could be greatly reduced and terrorists couldn't demand ransom for such acts."

"That certainly seems like a good idea," Karen agreed.

"I thought so, too. But if the system is not managed carefully, it could be used to control anyone, including honest citizens."

"But that just doesn't make any sense, Jeff. Who would want to do such a thing?"

"I don't know," Jeff replied, but inside he had that nagging feeling that maybe he did. "That's why I wanted to talk with your father. Maybe he'll be able to shed some light on this whole thing. I just know there is no logic behind having a file of twenty million exclusions, unless the system is being used to exclude a lot of ordinary citizens."

"I just hope you're wrong," she said. "Surely there is some other logical explanation."

It was nearly three o'clock in the afternoon when Jeff and Karen drove up to the entrance of the Livermore research facility. Jeff stopped at the guard gate to call Dr. Eison for clearance into the restricted area. The phone rang in Eison's office, but it was his secretary who answered it. Her eyes were wide with fright as two armed secret service men sat watching her. Dr. Eison was sitting at his desk, with two more secret service men holding guns on him too.

"Can't you tell me what this is all about?" the bearded physicist asked the man closest to him, who seemed to be in charge.

"It's a matter of national security," he responded gruffly. "Surely you must understand that, working here."

"But Jeff Wells has the highest security clearance," Eison protested. "Has he done something wrong?"

"I can't talk about it, Doctor. Now keep quiet until we have Wells in custody."

"Be sure you answer Wells calmly," the trembling secretary was warned.

Sounding as professional as she could, under the circumstances, she told Jeff he had been cleared but that Dr. Eison was in a meeting and would see him a little later. As Jeff drove up to the gate, the guard hit the switch to raise the guardrail. As soon as he was inside the compound, the gate closed again and immediately four armed men surrounded the car.

"Jeff, what's going on?" Karen cried out as one of the men jerked her door open, took her by the arm, and pulled her out.

The man on Jeff's side of the car commanded him, "Out of the car!"

"What's going on?" Jeff asked, trying to decide what he should do. The two men on his side of the car pointed their weapons at him and commanded again, "Step out of the car, and keep your hands in sight. Now!"

Jeff could see they were in no mood to debate the issue. He slowly lifted his big frame out of the car, being careful to keep his hands in plain sight. "Take it easy," he told the men. "I'm not armed."

As soon as he stepped out, one of the men frisked him carefully and told his companion, "He's clean."

"Come with me!" he ordered Jeff sharply.

The two men holding Karen led her away to a car waiting just outside the gate, and the two secret service men nearest to Jeff shoved him toward a second car. "Wait!" Jeff shouted toward the other car. "Where are you taking her?" But by that time, he was already handcuffed and shoved into the back seat.

Without another word, they drove off in the direction of Livermore Air Field, where an Air Force plane was waiting. Within thirty minutes Jeff was winging his way back to Washington—confused, and more than a little angry.

CRACKDOWN

W hat have you done with Karen?" Jeff shouted at Siever when he came into the detention cell at Andrews, where the secret service men had deposited the fuming programmer after they touched down.

"Calm down, Jeff." Siever tried to use his most sociable tone, but it came out sounding like an amateur actor. "Karen is fine. All I need is the code for system entry."

"Without me, no one will get in the system again," Jeff said defiantly.

"You will give me that code!" Siever said, more in anger than in fear. "I need it. If you want to see the girl again, you'll give it to me right now."

"I wasn't trying to sabotage the system," Jeff said sharply. "If I had wanted to do that, it would be down now. I just wanted to find out why you are trying to screen out such a large group of users."

"That is not your concern!" Siever glowered at Jeff. Now his pride was overcoming his fear. He was getting tired of playing games. First it was Rutland; now this kid. Just then one of the secret service men who had helped transport Jeff back to Washington stepped through the door.

"What do you want?" snapped Siever.

"Attorney General Lively is on the phone and wants to talk to you, sir," the agent replied curtly. "He says for you to hurry."

Siever left Wells and went to the office at the end of the hall. "Yes," he growled into the phone. "What is it, Fred?"

"Hold on," Fred Lively said as he handed the phone to Cal Rutland. Lively had never been so afraid in all his life. Rutland was as angry as anyone had ever seen him. Lively had called to tell Siever about capturing Wells, and within five minutes he was facing an enraged Rutland. Rutland's eyes told what his words did not; he was ready and willing to kill.

Lively had not even considered that the White House phones might be monitored; he wished he had because when Rutland found out what he and Siever were doing with Wells, he was fit to be tied. Lively had lied his way out of it by saying he thought Siever had White House approval for arresting Wells and the girl. He had placed the call to Siever immediately.

"Siever, you idiot!" Rutland said angrily. "What are you doing with Wells?"

"I had him brought back to Washington, just as you wanted," Siever replied defensively.

"I didn't want him arrested, you imbecile. He is the only person who can make the system work. Do you think he'll be productive if you alienate him?"

"I've got the girl too," Siever said confidently. "He'll give me the codes."

"And just what will you do with them? Put Rhinehart onto reprogramming the system? You really are an idiot, Siever. You get Wells over here immediately, and I want the girl brought here too. Where is she?"

"She's still out in Sacramento," Siever said. He was trying to find a way to salvage his pride, but he kept remembering how he had been treated earlier. The fear rose like bile in his throat. "I'll get him out right away," he said contritely as he hung up the phone and walked back to the agent who had brought Wells in. "Let him go," Siever said in a defeated tone. "He's to be taken directly to the White House."

As soon as Rutland hung up, he placed another call to the head of the White House secret service. "He's at Andrews," Rutland said coldly. "Do it!"

The director of the internal secret police force then placed a call to one of his agents at Andrews. "It's a go," he said. "Implement immediately."

A small cylinder was attached to the rear compartment air conditioning system of Siever's limousine. On the way back from Andrews the cylinder released a small amount of odorless gas into the passenger compartment, and Russell Siever suffered what would be diagnosed as a fatal brain hemorrhage. The driver didn't notice that his passenger had a problem until he reached the White House entrance. In the chaos of a country gone mad, hardly anyone would notice that the secretary of the treasury had died of natural causes, or that his wife, Elisa, had been appointed the interim secretary—until Congress reconvened.

Five minutes after Siever had left the room, one of the agents answered the call and removed Jeff's handcuffs. He was told there was a limousine waiting to take him to the White House. No one spoke another word. When Jeff asked the driver a question he simply responded, "I don't know, sir. I was just told to take you to Mr. Rutland's office."

Upon arriving at the White House, Jeff was met by one of the president's security guards. "Mr. Rutland's waiting for you, sir," the guard said politely; Jeff had the feeling he wasn't free to refuse the offer.

"Come in," Rutland said in a surprisingly pleasant manner. Pointing to a chair beside his desk, Rutland got up and walked around the desk, extending his hand to Wells.

Jeff reluctantly shook Rutland's hand and realized that it was the first time the other man had ever offered his hand. He was still a little confused about his release, but he assumed Rutland must have engineered it.

"I'm really sorry about what happened, Jeff," Rutland said in what seemed to be a genuinely concerned tone.

"Where is Karen?" Jeff asked brusquely.

"She's on her way here now. That idiot Siever just overreacted," Rutland said as he sat down in the chair beside Jeff. "He thought you spiked the system and then ran. So he called out the FBI."

Jeff thought to himself, *Those guys weren't FBI. More like CIA or something. Or KGB.* "What now?" Jeff asked.

"We want you back on Data-Net. I promise you, you won't have Siever breathing down your neck again."

"I've got some questions," Jeff said stubbornly, "and I won't work on the system again until I get some answers." Jeff thought he saw a flash of anger in Rutland's eyes, and then nothing. He knew he was playing a very dangerous game by confronting Rutland. He didn't know exactly what was going on in the White House, but with the country in economic and political chaos, three Supreme Court justices dead, and the president assassinated, he had no illusions that this was a game to them.

"Ask away," Rutland said calmly. "If I can answer your questions, I will."

"Why did someone attempt to put a patch in the Data-Net to keep twenty million people from using the system?"

"Well, first, the patch was attempted by one of Siever's cronies—a Dr. Rhinehart."

"Jack Rhinehart of Cal Tech?" Jeff asked in surprise.

"Yes. Siever hired him as a consultant, then tried to use him to change the system."

"Why?" Jeff asked, now very curious. He knew Rhinehart had no love for him. He also knew he was not astute enough to modify the system, at least not until Jeff developed the data base manager he was working on. Then just about any competent programmer would be able to make the system changes.

"We need a large potential base of users that can be excluded when we go worldwide," Rutland lied. "These will be the citizens of nations that refuse to eliminate all their currency. We can't operate with some half in and half out. It would undermine the integrity of the system."

Immediately, Jeff knew that Rutland was lying. He had dumped the laser disc files and printed out some of the names and addresses. They were all American citizens, widely scattered, and certainly not from any non-conforming countries. He also realized that Rutland didn't know that he knew.

"That sounds logical," Jeff agreed. "I changed the access code to the system so no one could mess with it while I was gone. I took Karen to see her father in California. I felt like we needed to get away for a little while. The next thing I knew, we were under arrest."

"Like I said, it was that idiot Siever. He's caught up in cloak and dagger stuff. It's probably a side effect of all the riots and killings. Try to understand, Jeff," Rutland said as he tried his big brother act. "We have billions invested in the Data-Net system now. We can't afford to have any glitches at this point. I promise you that no one else will try to modify the system until you say it's fully operational. I have already sent Dr. Rhinehart back to Cal Tech. But we would like to have you train an assistant. After all, what would happen if you got hit by a truck?" Rutland tried his best to chuckle, but it came out more like a grunt.

"I'll fix the system," Jeff said as politely as he could muster. "I just wanted to be sure that it wasn't being used as a political weapon. A cash-less system like the Data-Net could make life pretty difficult for a lot of people. Do you have anyone in mind as an assistant?"

"We have contacted Dr. Kim Loo. He has agreed to work with you. In fact, he is excited about the prospect."

"Dr. Loo!" Jeff said with genuine respect. "He is a great computer specialist." Then he suddenly felt a pang of fear inside. He had assumed he would be able to delay and stall the changes, but not with Dr. Loo. He was the one scientist who could grasp the concept of Jeff's Data-Net system. *Is Loo a part of whatever is going on?* Jeff wondered. He knew he would have to install the files and the people involved would just have to take their chances. At least he had given them a few days respite. Maybe he could stall for a few more days.

Perhaps, he thought with a spark of an idea brewing, *I can even give them a warning.*

It was nearly two days before Jeff completed the necessary changes to the system. All that was lacking was his system code to be input. But Karen still had not shown up, so he called Rutland to check on her arrival.

"I'm sorry, Jeff," Rutland said in response to his question. "We've had some difficulty in arranging her transportation back to Washington. Have you made the changes to the system?"

Jeff knew Rutland was stalling. He was making his point very clear without saying so: Karen would return only when the changes had been made. He answered, "Yes, I have, but the suggestion by Dr. Loo has not been easy to implement. I wonder if it is really necessary?"

Dr. Loo had instructed Jeff to write a subroutine accessing an external data file where the names would be supplied later. It was clear that they did not want Jeff to know who, what, or how many were in that file. He didn't object too strenuously since he had copied the original file earlier.

"It's absolutely essential that you follow Dr. Loo's instructions to the letter," Rutland said coldly. "He is operating under the direct orders of the president."

"I thought *I* was the Data-Net director," Jeff said in a voice meant to convey a bruised ego.

"Yes, you are," Rutland said hurriedly. "You are in charge of the system, but Dr. Loo is in charge of operations. Once the system is fully functional, your genius will be needed on other projects."

Jeff smiled at the strain he detected in Rutland's voice. *It must kill him to offer a compliment,* he mused. "The system will be operational shortly. I'd like to talk with Karen first, though. Her help would be invaluable to me. We have worked together on this project from the beginning."

Rutland's temper flared. Was Wells threatening to halt the system unless his girlfriend appeared? He wasn't sure. Wells was an enigma to Rutland. He was difficult to read but also essential at this point, so he decided to give in a little. "I'm glad to say that she will be here this evening, Jeff. I just wanted it to be a surprise." Rutland had decided that since the system was operating again, Dr. Loo knew the codes, and the master terminal was under daily lock and key, Karen Eison was no longer needed as a hostage.

For the past three days Karen had been kept in a room at Vandenberg Air Force Base. They had told her she was not under arrest, but it was also clear she wasn't free to leave either. She asked to call her father several times, but the impersonal security man responded, "Miss

Eison, my orders are that you are not to have contact with anyone."

"And just who gave those orders?" she demanded.

"I just follow instructions," the guard said unemotionally.

Karen had little doubt that his attitude would have changed abruptly, and unpleasantly, if she had attempted to leave the room. Then suddenly that morning she was whisked out of the room, hustled into a waiting Air Force van, and put aboard an Air Force plane.

"Where are we going?" she asked the guard.

"To Washington," he responded without further elaboration.

"D.C., I hope," she said sarcastically. The guard didn't respond.

When she had been pulled from the car at Livermore, she had envisioned being beaten or tortured, but not only had she not been abused, she had not even been questioned. In a way, that infuriated her even more. It was as if she was of no importance, except as a detainee.

First they kidnap me, then hold me illegally, she thought angrily as they prepared to take off. *Except for Jeff, no one in the world even knows I'm here. What can be going on? Is it the file Jeff discovered?*

And what about Daddy? she wondered. Panic struck again as she considered what he must be going through. If they wouldn't tell her anything, she knew they wouldn't let her father in on their plans either. For all his bluff, she knew he was a sensitive, devoted father. She was all the family he had left. *Don't let Daddy worry*, she prayed— something she had not done in a long while.

As the military jet—the equivalent of a commercial DC-12, twin turbo-fan passenger liner—took off from Vandenberg, she felt the plane jink first to one side and then to the other. The moves, almost neck wrenching in intensity, were standard military maneuvers designed to confuse a ground-launched, surface-to-air missile. White phosophorus flares were launched from a tube in the rear of the plane every thirty seconds to deflect heat-seeking missiles. Normally this procedure would have been limited to combat conditions, but since the terrorists had easy access to some of the older SAMs sold by the government to third-world countries to raise cash, California was considered a combat zone. Twelve military and two commercial aircraft had been lost or damaged over the last two years, clearly demonstrating the willingness of the terrorists to use the missiles. Commercial airliners flying into southern California had also been equipped with flares, although the violent jinking had to be tempered greatly on commercial flights because of the panic it caused among the passengers.

By the time the plane reached its cruising altitude of 40,000 feet, Karen was violently ill. As she lifted the barf bag to her mouth again, she thought, *After all that, I don't care if we are shot down*. In spite of her churning stomach, she felt satisfaction watching her guard of the last few days heaving into his sick bag too.

Upon arriving at Andrews, she was whisked into a waiting limousine and within minutes was speeding toward Washington. Not surprisingly, she was secreted into the White House long before the normal contingent of White House watchers appeared. What did surprise her was what awaited her: Kathy Alton, President of the United States.

The setting in the president's breakfast room was very informal. Only two places were set, and the president already occupied one. Karen was overwhelmed by it all. She had often read about Kathy Alton and admired what she stood for, but the events of the last few days had made her very cautious.

"Sit down, Karen," the president said politely. "You don't mind if I call you Karen, do you?"

"No, not at all, Madam President," Karen replied hesitantly.

"Please, call me Kathy," the president said warmly. "Actually I'm not used to the title of president yet. Things have happened so suddenly these last few days."

"That's for sure," Karen said as she shook out her napkin.

"I understand that you and Mr. Wells have been put through some difficulties," the president said as the maid began serving their breakfast of assorted fruits. "I hope you like fruit for breakfast, Karen. I enjoy fresh fruit."

"Yes, this is fine," Karen replied, somewhat amazed. Grapefruit was virtually all she ever ate in the mornings, but somehow she knew the president knew that also.

"I sincerely apologize for what has happened during the last few days, dear. With all the chaos in this city and around the country, I'm afraid some of our bureaucrats got carried away. Dr. Siever was acting in what he thought to be the best interest of the country, but nothing justifies violating the rights of our citizens. We are a nation that protects individual rights and I will allow no one to usurp them from even one person."

The words and the demeanor of the new president totally disarmed Karen, just as they were planned to do. Kathy Alton had been selected for her position long before the ill-fated flight to Mars thrust her into the public's eye. She had an amazing ability to make even large groups of people feel at ease. Karen found her previous anger and caution beginning to fade.

"What about Jeff?" Karen asked cautiously.

"He has been working diligently on the Data-Net for several days now," the president replied smoothly. "Obviously, he has also been concerned about you. I had some difficulty in determining your location," she lied. "Since Dr. Siever's death, things have been a little hec . . ."

Karen interrupted, "Dr. Siever is dead?"

"Yes. I'm sorry; I guess you haven't heard. The strain of the last few days was apparently too much for him. He died of a stroke. I appointed his wife, Elisa, to serve in his position until Congress reconvenes."

All of Karen's resolve melted as she heard the president describe how her administrative assistant, Cal Rutland, had confronted Dr. Siever and his blatant disregard for civil law in having Jeff and Karen arrested. "Actually, I think Dr. Siever had the best interests of the nation at heart. He just allowed his zeal to overwhelm his judgment.

"These are trying times, Karen," she said as she got up from her chair. Karen immediately stood and the president put her arm around Karen's shoulder. "I need people like you and Jeff to help me put this nation back on the right track. Data-Net is essential to our long-term prosperity if we are again to become the leader in the world's economy."

Karen's mind was reeling in confusion. She had been so certain that the government was corrupt. Now she was unsure.

"I want you to go back to work, Karen," the president said as the maid reappeared to clear the table. "You and Jeff keep an eye on things. If you see anything that you even think is wrong, please bring it to my attention immediately. If you have any difficulty from anyone on my staff, let me know. I'll tell Cal that you are to have access to me anytime you need it. Okay?"

"Sure . . . okay," Karen said hesitantly.

"Karen, I represent more than just the first woman president," Kathy Alton said as small tears formed in her eyes. "I represent all the people who feel like they have no voice in their government. I need your help. Will you help me?"

"Yes," Karen blurted out. "I will." She suddenly felt like a school kid who had been asked to erase the board for the teacher. Her faced turned a slight pink.

"Great!" the president exclaimed enthusiastically. "Now let's both get back to work."

16

FLEE TO THE MOUNTAINS

Karen!" Jeff exclaimed, as he looked up and saw her entering the room. He rushed over to her and wrapped his arms around her, his big frame dwarfing her. "Tell me what happened," he said as he saw the tears in her eyes.

"Nothing, really," she responded as she hugged him. Karen knew that she was in love with Jeff. She wondered if he felt the same way or was simply responding as a concerned colleague. "I was kept in confinement for several days and then suddenly flown back to Washington late last night."

"Did they uh . . . were you hurt in any way?" Jeff asked hesitantly, his natural shyness causing him to blush.

"No, I'm fine," she replied, as her eyes swept around the room. Nothing had changed, except that the master terminal was missing.

"What happened to you?" she asked.

"About the same, I guess, except that they flew me back the same day. I met with Rutland, and he gave me a song and dance about Siever being the heavy and going beyond his authority."

"I met with the president this morning. She told me the same thing."

"The president?" Jeff exclaimed with surprise.

"She said that Dr. Siever had exceeded his authority. She also said he suffered a stroke and died; she implied his actions were due to stress."

"Do you believe her?" Jeff asked in a tone that betrayed his skepticism.

"I think so," Karen replied. "That would explain a lot."

"Well, maybe," Jeff said in a low tone. "But look." He pulled a small electric device from his pocket and flipped a switch on. Instantly the device blinked green and then red on the indicator. "It's a bug detector," he said softly as he turned up the stereo he had placed next to the pickup he had found earlier.

"We're being monitored?" Karen asked in disbelief.

"In my apartment, too," he whispered again. "Yours, too, I suspect."

Now she really was confused. She had been so certain the president was sincere. "Should I take this to the president?" she asked Jeff.

"Better wait until we're sure who's doing what," he answered. "Look at this." He pulled up the Data-Net specifications written by Dr. Loo. "It calls for the new file to be loaded externally. Once it's operational, we won't have any control over who goes into it."

"How did Dr. Loo get involved?" Karen asked as doubts began to crowd her thoughts again.

"Apparently the government brought him in after I shut them out of the system. Rhinehart is gone and Loo is going to be operations director."

"But I thought that was your job, Jeff."

"Rutland says my function is design. Dr. Loo's is operations. That probably does make more sense in the long run, but we need to be careful all the same."

As he spoke, Jeff picked up a note pad, wrote something, and handed it to Karen. She read, "Look at the file coded 'Illuminati' when you get the chance. I've done a rundown of our leaders. They all seem to trace back to a secret society known as the Illuminati."

"Let's get to work," Jeff said for the benefit of those he knew were listening. "We need to get the system operational." He pointed Karen to the terminal he had programmed to bypass any monitoring devices set up by Dr. Loo. In the other Data-Net terminal room, Dr. Loo smiled agreeably even though he couldn't understand all the conversation.

That music drives me crazy, Dr. Loo thought, as he switched off the headset and cycled the recorder on. The listening device he had planted was extremely low power and not very selective in frequency range, but Rutland had warned him that any more powerful device would be detectable. He checked his program trap to see if Wells had been into any part of Data-Net except the subroutine for programming the new file. "Ah, good," he said out loud. "He cannot get around my trap." He checked the file and saw that Wells' only entry had been to the authorized file.

Dr. Kim Loo would have been amazed had he realized how simply Jeff Wells had been able to bypass his trap—almost as simply as he had been able to detect the listening device with the monitor he built. In truth, the best efforts of the second-best computer scientist in the world had not even been a challenge to Jeff. He had simply commanded the central computer controller to interrupt Loo's "trap" and then reinstate it once Jeff had access to the main compiler. In essence, he had trapped the trap.

As Karen scanned the screen before her, she was again amazed at what Jeff was able to do with a computer. He had traced every transaction for the previous twenty years by Cal Rutland and then run a comparison of locations and dates for virtually every government leader during the same period. Soon a pattern began to emerge that showed specific dates and places where several of the leaders, and future leaders, had assembled at one time. The list included Rutland, Siever, Lively, Hunt, and hundreds more.

Jeff had set up his program in such a way that any name could be queried and verified against the selected dates and locations. With her hand shaking slightly, Karen typed in the name of Kathy Alton. "Verified," the screen responded. "Correlation positive." With that, the program began to spew out the dates when Kathy Alton had met with the leadership of the Illuminati. Karen was startled to see that it began long before Kathy had ever met her husband—long before he had even been selected to head the expedition to Mars!

Fred Lively had been in an all-day meeting with Secretary of Defense Andrew Singer and other selected members of the Cabinet. Their discussions centered around the growing problem of what to do with the Christians they had been rounding up. Since martial law had been declared, they were able to by-pass the normal legal arraignment problems, but the sheer numbers of detainees were overcrowding the jails all over the country.

"Also," said Ben Randall, the FBI director, "there seems to be a sympathy movement growing in parts of the country."

"What do you mean by a 'sympathy movement'?" Jason Franklin snapped as he looked up.

"It seems that friends and neighbors are hiding many of the Christians now, even some neighbors who have no previous affiliation with the movement. It makes it hard to round them up."

What he heard from the next room infuriated Amir Hussein. He spoke into the device that allowed no one but Franklin and Rutland to hear him. "I want the Christians eliminated! They represent the only stumbling block to my plans. Activate the detention camps in the occupied zones."

Rutland heard the message and glanced over at Franklin who was visibly shaken. *He's weak too*, Rutland thought. Inside Rutland felt his spirits pick up. *Soon we won't need him any longer either.*

It was Franklin who finally spoke up. "We have set up temporary detention camps to hold the terrorists. Andrew, you allocate the trains necessary to transport them to the locations you're given."

"But Mr. Franklin, you're talking about millions of people. I can't . . ."

"Shut up, you sniveling coward!" Cal Rutland snapped. "We'll leak the information to the press. The American people will cheer when they hear about the terrorists being deported from their cities. You just be sure the trains are available when they're needed."

"But what about the military?" Singer asked tentatively, looking for some way to regain his dignity.

"The military will be with us," Rutland replied. "We have been placing members of the Society in positions of authority for decades. We will soon control the government and the military."

Hussein knew better than Rutland that what he said was true. For decades top recruits from the families of Society members had been educated in military schools and had risen to positions of authority until many of the top levels were dominated by them. But the plans of the Society had been laid so carefully that even lower-echelon leaders in the military had been carefully trained and recruited in the Society. The very fact that such a massive effort seemed impossible was what made it possible. Even the destruction of the American economy and morality since the early 1950s had been carefully planned through a systematic takeover of much of the media and virtually all of the movie industry. The movie industry sold Americans on immorality, and the media sold them on government handouts.

Once the average American was hooked on easy credit and government handouts, the plan was to collapse the U.S. economy. Just as Adolf Hitler had been positioned to lead Germany after a collapsed economy, so Hussein knew that Americans would welcome his leadership, given the proper incentive. The plan was simple: Give them their creature comforts, take them away, and then promise them again.

Shortly after the meeting with Singer and Franklin, the attacks by the so-called terrorists were stepped up. Many cities were plunged into darkness as power stations were sabotaged by groups calling themselves the CRC. Members of the media received threats, stating that unless the attacks on Christians were stopped, they would themselves become targets. Instead of reducing the coverage and attacks, the media increased their assaults, virtually daring the terrorists to touch even one of the sacred public figures. However, at the same time they demanded additional police protection. The airwaves were filled with vicious allegations against the terrorists in general, and Christian terrorists in particular.

Within days, a series of events set the media aflame.

Terrorists, using a hand-held SAM, shot down a commercial airliner as it was landing at the Dallas airport. More than two hundred people were killed, including the newly elected governor of Texas, James Basset, a staunch supporter of the "Crack Babies Bill." He had campaigned under the banner of allowing the organ transplant facilities to be located in his state, which meant thousands of new jobs and billions of dollars in potential revenue for Texas.

He had been strongly opposed by the religious community and had been swept into office, along with President Hunt, when the voters approved the new law. Since President Hunt's assassination, the governor had received several threats, and at least one plot against his life had been uncovered, according to the FBI.

All day the networks had shown scenes of the disaster and interviewed members of the governor's staff. The questions were carefully caged in terms meant to point the finger back at the group called the Constitutional Rights Committee.

Mary Howell, an aide to Governor Basset, was especially bitter: "We have all lost a friend and a great statesman," she said angrily as the tears welled up in her eyes. "The governor opposed those who would have kept Texas in the Dark Ages. I hope they all die!"

"Do you mean that you would like to see the death penalty reinstated for political crimes such as this?" the WNN interviewer asked cautiously.

"I mean I wish the people of Texas would rise up and exterminate the vermin who did this," Howell said bitterly. "They don't hesitate to kill our appointed leaders; why should we hesitate to eliminate them?"

"You don't mean to say that you support citizens taking the law into their own hands, do you?" the reporter questioned.

Her producer prompted her in the hidden ear piece: "Keep it up. This is great stuff."

"Wouldn't that result in anarchy in a country committed to law and order?"

"Just how much law and order do you think Governor Basset and the others aboard that plane got?" Howell shouted as the scenes of the children being hauled away from the crash site were flashed on the screen. "Kill them all!" she screamed as the cameras followed every detail of the interview.

The Insta-pol survey showed that 40 percent of Americans agreed with Howell—an increase of 30 percent from the first time the same sentiment had been voiced after the Hunt assassination. Clearly the campaign against the religious right was gathering steam as the violence continued. . . .

"It's time," Hussein said to Jason Franklin, as they watched the interview. "Execute Phase Four immediately."

Outside the offices of WNN in Atlanta, ABC in New York, and the Satellite Direct Broadcast office in Hollywood, men were already in position with automatic weapons. Calls had been made to those who had been planted among the members of the CRC. The targets had been selected long before the most current events made the United States a potential powder keg.

Under the dictates of martial law, the movements of all citizens were monitored, and anyone found on the streets after dark was stopped and questioned. The orders were clear: Anyone found carrying a weapon of any kind was to be arrested and held without bond. Anyone caught firing a weapon was to be shot on sight, as were all looters.

This particular evening small arms fire was heard several blocks from each of the major news networks' studios. Calls were issued for backup support and all available units were diverted to the outbreaks. The police on duty outside the offices of ABC in New York were puzzled. Why would the dispatcher command them all to go as backup?

"Do you think we should let the people at ABC know we're leaving?" the young policeman asked his sergeant.

"Ours is not to question why," the older man said sarcastically. "The dispatch will tell 'em all to stay inside for awhile. You just be sure you have your vest zipped up." With that he fired up the APC (Armored Personnel Carrier) and motioned for the other officers to get inside. Within minutes, they were moving toward the downtown theater district where the shots had been fired.

As they pulled out, the sergeant said, "Not even these news people would be nuts enough to walk these streets without guards around, anyway." One of the others grunted in agreement as he rolled up the bulletproof side windows. "I don't know how many of those terrorists are still around, but the pimps and dealers down here are carrying enough heavy artillery to start a war all by themselves."

The younger police officer shuddered as he thought about all the wounded and dead they had seen in the ghettos. It was like a war zone for sure. "I wouldn't travel these streets, even with a flak jacket," he commented as he ratcheted a live round into the overhead machine gun. He thought about the twin thirty-caliber Gatlings mounted fore and aft on the APC, and mentally cringed at the thought of drug dealers buying the same vehicles, as had been rumored.

The ABC nightly news anchor, Ted Chandler, left the studio offices and headed for the street level entrance where he had left his car. It was nearly eleven P.M., but he knew the police were all around the building, or so he thought. Once he left the protection of the bullet-proof glass entrance he felt naked and vulnerable. He was wearing a kevlar inner-coat lining, strong enough to stop a thirty-caliber bullet fired at close range. But the sniper with the night scope didn't aim at his chest. Instead he aimed at the unprotected head area, squeezing off three quick rounds. The most recognizable face in America suddenly became unrecognizable. Ted Chandler, television anchorman and long-time liberal, was dead before he hit the pavement.

Almost simultaneously, the same scene was being played out at the offices and studios of all the major networks and newspapers throughout the country.

Since threats against the media had been common, even before the riots, special blast-proof windows and doors had been installed at WNN in Atlanta. Inside the newsroom, reports were streaming in from message centers all over the country about attacks on media personnel. In one of those instinctive moves born out of years of facing danger, John Fletcher, the network night manager, ordered all the staff to drop what they were doing and head to the reinforced basement conference room.

Mari Itamo, the Japanese manager, objected. "We need to cover the stories as they come in," she said. "This building is secure, and there are security forces outside. It is safe."

"Then you stay here," Fletcher shouted as he swore at one of the reporters who was still at his desk. "This whole thing stinks, and I don't intend for my people to become one of those stories."

Mari was still fuming when she sat down at her desk to draft a telefax to her manager. *Americans are cowards*, she thought. She never had a chance to construct the memo. From the alley across the street two men dressed in combat sweats were aiming a Lodan missile at the building.

The Lodan was designed to combat terrorists holding buildings in downtown areas. Many buildings had been bomb proofed by drug dealers who often turned them into armed fortresses. Most were heavily armed and fiercely defended. Charles Lodan, a weapons engineer with Harp Industries, had designed a weapon to clear them out. It was both simple and inexpensive. He took surplus LAARs rockets from the Middle East conflict days and equipped them with recycled uranium warheads. When the uranium plug was superheated by the explosion of the warhead against a solid wall, it would penetrate up to thirty inches of solid, case-hardened steel. The weapon roared as its rocket was launched.

The projectile flattened against the six-inch glass panes of the WNN buildings and the uranium core passed through as if the windows were covered with cardboard. Inside the building, the uranium spread out like millions of tiny BBs, and the cordite charge traveling with it exploded with the fury of a miniature volcano. Everything on the main floor was obliterated and almost instantly incinerated, including Mari Itamo. Only the reinforced retainment pillars, installed to protect the upper floors, kept the building from collapsing. In the basement conference room, John Fletcher heard the thunderous roar above them and saw the lights go out. Sitting in the pitch black room, the rumble of the building seemed even more terrifying to those with him. Several of the reporters cried out in fear—both male and female.

Thirty seconds later the emergency lighting came on, bathing the terrified media employees with an eerie red hue. Above them the maelstrom of fire was racing through the floor where only minutes before they had been gathered. The outside ventilators provided breathing air to those who were trapped inside the conference room until the fire was extinguished by the automatic sprinkler system.

Scrawled across the walls opposite the burned-out offices of WNN were the words, "Death to the unbelievers!" The same basic theme was repeated in every city where studios and newspapers had been attacked.

The television media quickly activated portable studios and were back in business within a few hours. Only this time it was an all-out war on those whom they believed to be responsible. The media called for death sentences for those involved. And they left no doubt as to whom they adjudged guilty—the CRC, and Christians in general.

President Alton came on the air promising swift retaliation for the terrorist attacks and asking Americans to give the government time to catch the perpetrators. But right after the announcements by the president, the media ran scenes from the riots, the assassinations of the justices, and the assassination of President Hunt. John Elder's name was mentioned frequently and scenes of churches being razed by angry "citizens' groups" were prominent on all the networks.

"The country is approaching a state of anarchy," Kathy Alton said to the dark man seated across from her.

"Good," he replied dispassionately. "Are the camps ready?"

"Yes. We have set up camps in the most remote regions of the country. Already we have captured over one hundred thousand."

"That is not enough!" Hussein said, his black eyes glinting with hate. "When the camps have a million, we will begin the elimination process . . . I see you're troubled. What is it?"

"Nothing, sir," the president said as she tried to put her fears aside. "It's just that I'm afraid of what the public might do if they learn of our plans. How will we eliminate so many?"

"They will not learn until it is too late!" the dark man snapped as he got up and walked across the room. He stood silently looking out of the window, then turned, walked back, and stood by the president's chair. With a look of grim determination, he said, "We will not make the same mistakes again. First the Christians—then the Jews.

"It is time to make the people suffer some," he said as a cruel smile developed on his face. "These people are not used to suffering. They will do anything to save their way of life.

"It is time to launch Phase Five."

"Phase Five?" the president said with the question written on her face. "I have not heard the details of Phase Five."

"You had no need until now," he replied as he bent over and stroked her hair softly. "Now, my pretty one, you will see the anger of the world against the cursed Jews. The Christians were their only real allies, and the Jews helped us to destroy them."

UNCOVERING THE PLOT

Immediately after the aborted protest-turned-riot, the word had gone out from the CRC for its members to flee. Some did just that, taking up refuge with friends or family in an effort to avoid arrest. But many simply refused to believe that they would be arrested; they knew they were guilty of nothing.

One such couple, Bob and Ellen Cofer, in Chicago, decided not to run. Bob felt it was all just a big mistake; the government would never arrest private citizens. He and Ellen had decided not to join the march the day of the riots. They supported those who were protesting the arrest of John Elder, but felt that without parade permits they would be breaking the law, which they refused to do.

The televised scenes of the marchers being shot down along with the police shocked Bob out of his naiveté. He suddenly realized that the leaders of the CRC had been right when they said the plot against Christians went to the highest levels of government. But Ellen had a different reaction. She thought the Christians had actually started the shooting. As she watched the reports flooding in, she said, "I won't ever be involved with that group again, Bob. I can't believe they would shoot police officers."

Ellen had been active in the Catholic anti-abortion movement. At first she had felt too timid to picket the abortion clinics, and only worked in the local "care center" office twice a month. But once the "Crack Babies Bill" was declared constitutional, she could no longer stand by. She had joined the street pickets and actively wrote every senator and congressman in Washington. While marching in front of the state government's offices, she had been photographed and marked for detainment when the riots were being planned.

Before Bob could answer Ellen's comment about the shooting, the scene on television shifted to Father Vincent's school, where Ellen worked part-time as a teacher.

"This is Paul Bannon. I'm here at Father Vincent's Parochial School, where the police have just apprehended one of the riot leaders, Reverend Christopher Long."

The cameras focused on the police hauling out a priest dressed in traditional black clothing. It was obvious at first glance that the priest had been beaten. One eye was swollen and blood trickled from one corner of his mouth. He was bent over, as if in pain.

The newsman stopped a police captain and asked, "Captain, what is Reverend Long charged with?"

"He's one of the leaders of the riot that killed our officers," the angry policeman said. "He put up a fight and we had to subdue him."

"Are you saying he resisted, Captain?"

"Not only that," the officer responded as he held up a short-barreled weapon. "He had this on him. It's a good thing he had used up all his ammunition, or he might have shot someone else."

"It's a lie," Ellen shouted at the television. "Father Chris would never hurt anyone, and he certainly wouldn't carry a gun."

"I think we need to get out of here, Ellen," Bob said as he felt the knot tighten in his stomach.

"What do you mean? We can't go anywhere. This is our home, and we need to be at work tomorrow. Besides, it doesn't affect us," Ellen said, sensing the alarm in her husband's voice. Inside the panic started to grow like a cancer, gnawing at her sanity. Suddenly the emotional pressures of the past several weeks overwhelmed her and raw fear took over. She screamed, "Even if Father Chris is a terrorist, we didn't have anything to do with it!"

"Ellen, think about what you're saying!" Bob shouted. "Do you really think Father Chris could shoot anyone? It's all a setup."

"No!" Ellen insisted naively. "If the police say it's true, then it must be. We need to call them and tell them that we're not a part of that group. Call them, Bob!"

The two children—Marci, age twelve, and Robert, Jr., age ten—heard their parents arguing and came into the room. "What's the matter, Mom?" Marci asked, her quivering voice reflecting the panic she sensed in her mother.

Bob answered, "We're watching the television news, honey. The police have arrested Father Chris."

"Arrested Father Chris? They can't do that!" both Marci and Robert, Jr. exclaimed together. "Can't we do something, Dad?" Marci asked as she began to cry.

Before Bob could answer, Ellen said, "No, children, he must be guilty, or the police wouldn't have arrested him. We have to tell them we're not criminals too."

"That's crazy, Mom!" Marci declared. "Father Chris is no criminal, and I don't care what any police say."

Bob could see that Ellen had lost control, so he attempted to calm her, but her fear made her even more irrational. She started to cry. "I don't want my children hurt. I don't care what they do to those crack babies. I just want them to let us alone."

"Ellen, get a grip on yourself!" Bob said harshly. "This is no time to fall apart. We're a part of this whether we want to be or not."

"No!" Ellen screamed. "I don't want to be a part of it. It was all a mistake. . . ."

"Let's get some clothes and food together quickly and load up the car," Bob told the children.

"Where are we going, Dad?" Robert, Jr. asked.

"I don't know exactly, son. Maybe we'll go to Tennessee for a visit with Grandma for a while. We just need to get out of the city."

"All right!" the boy shouted gleefully as he headed for his room to pack. He loved to go to his grandma's house. It always smelled like cookies, pies, and fried chicken.

It took about thirty minutes to get the car loaded with everything Bob thought they would need. Ellen just sat in the living room crying. He knew she was close to the breaking point and wished he knew how to help her, but their safety had to come first. *Maybe when we get to Tennessee, Mom will know what to do,* he thought.

"Hurry, kids!" he shouted for the tenth time. "We have to get going."

Finally Bob got everyone into the car. The garage door was just swinging open when another car pulled up, blocking the driveway, and two men carrying weapons got out. When Ellen saw the weapons, she became hysterical. Bob tried to quiet her down, but she was beyond his control.

As the men approached their car, one of them asked, "Are you Robert Cofer?"

"Yes," Bob answered. "What's the problem?"

"Please step out of the car," the other man commanded. "And keep your hands in sight."

The nine-millimeter machine-pistol he was pointing said it all. He was ready to kill if Bob resisted.

"What's this about?" Bob asked again as he held his hands up.

"Shut up!" Secret Service Agent Carl Tooms demanded, as he pushed Bob against the door roughly. "You'll be told all you need to know."

Ellen was screaming so loud that Marci began to cry too. Robert, Jr. shouted at the men, "You leave my daddy alone!" He jumped out of the car and swung at Tooms, who was closest to his side of the car. His blow struck the man in a very sensitive area and he cuffed Robert on the side of the head, knocking the ten-year-old down in the driveway.

"That's not necessary," the other agent, Donald Shepperd, said gruffly. "The kid is just trying to protect his father."

"The little hellion better not hit me again," Tooms said angrily. "You remember that he's a small version of his parents. They're like roaches. It's better to stamp them out before they grow up," the man said as he laughed at his own sour joke.

Bob felt his heart pumping fast as he looked toward his children and wife. "What about my family?" he asked.

"Shut up!" Tooms said again. "You should have thought about them before you joined a group of terrorists."

"I'm not a part of any . . ."

But he never had the chance to finish his statement. Tooms jammed the butt of his weapon into Bob's rib cage, knocking the wind out of him. That and the pain of at least two broken ribs made it impossible for him to speak.

"I told you to let them alone!" Shepperd said sternly.

"If you don't like it, take it up with Washington," Tooms replied. "These types are all the same. They don't mind killing people, but they don't want anyone to touch their precious family." For all his bravado, Tooms was a coward and backed off as Shepperd came around the car. Shepperd helped Bob to his feet and steered him toward the vehicle on the street.

Bob and Ellen were loaded in the back of what was obviously a government car. Tooms, still angry, kept his weapon pointed at them the whole time. Something in Ellen had snapped. She had stopped screaming and sat, almost comatose, staring out the window.

The children were loaded into the front seat with Shepperd. "What will happen to us?" Marci whimpered.

Shepperd replied compassionately, "I don't really know, honey. I have orders to pick up just your parents, but we can't leave you here by yourselves, can we? You'll be all right." Shepperd had lied to calm the young girl. His orders included the entire family. *I don't like this,* he thought to himself. *They don't fit any terrorist pattern I've ever studied.*

As they pulled out of the driveway and headed down the street, they met a gang of youths carrying "Gay Power" signs and wielding sticks and bottles. Behind them, three houses were showing obvious signs of being looted, and one was on fire.

When the group saw the car approaching, several of the youths threw bottles and rocks at it. Tooms, in the back seat with the Cofers, stuck his weapon out the window and fired a short burst into the air. When the staccato of the automatic weapon reached the group, they scattered like ants in every direction, dropping looted electronic equipment and other contraband.

Tooms laughed, "I guess they'll think twice before they throw rocks again." Then he swore as he touched the hot barrel to his hand while drawing the weapon back into the car.

The pair drove the children to a converted holding area in an elementary school building. Agent Shepperd got out to talk with the woman in charge of the detention center.

"These are the Cofer children," he said quietly so the children couldn't hear him. Then he showed the list to the woman who compared it to hers.

"Okay, they're on the list. I'll handle them from here."

"Where will they go?" Shepperd inquired.

"Who knows? I just process 'em and get 'em ready for travel. I suppose they'll go to some permanent place, once the parents are processed."

Donald Shepperd was clearly troubled. He had been with the FBI for more than twenty years, and old habits don't change easily. He knew that most of the people they had picked up had had their constitutional rights violated. He didn't have a warrant—just a list of known subversives supplied by the attorney general's office. He knew that the treatment Tooms had given Cofer would be enough for any first-year law student to get him off.

They drove on to another building near the perimeter, where the Cofers would be detained. Bob wanted desperately to ask about his children, but Tooms held the gun against his sore ribs, just waiting for him to ask another question so he could jam the weapon into his side again. Bob prayed silently as they rode on, *God, please be with our children, and protect them from harm.* He also prayed for Ellen, who didn't even appear to notice that the children were gone. The only sign that she was still alive was the rise and fall of her chest as she breathed and the infrequent blinking of her eyelids. In a way, her unawareness was a blessing.

Shepperd pulled the car into the driveway of what was obviously a converted office complex. The entire facility was now surrounded by a triple-layered, razor-sharp, wire fence. As they drove up, a guard swung the outer gates open. Once they were inside, he closed them behind the car and opened the inner gates.

This is no makeshift operation. They didn't build all this since the riots started, Shepperd thought to himself. *Someone put this in motion several months ago.*

When the Cofers were taken from the car, Tooms spoke to the agent in charge—a large, tough-looking woman. "Here's one for you," and casting an admiring glance at Ellen, he added jokingly. "Let me know when you get her into the next stage of processing. I might need to oversee that." The woman laughed, "You're a nasty ole man, Agent Tooms."

He winked and said coarsely, "What do you mean? It's just part of my job."

Once they were in the processing center, Bob was hustled off to one side of the large room where several dozen other people were being processed and stripped, while the processors gawked at them. He panicked as he thought of Ellen experiencing this treatment. He looked around, but he couldn't spot her among all the others.

He realized he was next in line when he heard the angry clerk yell, "You! Strip!"

Bob didn't move and the man swore and shouted again.

"I said take your clothes off. Are you deaf as well as stupid?"

"You don't have any right to treat me this way," Bob said firmly. "And what have you done with my wife?"

"Oh, we have a lawyer in the group." The processor was a large man. He moved directly in front of Bob. "Would you like to see how we treat terrorists in here, you creep?"

Bob remembered the treatment he had received in his own yard and had no doubt that the man was deadly serious. "No, I'll do as you say," he said submissively.

"Now that's a good boy," the man said mockingly. "Now get undressed!"

Across the room the angry woman was shouting at Ellen, "I told you to get undressed!"

Ellen was now aware of her surroundings and she screamed, "No! I won't take my clothes off. You can't make me."

Tooms, who had been standing to one side talking to another one of the agents, walked over to Ellen and struck her across the face with the back of his hand. "You'll do what you're told here, sweetie," he said crudely. Then he reached out and grabbed her blouse, ripping it nearly off.

Suddenly Tooms was swung around, and as he started to protest, he was struck in the stomach. He collapsed in a heap. Donald Shepperd was standing over him, daring him to get up again. Tooms, fat and badly out of shape, was in no condition to do anything but groan.

Shepperd snapped at the big woman behind the receiving desk,

"You get some privacy curtains around these women, and you get the men out of here, now! Is that clear?"

"Just who do you think you are?" she protested.

"I'm going to be the agent that slugs you in about thirty seconds," Shepperd growled as his eyes narrowed. "You may have to strip search these people, but you're not going to make a public spectacle out of them. Now get going," he said with finality as he stormed toward her.

Hearing the shouting, the supervisor came over to where Shepperd was standing and asked, "What's your problem?"

"I want some privacy for these women. And keep the men out of here!" Shepperd ordered. "You do it now, or you'll answer to me too."

"Listen, agent . . ."

"Shepperd—Donald S. Shepperd," he replied angrily. "You report me or do whatever you want, but right now I want these people treated like human beings. As far as I can determine, they haven't even been formally charged."

The supervisor, only a recent recruit for the detention duty, backed down. "Okay, I'll get some curtains up," she said. "But you'll have to answer for this."

"Fine," Shepperd growled as he put his jacket around a young woman standing totally naked in front of him.

Something is dreadfully wrong here, Shepperd said to himself as he pushed Tooms ahead of him towards the door. *I'm not going to be a party to innocent people being treated like animals. My grandfather fought in Europe to ensure that the Nazis didn't get a chance to rule the world. This is no better. . . .*

OIL

When the Middle East War broke out in 1996, nearly two million Moslems were aligned against Israel. The spark that ignited the war was a report by OPEC that Israel had drilled slant wells in Israeli-occupied Iraq.

Slant wells had been declared illegal by the world conference on oil conservation, which Israel steadfastly refused to acknowledge. Even under pressure by the United States, Israel had refused to abandon its operation.

An OPEC report verified that as far back as the late eighties Israel had been drilling slant wells in an effort to tap into the last major oil pool in the Middle East. Jews around the world had poured hundreds of billions of dollars into the project. One of the major fund raisers was Jason Franklin. Amir Hussein also contributed heavily to the project. Working through Rabbi Moshi Amitt, Hussein had provided nearly $100 billion in development funds. Control of these funds had thrust Amitt into the leadership of the Knesset, the Israeli ruling Cabinet, and ultimately the religious leadership of Israel.

Virtually every renowned geologist in the world had mocked the project. The very idea of drilling under another country to tap an oil pool was ridiculous, they had said. They presented charts and graphs showing that the cost of drilling would far outstrip the market value of any oil that might be recovered. What they failed to take into account was that Israel had a bigger agenda in mind. The oil itself wasn't an end. It was a means to accomplish a greater end.

Then in 1994, Israel tapped the Bashra pool under Iraq with a thirty-six-inch slant well, and quietly transferred the entire pool into their prepared salt domes along the Gaza, virtually pumping the Bashra pool dry in less than two years—all without the Arabs suspecting a thing until the oil simply began to run out. Suddenly Israel was independent of foreign oil, at least for the next ten years.

A hoarde of red-faced geologists flooded into Israel to study their drilling techniques, but the government put all of the slant projects under close military guard and sealed them off. As reports leaked out, it was discovered that Israel didn't have just one slant well project going; there were dozens. Through an undisclosed new method, they had found a way to drill miles with commercial slant wells. It became clear that their goal was not just to tap into their Arab neighbors' oil supplies; they intended to drain them.

The combined forces of Iraq, Iran, Libya, and even troops from Saudi Arabia, aligned against Israel. The United States threatened to cut off all aid—military and economic—if Israel didn't cease the drilling. But by 1996, the Israelis were building virtually all of their own military equipment and selling billions of dollars worth on the world market as well. Even the Arabs had bought Israeli-made military hardware and were dependent on them for parts. Israel simply thumbed its nose at the U.S. and other nations, forming an alliance with Zimbabwe, Zululand (the old South Africa), and several other emerging African powers.

On August 17, 1996, the combined Arab forces launched an attack on Israel using chemical weapons. Even as the missiles and long-range artillery shells fell on the front-line troops, Israel and Zululand launched a tactical nuclear strike against the combined Arab forces. In thirty minutes, the fighting was over. Thirty thousand Israelis were killed by the chemical attack, and four hundred thousand Arabs were totally disintegrated by the Israelis and Africans. The Arabs, who had relied on the U.S. to keep Israel from using atomic weapons, sued for peace immediately.

The confrontation, which almost erupted into global war between the United States and China over the use of Israeli nuclear weapons, was stopped when the U.S. and Russia moved three separate carrier groups into the Gulf and threatened to use them against Israel if any more nuclear weapons were used.

By then the devastation of the Arab forces was massive. Iran's oil fields had been contaminated by surface-level fallout and its army annihilated. Israel agreed to the peace terms and also agreed to cease their slant drilling under the Arab countries, which they did—for nearly two years. But as the reserves they had stored began to wane, the Israelis covertly broke their agreement.

What the rest of the world didn't know was that the drilling operation by Israel had been successful beyond anyone's wildest dreams. The longest slant well in the world had tapped into the subterranean pool beneath Saudi Arabia nearly three years earlier. Six additional wells had been sunk immediately, and the pumping operation had begun in earnest.

At first, the Israeli geologists thought they had tapped a new pool of oil because pressures in the existing Saudi wells had not dropped. But instead they made an amazing discovery; the pool they had tapped was actually the sump for much of the oil under the desert lands. Simply put, the more they pumped out of the ground and into the storage domes, the more oil flowed into the crevasse feeding the wells. In essence they were draining the Middle East of most of its available oil, and the Arabs didn't even know it.

Later, as the pressures in the Saudi wells began to decline, they called in American geologists to investigate. The conclusion was that the Middle East oil supplies were running out faster than anyone had estimated. At the rate of depletion shown by the pressure drop, it was estimated that Saudi oil supplies would be exhausted in less than a decade. This news sent tremors through the industrialized world, especially Japan, which was totally dependent on foreign oil supplies. Prices shot up to one hundred and fifty dollars a barrel within a few weeks. Even the Japanese economy was having a difficult time digesting the large increases. The Japanese quietly signed an exclusive agreement with the Saudis to buy all their exported oil in exchange for the new desalinization process the Japanese had designed to convert sea water into fresh water economically. The Saudis knew they had to use their waning resources to develop new technologies. Food was the commodity they chose. They would make the desert bloom, just as Israel was doing.

After a much-heated debate in the office of Jacob Estine, the Israeli prime minister, the decision was made to bring all six main pumps on line to service the slant wells. Defense Minister Levi Klein strongly objected: "If we pump all the oil too quickly, we will bring the wrath of the world down on us," he explained for the fourth time. *Why can't these religious zealots see what they are doing?* he wondered. *If they push the Asians too far, they will fight. And fighting the Japanese and Chinese won't be like fighting the Arabs.*

The Chinese had become a formidable force under the mutual alliance pact with the Japanese and Koreans, known as the Asian Triangle. With two million men under arms and nuclear capability, they would not hesitate to protect their fragile economy, or that of their financiers, the Japanese.

"We simply cannot allow the Saudis to develop their land," Moshi Amitt, leader of the Knesset, said flatly. "We are the exporters of food to the Arab world now. If we lose that edge, we will be in constant danger again. We will drain the oil reserves and sell them to the Japanese so they won't buy them directly from the Saudis. We will strip the Arabs of their wealth. God is with us."

"If you do this, the Japanese will have the Chinese march on Israel. I beg you to reconsider this madness," Levi Klein pleaded to the Cabinet.

"You will defend Israel just as your brothers did before you," Amitt railed. "We cannot fail. God is on our side."

"Perhaps, my brother," the prime minister said wearily. "It will take God to win this war, if it comes to that. Our people do not have the same fervor for fighting they had when we were surrounded by enemies. We rule the Arab nations through the use of food now, rather than force. I fear we have lost our edge."

"We will stop these Asians from interfering in our lands just as we have the Arabs," Amitt thundered, his robes billowing as he swept away his unseen enemies with a wave of his arms. Amitt had always secretly pictured himself as a modern Moses. His size, beard, and flowing robes were meant to convey that image to his peers who sat on the Knesset.

In the past, the Knesset had been comprised of both the majority and minority party members, and in principle it still was. But the Zealots, or Hebrew absolutists, had total control by their unification within both parties. Amitt was their leader.

"Besides," he continued, "the Americans will never allow the Chinese to threaten Israel. There are many Jews still living in America."

"America has troubles of its own," Klein argued. "Their country is like a war zone. I do not believe they will defend Israel, at least not under these circumstances."

"If you cannot, or will not, defend your country, we will find someone who can," Amitt said defiantly. "God has given our enemies into our hands. We must act now!"

"I will defend my country," Klein said angrily. "I will even send my sons and daughters to fight, but this is still wrong. You sound like one of King Saul's advisers sending him into battle to die. What if you don't speak for the Lord?"

"But we do," Amitt said proudly. "Did we not raise the money to drill the wells? And did we not rebuild the temple of Solomon just as God's Word said?"

Klein slumped back in his seat. He knew logic could not prevail. *I pray we are not facing seventy years of exile again*, he thought wearily. *Many brave men will die . . . and for what?*

Within six months of the time the pumps were put on line, oil production in Saudi Arabia virtually ceased. With nearly half of all the available crude oil in the world safely locked away in their salt domes, the Israelis announced to the world that they controlled the crude oil market and would be taking bids on oil export—at five hundred dollars a barrel! Overnight the Japanese stock market plunged twenty thousand points! Japan was in the first stage of a total economic collapse.

An emergency summit was called in New York to discuss the situation. Leaders of all the Arab nations, as well as those from the Asian Triangle, were represented. Since the United States had threatened to veto any UN resolution against Israel, the summit was held at Camp David, without UN sanction.

"You must understand, Madam President, that Japan has the right to protect its interests in the Middle East," Japanese Economic Minister Hurichi Amato said heatedly after Kathy Alton refused to agree to force Israel to surrender the oil it had diverted.

"Are you threatening us, Mr. Amato?" the president asked politely while glaring at the Japanese diplomat, who looked like a sumo wrestler.

"You may take it any way you wish, Madam President," the irritated minister replied. He was not accustomed to addressing a woman politician, and he was even less comfortable debating with one.

"May I remind you, Mr. Amato, that any action taken against a sovereign nation, with whom we have a mutual defense agreement, will not be taken lightly by our people."

Amato, not to be outdone, retorted, "I would suggest that you have enough trouble controlling the dissidents within your own borders. You will find that doing so across five thousand miles may not be to the liking of your citizens. Japan will not stand by and see our economy destroyed because of the theft of the Saudis' oil reserves."

The lone representative from Israel, a young disciple of Moshi Amitt's, jumped up shouting: "The very land upon which they live belongs to Israel by divine right. We have every intention of controlling the resources if we desire. You will find Israel a formidable opponent for anyone foolish enough to attack her. God is on our side."

The Japanese minister slammed his notebook closed and exited the room, with his staff close behind him.

"Excellent," Hussein said to Jason Franklin as he watched on the closed-circuit monitor. "The stage is now set for war. Launch Phase Five immediately."

Franklin shuddered as he thought about the consequences of what they were about to do. *This will be brinksmanship unlike any the world had ever seen. One slip and the world will be left in cinders.*

Then, in his mind he clearly heard, "Yes, my timid subject. But if we win, I will rule mankind!" Franklin jumped as if he had been touched with a hot iron. *He can read my thoughts!*

The Leader simply left the room smiling. *Humans are so simple,* he thought to himself. *Created in the image of God—indeed!*

Within hours of the summit's abrupt ending, Israeli intelligence detected an alarming development.

"Prime Minister, our satellites have picked up massive troop deployments in China. And our contacts in America say the Japanese have diverted several hundred aircraft from the commercial airlines they have purchased."

"How many aircraft have they diverted?" the ailing prime minister asked of his defense minister. He knew Levi Klein felt as he did about the threat to Israel, but the religious right was in control now. Amitt had convinced the people of Israel they were invincible. It was as if they thought God could only be on their side.

Klein thought fearfully of what Amitt had proposed at the last council meeting. His mind still would not allow him to believe it. "They have diverted at least five hundred aircraft from the fleet they operate out of America," Klein reported. "President Alton is livid about this, since it has stranded millions of travelers, but there is nothing she can do. The Japanese have taken the official position that the diversion is due to the Olympic games."

"Five hundred aircraft! How many troops can they move, and how quickly?"

"Intelligence says they are moving a million troops into Afghanistan as a staging area into Iraq. They also estimate another eight to nine million are being moved by land. It is possible that the Chinese could have ten million armed soldiers on Israel's borders by November!" With that, the defense minister showed Estine the satellite photos taken earlier that day. The whole area around Beijing seemed to be covered with soldiers for a hundred miles in every direction.

"My God!" Estine exclaimed as he viewed the photographs. "Is it possible to move that many men in such a short time?"

"Yes, sir, it is," Klein replied wearily. "The Japanese are efficiency experts. They have equipped an army in China that may actually be ten times the number we see here. They have created a surrogate army to fight their battles. Since they have made no efforts to conceal their movements, we have to assume they are issuing a warning that we cannot ignore."

"What does the Knesset say about this?" Estine asked as he tried to think clearly. "Ten million men! With ninety million in reserve! We wouldn't have enough bullets to shoot them all, even if we wanted to."

"Amitt has suggested use of the doomsday bomb," Klein said slowly and deliberately. "He is trying to convince the Knesset to launch a pre-emptive strike."

"The doomsday bomb!" Estine shouted in astonishment. "We all agreed during the last war that the cobalt bomb could never be used. We have no idea what the effects will be."

"I know," Klein said as he replaced the photos. "But since we will be using it inside China they are apparently willing to experiment." Then, after a slight pause, Klein stepped forward. "I would like to submit my resignation," he stated as he handed the prime minister a typed document resigning his commission in the Army, as well as his position as defense minister.

Looking over the document Estine replied, "You cannot quit, Levi. You're the single voice of sanity I have among a company of lunatics. I will not accept."

"I'm afraid you have no choice, my good friend. I will not be a party to launching this weapon on the world. We are a nation because we wanted to escape the holocaust of the second World War. Now we're talking about killing ten times that many people, perhaps one hundred times as many! Will we be seen any differently than the Nazis?"

"I will call an immediate session of the Cabinet and the Knesset. At least wait until then, will you?"

"I will, out of respect for you, but I must tell you again, someone or something is directing this country on the road to destruction. And it is not the God of Abraham and Jacob."

At the great assembly hall in Beijing, the Chinese leaders were gathered to hear their president make an announcement to the World Press, which was represented by every major network.

The ambassador from China stood before the assembly: "I have the great honor of presenting our great leader, Chang Lo Tung, president of all China."

Chang had been just forty-three when he was elected in the first free elections held in China in more than sixty years. At fifty-three, he was still youthful by Chinese standards. The elections were hailed by the West as a sign that China was finally joining the community of nations. In reality, what had happened was Chang had become the strongest dictator in China since Mao Tse-tung. Under the tutelage of the Japanese, he had made China into the second most powerful nation in the world—militarily.

Speaking perfect English acquired at Stanford, where he had

earned his master's in International Law, Chang addressed the assembly.

"My brothers, as you know, the Zionists have stolen the world's greatest economic treasure and the life blood of our people, and are now trying to blackmail the world. If we allow this, our economy will collapse even before we get started. For centuries China has been struggling just to feed its people. Now, as we are developing the means to do so, the Jews threaten to stop us. We will not be stopped. Our people are willing to die to defend our right to progress."

As if by an unseen signal, the assembly thundered with applause.

"Even as I speak, the Chinese Republic is moving its army into position to recover the oil stolen by the Israelis. We do not wish war. We do not wish anything from Israel except peace. But if Israel persists in holding the oil so needed by our allies to help China, we will fight. And let there be no mistake: we will scrape Israel clean when we attack! There will not be one blade of grass left growing and not one brick left standing. We will tear down every building and cast the bricks into the sea. We will destroy the Zionists until their land will be uninhabitable for one thousand years.

"If the United States interferes, we will launch an attack that will end its ability to wage war. We have two billion people ready and willing to die for their right to feed their children. We will survive any war. The Zionists and their allies will not.

"This conflict can be avoided if Israel will relinquish the rights to the oil they have stolen. I pray that the United States will use its influence to accomplish this."

At the Pentagon in Washington, General Louis Gorman, chairman, called an emergency meeting of the Joint Chiefs of Staff. "Gentlemen, we cannot take this threat lightly. Our intelligence reports show that the Chinese have nearly five hundred long-range missiles capable of reaching the U.S., and more than one thousand capable of reaching Israel. I have read your reports and concur with the overall analysis: We could lose as many as one hundred million people in a nuclear exchange. Without question, we could inflict massive damage on the Chinese, but it is not an option as far as I am concerned. The United States should not go to war over Israel's right to Saudi Arabia's oil. We'd have a revolt from the American people."

"General, I recommend that we confront the president and her staff on this issue. I will not be a party to starting World War III. The president lacks the authority to launch any attack without the approval of Congress. And since the Congress is still on furlough, that means no war . . ."

"I agree, Ray," Gorman broke in to say as he closed the file before him. "I'll see the president immediately." General Gorman was addressing Lieutenant General Raymond Abbott, Commanding General of the Air Force. It was Abbott who had planned the strategy for ending the hostilities in the Middle East during the 1996 war. He was a cool thinker who was absolutely committed to his job. He believed in the constitutional form of government and was determined not to allow the politicians to run the military or the military to run the government.

Known only to General Gorman and a very few select military leaders, Lt. General Raymond Abbott had uncovered a plot within the military to take over the government and remove President Hunt because of his abuse of power. He suspected the sentiment against President Alton was running even stronger since the military police were being used to help round up and detain American citizens without right of counsel or arraignment. It was all Gorman could do to keep Abbott from storming the White House and confronting Alton and her group of boot lickers.

Gorman had gotten some bad vibrations from the White House. He had argued vehemently against President Alton's declaring martial law. Obviously there were problems in California with bandits and drug runners but nothing that warranted the suspension of civil rights for the general public. In fact, since martial law had been declared, more of his troops had been engaged in transporting and detaining the so-called "terrorists" than in stopping the crime sprees. Now he had reports that local units had been authorized to arrest and detain women and children, families of the Constitutional Rights Committees, to force them out of hiding.

Eventually we'll have a revolt, Gorman thought. *Many of those people being detained are friends and relatives of soldiers. They will eventually put it all together. Then watch out! Soldiers in China might follow blindly, but not Americans. Praise God for that.*

"I have scheduled a meeting with the president today," Gorman said in response to Abbott's comment. "I will tell her the joint chiefs are in disagreement with Israel's actions and we recommend strongly that Israel return the confiscated oil and defuse this situation. I'll make it clear that we will not allow Israel to use nuclear weapons—under the threat of U.S. retaliation. Are we in agreement, gentlemen?"

Unanimously, each member signaled his or her total concurrence. Most had thought Israel's actions were meant to give them a better negotiating position for the oil their country needed. Until the Chinese actually began deploying troops in Afghanistan, they had all assumed real negotiations would start. But when Israel had taken an uncompromising position, they realized that a conflict was inevitable unless the U.S. acted quickly. President Alton seemed to be stalling. In the face of such a potential holocaust, stalling was not an option.

General Gorman spent several frustrating hours trying to get an appointment with President Alton. Each call was met with the same response from her appointment secretary, "I'm sorry, General Gorman, the president is in a special closed door meeting with the Cabinet and members of Congress. She has your message and I'm sure she will see you as soon as possible." Gorman was furious. He had been in Washington long enough to know a stall when he saw one. *But why?* he wondered. *Is this another case of Nero fiddling while Rome burns?*

What he didn't know, but soon would, was that President Alton had another agenda in mind; one that did not include the joint chiefs or their chairman. Her meeting was not with the Cabinet, but with just one person—Amir Hussein.

"Is everything in order?" Hussein asked Kathy Alton as they dined in the blue room.

"It is, sir," she replied comfortably. "I will appoint you special envoy to negotiate the Israeli crisis tomorrow. Do you anticipate any difficulties from the Jews?"

"Naturally," the dark man replied as if he were discussing the purchase of a business. "The Jews are always a problem. You will give me sealed orders authorizing the use of nuclear weapons, if necessary. But we need to allow this conflict between China and Israel to develop further. We must bring the entire world under threat. Only then will they recognize Israel as the menace that she is. The harlot must be obliterated along with the Christians."

"They will be," Alton promised her benefactor. "But we may have some problems with the military. General Gorman has already been to see me about the detention of so many Americans. Now he wants a meeting about confronting Israel immediately."

Hussein's eyes narrowed. "Nothing must stop the roundup of the Christians! Do you understand? They represent the only true threat to my power. We will begin eliminating them soon. The Jews will become the key to solidifying our power. They have made themselves hated already. We will draw upon that hate. We will destroy them also, once and for all. Nothing must stand in the way. This is the time. I will succeed."

Kathy Alton was frightened. She had pledged her devotion to the Society as a young woman, but she had never truly understood how they could rule the world until now. "I will do as you ask, my lord," she replied. She was the president of the most powerful nation that had ever existed, and yet she cowered before one small man.

"I am but the servant of the prince," he said as he focused on her eyes. In them he saw what he wanted to see: fear and total devotion. "The prince of darkness will rule the world when the Christians are gone. We will defeat that pathetic band of groveling misfits who claim Jesus as Lord. The prince will be lord. This kingdom will be ours!"

THE DOOMSDAY WEAPON

The Israeli Knesset was designed much in the fashion of the British Parliament. It is a governing body made up of elected members and represents a balance to the powers of the Israeli prime minister, at least in theory. In function, the Knesset had become the ruling body since the two opposing parties had been united under the leadership of the Zionists. They called themselves the "Zealots."

Under the total domination of Rabbi Moshi Amitt, the Zealots dictated government policy, rather than approve or reject it. Any public official openly opposing the Zealots, including the prime minister, was instantly subject to a no-confidence vote and recall.

It was to this group and this mentality that Prime Minister Jacob Estine was making a desperate appeal.

He stood in the speaker's box addressing the hundred-plus group of men, the majority of whom wore the scarlet and black robes of the Zealots.

"You fools! You are leading us into a war we cannot win. Even if we were willing to use nuclear weapons on the Chinese, we could not kill them all. They have two billion people. If one hundred million survive, they will outnumber us twenty to one. Are you willing to kill a billion human beings?"

"If it will help us to fulfill our destiny," Moshi Amitt boasted. "But they will not attack when you tell them about the doomsday weapon."

"You fools!" Estine shouted again at the men assembled there. "We evaluated the cobalt bomb thoroughly. It is a weapon that cannot ever be used. The device would contaminate the planet we live on if it didn't destroy the earth itself."

"I am told the yield from this weapon is greater than the largest hydrogen bomb. Is that correct?" Amitt asked smugly.

Estine replied, "In theory, yes. But it may also create a chain reaction that could burn off the earth's atmosphere. We learned the technology after the Americans gave up the project in the late 1960s. Dr. Heinz said the device was beyond the capacity of mankind to control."

The other members of the Knesset looked at Amitt. It was clear they had not been told all the facts. "Just how powerful is this bomb, Prime Minister?" one of the members asked.

"We can only calculate its yield. The computer simulations suggest it would have a yield of one to two giga-tons."

"Define, please," the bearded rabbi requested.

"A giga-ton is the equivalent of one billion tons of TNT. As a comparison, the largest hydrogen bomb yet constructed has a yield of approximately one hundred million tons of TNT."

A murmur went through the room as the members considered the enormity of the weapon that Amitt proposed using.

"But that is the beauty of the weapon," Amitt said to his peers. "It is so destructive that no one will dare oppose us while we have it." Even as he spoke, Amitt knew he had a plan that required a "demonstration" of his doomsday weapon.

"But what if someone else also has the weapon?" Defense Minister Levi Klein shouted from his position in the back. He had come into the room unnoticed. "Or what if we force the Chinese to back down with it and others decide we have too great an advantage and develop their own? And what if the bomb does start a chain reaction that splits the earth at its core?"

"You are out of order," Amitt shouted at the defense minister. "This meeting is open only to members of the Knesset."

"I invited Levi to attend," Estine said as he stood facing the group. "He has the best understanding of the military ramifications we are facing. I ask that he be allowed to continue."

"No!" Amitt exclaimed loudly. "It is not allowed."

The other members began their ritualistic rapping on the table, signaling their disapproval of Amitt's actions. Overridden, he sat back down as Levi Klein approached the podium.

"Respected elders," he began, "as you know, I have dedicated my life to the service of my country. I have fought its wars with vigor because they were righteous wars. But what we are planning now is unholy and . . ."

Amitt interrupted with, "God decides what is holy!" He knew Klein could scuttle his well-laid plans if the Knesset listened to him. He had his instructions from the Society and they were clear. Israel would bring the world to the brink of war, then negotiate a settlement, with Amitt leading the way. When the one-world system was secure, Moshi Amitt would have one of the top positions.

In order for the independent nations of the world to accept a one-world government, the Society knew it would be necessary to threaten their very existence. However, since the threat of nuclear war had been virtually eliminated by an arms treaty between the U.S. and Russia, people had begun to sleep soundly, believing peace was secure. The cobalt bomb would create an imbalance and global panic once again, just as the hydrogen bomb had in the twentieth century. It would require a leader of enormous persuasion and power to knit the world together.

"Yes, God decides what is holy," Klein agreed, "but you want to interpret God's will for all of us. I wonder if the billion or so people you propose to kill feel the same way."

"If you don't have the stomach to defend Israel, then perhaps it is time you retired!" Amitt challenged. "We have the right to use whatever weapons are at our disposal."

"Who gave us that right?" Klein asked grimly.

Amitt shouted back, "God gave us that right. This nation is His, and the Jews are His people."

"Then let God defend us," Klein pleaded, as he looked around at the other members. "But don't unleash this demon from Hell on innocent people—not for the sake of oil."

Now on the defensive, Amitt began to sense his grip over the group slipping. "You don't seem to understand. It is not about oil. It is about the right to lead the world. Once we have annihilated the infidels, the world will know Israel is God's divine instrument." Then slowly a single member of the Knesset began to clap, then another, and still others, until the majority of the Zealots were signaling their agreement with Amitt. Amitt bowed his head and raised his arms toward heaven.

Klein sat down next to Jacob Estine. He felt a hundred years old. They were defeated and he knew it. How could anyone argue with the mentality of "God told me to do it"? He had seen people beaten and stoned because they drove their cars on the Sabbath or washed their clothes and left them on the line after sundown Friday. Now he had a better understanding of the fervor of those who crucified Christ twenty centuries earlier. Anyone who opposed their legalisms would be dealt with as an infidel. For the right to rule the world these men would be willing to destroy it. *God save us from men who would be god themselves*, he thought.

"Allen, I just received a communiqué from Andrea in Jerusalem that Moshi Amitt is addressing his nation about the crisis with Japan and China. It should be coming through on the satellite momentarily."

"Why Amitt?" Allen White, the senior news editor at WNN, asked. "Why not Estine, the prime minister?"

"I don't know. Andrea said that Amitt is the de facto leader of the Knesset. Maybe they have assumed responsibility."

"Switch on the viewer," White instructed his engineer. "Interrupt the news transmission and patch in Andrea. We'll carry this live. Who knows, maybe the Jews are going to back down." *But don't count on it,* he said to himself. The last time he was in Israel, it was a nightmare. *The religious zealots in Israel are as bad as the Ayatollah was in Iran in his day. The Ayatollah said Allah told him to do it, and the Jews say Jehovah tells them to do it.*

"The patch is in, chief. Andrea's standing by."

"Okay, feed her into the system."

"This is Andrea Bernstein in Jerusalem. Rabbi Moshi Amitt, leader of the Israeli Knesset, is addressing the Jewish people regarding the crisis with China and Japan." The cameramen first focused on Andrea Bernstein's strikingly beautiful face, and then the producer did a fade-out to the camera covering the Israeli parliament hall.

The face of Moshi Amitt appeared on the screen. Behind him was the full Israeli parliament. An interpreter was translating from Hebrew to English for the WNN American audience.

"Again, I repeat. Israel does not want conflict," Amitt announced, as he waved his arms dramatically. "We want peace. But we will not be intimidated by anyone. It is our right to use the resources God has provided, including the oil reserves now stored in our country. We will negotiate with any country for the sale of this resource, but we will not be blackmailed.

"The Republic of China has amassed an army on our border with the admitted intention of invading our land—'to strip it clean,' to quote President Chang. We have both the determination and ability to defend ourselves against any enemy, even against an army of a million infidels.

"By order of the Knesset, the Israeli military is equipping our SX-14 missiles with weapons so powerful each can obliterate an area of one hundred square miles. We have no desire to use these weapons. But unless China removes its troops from any territories adjacent to Israel, we will have no alternative.

"Any movement of these forces into Israeli territory will constitute an act of war and will be dealt with accordingly."

Even while Amitt was still speaking, Allen White was dialing his long-time friend, Colonel Bob Robbins, at the Pentagon in Washington.

"Colonel Robbins here," the Air Force missile and ordnance expert said as he leaned forward over his desk and picked up the phone.

"Bob, this is Allen. Have you been watching the news?"

"Nope. I've been busy pushing paper to justify my position," Robbins replied sarcastically, as he moved the pile of requisitions for supplies further to one side. He knew they wouldn't be filled anyway, not with the government running on short rations.

"Bob, the head of the Israeli Knesset, Moshi Amitt, is addressing his parliament right now about the Chinese troops stationed in Afghanistan."

"Yeah, I wouldn't want to be in Israel when a million screaming Chinese come running across the border. They'll take the Jews like Sitting Bull took Custer."

"Listen Bob, Amitt says Israel has a bomb that will wipe out a hundred square miles, and that they're willing to use it on the Chinese. Do you know anything about it?"

"My God!" Robbins shouted as he jumped to his feet and began to pace the length of the phone cord. "It's the cobalt bomb."

"What exactly is the cobalt bomb?" White asked as he flicked on the tape recorder. He was struggling to keep his voice under control. He didn't want to spook his contact.

"This is strictly off the record, right, Allen?"

"Absolutely," White lied as he motioned to the engineer to test the incoming signal. He wasn't about to lose this interview, even if it cost him a valuable contact and friend.

"The cobalt bomb idea was developed back when Dr. Howard Tolls headed the U.S. nuclear bomb project. You'll remember that Tolls helped to develop the hydrogen bomb and later lobbied against deploying it because of its destructive power."

"Yes, I remember. He was eventually removed from the project because of his political views, wasn't he?"

Before he answered, he eased back into his chair. "Officially, yes." Robbins thought back to the times he had heard Tolls argue against the deployment of hydrogen bomb technology. "The president was for deploying any weapons at his disposal. Having led the Allied armies in World War II, he believed the H-bomb would force the Russians to back down. Tolls argued that the use of hydrogen bombs would pollute the world to an uninhabitable state.

"When the cobalt bomb was first proposed, Tolls spoke out against it. He argued that cobalt was the fabric of our subatomic structure and could cause a fusion reaction that would destroy the earth itself."

"Wasn't that the same argument used by the Manhattan team before the first atomic bomb test?" White asked.

"Yes. But remember, they had few real facts to go on at that time. Later, when some of the same scientists argued against the hydrogen bomb, it was Tolls who provided the calculations showing a sustained atmospheric reaction was theoretically possible but highly improbable. His calculations were proven correct. Tolls also calculated that a cobalt bomb would have a fifty-fifty chance of starting a spontaneous reaction in the atmosphere."

"Meaning?" White asked as he glanced toward his sound engineer, who gave him the thumbs-up sign. The interview was being broadcast as a time-delay, with shots of the first atomic explosions superimposed on the screen.

"A cobalt bomb with a yield of one giga-ton—a billion tons," Robbins explained, "might conceivably set the world on fire and snuff out the very atmosphere we breathe. In which case, you win the war, but lose the world—so to speak."

"Could the Israelis have a cobalt bomb?" White asked. Suddenly he realized that he had uncovered the real "ticking bomb" that every journalist dreams about.

"It's very likely they have the technology," Robbins answered as a frown formed on his face. "After all, the Jews have dominated the inner circle of nuclear technology for a long time. But I can't believe that any rational human beings would use the cobalt bomb on another nation. It's probably the dirtiest bomb ever devised."

"By 'dirty,' you mean radioactive fallout?" White asked as he gave thumbs-up to his newscaster, who was readying a statement condemning Israel's actions.

"Yes," Robbins replied again. "A single cobalt bomb could make an area the size of Georgia uninhabitable for thousands of years. That is, if it didn't kill us all."

"Okay, thanks, buddy," White said as he signaled the engineer to shut down the recorder.

Robbins knew he had said too much. He asked in an almost pleading tone, "Please don't use any exact quotes. That whole project is still classified top-secret."

"You got it, pal," White lied. He hated to stiff a friend; *but such is the life of a newsman*, he thought. *Besides, it's too late to do anything about it now.*

Within ten minutes, agents from the FBI and the National Security Agency were escorting Colonel Robert Robbins out of his Pentagon office.

As the news networks began picking up the interview from WNN, there was an instant shift in the polls. More than 60 percent of Americans said they opposed Israel's receiving any more aid from the United

States, and 50 percent favored military action against Israel to keep them from using the cobalt bomb. Clearly the public sentiment was shifting against Israel.

The timing of the broadcast from Israel could not have been better if it had been choreographed. President Alton's news briefing had already been scheduled for later that afternoon. Cal Rutland simply moved it up so that it would be telecast following the WNN broadcast with White's Pentagon source.

At the briefing, President Alton announced that she was appointing Amir Hussein, a successful businessman and naturalized citizen from Israel, as special envoy to negotiate with the Israeli Knesset. The American and European media were reporting massive demonstrations against Israel. Anti-Semitism was growing throughout Europe as thousands of Jewish merchants had their businesses looted.

Amir Hussein stood beside President Alton in the Oval Office when she made the announcement. In the interests of security, only one representative from each of the various media was allowed to attend. As soon as the announcement was made, the networks began clamoring for more information on the Jewish immigrant to the U.S. who was given such a vital role to play in the world's future. Carefully prepared information packets were distributed that outlined Hussein's qualifications and background.

What they didn't say was that all official records had been altered to reflect what the packets presented. Amir Hussein was presented as a businessman who had been instrumental in helping to form an alliance between the U.S. and the Israelis that was satisfactory to the Arabs after the 1996 war.

Comments coming out of the Middle East made Hussein sound like the greatest negotiator since Dwight Eisenhower. With tensions running at an all-time high in Israel, Hussein was welcomed by the less radical factions there. Only Moshi Amitt, representing the Zealots, spoke out strongly against the U.S. emissary coming to the Middle East. He could see his position being eroded if another Jew, even a half Jew, were able to defuse the crisis. He didn't have the slightest inkling of Hussein's true identity. Amitt made a decision born out of desperation: He would launch the weapons on China as soon as possible. Israel would win the war and rule the world. He would rule Israel.

The Chinese continued to amass an army in Afghanistan. With more ground troops arriving daily, the number was estimated to be nearly two million armed men. Without heavy artillery support, they were little more than a show of force meant to intimidate the Israelis. But with heavy equipment on its way by rail, the Chinese would be capable of staging a full-scale invasion within two weeks. It was even rumored that Egyptian missiles were being equipped with nuclear warheads by the Germans, who relied heavily on the Japanese for their capital. These weapons would be used to neutralize the Israeli nuclear arsenal, if necessary, forcing them to negotiate.

The Israelis were being hemmed in from all sides and, like a cornered animal, they were most dangerous when their backs were against the wall.

Anti-Semitism was accelerating around the world. In Europe anyone of Jewish ancestry was in danger of being mobbed, beaten, and even killed. In America, Israel's longest running ally, Jewish merchants were attacked with the same ferocity that had been directed toward the Christians after the president was assassinated.

Even within the Israeli Army sentiment against the Knesset was at a high pitch. The resignations of Estinc and Klein had been followed by several of the military's highest-ranking officers. These men and women who had led the Israelis so capably in the Middle East War against the Arabs had the confidence of the troops. But the average Israeli soldier had no such feelings about Amitt and the other religious leaders who were now running the country. The Fifth Israeli Armored Division simply refused to obey orders to move to the Iraqi border. Several of the officers who were leading the "strike" were arrested, tried, and executed by order of the Knesset. In protest, three more divisions refused to obey orders also. This time in a more militant state of mind, they challenged the leaders and formed defense groups, heavily armed, and spoiling for a fight.

Support for Amitt was fading rapidly within Israel. Unknown to him, the movement against Israel was well organized and well planned by the Society. Israel was to be a pawn in the chess game about to be played out on a worldwide scale, and the Society intended to control both sides of the issue.

THE BOMB

Moshi Amitt was scheduled to receive the new Washington emissary later that day. His sources had warned that Hussein was no one to be trifled with; he had tremendous authority and power within the American, as well as the Arab, governments. *Well, Moshi Amitt said to himself, I also have power—perhaps more than any man alive. I have the doomsday bomb.*

Six Israeli SX-14 missiles had been equipped with the only six cobalt bombs ever assembled. It had been no small task for the Mossad, the most feared secret police in the world, to steal the components from the U.S. arsenal nearly twenty years earlier. At first the Americans feared that a terrorist group had stolen the weapons, but when the bombs were never seen again, the secret went undisclosed.

Now Israel had the bombs, and Amitt intended to use them. After the two intended for the Chinese and the Iraqis, he would use the remaining four missiles to dictate his terms to the rest of the world. His terms would be simple enough: All the Arabs would be relocated to Europe and America. The Middle East would be the land of the Jews again. And he, Moshi Amitt, would be the leader of the Jews.

In the office of Levi Klein, former minister of defense, a hasty meeting had been called to address the latest crisis facing Israel.

"General Klein, do you realize that Amitt has ordered the six cobalt bombs to be mated to our latest SX-14 missiles?" Jerome Facimadi, the provincial head of the Mossad, literally screamed.

"I suspected such," Klein said wearily. "He is mad with power and his own self-righteousness. He would kill a billion innocent people to accomplish his own insane goals."

"We must stop him!" Facimadi demanded.

"Then have the Mossad kill him," Klein said angrily as he poured himself another glass of wine. "I can do nothing now." He took a sip of the sparkling red wine and commented, "The vineyards in the desert do produce the best wines. At least the wonders of modern science have produced something worthwhile. The desert is once again blooming."

"You know we cannot kill Amitt," Facimadi replied in a more subdued tone. "He is the holy man to millions of Jews. It would rip our country apart."

"Then let him launch his bombs," Klein muttered, as he put the second glass of wine down untouched and slumped wearily into his chair. "Perhaps Israel will rule the world as he says."

"Or perhaps Israel will destroy the world," Facimadi countered.

"What of this Hussein?" Klein asked as he reviewed the Mossad report. "Can he be of any assistance?"

"The sentiment against America is running very high," Facimadi replied with a frown. "It is reported that there is a general roundup of Jews going on in America."

"I thought it was a roundup of Christians," Klein said in surprise as he leaned forward. What he feared most for his people was a worldwide anti-Jewish uprising.

"It started with just Christians, but now they are detaining all the Jews too."

"Ah, it was acceptable as long as it was someone else," Klein said with disgust. "Just like it was in Germany with Hitler. We Jews never learn from our mistakes, do we? The Jews are always on the list. Sometimes first, sometimes second, but always on the list."

Facimadi frowned at his friend's comment. It was too correct to dispute.

"Talk to this Hussein. Perhaps he will be able to help with Amitt, though I fear Amitt is drunk with the wine of power and nothing will stop him except death."

Even while the two Israeli leaders were trying to sort out their options, Amir Hussein was meeting with Moshi Amitt. Hussein was not seeking a compromise from Amitt. In fact, the exact opposite was true. His plan required that the Jewish Zealot reject all options except force.

The first meeting with Amitt went better than Hussein could have hoped for. His people within the Society in Israel had chosen Amitt very well. He was power mad and took Hussein's demands as an affront to his position.

Hussein had demanded that Israel release the oil it had taken from the Saudis and dismantle the cobalt bombs. "If you do not," he had said, "you can expect swift retaliation from the United States."

Amitt had ranted for nearly thirty minutes about how he would see the United States humbled and begging at Israel's door for the oil to keep their children warm. Hussein had again warned the radical rabbi that America was quite capable of neutralizing Israel's forces. At that point Amitt had stormed out of the meeting, shouting, "We will see who disarms whom!!!"

Amitt hurried directly to the Gobi Missile Command Center housing the SX-14s. The officer in charge was a young man who had been a captain until the revolts erupted within the Israeli army. Since that time he had demonstrated his absolute loyalty to the Knesset and had been promoted to the temporary rank of full colonel. Amitt addressed him: "Colonel Shuman, do you accept the destiny of Israel to rule the world one day and defeat the infidels who would deny our very right to exist?"

"Yes, Rabbi, I do."

"Then you must order the launch of one of our newly equipped SX-14 missiles on the infidel nation of China immediately. Can you do it?"

"Yes, Rabbi," the young soldier gasped. "But are you sure that . . ."

Amitt cut him off. "I'm sure that God has appointed me to defend our nation. Even now I believe the Americans are planning to attack Israel. We must demonstrate both our weapons and our resolve to use them."

"But we need more tests, Rabbi . . ."

"We must launch quickly!" Amitt screamed, waving his hands wildly. "If we wait, the traitors will find a way to destroy our weapons. There are traitors even within the Army, as you well know."

"Yes, Rabbi, but I don't know if we are ready . . ."

"God is on our side," Amitt shrieked, his face so red the young officer feared he might have a stroke. "He is always ready. Launch the weapon on our enemies! Do you have the men to do it?"

"Yes, Rabbi," the ashen colonel responded. "We are running the systems' tests now. We will have to connect the firing circuits to the warhead and install the destruct ordnance."

"There is no time to install the destruct system. The missile will fly true. Arm the bomb!"

"Yes, Rabbi," the young colonel said as he hurried out. He felt a cold chill as he thought about the awesome weapon they were about to unleash. Without the destruct system, it would be truly in God's hands, since they would have no means of destroying it once it left the underground silo.

Amitt ordered the entire battalion of soldiers protecting the installation to seal off the missile complex from the outside. Only a nuclear bomb could penetrate their defenses. He allowed the colonel twenty-four hours to prepare the missile. "Then," he ordered, "the countdown is to commence." *In exactly twenty-seven hours the first doomsday bomb will be flying toward the infidels,* he thought. *Then for the Americans. . . .*

Amitt's actions in sealing off the missile complex signaled the start of irreversible events to the Israeli leaders who opposed his actions.

Facimadi had returned to his Mossad headquarters when he received word of the latest activities at the Gobi complex. He placed a hurried call to General Klein at his office.

"Yes, Jerome?" Klein said after his secretary transferred the call to his home. "What is it now?"

"Amitt is going to launch a bomb!" the normally self-controlled Mossad leader shouted into the receiver.

Klein sat up in bed. He knew his friend would never violate security procedures by discussing such information by phone, unless it was a severe crisis. They had often been through life-threatening situations, and Facimadi had always responded exactly according to the book before.

"Explain!" Klein commanded, as he bolted out of bed.

"The missile facility at Gobi has been sealed off; Amitt is inside. They have gone on internal power and cut off all communications to the outside. I believe he is going to launch a missile!"

"But why? Why now?" Klein asked in disbelief, as he tried to sort through his options. Had Amitt really gone mad?

"He had a meeting with the American emissary, Hussein," Facimadi replied. "The American told him they would not allow Israel to launch an attack on the Chinese. According to my sources, Amitt went crazy; he is truly insane."

"What are the options?" Klein asked, suddenly feeling weary to the bone.

"Not many," Facimadi replied, as he reviewed the latest intelligence reports. "And none of them good. We could never storm the complex. It is well-guarded and practically impenetrable from the ground."

"What about shooting the missile down as it leaves the silo?" Klein suggested.

"My people tell me that the bombs will be armed once they are launched. It is possible that the cobalt bomb will go off if the missile is destroyed in flight."

"You mean they have not installed the fail-safes?" Klein asked incredulously.

"Apparently not. Amitt ordered the launch before the safety systems could be installed. The only fail-safe will be the barometric sensors. But destroying the missile could confuse the sensors and initiate an explosion."

"So what do you suggest, my friend?"

"We have no choice but to wait and hope that Amitt is only bluffing. If he attempts to launch a missile, I will ask the Americans to destroy the site with nuclear weapons."

"You mean bomb our own people with nuclear weapons?" Klein asked in disbelief.

"What other choices do we have? If we allow Amitt and his fanatics to continue, they will destroy the entire world. At least in the Gobi the damage will be isolated to a remote area."

"But what about the fallout? It will kill millions."

"The Americans have neutron bombs in Europe. They have never admitted it, but we know they have them. We will ask them to saturate the complex with these weapons. At the very least, they will disable the electronics for the launch systems."

"And kill all the Israelis inside the complex and those guarding the facility?"

"Unfortunately that is true. I would estimate the casualties at ten thousand," Facimadi said grimly.

"What makes you think the Americans would consent to do such a thing?" Klein asked.

"Because we have already announced to the press what Amitt has in mind. We also told them that the United States is next on his list of targets. Hussein has assured me that the U.S. will retaliate swiftly rather than be blackmailed by Amitt."

"You do realize what this will mean to Israel?" Klein asked sadly, as visions of world reaction flooded his mind. "We will cease to be a totally sovereign nation. The world will demand our adherence to international rule."

"It is still better than becoming the butchers of the world," Facimadi said as he reached to disconnect the line. *Perhaps it is time we admitted that it is we who are attempting to become the master race today,* he thought as he dialed the number he had been given to reach the American emissary.

As CIA reports of the actions at the Gobi missile complex flooded in to the secretary of defense, they were immediately forwarded to the office of President Alton, where her press secretary, Mary Foust, was putting the finishing touches on a press release outlining the threat Israel posed to America. In her impromptu press meeting, the president stressed the point that her ambassador, Amir Hussein, had done everything possible to convince the Israeli government to dismantle the so-called doomsday bombs and seek a peaceful solution to their dispute with the Chinese. But the Israeli leader, Moshi Amitt, had threatened to use the weapons on the United States if the U.S. interfered.

Later, the new secretary of defense had taken the podium to explain that the Israeli SX-14 missiles had a range of seven thousand miles and were fully capable of reaching targets in the United States.

The response was immediate and overwhelming from the American public. The latest Insta-pol showed that anti-Semitic sentiment was running at nearly 90 percent. More than 80 percent of all voters favored a pre-emptive strike against Israel before they could launch the cobalt bombs.

The face of Amir Hussein was shown on every network nearly all day long. The president made it extremely clear that she felt the country's only hope of resolving this issue lay in his hands.

As mock-up shots of what a cobalt bomb was capable of doing were shown on prime time TV, the panic that ensued rivaled that of the Cuban missile crisis during the early 1960s. Americans, used to living in a society relatively free from the threat of nuclear war since the Eastern European agreements, were frightened and angry.

Stores were stripped of all available goods within hours. Gas masks, which would be of no real use in a nuclear attack, sold for hundreds of dollars. Basements were hurriedly converted into bomb shelters. The media had a blitz on to scare the daylights out of as many people as they could with each new dramatized broadcast.

The sentiment against anyone Jewish grew to the point of frenzy. American Jews were blamed for the presumed aggression coming from Israel. Christians were carried along in the rising tide of anger since so many had previously come out in support of Israel. Flights to and from Israel were banned, and Insta-pol surveys continued to show an increasing support for pre-emptive strikes against the Jewish homeland.

At the Gobi missile site, the inexperienced crews were making little progress in preparing the first SX-14 for launch.

"I am sorry for the delays, Rabbi," the young colonel apologized. "We are having difficulties with the guidance system. It is controlled by inertial gyros, and we have been unsuccessful in reprogramming them."

"What is the problem?" Amitt bellowed at the frustrated young officer. "We are ten hours behind schedule now!"

"We need the trained system engineers to reprogram the guidance package, but they refuse to assist us," the young man responded.

"They are traitors to their country!" Amitt screamed as he threw the headset he was wearing against the wall. He was clearly becoming more and more unstable. He knew his future and, perhaps, his life were on the line. Several units of the secret police had attempted to break through the blockade of the facility, but had been beaten back. If he failed to launch the rockets on China, he would quickly lose the support of the Jewish people. Already the news media carried reports of citizens speaking out in favor of Jacob Estine, the former prime minister, who openly condemned the proposed aggression.

"We can hit a target as large as China with a minimal guidance system, can't we?" Amitt railed at the shaken colonel.

"Yes, sir," he replied with some confusion. "But we need to target a remote area to limit the civilian casualties for such a demonstration."

"I don't care what we hit! Launch the missiles immediately."

"We have only a single missile that is capable of being launched at this time, Rabbi. But if we launch without specific parameters, we will have to disable all in-flight controls and rely only on telemetry guidance. Otherwise the systems will conflict and cancel themselves out."

"I don't care what you have to do," Amitt said, forcing himself to respond in a calmer tone. "Just do it." He knew the young officer was worried. He also knew if he lost his support he would have no chance of seeing his plan succeed. *If I can launch the bomb on the infidels, they will have no choice but to withdraw,* he thought. *And Israel will be committed. The experts we need will have to help us.*

"How long until you can launch?" Amitt asked the colonel calmly.

"In thirty minutes, Rabbi," the unsure young man replied. To launch a missile with a faulty guidance system and a fully armed weapon like the cobalt bomb was against everything he had been taught in missile school. He was wavering in his convictions. *What if the missile goes off course?* he asked himself. *It could conceivably hit any target within six thousand miles—including our own country.*

Amitt softened his approach as he said to the doubtful young colonel, "Don't worry. God is with us. We will not fail. If we don't teach the infidels a lesson, Israel will exist no more."

The colonel slipped back into Amitt's camp as he heard the assurances he so desperately wanted to believe. "You're right, Rabbi," he stated resolutely. "We will succeed. We launch in thirty minutes."

With the inertial guidance system disabled, along with virtually all of the missile's fail-safe mechanisms, the countdown progressed steadily. The minimal crews raced up and down the access platforms, folding them back so that the missile would not hit them during liftoff.

From T-five minutes until launch, the missile launch system's automatic sequencer took control. Except for a major fault detection, or a manual override from the commander's console, nothing could stop the launch.

"T-four minutes and counting," the sergeant acting as the flight controller said over the P.A. system. "All personnel evacuate the launch area."

The remaining few personnel who had been securing the platforms hurried toward the control center. Once they had all left the silo, a single figure made his way to the second level, which housed the umbilical cable providing power to the explosive bolts. These bolts held the missile to its launch platform and would be blown only after the rocket motors ignited. The final test before committing the missile to its target would be a verification that the explosive bolt circuits had continuity, because if the rocket motors ignited without the hold-down bolts blowing, the missile would tear itself apart on the launcher.

Using a large pair of cable cutters, the Mossad agent cut through the umbilical cable feeding the hold-down bolts.

"T-one minute and counting," the sergeant announced. The agent ran for the silo exit door. His job was done. Now he wanted to get as far away from the launch as he could.

"T-minus thirty seconds," the sergeant announced, his voice wavering. There was a tremendous shudder throughout the control room as the forty-ton blast doors protecting the missile in silo three were blown off. To the ground troops less than one half mile away, the blast sounded like a small atomic explosion. They watched in fascination as the huge steel and concrete doors were launched skyward, only to thunder back a few hundreds yards away.

"The missile is on internal power," Colonel Shuman announced to Moshi Amitt over the intercom.

Amitt could feel his spirits rising. They would annihilate the infidels. Then they would deal with the United States. Nothing could stop them now!

As soon as the blast was heard, the army assault team leader, Colonel Hahn, knew what had happened. He immediately placed a satellite-link call to Mossad headquarters.

"My God!" Colonel Hahn shouted to Jerome Facimadi when he answered the urgent call. "They have blown the blast door on silo three; they're going to launch!"

"That fool! He's really going to do it!" Facimadi said as he reached for the red phone linking his office to that of Levi Klein, and placed a call.

Klein heard Facimadi's news with unbelief. "I never thought he would actually launch the missiles," he said as he envisioned the missile hurtling toward its target. "I'm afraid it is the end of us all."

"Perhaps not," Facimadi replied. "I met with Hussein, the American emissary, earlier today. He assures me that the United States has no desire to attack Israel, but he said the president has authorized him to use the carrier Enterprise to neutralize the launch facilities at Gobi, at our request."

"What good will that do?" Klein asked. "He will have launched the missiles by then."

"I think not, my friend," Facimadi replied. "The Mossad is not without resources. The missiles will not launch, but we must act swiftly before they can correct the damage my men have inflicted."

"But you said the doors have opened."

"Only the first silo's blast doors were blown. Apparently they are having difficulties getting the others operational. That missile will not be launched right away. But I need your help, Levi. The Americans have converted one of their cruise missiles to a low-yield nuclear weapon that can take out the Gobi complex. I need your approval to use it."

"You mean launch an atomic bomb on our own men?" Klein exclaimed. "What about using the neutron bombs?"

"Hussein assures me there is not enough time to secure a neutron bomb. It is either use a single, low-yield bomb, or risk an all-out war with our own allies," Facimadi said. "If even one of those cobalt bombs is used, we will be outcasts from the world, if there is any world left."

"What can I do?" Klein asked wearily. "After all, I am a retired politician, which is worse than no politician at all."

"Just be willing to go on television and explain to our people what we had to do. Hussein is willing to accept the blame for launching the attack."

"I will do that," Klein agreed. "I don't know how the people of Israel will accept it though."

"Only history will tell if we have been patriots or traitors," Facimadi said. "I am willing to accept their judgment but not that of a madman like Amitt."

After his conversation with Klein, Facimadi placed a call to Amir Hussein aboard the USS Enterprise. "You are authorized to launch the strike on Gobi," he said.

"It will be done immediately," Hussein replied, a smile on his face. "Be certain your military is not on alert. We would not want an attack on our carrier group."

"The military will not be alerted," Facimadi assured him. "All combat aircraft have been ordered grounded for the next hour. The furor within the military is great. We will not be able to keep the planes grounded longer than that."

"It will be long enough," Hussein said, his eyes revealing an evil glint. He ordered the still-protesting captain of the Enterprise to launch the attack. Only the direct order carried by Hussein from President Alton persuaded him to do so.

At the Gobi missile site, Colonel Shuman counted the launch down: "Five-four-three-two-one-launch!"

But instead of a deafening roar from the massive solid rocket boosters, there was nothing but silence.

"What happened?" Amitt railed at him.

"I don't know, Rabbi. Apparently the igniters didn't fire."

Suddenly he heard one of the technicians shouting in the intercom: "Colonel! The wiring to the hold-down bolts has been cut! Someone has sabotaged the launch."

"Traitors!" Amitt screamed hysterically. "Colonel, get the wiring fixed and launch the missile immediately."

"It will take at least an hour to repair and test the circuits. Then we will need thirty minutes to evacuate the repair crews."

"Have them hold the wires together if necessary, but launch that missile!" Amitt shouted. He was seething with anger. "This is the work of Satan. We cannot sit here exposed like this."

The first cruise missile launched from the Enterprise roared from the deck, dropping the rocket assist take-off canister into the ocean. As the small vehicle's own engine took over, the sleek, delta-winged aircraft weaved and bobbed its way across the ancient holy land, covering the pre-mapped route to the Gobi missile site in less than ten minutes.

Once inside the missile complex's perimeter, the infra-red target-seeking system locked onto the heat emitted by the exposed silo. Inside the warhead, the Sandia arming system enabled the high energy strobes which fire the atomic core. Fully armed, the nuclear-tipped missile pitched its nose up to a nearly vertical angle.

The last sound the launch crew heard was the rocket motor of the cruise missile as it pitched the machine high into the sky before it plummeted down into the open silo. The two-kiloton device instantly cremated the Israeli crews confined in the six silos. The open blast doors to the silo funneled the explosion throughout the entire missile complex.

What was totally unexpected, even by the leader of the Mossad, was the simultaneous launch of five additional cruise missiles, each carrying a low-yield nuclear device to a selected target. In less than two minutes, Israel's military capability was eliminated. The mobile launchers at Golan were vaporized, as well as the nuclear storage facilities in the Negev. The Israeli intercept fighter bases were also wiped out by the remaining three missiles. Israel had been betrayed by her oldest ally without a single shot being fired in retaliation.

When Levi Klein saw the explosions on the horizon, he immediately called Facimadi. There was no answer. At the air base, where the office of the Mossad had been, there was a gaping hole and a drifting dust cloud laden with nuclear radiation.

Even as he was trying to grasp what was happening as he saw the bright flashes, Jacob Estine heard his phone ring. In a daze, he answered it.

"This is Amir Hussein," the voice on the other end said. "I regret to inform you that the government of the United States has initiated a pre-emptive attack on the nation of Israel, at the request of your secret police. Any military response will be met with further actions by our country. We do not choose to destroy Israel, so please advise your leadership that any resistance is suicidal."

Estine slammed the receiver down and made numerous calls to many of his previous military commanders throughout Israel. Less than 10 percent had survived the surprise attack. Virtually all of Israel's air force had been eliminated since Facimadi had ordered them grounded. What no army had been able to accomplish in sixty years, Hussein had accomplished in two minutes.

Levi Klein carefully arranged the papers on his desk; then he opened the bottom drawer, took out his well-worn military revolver, and put it to his head. He prayed silently to the God of Abraham to forgive him, and then he pulled the trigger.

As word of the aborted launch and so-called "surgical attack" on Israel was made public in the United States, Amir Hussein became a household name almost immediately. The White House press releases stated that the strikes had been arranged with the support and consent of the Israeli government. "Unfortunately," the release said, "many Israeli officials have been assassinated by religious radicals opposed to the strikes."

It was also reported that forces from the United Nations would temporarily be stationed in Israel to oversee the restoration of civil order. The new government of Israel, headed by Mordecai Cahn, a long-time friend of Amir Hussein, immediately negotiated with the Japanese to release the oil reserves necessary for their economic stability. Hussein also secured a commitment from the Chinese not to invade

Israel, provided the conditions set down by the Japanese were met.

Amir Hussein returned to Washington amid a media blitz declaring him the greatest peacemaker since Gandhi. Whenever the issue of using nuclear weapons on Israel was discussed, the typical media comment was, "Better them than us"—an attitude to which the vast majority of Americans ascribed. The latest Insta-pol reflected a public approval of nearly 90 percent.

From a position of relative obscurity, Hussein was thrust into the public eye and suggested as a viable candidate for the position of vice president when the Congress reconvened.

Amir Hussein proved to be a media favorite for interviews. He was readily available and praised the media for alerting the American people to the danger the Israelis posed with the cobalt weapons. "I regret the loss of any life," he told the WNN interviewer. "But all the targets were military installations capable of launching counterattacks on American forces." Hussein emphasized that only clean nuclear weapons had been employed. "Thus," he said, "the residual effects of the detonations were localized."

"How long will the targeted sites be contaminated?" Allen White quizzed Hussein.

"All the sites, other than the Gobi missile installation where the cobalt bombs were housed, are inhabitable even now," Hussein lied. "However, as a precaution we are recommending that the sites be left vacant for a period of at least one year. We have very little data on the effects of low-level radiation in the ground water."

"What about the Gobi missile site?" White asked. He had already been well-coached on what his bosses would and would not allow him to pursue. The actual degree of radiation contaminating the other sites was one of the off-limits questions.

"The cobalt bombs did not actually detonate," Hussein said as video images of the missile site flashed on the viewer panel behind him. "If even one had, we might not be here today. Our scientists tell us that the madmen planning to launch these weapons were prepared to use them on the United States. We now know that three of the first six missiles were targeted at cities within the United States," Hussein lied again.

White forgot his initial question when he heard this. "You mean that the Israelis were actually planning a pre-emptive attack on the United States using cobalt bombs?"

Hussein stopped and paused, allowing the maximum effect of White's question to sink in. Then, staring directly into the camera, he replied, "As hard as it is for most of our countrymen to believe, the Jewish radicals were committed to the total destruction of this nation.

They claimed it was their divine right to rule the world, and we represented a threat to that goal. It is the duty of this country to assure that such madmen never come into power again. I have personally proposed to the World Council of the United Nations that Israel be disarmed and a permanent peace-keeping force made up of neutral countries be positioned there."

"Does that mean the Jews would lose their homeland?" White asked, somewhat in disbelief himself. "This certainly wasn't in the script," he mumbled into the mike as the sound man shifted back to Hussein.

"It depends on what you call the Jewish homeland," Hussein replied, much like a sixth-grade teacher instructing a class. "If you mean will the Jews be allowed to keep the land they stole from the Palestinians and Egyptians, as well as the other Arab nations, no, they won't. Israel will be reduced to the territory granted them by the 1916 treaty—basically that land which was theirs by treaty, not by theft."

When the interview was aired on WNN worldwide, Amir Hussein was hailed as the greatest friend of the Arab nations in history. Even the normally belligerent Iraqis invited him to visit their country. The few remaining Palestinians within Israel pledged their allegiance to Hussein, the World Council, and America—in that order. Immediately, plans were formulated at the UN to divide Israel and distribute the conquered lands to their former captives.

Each day Hussein became more and more visible on international television. Except in Israel itself, he was hailed as the most far-sighted and gifted peacemaker in modern history. Hussein was even promoted by many in the media as the next president. When it was pointed out that he was constitutionally barred from running for president because of his foreign birth, the media suggested a constitutional amendment be started when Congress re-convened.

Hussein made two proposals to the American people that secured his power base in the government. First, he proposed that the sale of narcotics be legalized and taxed by the federal government. The proceeds would be used to fund more traditional businesses to compete directly with the Asian common market. He also proposed that existing drug dealers would be given a one-month period during which they could apply for amnesty from the government. Both the media and the public loved it. The Insta-pol rating was an astounding 94 percent.

Second, he proposed a ban on all Asian products sold in America and the European Common Market. This proposal later unified the radical American labor party behind him. They could finally see a leader who had their interests at heart. The American labor party had long said that weak-kneed politicians had allowed the Japanese to kick Americans around too long. Hussein assured them that full implementation of the cash-less system called Data-Net in Europe and America would be capable of crippling any country that refused to cooperate.

His final statement endeared him to the depression-wearied public. "I absolutely refuse to run for any political office," he said with emotion. "I believe I can do more good for the country I love by serving in the background rather than seeking any official position. I neither need, nor do I seek, anything for myself." With that announcement, Amir Hussein attained more stature in the public's mind than any political office could have provided.

Television screens around the country flashed his Insta-pol rating at a never before seen 100 percent, from a viewing audience of nearly 90 percent of all registered American families.

"One thing I would ask," Hussein said as he clasped his hands together and placed them under his chin, presenting the picture of a fatherly image to his nearly two hundred million viewers, "is that we not be slack in our efforts to track down and prosecute those who would undermine our country. We stopped the fanatics in Israel but the fanatics in America are just as dangerous. They kill our leaders and defy our laws. They, as the Zealots in Israel did, demand that we obey their rules and bow to their gods. We cannot allow this. Help us to find and remove those who are a cancer on our society."

The Insta-pol response dipped temporarily as the polling viewers mulled what Hussein said. Then it returned to nearly 90 percent again. Hussein knew he had sold the public on his anti-Christian, anti-Jewish campaign. Now to execute it. . . .

ID

As the media attacks on the dissidents—now both Christians and Jews—grew daily, the Insta-pol showed President Alton's popularity soaring. She named Senator John Grant, opposition leader, as the interim vice president, in a move calculated to quiet the conservatives; Grant accepted the position in hopes that he would have some input into policy decisions. Public support for the Congress was at an all-time low of 26 percent. Their indecision and in-fighting, prior to being furloughed, had alienated the majority of the population. America had become a one-leader system and precipitously close to a non-democratic government.

With the country clearly behind the new president and adapting to the cash-less system, Hussein decided it was time to take Data-Net one step further. It was time for the numbering system to be introduced.

Allen White, of WNN, was in his office working on a story when he received a call from a long-time contact at the White House.

"I've got something for you," Rutland said with no formalities.

White had paid Rutland small amounts of money from time to time for information, and assumed that Rutland was just another minor bureaucrat trying to supplement his income with a little media money. The information was always worth a lot more than Rutland asked. In fact, White had been requisitioning three times what Rutland charged for it and pocketing the difference. The information was so valuable, his bosses never questioned him.

Rutland accepted the money to make it appear that he was taking bribes for leaks of sensitive information. In reality, it was Rutland who was in control, using White as a source to release new information to the public as needed.

Rutland continued, "The FBI has uncovered a major counterfeiting ring that is duplicating Data-Net users' cards. They have proof that the drug cartels are using the system to siphon off money into dummy accounts. There's also evidence that the banks are being systematically milked of needed funds. This thing can wreck the entire federal funds guarantee system if the leaks are not plugged."

"How serious is it?" White asked as he typed furiously. He knew better than to compromise a vital source like Rutland by taping the conversation.

"If the administration can't find a way to stop the fraud, we could lose half of the banks this year," Rutland replied as he glanced over at the president, who was seated at her desk listening on the monitor.

"Half the banks!" White exclaimed. "Why, that would sink the country for sure. Can you provide any back-up data?"

"It's on its way," Rutland said casually. "White took the bait," he whispered, with his hand cupped over the mouthpiece. Rutland set the hook deeper. "We think there is a way to protect the system."

"I'm listening," White said excitedly.

"The Data-Net operations director, Dr. Kim Loo, suggests doing away with the cards altogether and going to a system that can't be counterfeited."

"How could that be done?" White asked as he saw his next promotion looming before him. His scoop on the cobalt bomb had catapulted him into a national figure. If he beat the other networks to the punch again, he could write his own ticket.

"Dr. Loo suggests that the entire Data-Net system be converted to use a magnetic-ink-tattoo ID."

"How would that work?" White asked as he stopped writing momentarily. He had heard of a similar idea somewhere before, but he couldn't remember where.

"A magnetic-ink tattoo would be imprinted on each person's hand. A scanner would be able to pick up the number and verify it immediately, just like a card, but it could not be counterfeited. Each person would have his or her own code."

Suddenly it struck White where he had heard of this idea before. "Isn't there something like that mentioned in the Bible?" he asked. "There was a big debate about Social Security numbering people several years ago."

Rutland's eyes narrowed, but he forced himself to respond calmly. "I remember some stupid discussion by the radicals. You don't support their position, do you?"

White stiffened at the tone in Rutland's voice. It wouldn't be healthy to be labeled a Christian supporter in the current climate, he knew. "No!" he replied gruffly, "I don't! I was just asking a question.

Thanks for the information. Your money will be in the normal drop."

With that, White hung up. He immediately assigned one of his best writers to work up the story about fraud in Data-Net. By the time the story was completed, he had carefully woven in the information about a shadowy network of religious fanatics who opposed the ID systems.

Allen didn't concern himself too much about his lack of documentation on the Christian groups, since his network was owned by Thomas Galt, head of the Galt Network of twenty newspapers, WNN television, and the World Satellite broadcasting system. Galt, a seldom-seen recluse, had led the media assault against Christians for years. When the government began to leak rumors about secretive Christian groups, Galt had sent a personal memo to the managers of his enterprises to give maximum coverage to the stories. Galt had a grudge against Christians that went back more than thirty years to when he had owned a major Hollywood film studio. Christians had led boycotts of his first two films. Those boycotts had cost him nearly $100 million in lost revenues. Galt never forgot. Or forgave.

Allen White smiled as he read over the text of the Data-Net story. *Galt will love it,* he thought. *Now I need several noted financial advisors to confirm the problem and praise the ID system as a means of controlling the fraud.*

One of the experts he solicited, Dr. Rhinehart of Cal Tech, offered some great information that helped sell the package to the American public.

"Obviously drug pushers, terrorists, illegal aliens, and escaped criminals will fight the system," Rhinehart said smugly during the WNN interview.

"Once the magnetic tattoo is implemented, all the police need to do is to install scanners on the sidewalks to check IDs as people pass by. Anyone without a magnetic ID will be picked up. We'll clear up the cities in just a few weeks. I personally helped to develop the Data-Net system," Rhinehart added piously, "and I heartily approve of this new ID system."

The interview with Rhinehart faded as scenes of the riots and massive looting were flashed on the screen.

Initially the response, according to the Insta-pol, was only fifty-fifty. But as more and more experts came on board, the acceptance climbed to nearly 70 percent. WNN then led a campaign to force the Alton administration to adopt the magnetic ID system.

Within days a temporary "law" had been enacted that made the new ID system available to all Data-Net users. Since there was no other monetary system, that meant everyone. Data-Net officials began recruiting thousands of unemployed workers to man the marking stations.

In less than a week, the first "volunteer users" were showing up at ID centers around the country. Tens of thousands of people lined up to get their identification number implanted under the skin of their right hand. The attitude of most of the masses crowding the ID centers was that of resigned acceptance. It was, as the media pointed out, necessary to ferret out the criminals.

Jeff Wells had become a regular TV viewer for the first time in his life. He knew that much of what was being shown about his system was trivia, rumor, and even outright lies by the media.

"The one thing TV is really useful for is sleeping," he told Karen one morning. "All I have to do is flip it on and I'm sound asleep in ten minutes."

She laughed with him. There had been precious little for them to laugh about lately. She had talked with her father, but it was obvious from his stiff response that he knew they were being monitored. She had been unable to say much except that she loved him and would like to see him.

"Are you well?" Bill Eison asked in an uncharacteristic display of emotion over the phone.

"Yes," she responded. "Jeff and I are doing fine. He has nearly completed the project. We should be free in a few weeks. We'll try to come out and visit."

"I don't think that would be wise just now," her father responded hastily. *Was he trying to warn them, or just being an overly cautious father?* she wondered. When she hung up, she sat at her desk with tears rolling down her face.

Jeff asked, "What's wrong?"

Karen wiped her eyes and said, "It's just this crazy world we live in."

Jeff understood and just nodded in agreement. Karen didn't know that he had already found and disabled half a dozen monitors planted in the room. He wondered if the people listening to the devices thought they had a run of bad listening bugs, or guessed he was disabling them. He didn't really know or care. When the project was over, he and Karen would slip quietly out of Washington and get away—maybe to Wyoming. At least the horses and cattle would still be sane. Then he realized that every time he thought about the future, it included Karen. He wasn't sure when the realization had struck him, but suddenly he knew he was in love with her. *Does she feel the same way?* he wondered.

Karen was already back at her console loading in some data Jeff had compiled earlier. Since Data-Net had become fully operational, the demands had grown exponentially. Somehow Jeff had devised an internal system that allowed the multiple computers to re-program themselves as the needs arose.

"Very simple," Jeff had said when she asked him about the technology. "It's just a smart program."

"Right," she replied. "And a smart program is one written by a smart aleck."

Jeff laughed and retorted, "No, a smart program is one that is able to interpret new data and change its logic to match the new need."

It was simple to theorize, but no one else had ever designed a compiler capable of doing it. Literally, Jeff's program was able to program itself! If the computer capacity had been available to expand the system, the program would have been capable of active thought and independent decisions. For weeks the internal compiler had been designing much of the software necessary to make the Data-Net run more smoothly.

The new idea Jeff was working on was to provide a voice synthesizer at each terminal location. Voice synthesizers weren't new. They had been used as far back as the 1980s. Even most appliances and automobiles had them. But input and output were limited to a few simple voice commands. No computer program ever devised was capable of a full range of verbal communications—until now.

Assuming Jeff's program worked, and Karen had no doubt that it would, the system would be voice responsive in virtually every language of the world. With its library of languages and a capacity for self-programming, Data-Net would be the first genuine artificial intelligence.

Suddenly Karen noticed an anomaly on her screen. In the midst of some data she was compiling, there appeared an assortment of unrecognizable symbols. She called to Jeff, who was inputting the language files supplied by outside programming groups from several universities.

"Jeff, I've got a problem. Take a look and tell me what you think it is."

Jeff stepped over to Karen's station. "What's up?" He smiled at the cute frown on her face.

"I don't know," she replied, instructing the system to print a hard copy of the file. "Something just cropped up in the middle of the files I was compiling. Maybe it's some bad memory."

"No, it couldn't be that," Jeff said as he watched the printer spewing out several sheets of data. "The system would patch around the bad memory and send a message to maintenance to replace the defective core."

As he picked up the printed pages, he whispered to Karen, "It's a message from your father!"

"A message! How could . . ."

"Shhh," Jeff put his finger to his lips. Then he walked over to his briefcase and removed a small device with an antenna. Flipping on the switch he said, "It's okay now. I scrambled their transmitter."

Down the hall, in the monitoring room, the agent ripped off the headset, cursing, "It's doing it again," he griped to the other agent lounging in a chair nearby.

"Probably static from something in the building. Try another frequency."

"I did," the first agent said angrily. "The static seems to be on every channel."

"Must be in the building's power system then. Just file a report and let maintenance handle it. We've been at this for weeks now and they haven't done anything but work. So what's the point anyway?"

Back in Jeff's office, Karen voiced her astonishment. "What do you mean a message? How could Daddy send a message? Could it be a computer error message?"

"No, Karen. The computer would send any error messages through the system printer. It's in hexadecimal. Someone is talking through the compiler in machine language. That could only be your father. It's a code we used to use."

"Can you interpret it?" Karen was trying to comprehend what Jeff was saying. How was it possible for her father to talk to them through the computer?

Jeff was already at his terminal typing. "Normally we use the data base and it converts our instructions over to machine language—in this case, hexadecimal. So I've instructed the compiler to convert the hexadecimal to English."

Jeff called up the conversion routine, and suddenly a message appeared on the screen: "Karen, great danger for you and Jeff. Contact me at station two, Dad."

"It is from Daddy!" Karen exclaimed. "How is that possible?"

"Back when I was first designing Data-Net, your father and I discussed the feasibility of simultaneous processors and how the main controller would need to function. We would often transmit ideas via Data-Net, through the compiler itself. I thought I had closed the channel a long time ago. Apparently your father figured out a way to reopen it. Station two is another system console I enabled in his facility. He's a pretty crafty old programmer himself," Jeff said admiringly. "I don't think there is another programmer in the world who could have reopened the channel directly into Data-Net's memory banks. With access to the internal compiler, anyone could input data and defeat the monitoring systems. Having access to the compiler on Data-Net is a little like being able to withdraw money from the world's biggest bank, without any record of it."

"Can you reach Daddy now?" Karen asked breathlessly.

"I think so," Jeff said, as he typed more instructions into the system. "First I want to be sure that the data is scrambled in both directions and the calls are not recorded. As far as Data-Net is concerned, no one will ever know we communicated."

As soon as his instructions were compiled, Jeff typed in: "Hi, Dr. Eison, how are you?"

"Good, Jeff," came an almost instant reply. "Is Karen there?"

"Yes, sir," Jeff typed in the reply. "What's wrong?"

"I have information vital to you and Karen," Dr. Eison responded. What had sparked his need to contact Jeff was what he had seen and heard from several close colleagues around the country. They reported friends and associates being arrested and held without appeal. Some suggested that internment camps had been set up in various parts of the country to hold political prisoners. He had discounted the reports as just rumors until the incident with Jeff and Karen. Then he knew something was terribly wrong. He had begun a systematic check of friends he knew were Christians or Jews. He was alarmed to discover that several were missing, along with their families.

As his inquiries widened, he began to exercise extreme caution. He had seen the ruthless manner in which the secret service acted with him, and he had no doubts that they were capable of much more. What he didn't realize was that a group outside the federal agencies had carefully monitored the progress of his investigation.

The group monitoring Dr. Eison decided to take a chance that he was on the level, since he was checking on the whereabouts of some colleagues who were missing. It was clear he was not conducting a formal investigation. Bill Eison was tired and frightened about what he had discovered. He did not fear for himself; he was long past worrying about his own safety, but Karen . . . that was another matter. One evening he entered his motel room in Washington where he was attending a meeting on Star Cluster and as soon as he opened the door, he saw the outline of someone in the room shadowed against the dim light of the setting sun.

"Who's there?" Eison demanded as he reached for the light switch.

"Please don't turn on the lights, Doctor," the shadowy figure asked politely. "I would prefer that you didn't see my face just yet."

Eison complied and sat down in his big easy chair. "What do you want?" he asked. He was surprised to discover that he was unafraid. The events of the last several months seemed to have drained him of all emotions. *Or maybe I'm just too angry to care*, he thought.

"Doctor, I know you have been making inquiries about some colleagues of yours. I have information that may be helpful. Do you know a Dr. Epps?"

"Paul Epps? Sure. He's an old friend from the space program. Why?"

"I have a letter from Dr. Epps. He said you would know that he wrote it." With that he handed Eison a handwritten note.

> Dear Bill:
> Just so you'll know it is really me writing this, I wanted to remind you of our camping trip in 1960. Remember when we decided to catch the friend who had wandered into the camp—the perfumed friend?

Eison smiled at the memory. He and three other students had been camping out in Yosemite when a skunk, drawn by the smell of food, had wandered into camp. Paul Epps told the others that, being a farm boy, he knew if you caught a skunk by its tail and held it up high, it couldn't spray you. Eison, being young and gullible, grabbed the creature by its tail and hoisted it off the ground. The skunk, who was unaware of Paul's theory, promptly sprayed them all with its pungent odor—dead center. They missed several days of classes as overly sensitive professors commanded the stinking students to depart their classrooms. Even with tomato juice baths, the odor lingered for more than a week.

Eison read on. He had no doubt the letter was authentic.

> Because they are Jewish, some of my family have been detained in a camp outside of Phoenix. Bill, these are fine people whose only crime is that they are Jews.
> I fear that we're seeing a repeat of what happened in Germany during World War II. If you can help the man who brings this letter, I encourage you to do so. It is possible that I will be arrested myself.

Eison put the letter down. He was visibly shaken.

"Do you believe the letter, Doctor?" the visitor asked.

"Yes, I do. I know Paul well. It's just hard to believe this is really happening. We are not Germany. We don't detain innocent citizens."

"I'm sure many people in Germany said the same thing, Doctor. But they waited until it was too late to do anything."

"What do you want me to do?"

"I believe you know Jeff Wells?"

"Yes, I worked with him on the earthquake program. My daughter is working as his assistant now."

"I understand he is the designer of the system known as Data-Net. Is that correct?"

"Yes," Eison replied. He knew that if the man were a government agent, he had just signed a long prison sentence.

"Our sources tell us that Mr. Wells attempted to contact you when he began to have doubts about the use of his work. We also believe that he is the key to helping a lot of innocent people get their freedom back."

"What can I do?" Eison repeated as he thought about the horror of Nazi Germany being replayed in the United States. *There will be no one to come to our rescue*, he thought grimly, *not like the U.S. did in Europe*.

"We need someone whom Wells will trust to contact him. He is in grave danger and, as soon as Data-Net is fully operational, he and your daughter will be eliminated. Once that happens, the process cannot be reversed."

"Why would they do that?" Eison said, visibly shaken again. He had assumed Jeff was too valuable to risk harming him.

"He's a threat because he is the one man who can wreck their system. I assure you, Doctor, our sources confirm that Wells will be eliminated as soon as Dr. Loo can run the system."

"Dr. Loo?" Eison asked. "Do you mean Kim Loo?"

"Yes. He has been brought in to take over management of the system as soon as it is operational."

Eison knew Kim Loo well. He was a brilliant scientist but politically committed to a one-world government. He had heard Loo discuss the philosophy too many times. Even liberal Berkeley had ousted Loo because of the trouble he stirred up among the students there.

"I'll help. Tell me how."

"Can you contact Wells so that no one, and I mean no one, will know?"

Eison thought for a moment. Then he answered, "I think so. But what should I tell him?"

"The truth, Doctor. The absolute and dirty truth. His system is being used to control millions of American citizens. If the laser identification system becomes operational, your daughter and Wells will live or die at the government's whim. Right now it's the Christians and Jews. Who knows who will be the next targets?"

That had been two weeks earlier. In the intervening time, Bill Eison had worked feverishly, trying to reopen the channel he and Jeff had used when Data-Net was in the early stages of development. Finally, earlier that day, he had discovered Jeff's password to restart the secret message compiler. It was "Karen." He immediately sent the coded message Karen had seen on her terminal.

Jeff could scarcely believe what he was reading on the computer screen. Dr. Eison laid out the whole plan, as it had been explained to him. Jeff had guessed parts of the plan, but his mind would not let him believe that the United States government would be rounding up citizens for extermination.

"My God!" Karen exclaimed as she read what her father transmitted. "Is this possible, Jeff?"

"You know your father, Karen. Do you think he could be duped into believing it if it weren't true?"

As she thought about it, she knew he could not. Her father was an absolutist about scientific evidence; he would have verified every detail before telling anyone else. "No, it's true," she said as tears welled up in her eyes once more.

After a few seconds' pause, Jeff typed in: "What should I do?"

The terminal responded: "Keep options open, and get out of there. Group will contact you with best means of escape."

"What does that mean?" Karen asked as she saw the final entry.

"It means he wants me to keep the link to terminal two open so we can get into the compiler again later."

"Can you do it?" Karen asked as Jeff closed the channel to the compiler.

"I honestly don't know. I put every protection I could think of in the main program. It regularly sweeps its files, looking for unauthorized entries. I don't know if it can be defeated. It's like trying to beat yourself at chess."

"You're the only one who can defeat you at chess," Karen said admiringly as she put her arm around his waist. "I love you, Jeff Wells."

Jeff was startled and pleased at the same time. "You do? So do I."

"You can't love yourself, silly," Karen teased.

No . . . ," he stammered. "I meant, I love you, too."

"I know," Karen whispered. "I was just waiting until you were sure you knew."

THE TRAP

There is no way the message could have been faked is there?"
Karen asked Jeff after the terminal had been shut down.

"No. Only your father knew about the channel. It would be impossible for anyone else to know about it."

"But what if they forced him to reveal the codes?" she asked, not really wanting to know if they had. She shook off a mental image of her father being drugged—or worse.

"They might have," Jeff replied as he thought about it. "But what would they have to gain by warning us? Besides, what he said corroborates what we already knew to a large extent."

"What are we going to do?" Karen whispered. She was nearly paralyzed with fear. The country was in chaos, her father was a virtual prisoner in his own lab, and now they were also in danger. It looked hopeless.

"We'll get out of this," Jeff said with a lot more confidence than he actually felt right then. "But we've got to be extremely careful. If anyone suspects we know what they're doing, we'll be locked up tighter than a sealed drum.

"They still need me right now, and as long as I can stall Dr. Loo and keep the Data-Net glitching a little bit, we'll be okay. In the meantime I'm going to do a little checking inside the system."

"Can you do that without arousing suspicion?" Karen asked as she once again became the professional systems analyst. "I thought Data-Net kept a record of everything that goes on."

"True. At least to some extent. But when I designed the system I built in some internal diagnostics that are not documented and are accessible only by my personal codes. I didn't want a system that was too autonomous. If indeed there are masses of people being transported and confined, there has to be a record of it in the network," Jeff said, more to himself than Karen. He began typing in special codes to activate the internal diagnostics. "If there were meetings attended by several key players, I want to know if the new attorney general is one of them."

With that, Jeff called up the file for Fred Lively, U.S. Attorney General. The official file showed only the normal activities Lively had while the head of the NCLU but, looking into the storage files, Jeff noted several additional charges to locations that were deleted from the official file. One entry was a telephone call to his headquarters from the conference center at Jekyll Island, Georgia.

"Mission accomplished!" Wells said as he spooled further into the files. "Old Fred is one of the Society's upper crust too. Now let's see what he's been up to lately.

"Karen, look at this!" Jeff said excitedly. "There has been a whole raft of calls to various locations since Lively became attorney general. Here are the calls to Livermore when we were picked up."

The files showed calls to Sacramento, Livermore, and Los Angeles, all during the time when Jeff and Karen were en route to California.

"Hello . . . What's this?" Jeff asked out loud. "I'm going to run a trace on this L.A. number."

Within seconds, Data-Net responded with a correlation between the number in L.A. and the secret number of the CIA in Washington, D.C.

"It's a link with the CIA," Jeff said jubilantly. He was really beginning to get into the game. Spooling through the internal CIA files, he found the number listed. The caption read: "Headquarters— suspected terrorist, Juan Marques."

"Lively was in constant contact with known terrorists," Jeff said as he spooled further into the file. "And the CIA had a tap on the line all the time. Now why do you suppose they didn't tell the president? Could it be the president knew all along?

"Wow, look at this," he exclaimed as the next file came up. "It's an internal authorization to re-route nearly a hundred trains for official government use. I wonder who authorized it . . . and why?"

His fingers literally flew across the keyboard as he instructed the search routine to respond. Almost instantaneously the screen displayed the startling truth: "Authorization KAPUS."

"KAPUS? What is that?" Karen asked as she stood mesmerized in front of the display.

"KAPUS is Kathy Alton, President, United States," Jeff responded. Her code will access any appropriation within Data-Net. It's a change I saw the other day from one of Dr. Loo's new subroutines. It means she has a blank checkbook within the system." Jeff then typed in, "access authorized terminal."

The computer responded: "Sub:4."

"Sub:4," Karen whispered as she watched the screen, "but that's . . ."

"That's Cal Rutland's terminal," Jeff finished before she could. "He's been given the keys to the government. Hello . . . What's this?"

Jeff noticed an internal memo that had been re-routed and then the transfer deleted from the official file. Because Jeff had been storing all data in his diagnostic file as a cross check against the main operating system, the transfer was still noted.

"Dr. Loo is further along than I thought," he said. "He has apparently found a way to delete permanent data from Data-Net, except that he didn't know about my backup storage."

Jeff typed in a request to trace the transfer, and the computer responded: "Sub:2."

"Why, that's the president's terminal," Karen said as she glanced down at the index of assigned terminals.

"Correction," Jeff said quickly. "That *was* the previous president's terminal. President Alton had it removed from her office. She said she didn't understand computers and didn't need a terminal. Besides, look at the date."

Karen gasped. "It's the day President Hunt was assassinated. Why would Cal Rutland move a memo from his terminal to President Hunt's on that day?'

"Not just from his terminal," Jeff said scanning the data. "He also moved one from Hunt's to his file . . . I know!" he exclaimed as the revelation hit him. "He changed a file from his terminal to the president's and transferred the president's file to his. Let's see. . . ."

As Jeff accessed the file that had been shifted from Sub:2 to Sub:4, Karen almost fainted.

"Jeff, it's a speech written by President Hunt. But it's not the speech supplied by Cal Rutland to the press. Look, the president is exonerating the Christians from any complicity with the terrorists' attacks."

"Yes, and I'll just bet the speech Rutland released is stored in the president's file for anyone who would care to check."

With that, Jeff commanded a hard copy of the memo to be sent to the laser disc attached to his terminal. Moments later it was sent and recorded.

"We need to get this information out," Jeff said as he instructed Data-Net to print out a copy of all the locations to which the trains had been diverted. "I suspect these represent the camps where Americans are being held illegally. Now if we can just find a way to get this information public."

Jeff sent a command to the compiler to reopen the channel to Livermore. A few seconds later the linkup was made. Once again Jeff communicated with Dr. Eison.

"I hate doing this," he told Karen as he typed in his message. "When I designed this system we were still in the early stages of Data-Net so I didn't bother to build in any cloaking routines."

"But I thought you said no one could tell that you were communicating through the central compiler," Karen said apprehensively.

"True," Jeff said as he continued to input data to the compiler, "but any time the system is on line, it stores the available access time. What it would show, if anyone chose to check, is that central processor time was being used without being logged to any particular user. That's impossible."

"Oh, you worry too much about your machine," Karen teased. She was feeling more lighthearted than she had in several weeks because now at least they had some hard evidence; all they had to do was get it out. If Karen had known that in the central processor room Dr. Loo was busily engaged in trying to track down the mystery he had discovered, she would not have felt so lighthearted.

"Can you trace the source of the user?" Loo asked the programmer.

"No sir. It's the weirdest thing. It's like the CPU has slowed down by itself. I'd swear there was a program being compiled, except that we shut the compiler down."

"You're sure there is nothing we have on line using the machine time?" Loo asked as he was sorting through the possibilities in his mind.

"Positive, sir. We've even shut down the outside users. I'll bet the trouble line is ringing off the hook by now."

Just as I suspected, Kim Loo thought to himself. *Wells is the only person capable of bypassing the monitoring system and my traps. Somehow he has direct access to the compiler. I wonder what he's doing?* He dialed Cal Rutland's number.

"Yes," Rutland answered. "What is it?"

"Mr. Rutland, we have a problem," Loo said without emotion. "I believe Wells has a program running that can bypass the traps I have set. It is entirely possible that he is transmitting to someone outside the system."

"What?" Rutland shouted over the phone. "Doctor, you keep monitoring. I'll check out Wells."

"Very well," Loo replied as he hung up. *This Wells is the best I've ever met,* he thought admiringly. *It is too bad he can't be recruited.*

Rutland hung up the phone and made his way directly to the lab in the basement, where Wells had set up his office. As he reached the door, he carefully turned the handle. "Locked," he swore under his breath. He knew he wouldn't be able to sneak up on Wells.

Inside Jeff heard the click of the handle as it hit the lock. Immediately he punched the "clear" key on his console, and the program closed the channel and resumed normal operation.

Outside, Rutland knew he might as well play it cool. Wells was nobody's fool. He knocked on the door.

Karen opened the door and said calmly, "Oh, Mr. Rutland, it's you. Please come in."

If there was one thing Cal Rutland was good at, it was reading people. Karen's nonchalant manner told him that Loo's hunch was right. He knew Wells was far too dangerous now. He and the girl would have to be eliminated.

Within an hour, he was meeting with Amir Hussein in his office. Rutland knew it was the one place that was totally secure. "I believe Wells has become a liability we cannot afford," Rutland told Hussein as soon as their meeting began.

"How so?" the dark man questioned as he pushed some papers into his briefcase. He was preparing to go to Israel to oversee the occupation. He would have preferred to postpone the problem with Wells, but he knew that Rutland had proved his worth many times in the last three years in analyzing people and situations.

"Dr. Loo is certain that Wells is communicating with someone outside the system."

"Can he prove his accusations?" Hussein asked casually. "You know how these academic people are. They have so much professional jealousy among themselves. Perhaps he wants to get rid of Wells so he can be the guru."

"I have considered that," Rutland said as he reached for the documents Loo had given him. "Dr. Loo has conclusive evidence that someone altered the main system's program. He is certain that Wells has enabled the Christians to use the system. We won't be able to control access until the ID scanners are in place."

With that comment, Hussein's eyes narrowed. "He allowed the Christians to use the system after I ordered them eliminated?"

"Yes. Dr. Loo took a card from one of the people we picked up and ran it through the system. It was processed normally, but the transaction never appeared on any permanent files. Once the name was put into the detention file, showing the person was arrested, the system rejected his card. Apparently Wells enables the users until we arrest them, and then he disables their files. Until they are actually arrested, they have free access to the system and virtually unlimited credit."

"Kill him immediately!" Hussein ordered. His rage was becoming uncontrollable. Even the normally stoic Rutland felt a chill when the leader became this agitated. "Control of the Christians is essential to our plans," he ranted as he swept the desk clear and everything crashed to the floor.

The tiny device planted inside the stapler on Hussein's desk stopped working when it hit the floor, but the listener had heard enough. She quickly closed up the portable receiver that was concealed in the briefcase and headed for the basement.

Amelia Durant had been born thirty years earlier, Sharon Vinetta, daughter of Jewish parents, in Israel. At seventeen, she had been recruited by the Mossad, the Israeli secret police, to be trained as an undercover agent in America. Once she accepted the assignment, she was transported to the United States, placed with a family in New York whose daughter had been killed in an auto accident ten years earlier, and raised as an American citizen; all records on Amelia Durant had been altered to make her and Sharon Vinetta one and the same. The Mossad was clearly as efficient as the Society and had long known the future goals of the group.

Amelia was educated in the best schools, trained in cryptology, and positioned in Washington, where she quickly worked her way to the head of the most secret files in the nation. She was recruited into the Society and had been instrumental in securing essential records for them. At the same time, her nearly perfect recall allowed her to keep the Mossad informed of agents the Society planted in Washington and Israel. Over several years she had been instrumental in compiling a profile on the Society and its ultimate goals. Now two shadowy organizations were locked in mortal combat for control of the United States and, ultimately, the world.

Amelia reached the basement. As she approached the hallway leading to Wells' office, she took out a small cylinder and concealed it in the palm of her hand. At the door, the guard stopped her abruptly.

"What do you want here?" he demanded, his hand resting on the holstered weapon inside his coat.

"I'm looking for the records office," Amelia said meekly. "Isn't it here anymore?"

"No!" the guard answered sharply. "This area is off limits to all unauthorized personnel."

"I'm sorry," the young woman said, appearing to be very flustered. "I'm new here and I was told records was here in the basement."

Softening his previously stern look the guard said, "Someone was putting you on. The storage records were removed from this area more than two years ago."

"Well, thank you," Amelia responded in a small, quiet voice. "I'll just have to find it."

As she turned to go, she dropped the stack of files she was carrying and let out a soft moan, "Oh, no. I did it again."

"Here, I'll help you," the guard offered as he bent down to pick up some of the scattered files. As the woman brushed by him, she touched the concealed cylinder to his neck and pressed the trigger. Instantly the startled guard reached for his gun, but even as his mind told him he had been duped, his muscles refused to obey his commands. He slumped to the carpeted floor, unconscious.

The young woman deftly punched in the codes to give her access to Wells' work area. As she entered the room, she put her finger to her lips signaling Karen to keep quiet. In a quick series of hand signals she motioned for Jeff and Karen to follow her.

Jeff was naturally cautious and started to say something. Again Amelia frowned and put her finger to her lips, and at the same time shook her other hand at Wells. She drew her index finger across her throat in the international sign that meant death. She handed Karen a short, handwritten note from her father saying, "Karen, follow the person who gives you this note without question or hesitation. It means your lives are in imminent danger." Karen looked up from the note and signaled for Jeff to follow them as she moved quickly toward the door.

Jeff took another few seconds to type in some final instructions—the last commands to activate a hidden program he had been developing since they had received Dr. Eison's message. He wished he had enough time to verify it, but the frantic look on the face of the young woman told him he didn't. He issued the shutdown command to disable his terminal and then followed the two women out the door.

Once they were in the hallway the young woman said, "You must do exactly as I tell you if we are to have any chance of escaping. The security police will be coming after you any minute. If we're not out of the White House before they discover you're gone, we won't have any chance at all."

"The guard . . ." Karen was startled when she saw him slumped down on the floor. "Is he . . ."

"He's just unconscious," the woman said sharply. "Help me pull him inside the door. It may give us a few more minutes until they can get inside."

"I can help," Jeff said as he punched in the access code and then added in a series of new numbers.

Seeing the puzzled look on Karen's face, Jeff said with a sly grin, "I reprogrammed the system to allow me to change my access code. The system's a lot more versatile than anyone else realizes."

Moving rapidly toward the security elevator, the young woman said, "My name is Amelia. I'm part of the group helping to restore our government to its people. There will be a limo waiting in the garage. As soon as we call the security elevator, we will have two minutes to get away from the garage. Security will know something is wrong when the elevator is used without the proper access codes for today."

"I wish you had told me," Jeff said as they ran. "I could have programmed the system to ignore the call."

"No time." The young woman panted as they ran. "Things were moving too fast. We had hoped to make contact before the actual move, but Rutland has orders to eliminate you immediately."

"But why?" Karen gasped as they ran faster. "Jeff is still needed."

"They found out you allowed the Christians to continue using their Data-Net cards," Amelia replied as she got her second wind.

Karen glanced over at Jeff, who was also winded. "Too much sitting at a computer day after day," he said as he sucked in the oxygen his lungs craved. "I promise to exercise more, if I get a chance." Then with a wry grin, he added in response to Amelia's comment, "Well, I couldn't just let twenty million people go hungry, could I?"

They reached the elevator and Amelia punched in the only access codes she knew—Vice President Grant's emergency code. The monitor responded: "Confirmed: Access Vice President."

"The vice president?" Jeff commented as he arched his eyebrows in surprise, as well as admiration.

"Yes. He's one of us; he wants the government back in the voters' hands. He could have been a great help to us, but I'm afraid when they discover he has helped us, he'll be compromised."

"Not if you can get me to a computer with a two mega-hertz modem," Jeff said confidently.

"You can change the internal codes?" Amelia asked in amazement.

"There is really nothing you can't do with a computer system like Data-Net. Maybe too much, in fact," he added. "Dr. Eison was right; it's too much power to trust to anyone, especially politicians."

"This is more than politics," Amelia added as the elevator doors opened. "This is evil against good."

Jeff half expected the elevator to be full of secret service men. His mind conjured up images of the men who had brought him back from

California. They would not hesitate to kill, if so ordered. That much he knew. But the elevator was empty. As they stepped inside, Amelia punched the button labeled "Official Parking."

In the security control room, the signal to call the elevator had triggered an immediate reaction. The guard assigned to White House security systems said, "Somebody called the security elevator. Are any of the 'big shots' signed out to leave the building?"

The other guard glanced at the computer terminal and replied, "Not on my log."

"Well, someone called the elevator. Better check it out."

"May be a scheduled maintenance check," the other man suggested. "I'll call and verify."

It took a few seconds to reach the day shift supervisor. When he came on the line, he confirmed with several select words that his crew didn't schedule maintenance in the White House without checking with security first. As he was slamming the receiver down, the guard heard him mutter, "Stupid!"

The security guard put several processes in motion at once. He punched the silent alarm button, signaling all the other guards that a breach of White House security was in progress. Then he turned to his companion and said, "I'm headed to the garage. It wasn't maintenance." After turning the console over to his partner, he hurried out the door. He knew that it would take at least five minutes for any of the other guards to reach the garage deck; he could be there in less than two.

The ride up to the VIP garage level seemed like an eternity to Jeff. He could envision the events taking place as soon as the elevator was called. With all the recent trouble, he had no doubt the guards would shoot first and then try to sort it all out later. *I could have disabled the alarm system if I had just known,* he thought to himself. He knew their lives would be determined by a minute either way now.

The elevator stopped at the garage level, and the doors retracted into the walls. As they stepped out, Jeff breathed a sigh of relief. "No guards," he announced.

"There will be soon," Amelia warned. "Follow me, quickly! We don't have any time to lose."

Jeff and Karen followed as she dashed toward one of the limos. She had a set of keys ready and stopped in front of one of the limousines—a Lincoln. Jeff heard the click as the electronic locks responded to the magnetic key.

"Get in!" Amelia commanded as she slid into the driver's seat. Jeff and Karen scrambled into the back seat. Amelia had already donned a chauffeur's cap and was starting the limo.

The guard was still making his way down to the first level. He cursed himself for being so stupid. He had tried to use the security elevator because it would be faster than going around to the stairs. But Amelia had flipped the "hold" switch as she exited the elevator. That small detail had saved their lives.

When the guard hit the crash bar on the door to the garage, the black car was already turning the corner. He was puffing as he raced into the garage. He heard the squeal of tires but saw nothing of the car or its occupants. He stopped a moment to catch his breath; then he called the security desk to report.

When the alarm sounded, Cal Rutland saw it on his own security console. It was a precaution he had personally ordered after Hunt's death. It gave him total visibility of all the monitors and security alarms in the White House. Within seconds of the alarm, he was headed toward Wells' office. A quick call to security on his pocket phone confirmed that the security elevator had been called from that level. He instructed the security monitor to have the nearest guard meet him at the Data-Net room. They arrived at virtually the same time. The guard paused to punch in his access code.

"I can't get the door lock to respond," the frustrated guard said to Rutland.

"Try the main security override, you fool!" Rutland shouted at the nervous guard.

"I did, sir," he stammered. "It won't work."

"It has to!" Rutland barked as he shoved the man aside. "It will open any door in this building."

"Not anymore," the slightly built Oriental man said as he casually walked up. Dr. Kim Loo couldn't help but silently admire Jeff Wells. *Who would have thought that Wells was capable of using the resources of Data-Net to reprogram the White House security locks?*

"What do you mean?" Rutland snarled at Loo.

"Dismiss your guard, please," he said to Rutland politely.

"Go!" Rutland commanded the guard, who was more than happy to comply. He feared Rutland. Most of the people who worked in the White House did.

"Apparently we have underestimated young Mr. Wells again," Loo said calmly. "He has linked his network with the internal security system and reprogrammed your master security key."

"Can you restore it?" Rutland was barely able to control his fury.

"Yes, but it will take at least one hour. You can be sure that Wells is no longer inside. It is imperative that he be caught!" Loo was now giving commands. "There is no limit to what he is capable of doing."

Through clenched teeth, Rutland said, "We will stop him, Doctor. You can be assured of that. We have resources he knows nothing about." Then he turned and hurried back to his office. He knew he had to handle this matter quickly and effectively. He would not fail the Society he had pledged his life to promote. He placed a phone call.

"Lively? Rutland. We have reason to believe that Wells and the girl have escaped. They had help from someone inside. They're in one of the limousines. Can you track it?"

"We can," Lively said assuringly. "I've had every government vehicle fitted with a locator. We'll pick it up as soon as they cross one of the ID scanners. Do you want us to stop them?"

"No!" Rutland said coldly. "Just track them to their destination. I want to find out who is involved. Then we'll eliminate the traitors."

"I'll let you know as soon as we have a track on them," Lively said, softly humming to himself. "Things are going great," he mused. "We're rounding up the Christians and the Jews, too. This country will be a fit place to live, as soon as we get rid of the do-gooders and the money-grubbers."

Lively called his secret service command center. "Let me talk with Marla," he snapped at the receptionist.

Marla West was Lively's head of security. She had been with the NCLU since the early eighties when President Reagan's pro-family, pro-life rhetoric had caused them a lot of grief. They had waited him out, as they had all the other right-wingers. The one thing Lively despised most about those who called themselves Christians was their lack of commitment to their cause. They always crumbled when troubles came.

Marla West was absolute in her commitment to the anti-Christian crusade. She had been convicted of torching several churches that had caused the NCLU so much grief in the nineties. She had served her time, and she came out more committed than when she went in. Persecuting Christians was pure pleasure to her.

"Yes, Fred," the stone-faced woman said into the phone as gently as she could. Marla West was fifty and looked ten years older. She had always been overweight, and had developed gray hair and wrinkles at thirty. She pretended that she didn't care that other people thought her ugly. In reality, she did care—a lot.

When she was a teenager, she had attended a church camp for a week. The other girls had called her "Fatty," and "Grandma," because of her older-looking face. She had lain in wait for two of them one night as they returned from a cookout. All she had was a broken broom handle but she had used it viciously. She split the scalp of one girl; the blood made it look like a massacre. She had pelted the other girl with the handle until she had black welts all over her face and arms.

Since it had been dark, neither of the girls really saw their attacker and Marla might have gotten away without discovery, except that she had to let them know it was her. The next day she visited the two girls in the local county hospital and told them both, "Now who looks like an old woman?" That very day she was shipped home and barred from ever attending the camp again. From then on she had developed a consuming hatred for those who called themselves Christians.

"Marla, we have an emergency," Lively said calmly. "Two people working on Data-Net have decided to defect. They are in one of the government limos right now. We need to locate them before they change vehicles."

"Who are they?" she asked.

"Jeff Wells and his assistant, Karen Eison," Lively said matter-of-factly.

"Whew," West said. "That's pretty heavy. I thought Wells was the brains behind the network."

"Just catch them," Lively told her. "Rutland wants them eliminated after we find out who's involved. We can't have any screw-ups on this."

"I don't make mistakes," West countered. "I already have a trace on them, just like we do every government vehicle. They're headed down MLK right now. I'd say it's a good bet they're headed for the old airport."

Lively signaled his chief of security. He wrote "MLK Airport" on a note and handed it to him. Instantly a call went out to any units in the vicinity, and in less than five minutes contact was made.

"Sir, one of our units is in sight of the limo," the security chief said.

"Keep them well back," Lively instructed. "I don't want to lose them, but we don't want them to know they've been tagged yet either."

"What are we going to do?" Jeff asked Amelia as she drove through the crowded streets.

"We've got it all set up," she replied as she noticed the nondescript vehicle several blocks back. *I wonder why cops don't buy a few Corvettes or Astons?* she mused to herself. *Their cars are so plain they stand out.* She said nothing to Jeff or Karen. *It will be easier to do my job without them worrying,* she decided.

"We'll ditch the limo in a minute," she said. "Get ready to exit when I tell you."

She pulled onto a small side street that circled back onto MLK

Boulevard. She was sure the tailing car wouldn't risk following, but the monitor she knew they had planted would keep them on track. Just as expected, the car drove slowly past the side street and continued down MLK.

"We'll pick them up when they re-enter the main street," the driver said to his control center. "There is not enough room for us on the side street without them seeing . . ."

"Watch for a switch," Lively said, interrupting the dispatcher.

"We saw a brown Caprice parked in the alley," the other agent said to Lively. "We'll check every car that exits."

Amelia told Jeff, "Get ready. When I slow to almost a stop, you and Karen jump out and head toward the garbage truck. Get in the back."

"A garbage truck!" Karen exclaimed, wrinkling her nose. "Yuk."

"It's a lot better than a bullet in the head," Amelia said in response. "Garbage smells will wash off. Get ready. . . ."

Jeff reached forward and opened the door. As Amelia slowed the car almost to a walk, he grabbed Karen and stepped out running. Karen stumbled, but Jeff caught her and kept her upright. They bolted toward the garbage truck as the tail section was opening. Jeff pulled Karen into the trash with him as the tail was closing again.

Even though they could not hear her, Amelia said, "Good luck . . . and Godspeed." Then she pulled the limo up behind the waiting Caprice and ran to the opened driver's door. As she got in, two people, a young man and a woman, sat up in the back seat, and she drove off.

When they exited the alley, the dark car pulled out several blocks behind them. She smiled.

"We have them," the driver said to his companion who immediately called headquarters. "We're following a 1993 Caprice. Wells and the girl are in the back seat. They're headed toward the airport."

"It's too easy," Lively shouted into the microphone. "There's been another switch. I want a second car to wait where they are. See who comes out of that alley."

"This is Car Two. We copy," said the agent known as Kruger.

A few minutes later the garbage truck exited the alley.

"We have a city disposal truck coming out of the alley," Kruger reported.

"Follow it!" Lively commanded. "And stay well back. I don't want them to know we're on to them. I'll have extra units all along the way to change off."

Lively was excited. He knew they had spoiled the plan to free Wells. Now he would show them who was smarter.

The garbage truck continued along its normal route, collecting garbage as it went. Karen thought she was going to be sick, the smell was so bad.

"Hang in there, Karen," Jeff said as he squeezed her hand. But he was unsure of his own stomach if they stayed in the truck very long. "Try thinking about something else."

"I have," Karen replied as she held a tissue to her nose. "But all that comes to mind is garbage . . . and rats. . . ."

The garbage truck continued on its assigned route for the better part of an hour, picking up trash on the way. Jeff was afraid for awhile that they might be suffocated as the trash piled up around them. Then suddenly the truck turned off the assigned route and headed toward the Maryland suburbs at maximum speed, which was about forty miles an hour.

In the trailing car, Kruger reported the change. "Control, the truck has turned onto Arlington Boulevard. I think it's heading to a rendezvous point between here and Fairfax."

"What's out there?" Lively asked Marla West on the phone.

"I'll check," she replied as she punched up the possible locations on the computer screen. "There's a small airport about twenty miles from where the truck is now. They could have a small jet there."

"Get a LAARS team on the way," he commanded.

"Are you going to shoot them down over a populated area?" she asked incredulously. "There are a lot of people living around that airport."

"Just get the LAARS team under way," Lively snapped again. "Wells is a lot more important than a few civilians on the ground."

"Okay," she said as she placed the call to her special forces group at Andrews. "They'll have to go by helicopter if they're going to beat them though."

"Have them stay out of sight until we know what they're going to do with Wells," Lively commanded. "But stay ready."

Thirty minutes later when the garbage truck pulled onto the runway at Merrifield, the helicopter was already in place behind a hill three miles away. The side door to the ancient Huey was open and the agent had a LAARS ground-to-air rocket launcher armed and ready.

When the truck stopped, the driver yelled, "When I lower the tail, you get out and run. Follow the agent, she'll lead you."

Wells heard another clank in the truck, which he assumed was the driver slamming his door. Then he heard the tail hydraulics as the lift went down. A young woman was waiting outside for them. He noticed her nose wrinkle up as they exited the trash pile. They followed without a word as she led the way.

Two minutes later a small business jet was taxiing down the runway. It paused for a moment to allow the engines to spool up to 80 percent power for takeoff. Then the pilot released the brakes and the plane roared down the short runway. Since the plane was powered for a full load of twelve passengers and carried only three, it virtually leaped off the runway, climbing rapidly into the cloudless sky.

The helicopter rose above the hill and positioned itself directly below the flight path of the plane that was, by that time, a thousand feet higher. The agent with the rocket launcher aimed at the hot exhaust of the business jet. A small puff of smoke and fire like a large Roman candle were all the signs to mark the launch of the converted heat-seeking missile. It streaked up toward the accelerating jet. Even at its maximum speed of 430 miles an hour, the jet would have been no match for the Mach-three missile. It took the rocket only seconds to catch it.

Those on the ground saw the fireball as the plane disintegrated when the rocket hit the engine turbines and exploded with the force of a 200-pound bomb. The fragile machine was blown into a thousand tiny bits. Fire from the onboard fuel rained down over Interstate Highway 66, destroying cars unfortunate enough to be directly in the flight path.

"It's done," the pilot of the Huey reported to control.

"Any survivors?" Lively asked calmly.

"Not a chance," the pilot reported. "It came down in a million pieces. They never knew what hit them."

That's too bad, Lively thought to himself. *It takes half the fun out of killing them.*

"There are several fires on the freeway and in a couple of subdivisions," the pilot reported. "Shall I notify the fire department?"

"No!" Lively said coldly. "They'll know soon enough. It's their tough luck they were in the wrong place."

From the other surveillance vehicle, the driver called in. "This is Surveillance One," he said. "We're still in sight of the Caprice. What do you want us to do?"

"Take them out," Lively said casually.

The dark green government car accelerated until it pulled parallel to the old Caprice driven by Amelia Durant. The agent on the passenger's side rolled down his window, preparing to rake the vehicle with his uzi. Instead, he found himself staring into the muzzles of two assault rifles held by the two Mossad agents in the back seat of the Caprice. The last thing either man in the surveillance vehicle ever heard was the startled government agent shouting, "What the . . . ?"

Lively knew nothing about what was happening to his surveillance team. He assumed they were eliminating the traitors. He turned and walked out of the control room and back to his own office. When he sat down he poured himself a drink and called Rutland. "It's Lively," he said sharply to the secretary who answered. "Let me speak to Rutland."

Rutland picked up the receiver when the chime sounded, signaling a waiting call. "Yes?"

"It's Mr. Lively," the nervous secretary reported.

"Go ahead," he responded as she patched the call through.

"It's done, sir," Lively reported with a smirk on his face.

"You're sure?" Rutland snapped. "I don't want any mistakes."

"I'm sure," Lively said cordially, in spite of the resentment he was harboring inside. He didn't really like Rutland much. One day he would need to teach the arrogant political lackey a lesson, he decided.

Rutland hung up the phone and jotted a note to be forwarded to Hussein in Israel. *He will be pleased*, Rutland thought as he relaxed a little. Wells was no longer a liability.

THE UNDERGROUND

Randy, you just can't go out again," Harriet pleaded. "Why don't we stay here? We're doing fine."

"We're not doing fine, Harriet," he responded compassionately. "We're hiding out in the woods while a lot of our friends are probably in need of help."

"But you saw the television," she protested, her eyes beginning to tear. "All of our group have been labeled terrorists. You'll be arrested."

"Harriet, I know this has all been hard on you, but you've got to get hold of yourself. God does not want us to hide out when we could be helping others. This place can house ten or twelve more people if we sacrifice a little."

"Twelve more people!" Harriet couldn't believe her ears. "Randy, you brought in five people the last time you went out."

"And I'll try to bring five more every day, if I can. Someone or something has made it possible for my card to still work in the system. You know that most of the Christians have had their accounts frozen. Now they're talking about applying a laser ID number to everyone. When that happens, none of us will be able to buy anything. I've heard rumors about an underground network. Apparently a lot of others feel the government is wrong, too. I want to make contact with the underground if possible."

Unknown to Randy, Jeff Wells was his benefactor. When Dr. Rhinehart had first attempted to freeze the Christians' accounts, Jeff had instructed the Data-Net system not only to unfreeze the accounts but to give them unlimited credit within the system. Until the laser ID was implemented, they would still be able to buy and sell.

"I know you're right, Randy, and I do want to help. But it's all so frightening. I wasn't ready for what has been happening."

"No one could have been ready for what we're going through,

honey. But if we think only of ourselves, then the ones behind all this have won. As long as we're willing to sacrifice ourselves for the sake of others, God will intercede; I just know it."

Harriet had told herself the same thing a hundred times since their nightmare had begun. She mentally recited what she knew was God's direction, "Why do you worry so for tomorrow . . . ?" But somehow it didn't seem to help. She knew her anxieties were not for Randy's safety, or even her own. They were for Matthew. She couldn't seem to let go and trust God—at least not the way Randy seemed to be able to do. Inside, Harriet knew the truth.

She had always gone to church and Sunday school, even as a little girl. When she was thirteen, she had even dedicated her life to Christ. But mostly, she knew she had reacted to the other kids who were dedicating their lives. She hadn't really surrendered to Christ. She had surrendered to peer pressure. In some circles, peer pressure meant drugs or sex. In hers, it meant becoming a Christian. It was what her parents had wanted most of all. They needed a showpiece to display in church: their lovely Christian daughter. *It had all been so easy*, she thought, *first Christian school, then Christian college.* All the while, she felt resentment and rebellion but never showed it.

Her single act of rebellion had been Randy. When she met him, he was a senior at Clemson and most definitely not a Christian. Her father had demanded that she not date Randy, so they dated secretly. After he graduated from college and was accepted at a law school in Alabama, they eloped. For a while, she had been afraid that her father might die from a heart attack. But after a year or so, her parents accepted the situation, with reservations.

Then, in his second year of law school, some of the campus groups invited a Christian speaker and Rhodes scholar to speak one evening. She had attended out of curiosity and Randy had gone with her. That evening, Randy heard a message that changed his life. When the invitation was given, Harriet was shocked to see her husband go forward.

From that point on, Randy never looked back. He devoured Christian books and never missed an evening of studying his Bible. Within a year, it was Randy who was pulling a reluctant Harriet to seminars and rallies. She went with him, but somehow she knew he had something she did not.

All these years, she thought, *all these years I knew something was wrong inside. I was just mouthing the words and playing the role.* Then she realized, *I might have gone on that way for the rest of my life.*

Suddenly Harriet blurted out, "Randy, I have to tell you something. I'm not sure I'm a Christian."

"I know, honey," Randy said with no condemnation in his voice.

"You know!" she said in astonishment. "You mean you knew I wasn't really a Christian and you didn't say anything all these years?"

"Would you have listened if I had?"

Harriet thought about it for a minute, and then answered, "No, I guess I wouldn't have, not until this happened. I played the role so well even I had come to believe it.

"I know now that I need Christ," Harriet said as her eyes filled with tears again. "It's not what we're going through that terrifies me. It's the fear itself."

"Harriet, you need to know that I'm just as afraid as you are most of the time. It's just that I know God is still in control, and even if we all die, I'll still believe that."

"I know that too, Randy. I saw the peace Mom had when Dad had cancer. I see that same peace inside you. That's what I want."

"I do have a peace that I didn't know was possible. I guess that's the one thing that has sustained me through all of this. When I'm the most frightened—like when those kids tried to attack the van—God seems to take over my will and strengthen me."

"That's what I want with all my heart," Harriet exclaimed.

Randy led his wife through the plan of salvation that she had heard so many times before. But this time it was for her. She committed her life, her family, and their future to Jesus Christ.

"Remember, Harriet," Randy said as they hugged each other. "Fear is a normal, human emotion; panic is not. Knowing God is absolutely in control is what conquers the fear and eliminates the panic."

"I know what you're saying, Randy," Harriet said as she dried her eyes on the kitchen towel. "But I feel so much better now. I know God can give me what I have lacked all these years—peace."

Randy kissed his wife like it was the first time. He felt closer to her than he ever had. But there were still people out there who needed their help. "I've got to go, Harriet," he said. He was concerned about leaving her.

"I understand, Randy," she said. "I want you to go. I'll pray God will lead you to someone who needs our help."

Randy left the cabin feeling like he had just received the Nobel Peace Prize—only from the Lord.

Driving into the small community of Winder, Randy saw a long line of people waiting at the entrance to the courthouse. "I wonder what's going on," he said aloud. As he passed the local post office, he saw a notice posted in the window that Data-Net IDs would be issued every Monday from 8:00 A.M. until 5:00 P.M. Since it was Monday, that explained the line. He decided to take a chance and find out what he could. He parked the old pickup truck a block away and walked back to where the line stopped.

"What's up?" he asked an older man standing at the end of the line.

"This is worse than getting car tags," the frowning man responded. "You'd think they would have a better system."

"What's the line for?" he asked as he took his place in line.

"What do you think it's for?" the older man gruffed. "It's that new ID. I wasn't gonna do it, but then I got a notice from Social Security that I wouldn't get my allotment anymore if I didn't have the right ID."

Randy could feel his heart thumping. *So it's finally come,* he thought. *The tattoo under the skin. It's the next step toward the MARK!*

"I thought the president said the ID would be strictly voluntary," Randy said more to himself than to the old man.

"That may be the official position on the news, but just try to buy somethin' now and you'll see. The only scanner that works is the one that reads the ID on your hand. It's voluntary all right, if you don't want to eat."

If it's come to Winder, it's probably everywhere in the country, Randy concluded. *With the focus on the Middle East crisis, who's going to object?* He knew he could no longer use Data-Net, since he wasn't about to get tattooed. Then it struck him like a hammer. *They'll start screening for people without the tattoo as soon as the system is totally in place! It won't be safe to walk the streets anymore.*

"How many people are left to be ID'd?" he asked.

"Well, I'm a 'W'," the old man said, stopping to stare at Randy. "Henry Wallace. I guess I'm nearly the last. Say, what's your name? Didn't you get a notice to report for your ID?"

Randy panicked a little. Two other people had turned to stare at him too. "I've been out fishing for the last few days," he said. It wasn't a lie. He had been fishing with some of the others living in the cabin.

"Well, you should have a notice at home," the old man said gruffly. "Don't bother to use your card unless your name starts with a 'Z.' I tried mine this morning and it don't work. I just hope they can get me in before closin' time. I can't wait a whole week. They only come here on Mondays."

"Yes, I saw that at the post office," Randy said. "That's why I came."

"Well, I don't care what letter you are. I was here first," the man said threateningly.

"It's okay," Randy said politely. "I can make it another week. I'll come back next Monday. With the length of this line, I don't think I could get in before five."

"Yeah, and these birds won't stay another minute either," the old man groused again. "Government!"

Randy walked slowly away from the line and toward his truck. He was suddenly aware of being followed. In spite of himself, he picked up his pace. Behind him, the footsteps also quickened.

"That was really stupid of me," Randy chided himself. "I should have known they would have someone watching to see who didn't get an ID."

He felt the panic rise inside and fought back the temptation to run for the truck. He knew it wouldn't do any good. Whoever it was could catch him before he could get out of town. And with the truck's tag number, it would be only a matter of time until they traced him back to the cabin.

Stupid! he told himself. *You were stupid not to even change the tags. Now Harriet and the others will be caught too.*

He was almost to the old truck. Instead of stopping, he walked on past. *Maybe they won't know I came in the truck*, he thought. *At least it will give Harriet and the others a little more time. If I'm late enough, maybe they'll run . . . but where can they run?* he thought dejectedly.

He glanced around. The man he had seen out of the corner of his eye earlier was nowhere in sight. He relaxed a little.

Maybe it was just my imagination, he told himself. *Probably just somebody heading home.*

Suddenly a figure stepped out from behind one of the buildings lining the old street.

"I think you passed your truck," he said almost nonchalantly.

A surge of adrenalin pulsed through Randy. He fought back the urge to run and replied, "I don't know what you're talking about. What truck?" For the first time since the madness began he wished he was armed. He didn't mind that he was caught, but he had jeopardized seven other people now.

"Mr. Cross, we've been looking for you," the man said. He was only of average build but Randy could see that he was heavily muscled, and the way he carried himself showed he had no fear that Randy would be a problem.

"What do you want?" Randy asked, resigned to his capture. *What would they do with him and the others?* he wondered. Even as he thought about what capture might mean, he felt relief flood over him. *At least Harriet knows the Lord*, he thought, smiling. *God will sustain her just like He has me.*

"Mr. Cross . . . Randy, I represent a group committed to helping Christians . . ."

"What?" Randy blurted out. "You're not part of the government, then?"

"Yes and no," the man said. "But let's go to your truck. I don't want to attract too much attention."

As they walked toward the old Ford, Randy asked, "Who are you? And how did you know who I am?"

"In time," the man said quietly as they got into the truck.

Randy turned the key and the faithful old machine roared to life with the first turn. "Where to?" he asked.

"Head out Highway 20," his passenger said.

As Randy drove slowly along the streets heading out of town, a thousand thoughts crowded his mind, but he sensed his passenger would tell him what he needed to know in time. Once they reached the outskirts, the man began to tell a story that seemed so incredible Randy probably wouldn't have believed it, except for his own experiences since the riots.

"My name is not important at this point," Agent Shepperd said as they drove. "I am, or at least was, an FBI agent on special assignment with a branch of the secret service. Something happened to me several weeks ago that changed my life."

Shepperd began to relate the story of Bob and Ellen Cofer, including their arrest and internment in the detention center. "As far as I know, they were shipped out to a more permanent facility somewhere in the West," he said.

"I can't believe it," Randy said, shaking his head. "Or more accurately, I guess I can believe it, but I'd rather not. I heard rumors about concentration camps for Christians, but it's still hard to believe."

"I know how you feel," Shepperd agreed. "I was called back to Washington after that episode. My common sense told me I wouldn't be able to make any difference if the powers to be knew how I felt. So I decided to make up a story about disliking Agent Tooms, which was not entirely untrue. I pledged my full cooperation with the roundup of the terrorists—apparently people like you. Tooms is a pig, and because of his bad record, he was sent as a guard to one of the camps in the West.

"I spent several weeks in Washington researching this so-called terrorist group. What I discovered frightened me enough to make me realize I had to do something to help—not the government, but your group. I convinced the attorney general's office that I could locate the terrorists' strongholds, so I was reassigned to Atlanta. Apparently there's been a strong resistance movement here because of Elder's capture and, try as they might, the secret service has been unable to locate the underground's base camp."

"Then how did you find me?" Randy asked.

"I made contact with the underground here a few weeks back. Actually I arrested Rod Wilton, one of the leaders."

"I know Rod," Randy said angrily. "He worked at the Johnson Space Center before transferring to Scientific Atlanta; he has a Ph.D. in mathematics. He's no more a terrorist than I am. Those idiots in Washington are purging some of the best brains in our country, just like the Nazis did in Germany."

"Hold on," Shepperd replied, raising his arms in a mock sign of protection. "I'm on your side. I didn't turn Wilton over. Instead I helped him to reach a safe house just outside the city. It took some doing, though. The CRC group was convinced that I was a plant from the government for a long time."

"I can believe that," Randy said coolly. "I'm still not sure you aren't."

"Listen, if I wanted to get the rest of the group you have hidden, all I would need to do is trace the tags on this truck. I'll bet you didn't even bother to steal a new set of tags, did you?"

Randy turned a shade of pink. "No. It belonged to my dad. It's been parked out on his old farm for years."

"You people don't know a lot for a bunch of wild-eyed terrorists, do you?" Shepperd said with a smile.

"No, I guess not," Randy agreed. "We've always operated within the law, not against it."

"That's how I knew the whole thing was a plot to get rid of some pretty ordinary citizens," Shepperd said. "No organized group would do the stupid things you people are accused of."

"But who is behind this?" Randy asked as Shepperd signaled him to slow down for a turn onto a small farm road.

"Apparently it comes from the highest levels of our government. Your people made some bitter enemies. Someone inside the government has given them a free hand to get rid of you. Take the next left. . . ."

Randy turned down an old farm road that looked as if it hadn't been used for years. Ahead of them the brush had grown over nearly half the roadway. He slowed down to stop and noticed that a tree had fallen, almost blocking the road.

"Keep going," Shepperd ordered.

"But I can't get around that tree," Randy said as he shifted into second gear.

Even as he spoke, the tree was pulled back out of the road. He drove past and it moved across the road again. On the other side he saw several men and women pushing the tree back into its original position. Others were brushing away the tire tracks they had just left. Within seconds, only a trained tracker could tell that a vehicle had passed on the road.

"Who are they?" Randy asked as he accelerated slightly.

"They're some of your friends," Shepperd replied with a grin. "They learn pretty quick."

They had driven about another quarter of a mile when Shepperd signaled Randy to pull into a driveway leading to a huge old farmhouse with two large barns out back. As far as Randy could tell, the place was totally deserted. There was not a telltale sign of a car track leading in or out of the drive. He was about to stop when one of the barn doors opened and a man signaled him to drive the truck inside. Once inside, the doors closed again. Through the rearview mirror Randy could see two children brushing away their tire tracks.

Shepperd reached out the window and pulled the door handle. Once out of the truck, he signaled Randy to follow him. But as they walked through the barn Randy almost stumbled as he stared at the enormous supply of food and other kinds of supplies filling the barn.

"The other barn is even better equipped," Shepperd said. "We have a benefactor in high places."

Puzzled, Randy followed the agent out of the barn and into the house.

Randy was fascinated. From the outside there appeared to be no sign of life, but inside, the old house was a hubbub of activity. As they passed the kitchen, he caught a glimpse of several people preparing food in several large commercial microwave ovens.

"No smoke," Shepperd said, without being asked.

Randy just grunted in response. They proceeded to what had obviously once been the living room for a large family.

Randy recognized several men and women he had met at rallies before the riots, including his old friend, Rod Wilton.

"Rod, it's good to see you," Randy said enthusiastically. "How is Cory?"

"She's in one of the camps somewhere," Wilton responded sadly. "I haven't seen her since before the riots. I would have been with her, but we were in the middle of a launch at the Cape with the Japanese."

Randy felt compassion as he saw the hurt on his friend's face. "I'm sorry, Rod. I didn't know."

"Yeah, I know," Wilton said as he hugged his long-time friend. "How's Harriet? And Matthew?"

"Harriet! Oh, I need to contact her. She'll be worried sick by now. They're both fine," he added.

Turning to Shepperd he said, "Is there any way I can contact Harriet?"

"You won't need to," Shepperd replied as he handed Randy a cup of coffee. "Somebody's on the way to the cabin right now. Your family will be brought here in the next day or two. The others at your cabin will be dispersed to other sites."

"Other sites?" Randy questioned. "You mean there are more like this?"

"Bigger and better in some cases," Rod Wilton offered. "There are a lot of Americans who don't agree with our government."

"But a lot more who do!" Shepperd interjected angrily. "And don't forget that!"

SURPRISE MEETING

At the Livermore laboratory in California, Bill Eison was troubled. He had been trying to reach Jeff and Karen since that first day when he had been able to break into the main compiler. He knew that Dr. Loo probably suspected something by now, but without the keys to crack the compiler's code, he would have no way to prove his suspicions.

Dr. Eison desperately wanted to tell Jeff that he had made contact with a group of people who were trying to help the Christians and Jews evade the government trackdown. Actually, the contact had come as a result of the arrest of an old friend, Dr. Ben Moore. Eison had to call in every favor due him from anyone in Washington to get Moore released. Finally, he had convinced the FBI that Moore was essential to the completion of a top-secret project being developed jointly by Livermore and Cal Tech: the highly touted antimissile system called "Star Cluster." Sooner or later he knew someone would discover that Moore's name had been added later to the list of contract personnel, but with the threat in the Middle East and the terrorists in the West, it would take a while.

About a month after he had secured Dr. Moore's release, Bill Eison had been sent to Washington for a briefing on the Star Cluster program. One evening he received a visitor, an FBI agent by the name of Shepperd. The agent had shown him the file that had been altered to add Moore's name to the Star Cluster program. Eison feared his time was up. But instead of arresting him, Shepperd had told him an incredible story about concentration camps and that only one person could really help—his friend, Jeff Wells.

Shepperd knew the risks in contacting Dr. Eison when he heard the doctor was coming to Washington. If Eison decided to turn him in, he would be on the way to a camp himself; of that he had no doubt.

But while working in Washington, after the episode in Chicago with the Cofers, he had learned that a young computer genius named Jeff Wells was the one who had designed and built Data-Net. The name rang a bell, and after checking the archives, he had found what he was looking for. Jeff Wells' grandfather and namesake, Colonel Jeffrey Wells, had been a friend of Shepperd's father. Colonel Wells and Shepperd's father had worked together during the war, and for several years afterward at the space center in Florida.

He had a hard time believing that any man his father trusted so totally would have a grandson who was a traitor to his country. He had taken a very great risk in checking the top-secret file on Jeff Wells, which noted that Wells had tried to skip out on the project but had been caught and returned. It was also clear that the single hold the administration had over Wells was his assistant, Karen Eison. The file revealed that the girl's father, Dr. William Eison, was being watched closely, and he demonstrated every indication of becoming a defector himself. He was scheduled for internment as soon as Wells completed the Data-Net system and Star Cluster was operational.

Dr. Eison had been called to Washington to report on the progress of Star Cluster. Shepperd realized it was the only chance he would have to get to Eison. With surprisingly little difficulty, he got himself assigned to watch Eison while he was in Washington. His orders were explicit: Eison was to have no contact with his daughter or Wells.

It was only by chance that Shepperd had come across the altered personnel file on Star Cluster while it was still in the processing basket and had not been reviewed.

Unknown to Shepperd, his efforts had not gone unnoticed. Within the cadre of agents assigned to round up the terrorists were a group of men and women who secretly opposed the government's actions. They had helped many Christians and Jews to escape. Shepperd had already guessed that several well-organized resistance movements existed throughout the government. Determining which side somebody was on was a little like the old Abbott and Costello routine of "Who's on First," he decided.

Shepperd knew he had to do something. *But what?* he asked himself one evening as he walked toward his car in the government parking lot. *This "Society" is bigger than the government itself. Somehow Wells is the key to their control. Without the Data-Net system in place, they can't hope to control several millions of Americans. And without the help of the media, they can't hope to dupe the rest.* "Freedom of the press has become a charade," he yelled out in frustration. "They're the problem."

"I agree," a soft voice said from the shadows.

Startled, Shepperd automatically reached for his weapon. "Who is it?" he growled.

"I'm a friend," she said in an easy, unassuming manner. "I believe we share some of the same concerns."

"I don't know what you're talking about," Shepperd said cautiously as he eyed the woman. He recognized her as the head of the Records department where he had spent much of his time during the last several days. His superiors had assumed he was gleaning the files for evidence of terrorist activities that could be used in the searches, and he had fed them enough information to keep them satisfied. But the majority of his time had been spent piecing together a secret organization, known only as the Society, that was working within the government. He suspected that it went far back in history and had spread its infection to the very heart of the government, including the presidency.

Shepperd cautiously made his way to an area that was better lighted. The young woman followed but was careful to stay just beyond the direct light. *It is her,* he thought with certainty as more light reached her face. *She's the one in charge of Records.* It had been hard the first several days for him to avoid staring at her. Her piercing blue eyes, chiseled features, and flawless skin made her look like someone on the cover of *Vogue* magazine. He had been impressed that she never seemed to look up from her desk, and rarely, if ever, took breaks. He never had a chance to speak to her personally. Any question he had was relayed by one of the other workers, but it was clear they respected her, and she always had the answers to any questions asked. His years of training served him well, though. Every part of him cried out: *Be careful.*

"I don't blame you," she said gently.

"For what?" Shepperd asked cautiously.

"For wondering what is going on inside our government."

"I don't . . ." he started to say.

"What is going on is a conspiracy to imprison and then eliminate millions of Americans on the basis of their religion or race," she said angrily. "I know who and why, but I don't know what to do about it."

"Why tell me?" Shepperd asked, every nerve now on edge. "I'm just a field agent."

"You underestimate yourself, Agent Shepperd," she replied. "Now you had better kiss me or someone will think we're conspirators."

With that, she walked up to him and kissed him as if it were the most natural thing to do. The low-light television cameras equipped with motion sensors picked her up as she entered the light.

In the closed circuit monitoring room, the security guard said to his companion, "I knew that agent was spending a lot of time in Records. Now I know why. Look," he said as he zoomed in on the couple who appeared to be totally engrossed with one another.

"That lucky stiff," the other guard said. "She's gorgeous. Who would have believed that little 'Miss Prude' would go for some guy twice her age?"

"I don't know, but if that's what it takes, I'd gladly trade with him."

"Listen, she might be crazy, but that doesn't mean she's also stupid," the other guard said jokingly as Shepperd and the young woman disappeared into her car.

When they were driving out of the parking lot, Shepperd said, "Since we've been seen kissing, you can at least tell me your name, can't you?"

She laughed. "It's Kathy Birk. I thought you knew, since you spent so much time in the file room."

"No," he replied honestly. "I wondered, but I learned a long time ago that people who ask questions get asked a lot of questions."

"Besides," she said mockingly, "you looked into some files where you didn't have a 'need to know.'"

"How could you . . ."

"How could I have known that?" she finished his sentence. "Mr. Shepperd, I'm not a librarian. I'm a trained field agent placed in Records just to catch defectors like you. It's a good thing that I'm also a defector, wouldn't you say?"

"That's for sure," he agreed as they turned the corner onto a side street. Just as they passed, a bakery truck pulled out behind them blocking the street.

When she saw the puzzled look on Shepperd's face, she said nonchalantly, "That's just in case anyone may be following."

Shepperd was impressed. Apparently this was not some fly-by-night outfit. They had escape routes and alternate road blocks arranged. They had to have known he would come with the girl.

"My car's been swept clean," she said. "We can talk freely."

Shepperd nodded.

"Are you willing to help ferret this cancer out of the government?" she asked bluntly. "Even at the risk of your own life?"

"You're pretty direct," he said. "How do I know that you're not a part of the cancer?"

"If I were, you'd be on your way to a camp, or else you'd have an extra hole in your head, Mr. Shepperd," she replied coolly.

"I hear you," he said. "The one thing this group is not is subtle."

"Yes, and you only know part of it. The intent is to remove all the

Christians and Jews to detention camps, turn the government over to a man known as 'the Leader,' Amir Hussein, and . . ."

"Hussein?" Shepperd interrupted. "As in Amir Hussein, the new emissary to Israel?"

"The same. A group of fanatics, calling themselves the Society, believe he is their long-awaited leader who will rule the world and bring in a one-world government."

"How do you know that?" Shepperd asked, trying to absorb what he was hearing. "Control the economy, maybe . . . but take over the government?"

"They allowed three million people to die in the Japanese earthquake without a second thought, and they're planning to kill twenty million Americans. What makes you think they won't take over the government? The country is in shambles. America is ripe for a dictator who will promise them prosperity. What are a few million Christians and Jews, compared to a new car every three years?"

"How do you know this?" he asked again. "What proof . . ."

"You will have all the proof you need in good time."

Kathy knew that Shepperd was a vital link in stopping the Society. But could she convince him of that?

For the next two hours, Kathy filled Donald Shepperd in on all she knew about the Society and its leaders. Often Shepperd would stop her to fill in some gaps, like the processing centers he had located through his research. Finally, she dropped him off several blocks from his hotel.

"You must convince Dr. Eison to help," she said emphatically. "Jeff Wells is the key to their control, just as John Elder is the key to organizing the CRC."

Shepperd was too shocked to answer. She had guessed his intention to contact Dr. Eison. *Could I have been that obvious*, he wondered.

"You checked out his file," she answered without being asked.

As he was getting out of the car, Kathy said, "We arranged for you to watch Dr. Eison when he arrives. Good luck." With that, she drove off.

The earlier meeting with Dr. Eison had led to the scientist's message through Data-Net. That contact through Data-Net had been an act of desperation that worked. On such acts the fates of nations are often decided. But now he hadn't heard from Jeff or Karen for several days. His encrypted messages went unanswered.

RESCUED

Plans to free John Elder had been discussed several times, but, since he was being held in the top security wing at Andrews, it seemed impossible. When one of the guards tipped off the group that Elder was being moved, they had acted swiftly. As soon as it was certain that Elder was being transported to the capital, the plan had been activated.

The call had come in on Warner's cellular phone while he was meeting with some of the local Atlanta CRC organizers. Warner had also learned that an FBI agent from Washington was working with the CRC and would soon be joining them in Atlanta. He wanted desperately to know the agent's name but decided that it was too risky to ask any more questions.

After the call, Warner could hardly contain his excitement. He relayed the message to the group leaders, then made his way out of the abandoned office building that served as their temporary headquarters. He needed to call Rutland—quickly. This would be his ticket to get Franklin off his back.

Once outside, he decided to make the call immediately. Stepping into a small alley beside the building, he flipped the "on" switch of his pocket-sized phone. Normally he would have been more cautious in such a tough neighborhood, but he was too excited to wait until he reached the security of his car. When the phone was activated, it made a soft beeping sound as it scanned the local cellular frequencies for an open channel.

The two men watching Warner come out of the building had lost sight of him. One said, "Where did that guy go?"

"I don't know," the other replied angrily. "But let's find him. I really need a fix."

Just then they heard the beep of the scanner coming from the alley. They stepped around the corner just as Warner was dialing Rutland's Washington number. The last thing Archie Warner ever heard was the soft "pop" of the silenced hand gun. In less than a minute, the two thugs had stripped him of all his valuables, including the pocket phone. The gunman picked up the phone as Rutland's receptionist was asking. "Who's calling, please?"

"Sorry. Wrong number," he said, laughing, as he flipped the switch off. John Elder never knew it, but he owed his life to those thieves.

A few hours later Elder found himself being hauled out of bed before sunrise and hustled into a waiting car. It was all done so quickly and secretively he thought he was probably going to be killed. He knew better than to ask questions without first being asked to speak. The several interrogations he had gone through had been brutal experiences.

The first time he had demanded his rights, the interrogator had touched the high voltage immobilizer to his trapezoid muscle and flicked the switch on. The pain had been excruciating. The man laughed and asked Elder to repeat his demand for civil rights. Once the pain subsided, he again demanded the right of counsel. Once more the immobilizer had sent waves of pain through his body.

Elder had heard and read about torture, especially within the ranks of Christianity throughout the centuries, but until he experienced it himself, he had no real appreciation for how psychologically demoralizing it could be. The pain was bad enough by itself, but it was the feeling of helplessness, quickly followed by hopelessness, that took the greatest emotional toll. John Elder had a great appreciation for why prisoners of war capitulated to their captors. Without a total dedication to a greater power, all else seemed trivial and easily renounced.

The confusing part of his ordeal was that his interrogators didn't really ask anything of him. It was as if he were being softened up for something. He wasn't asked to sign a confession or to renounce his faith, which he had originally expected. He was asked his name, his occupation, and the name of his wife. The latter had the desired effect of placing her foremost in his thoughts. If he dared challenge a question or resist in any way, he was jolted with the immobilizer.

This morning he was simply whisked away without a word. He knew this would not be a normal interrogation and was truly frightened. The windows of the limousine were totally darkened so he could not see out; nor could anyone see inside. From the sounds outside, he guessed they were approaching a city. Since he knew he was being held at Andrews, he assumed it had to be Washington.

The car stopped, and Elder heard a slightly familiar sound. It took a moment until his senses made the connection. It was a garage door opening. The car moved again and he heard the door close. Before the car stopped, the interrogator shoved a black cloth bag roughly over Elder's head and muttered, "Not one sound . . ."

Elder felt himself pushed along a concrete floor, and heard what he assumed to be an elevator door opening. He was shoved inside. *An office building*, he thought. *But where, and why?* The elevator stopped, and Elder was shoved out into the hallway. He stumbled and another man took his arm, pushing him down the hall. Still he had no hint as to where he was. The bile of fear rose in his mouth. He choked it back and silently prayed for God to give him strength. He was pulled to a halt and his handcuffs were removed. He stood silently awaiting the next move from his captors. Someone pulled the bag off his head. At first he had a difficult time focusing. He had been kept in a poorly lighted cell and then hooded for several minutes; his pupils were trying to adjust.

"Welcome, John Elder," the man said smoothly. "I have been waiting a long time to see you."

Elder squinted, trying to adjust his eyes to the lighted room. Suddenly, as the image came to him, he felt a pang of fear rise from his spine. "You!" he said hoarsely. He would have shouted it out but his vocal cords were unaccustomed to talking, much less shouting. The image he saw filled him with near terror. It was straight out of his childhood nightmares. The dark man sitting behind the president's desk was the one in his nightmares.

"It is me," the man responded. "I trust our friends have kept you well."

Elder said nothing. He knew that his nightmare had become a reality. The man sitting in the chair of the nation's highest office was the enemy of all he held true. He recalled the words of the prophet, Daniel, who said, "Then the king (leader) will do as he pleases, and he will magnify himself above every god, and will speak monstrous things against the God of gods; and he will prosper until the indignation is finished, for that which is decreed will be done."

"I know you!" Elder blurted out. "You're the evil one!"

Hussein's eyes burned with anger. The guard stepped forward, but the dark man stopped him. "Leave us!" he commanded.

"But, sir," the guard protested.

"Leave us at once!" he commanded again, and the guard left the room.

"Evil is a relative term, John Elder," Hussein said smoothly, once more in control. "Most of the people in this country would say you are evil. I could have you killed and the people would cheer me as a hero."

"Perhaps you can fool the people," Elder said cautiously, "but no man can fool God!"

"What do I care about your God!" Hussein hissed as he rose from the chair. "Has He been able to help you or your pathetic followers? No. I am in charge now. Your God is a myth. Even your own school children know that!"

"School children are easily deceived too," Elder said more boldly now. He did not underestimate the man in front of him, but facing his nightmare, he found it was not nearly as frightening as he had imagined.

"What do you want from me?" Elder asked. "I know you haven't planned this whole episode just to impress me."

Hussein's eyes narrowed as he felt the anger well up inside. Then he smiled, "Very good, John. Try to make your opponent lose his composure, then you will be able to manipulate him."

Elder said nothing, but he realized that the man in front of him was susceptible to the same feelings of anger as anyone else. It wasn't much, but it was a crack in the armor.

"I want to offer you a deal," Hussein said.

"What kind of deal?" Elder asked cautiously. He knew the one they called the Leader wanted something from him, but he couldn't imagine what.

"I have the power to destroy you and all the other Christians in America. We have you isolated and cut off from those around you. But I have no desire to destroy you, unless I am offered no other choice. Your beautiful wife, Julia, does not fare well in prison, I'm afraid."

Elder blanched at the mention of his wife. He had prayed for her daily during his imprisonment, but inside he also prayed that she would not be arrested. He shuddered at the thought of her frail body undergoing the treatment he had received. Suddenly his mind flashed the connection. *That's why I have been tortured,* he thought. *They want me to know what Julia will suffer—or perhaps is suffering.* Hussein instantly sensed he had struck a nerve in Elder. "I am willing to have your wife released."

"In exchange for what?" Elder asked as Hussein paused for several seconds.

"In exchange for your sworn loyalty to my cause," he said, his eyes seeming to pierce Elder's soul.

Elder fought back the fear that was welling up inside him. He did the only thing he could think of at the moment: he kneeled and prayed. His mind was so numb, all he could remember at the time was the Lord's prayer. So he began, "Our Father, Who art in Heaven . . ."

"Stop it!" Hussein shouted at Elder as he struck him in the face. "You will not mention your false god in my presence."

"If He is a false God, then why do you fear the very mention of His name?" Elder asked as he got to his feet.

"You will suffer, and your wife will suffer even more," Hussein hissed in anger. "You had your chance; now you will pay, and your miserable followers will be wiped off the face of the earth . . . starting with your wife."

Elder began, "If you kill me, I'll rejoice that I am found worthy to suffer for His sake. If you kill my wife, I'll rejoice for her sake. The more of us you persecute, the more will join our ranks, so you can't win. You are defeated—then, now, and forever."

Hussein struck Elder again. "You will die last! You are the one who condemns your followers to death! You are a fool!"

"I have no followers," Elder replied, as he wiped the blood off his mouth. "We all serve the one true God. You have tried before and have been defeated. In the end, it's you who will bow before the Lord."

"Never!" Hussein shouted. "Never! I serve the ruler of the earth. I will have the nations as my footstool." He pressed the button on the side of the president's desk, and two bulky guards came in.

"Take this terrorist to the place we have prepared for him and his kind. You may teach him manners, but don't kill him. He must live to confess his guilt."

Elder felt his arms being wrenched behind his back, and the cuffs put back on his wrists. One of the men shoved his face down onto the massive desk where Jefferson and Lincoln had sat. The impact split his eyebrow and blood dripped onto the carpet. He was dazed when they snatched him up again.

Hussein said softly, "We will speak of this again. The next time I will arrange to have your wife here with us. Right now some of the guards are busy with her."

As Elder staggered out between the two guards, he said in a clear, strong voice, "Greater is He who is in us, than he who is in the world." He could still hear Hussein's curses ringing in his ears when the guard on his right smashed a fist into his temple. He lost consciousness as they dragged him to the elevators.

"Where's he going?" one of the secret service guards asked the two who met them at the garage level.

"To the camp in Arizona," the huge man said as he lifted Elder by the collar. "He will learn what it means to assassinate members of our government. It will be a one-way trip."

Elder had regained some of his senses, but he decided to fake unconsciousness. As the big man hauled Elder toward the waiting car, one of the guards said, "Wait a minute! I don't know you two. What department are you with?"

"We're from special forces," the smaller man said. "We're new recruits from the attorney general's office."

"And they gave you the job of transporting the leader of the terrorists? Something sounds funny," the secret service guard said, pulling his weapon. "You stay right there while I make a call to headquarters."

"Do what you want!" the big man said angrily. "But why don't you just check our orders first? It will save us both a lot of reaming from up top. We didn't ask for this assignment, and as you know, Lively doesn't like to have his orders challenged."

"Yeah, that's for sure," the other guard said. "Let me see your orders." As he reached for the papers the two men held out, the big man grabbed his arm and literally swung him through the air. His companion was caught off guard and fired his weapon just as his partner came flying toward him. The bullet struck the other man in the chest, point blank. He never had a chance to pull the trigger again; his compatriot's body struck him like a 200-pound sack of potatoes. He was slammed against the concrete wall, out cold.

"Who are you?" Elder stammered.

"So you are awake," the smaller man said. "I thought you were. Get up, and hurry. We're going to have guards all over us in about thirty seconds."

The big man grabbed Elder by the waist and hauled him into the car like so much baggage. The other man jumped into the driver's seat and dropped the shift lever into gear. The tires were still smoking when the first of twenty guards hit the garage level. Before they could fire a shot, the car turned the corner and disappeared out of sight.

The secret service agent who had been unconscious was just coming to, and yelled, "Get them! They took Elder!"

Three groups of guards jumped into the three vehicles still in the parking area. The dazed guard heard the starters spinning, but not one started. He heard one after the other of the guards swearing as they raised the hoods to see loose wiring hanging in the engine compartments.

"We'll need to alter our plans slightly," the driver said to his partner in the back seat with Elder. "They'll have an alarm out for us momentarily."

"Who are you?" Elder asked again, wondering if he was being rescued or kidnapped by another group.

"We're friends, Pastor," the big man said pleasantly. "We're members of Randy Cross' Bible study."

Elder began to laugh. "Well, I guess it's been a while since Randy's had a chance to teach that Bible study."

"Yes, I guess it has," the big man said chuckling, "but we thought you would believe us quicker if we explained that we knew Randy. Hold it, Pastor, and I'll have these cuffs off in a second." With that he tried his master key, supplied by one of Shepperd's recruits from the FBI. It worked just as he had been told it would. Elder rubbed his wrists to get the circulation back.

John Elder had many questions, but he knew they would have to wait until they were safe—if they were safe. He also knew that Hussein would stop at nothing to find him again. *Why was so much attention being directed toward a Baptist preacher from Atlanta?* he wondered.

When Hussein heard that Elder had been rescued by two men in the garage, he was in a rage. He immediately called Rutland, who was with Kathy Alton at an official Washington reception for the Arab ambassadors to the United Nations.

Rutland glared at the secret service man who brought the message over to their table. "I told you I was not to be disturbed!" he said angrily. He knew the next step in the plan required that the Arabs occupy Israel. Then the Jews would become slaves to their former serfs.

"Sir, you have an urgent call from Mr. Hussein. He said to reach you, no matter what."

The Leader would never interrupt unless it was critical, Rutland thought silently. "Tell him I will be there momentarily." He made his way to the telephone as quickly as he could after offering his apologies to the Arab delegation.

"Yes, sir," Rutland answered as he listened to Hussein's screaming about Elder. "I'll handle it personally."

Rutland was clearly disturbed as he hung up the phone and walked out of the meeting room. *I've never heard the Leader so upset. How could one pastor be so important? The Arabs will just have to get along without me. Kathy Alton will learn about Elder soon enough,* he decided.

John Elder was beginning to believe that he had actually been rescued from the clutches of the Society. After his weeks, or months, of captivity—he really wasn't sure anymore—he was free.

The big man looked at Elder, and it was almost as if he could read his mind. "It's not over yet, Pastor," he said softly. "We're in the middle of enemy territory, riding in the enemy's car. We've got a ways to go yet."

"I understand," Elder responded with a smile. "But who are you—besides being friends of Randy's?"

"Well, actually we were in the secret service under President Kilborne, but we were lifted from government service when Hunt was elected. We're part of a movement to help rid our government of the cancer growing within it."

"How did you get into the White House garage?"

"I'm not really sure. Apparently there is some link to the national security system from within our group. Everything is on a need-to-know basis, just in case we get picked up."

"What's the plan?" Elder asked as he felt his old vigor returning.

"We have a second car stashed not far from here. We'll make a switch and others will continue on in this one," the driver said as he maneuvered the car through the back streets. He spotted the side street where the second vehicle should be and turned in.

"That's it," the driver said as he pulled up behind the big truck.

"That's it?" Elder asked.

"Yep, that's it, Pastor," the big man said with a warm smile.

"A garbage truck?" Elder said with a puzzled look.

"Yeah, we've had better than average luck heisting garbage trucks lately. They apparently don't expect many people to swipe them."

"I can understand that," Elder said as the aroma drifted back to them. "Let me guess. You don't plan on me riding up front, do you?"

"You guessed right, Pastor," the big man said as he pulled the handle to lower the compactor. "In you go."

"You're sure you two are part of the 'good guys' and not the Society. Right?" Elder asked good humoredly as he crawled into the stinking trash pile.

"Remember what the Lord said, Pastor: 'It's not what goes onto a man . . .'"

"Or something like that," Elder shouted as the compactor growled closed.

The driver donned dirty coveralls and a cap, slid into the seat of the huge truck, and drove slowly away. In the passenger's seat the big man was pulling off his jacket and tie and trying to push his oversized frame into the coveralls provided for him. "They don't fit real well," he said to the driver.

"They'll have to do. Neither of us would pass a real close inspection anyway. Now get out there and earn your pay."

"Yeah, sure," he responded. "If they double it, I'll still make nothing. This is *not* what I went to college for."

The truck continued on down the street picking up dumpsters

with trash in them. Each load provided better cover for Elder in the collector.

"I just hope you guys remember I'm back here," Elder shouted as the truck began to fill up.

The government car the trio had been riding in sped away with three men inside. Rather than traveling in the opposite direction from the trash truck, the men drove directly north, intending to dump the car as far away from the transfer point as possible without pointing the search teams back to the swap point. As the three men raced through the city, they had no way of knowing that Fred Lively's secret service agents had already picked up the locator and were tracking their movements.

"There are three men still in the car," the agent said as he watched the car go by a block away. "Do you want us to take them out?"

"That's affirmative," Lively said on the other end. "But we need positive identification on Elder first; no slip-ups either."

"That's going to be a little difficult," the agent responded. "Unless we stop them, there's no way of being absolutely sure."

"Then stop them, you idiot!" Lively shouted into the phone. Rutland had been brutally clear. Elder was to be eliminated at all costs.

The agent signaled his partner as they roared onto the highway in pursuit of the speeding car ahead of them. "We'll need some help," he relayed to the control center. "Any other cars in the area?"

"Yes," the dispatcher said as she checked her screen. "I've already flagged them to intercept the vehicle. Move in behind to block their escape if they try to double back."

"We're in position now."

In the car that was thought to hold Elder, the driver, Sam Rosen, said, "We've been tagged."

"Where are they?" one of the men in the back seat asked.

"About three blocks back and coming up fast. They must have a bug on this car. They're going to try and stop us."

"We can't let them do that," the other man said. "They'll know the pastor got away, and they will eventually put the missing trash truck and us together. We've got to give the truck more time. It'll take a good hour before they can make the transfer."

"Hang on!" Rosen yelled. "Let's give them a run, then." With that, he floored the gas pedal. The powerful engine roared in response, and they sped toward the early morning traffic heading into D.C.

"He made us!" the agent shouted as he saw the car almost leap into the oncoming lane. "Man, I'm going to hate this. Hang on. This guy's not going to be easy." He jammed the accelerator down and whipped the car into the opposite lane too.

The motorists in the inbound lanes were used to rotten drivers (after all, they lived in D.C.), but two cars bearing down on them at breakneck speed was too much. Many whipped onto the shoulder at the last possible moment to avoid the crash. Some displayed the international gesture for bad drivers as they shouted strings of obscenities.

Both cars were weaving in and out of traffic as they barreled along the crowded street headed for the Washington Parkway bridge. The driver of the FBI car advancing on the scene from the opposite direction saw what was happening and decided to block the road ahead with his vehicle. Unfortunately, Sam Rosen was looking back at that moment and didn't see the car stopped in his path. His car slammed into the parked car at nearly eighty miles an hour, glanced off the side of the guardrail, and plunged down into the Potomac near Little Falls Dam. The car he hit was spun around in the road and smashed several other vehicles before it came to rest on the opposite side of the freeway.

As soon as the report was relayed to Lively, he called Rutland. "We're sure it was Elder," he said as the sweat beaded on his forehead. "But the car plunged into the Potomac just above the dam. The water's nearly sixty feet deep there. It'll take a couple of hours before divers can reach it." *Nothing seems to go right these days,* Lively thought to himself. "It had to be Elder in the car though," he lied to Rutland. "Our man made a positive ID before the car went over. Elder was in that car, I'd stake my life on it."

"You already have," Rutland said coldly. Even over the phone, Lively could feel those dead eyes staring at him. He shivered involuntarily.

"I'll call as soon as we have them," Lively said with a false gusto. The line had already gone dead.

"Did they get Elder?" the dark man inquired.

"Lively says they did. But I think he is lying."

"He is alive," Husscin agreed, as he sat back in the president's chair. "I know it."

THE MARK

P astor, we have some clean clothes for you," Randy Cross said as
John Elder entered the old farmhouse on the outskirts of Clayton, Georgia.

"I appreciate that, Randy," Elder said. "I'm beginning to smell a
little ripe . . . maybe even a little overripe."

After hiding in the garbage truck for nearly two hours, Elder had
been transferred to a semi-truck, owned by a CRC sympathizer, hauling produce into Atlanta.

It was obvious from what was said that most Americans still believed the general roundup was exactly what it was reported to be:
legal arrests of suspected terrorists. The media played a key role in
convincing the public that no one's civil rights were being violated.
Key officials within the Alton administration testified that no indis-
criminate arrests could, or would, ever be made in America. Since
most of the Christian leaders were targeted for immediate arrest, there
was virtually no one able to come forward and refute the official position. Anyone who might have cared to check would have seen obvious
indicators to the contrary: the hundreds of thousands of Christians and
Jews who were missing.

With each passing week, the noose tightened as the Data-Net system was augmented by the magnetic ID system. Anyone attempting to
use the system without the proper ID risked immediate arrest, since
magnetic scanners were appearing in virtually every city in America.
As the food that had been stored during the early days began to dwin-
dle, the leaders of the movement began to wonder what their next step
would be.

Amir Hussein was maniacal when it was confirmed that Elder
was not in the car recovered from the Potomac. He redoubled his ef-

forts to ferret out the Christians. All pretext of the ID system's being voluntary was abandoned.

"Disallow all users without a permanent ID," Hussein ordered.

President Alton announced the immediate implementation of the system, declaring the Insta-pol results were a mandate from the people of America. It became Public Law Number 186, passed by interim legislation until the Congress reconvened.

Randy Cross related as much as they knew at that point to John Elder. Then he told him, "Pastor, you were brought here because the CRC needs your help. We're going to expose the Society to America and the world."

"I don't see how I can help much," Elder said as the enormity of what he was told sunk in. "I can contact some of our local group but without funds and IDs we can't contact other groups."

"The country has become a virtual dictatorship since President Alton took office," Donald Shepperd said. "If we're to stop it, we need your help."

"And who are you?" Elder asked.

"I'm Don Shepperd. I was one of the FBI agents on loan to the attorney general's office to help round up the terrorists."

"Don's help has been a godsend," Randy added. "He planned your escape, as well as the escapes of several other key people."

"But how do I fit?" Elder asked. "I'm just a pastor without a church."

"You're being a little too modest, John," Bill Frost said as he stepped into the room.

"Bill! I thought you had been captured," Elder said as he hugged his long-time friend.

"I was. They took me to a facility in Arizona. Don helped arrange my escape."

"What about your wife?" Elder asked, as he thought about his own wife.

"She's somewhere in another camp, John. We can't spare the men to rescue her, at least not right now. We're in a struggle for survival. It's a battle we can't afford to lose." Seeing the anguish on Elder's face, Frost added. "Your wife, Julia, is safe though. She's doing fine; just worried about you."

"You mean she's not in custody?" Elder said as his legs buckled a little.

"Sit down, John," Randy said. "You've been through a lot. We'll fill in the details later. For now you can be assured Julia is safe. We wouldn't let the Society get their hands on her. They would have tried to use her to get to you."

"They, or rather Hussein, already tried," Elder said as he relaxed a little. "I'm fine, just a little tired."

"Nothing a good hot shower won't cure, then," Frost said. "We have that much."

"You said Hussein?" Shepperd interrupted. "Was that Amir Hussein?"

"That's what he calls himself," Elder said as he gritted his teeth involuntarily. "But I rather suspect he is known by another name."

"What do you mean?" Shepperd asked.

"Oh . . . nothing," Elder replied solemnly. "It's one of those ideas that labels a Christian as a radical. Perhaps even a nut!" Elder added as he looked around the room at the pitifully small group committed to facing the might of the government.

"John, we have something in mind that is so radical that it just might work," Randy said. "We want you to help organize Christians throughout the country to win back their freedoms."

"I don't know if you have noticed," Elder said with a smile. "But I'm not exactly the most popular man in the country right now. In fact, I understand that I am dead." Immediately Elder wished he hadn't said that. He knew three good men had died to gain his freedom.

Seeing the grimace on Elder's face, Bill Frost commented, "All of us here would lay down our lives if it would help the cause of freedom. The men who died knew the risks; they were more than willing to take them."

"I know how you feel," another voice added from the next room. As he spoke, Jeff Wells stepped into the room.

"This is Jeff Wells," Randy said to Elder.

"I know the name from somewhere," Elder responded, trying to put the two together.

"Jeff is, or was, in charge of the Data-Net program," Shepperd said.

"Oh yes, Wells. Now I know who you are," Elder said as he raised an eyebrow, signaling his confusion. "You're the young computer wizard who predicted the earthquake."

"Jeff is officially dead too. The plane he was supposed to be on was shot down just outside of Washington."

"Shot down?" Elder said quizzically.

"Shot down by a heat-seeking missile. Four of our people died in the crash."

"Yes," Jeff said as his face momentarily flashed the anger he felt. "If Don hadn't planned a double switch, Karen and I would have been on that plane." He began to outline what had happened from his first contact with Amelia Durant until they rolled up to the airport.

Just before Jeff and Karen were to exit the garbage truck, another couple had exited the cab and run to the plane. Jeff and Karen had been whisked away to another car and later transferred to a commercial truck headed toward Atlanta. As they drove away from the small airport, they had seen the explosion and disintegration of the private jet.

"The pilot and three other people were aboard that plane," Jeff said through clenched teeth. "They died in our places."

"They were Mossad," Shepperd said. "They have been helping us to sort out this mess. They have contacts almost everywhere."

"What does the Israeli Mossad have to do with this?" Elder asked.

"Oh, you probably don't know. The United States launched six nuclear bombs on Israeli defense installations under the guise of stopping a maniac by the name of Moshi Amitt from launching several cobalt bombs."

"I know of Amitt," Elder said in amazement. "He was part of the Zealot movement in Israel: anti-Christian and anti-American."

"Well, he's so much radioactive dust now," Shepperd said caustically. "But the U.S. has proposed an occupation force made up mostly of Arab nations to control Israel."

"The Israelis will never stand for that!" Elder nearly shouted. "I've been there many times. They know the Arabs would wipe them off the face of the earth the first chance they had. They will fight with sticks if necessary."

"That is exactly the plan," Shepperd explained. "The Mossad believes that it is Hussein's intention to totally eliminate the Jews, beginning with Israel."

Elder felt like his head was going to explode. "So many things have happened in such a short period of time. I was the pastor of a growing church here in Atlanta and had a television ministry reaching people around the country. I thought we were safe, but I guess my ego blinded me. Sure, I was doing God's work, but I was so busy in my own activities I missed what was going on around me."

"We were all guilty of that," Shepperd said, looking at the others in the room. "I guess none of us really believed something like this could happen—certainly not here in America. But we're no different from the German people before Hitler or the Russians before Lenin. Nobody ever really believes it can happen to them."

Elder was overwhelmed with emotion. "We became so attached to our 'things' that we didn't notice, or didn't care when we began to give up our freedoms to keep those things.

"We kill unborn children because they're an economic inconvenience; our kids take drugs so they won't have to face the realities of life without purpose; our politicians care more about getting elected than they do about the country. And worst of all, God's people cared more about maintaining their lifestyle than they did about reaching the world for Christ.

"And I'm as guilty as the rest," Elder added.

"You're being too hard on yourself, Pastor," Bill Frost said. "You warned us, and we tried to change. It was just too late by the time we woke up."

"Do you believe this is the tribulation, Pastor?" Randy Cross asked. He had voiced the question that many others were thinking, but hadn't asked.

"I don't honestly know," Elder replied with a sigh. "I think that Hussein is a part of Satan's plan to conquer the earth. But remember, no man knows the time; only God knows. If this is the tribulation and Hussein is really the anti-Christ, he will win right up to the last stage before Christ comes again. But if he is simply a puffed-up dictator like Stalin or Hitler, he can be defeated. We just need to pray for God's will to be done, and then do as He directs us."

Looking at Shepperd, Elder asked, "What can I do? If the ID system is so airtight that we can't even buy food anymore, how can we possibly reach the hidden groups throughout the country?"

"I think I can help there," Jeff said, as Karen came into the room holding a small electronic device that he had pocketed when they fled from the lab. "This is Karen Eison, my . . . my fiancée," he said.

The surprised look on the young woman's face told Elder the announcement was a revelation to her too, but she said nothing.

"This is a scanner similar to the ones being used in Data-Net," Jeff said as he took the small device from Karen. "The scanner output is transmitted back to a central location, where a number is verified. It's very similar to using a card, only the number is permanently imprinted under the skin using a thermal laser. The dye is magnetic so it doesn't show on the surface, but it can be detected by a sensitive magnetic scanner."

"Absolute control," Elder said. "You can't buy or sell without a number."

"Well, almost absolute," Wells added with a grin. Karen punched him in the ribs, and he pretended to get very serious again.

"What we're about to show you, Pastor, is known to no one outside this room as of this moment," Shepperd said. "It is imperative that it be kept secret. The trick is how to transmit the information nationwide to our groups and still keep it secret from the government. That's where you will come in. We know the groups were infiltrated by members of the Society; perhaps some groups still are. If one word of what you're about to see leaks out, we're finished."

Elder sat down in the chair closest to him. "I'll do what I can," he said with as much confidence as he could muster. *A dozen people against the might of the government,* he thought. *We really are Gideon's handful.*

"Give me your hand," Wells said. As he ran the scanner over the pastor's hand, the little device let out a screech that startled everyone.

"Very effective for alerting people that someone without an ID tried to use the system or simply walked past a scanner without knowing it was there. If this scanner had been hooked up to the system, a signal would also have gone to the central processor and set off an alarm there. I rather suspect that by now there are teams of agents stationed throughout the cities, ready to pounce on anyone detected."

"I understand," Elder said as his nerves settled down.

"Now," Wells said as he ran another small device he had retrieved from his pocket over Elder's hand. There was no sensation at all that Elder could tell.

"What was that?" he said.

Wells ran the scanner over Elder's hand again, only this time the device winked a green light on and issued no sound.

"You passed," Wells said triumphantly. "You're now officially a part of the Data-Net system."

Seeing the question in the Pastor's eyes, Wells continued. "I just printed a number on your hand. It's not permanent, but it will last about three months, or thirty baths, whichever comes first."

He made a grunting sound as Karen punched him in the ribs again. "It will eventually wear off as your skin replaces itself," Karen said softly. "It is waterproof and scratch proof."

"That means I could use Data-Net now?" Elder said as he scoured his hand. He could detect no mark of any kind.

"That only solves the problem of getting a number on your hand," Wells said. "If you tried to use Data-Net, your number wouldn't match your fingerprint on the system access scanner and you'd set off another alarm."

"Then how . . ."

"Patience, Pastor," Wells quipped. "Let me explain. The system has records of everyone who has received a number, back from when they first got their cards. I knew that counterfeiting cards would quickly become a big business, so I included a second check: The index fingerprint of every card holder. The ID number must be matched to the correct print also. Try to use the system with someone else's number, and you get instant rejection."

"I think I understand," Elder said. "So I can get past the scanners, but I can't use the system, right?"

"Not exactly," Wells said as he shifted into the swivel chair behind the desk. "I would assume by this time Dr. Loo has identified good numbers and bad numbers in the system. So you go walking through a scanner with the wrong number and the alarms go off."

"So it would seem we're back to ground zero again," Elder said.

"Not exactly," Jeff repeated.

"Cut it out, Jeff, you're getting irritating," Karen said. "I know you've already worked out a solution. What is it?"

"Actually it was pretty simple." Jeff looked over at Karen who rolled her eyes back in pretended agony. "Okay, maybe it wasn't so simple. But it will work," Jeff said, grinning from ear to ear.

"I left a window open to get into Data-Net from a remote location after Dr. Eison warned us that we were under suspicion."

"Dr. Eison?" Elder repeated. "A relative of yours, Karen?"

"Yes, sir, my father. He is a physicist at Livermore labs in California. He discovered the government's plot to arrest the Christians and Jews; then he began to put two and two together."

Jeff continued, "I can still get into Data-Net through a remote location. But there are two problems: First, I'm sure that by now Dr. Loo has activated my traps to monitor any attempt to enter the system from the outside. This was a necessary precaution I built into the system. Otherwise we would have every hacker in the world trying to get free access. Second, virtually every telephone system in the country has the ability to trace calls instantly and even send the number to the receiving end. So the first time I call, they have our number and location."

Elder was beginning to feel like he was in the *Catch 22* movie. "Is there a way around the problems?" he asked Wells.

"I think so. That's why we're here today, to find out. I said virtually every telephone system has the capability to trace calls, but not all. The system used here in Clayton is still mechanical. When AT&T was broken up in the early eighties, a lot of small, private telephone services were still using mechanical systems. Most converted to electronic relays over the years, but not all. Shepperd found out that this little community still has the old system. It takes several minutes for the electronic system to hunt its way through relays. So I figure I'll have about ten minutes to get in, modify the system, and then erase any trace of my entry. From that point on, the system will accept me as a normal entry, but it will wipe out all traces of my visits when I exit."

"You can do that?" Elder said in awe. He didn't understand it all, but he could see the genius in Wells.

"We'll see, Pastor. If the bad guys don't show up in thirty minutes or so, you'll know we made it."

"That sounds real comforting," Elder said with the first humor he had felt in weeks.

"Actually," Jeff said, grinning, "I'll know as soon as I activate my program in Data-Net."

Wells sat down at the terminal and typed in the access code that had been hidden inside the operating system. As soon as the computer connection was made, the screen responded:

"Access approved, Luke. The force be with you."

"Just a little private joke of his," Karen said as she narrowed her eyes at Jeff.

"Maybe 'The Lord be with you' would be more accurate," Elder said.

"Good idea," Jeff agreed. "I'll make the change when I exit."

Next he typed in: "Activate code 777."

The terminal responded: "Code 777 running. Input data."

"What is code 777?" Elder asked as he sat, fascinated, next to Wells.

"It's the program I have hidden away inside the system," Wells replied.

"Why 777?" Elder asked.

"That is God's perfect number isn't it?" Jeff responded. "Just like 666 is Satan's number?"

"How in the world did you know that?" Karen asked in amazement.

"I've read the Bible too," Wells said, pretending to be hurt at her insinuation.

"Now we just activate a block of numbers that you can use for your groups, and they should have no difficulty with Data-Net. You'll need to caution them not to use the system too much, too soon. These accounts will have unlimited credit. We wouldn't want to drain the system of all its resources. Someone might get a little suspicious."

"You could do that?" Shepperd asked, as an idea struck him.

"I guess I could," Jeff said as he thought about it. "As long as my program is in the system, the transfers are not recorded."

"How will you keep the books in balance?" Shepperd asked as his mind raced.

"It's really pretty simple . . . not too complicated," he said as he glanced over at Karen who was smiling. "When one of your people uses the system, an automatic transfer is made from the central bank to the merchant's account; that is, assuming the system verifies that the credits are in the user's account. In this case, the system will always acknowledge a balance in excess of the purchase. That's why they must be cautious about over-using it.

"Next Data-Net makes a transfer to the central bank from the user's bank account at the end of the day. Meanwhile, it has been keeping track of all transfers during the day to be sure that no one can run up too much credit in one day. Again, in your group's case, the tally is not recorded because the transactions are never recorded.

"Since these accounts don't actually exist, the transfer, plus the system's commission, is created by my program."

"Created?" Shepperd asked.

"Yes. I literally create the funds by rounding off the least significant bit in every transfer going through the system, and storing it in a special file, just for this purpose."

"The least significant bit? Could you explain?" Shepperd asked.

"We use a sixty-four bit computer system for Data-Net. But in reality, a number extends forever. We arbitrarily round it off at sixty-four units because it fits our particular need for accuracy. If we were plotting coordinates for the Mars mission, we would use a 128 bit computer system. So my routine looks at the total cash flow through the system and then stores the hypothetical sixty-fifth bit in a file.

"For instance, if I were storing the sixteenth bit, my system would accumulate one-tenth of a dollar, or a dime for every transaction. But we can't do that because someone would miss the dime. However, since we have arbitrarily elected to stop at sixty-four bits, no one will miss the sixty-fifth. You see, it's really simple."

"But how much would you accumulate storing such an insignificant number?" Shepperd asked skeptically.

"Well . . . let's look in my accumulation register and see," Jeff said as he typed in the appropriate commands. "To date, the system has been accumulating for nearly three weeks, and we have a balance of $13 billion."

"Thirteen billion!" Shepperd said as he nearly fell out of his chair. "Why, that makes you the biggest bank robber of all time."

"I hadn't thought of it that way," Jeff said as he shut the input down. "But I guess it probably does. Remember though, the money doesn't really exist. I made it up."

"Just like the government, huh?" Shepperd quipped.

"Pastor, you have a blank checkbook for your people," Shepperd said. "Now all we have to do is get you to them without encountering any of the several thousand government agents looking for you. Thirteen billion, huh?" he said. "Let's go shopping."

OUT OF CONTROL

I want the arrests stepped up!" Hussein commanded Rutland as they sat eating breakfast. Hussein had taken over one of the guest suites for dignitaries in the White House. From there he could be involved with the daily activities of running the government.

"I'll do whatever you say, sir," Rutland replied in a monotone voice, as he laid his fork on the table.

"But, you disagree," Hussein said, seeing the expression on Rutland's face.

"If we push too fast we will alienate many people, sir. Already we have spies within our own system. Wells and Elder were helped by people within the government. And several of our security people have defected."

"I know all the excuses," Hussein hissed through clenched teeth. "But we must eliminate the Christians as quickly as possible. Once the Christians are gone, the others will conform to the new system. They are too attached to their pleasures to risk losing the handouts from the government. Soon we will control all the drugs. This will give us the money and the means to control all the cities.

"Fear is the key to total control," Hussein said as madness showed in his eyes. "Make the citizens more afraid of you than they are of anything else. Those who harbor the Christians and Jews will give them over to us if they themselves are in danger."

Rutland was clearly disturbed, although he displayed no change of emotion outwardly. He had never seen the Leader out of control, but since Elder's escape, Hussein had been almost frantic, as if he actually feared the man.

"I will tell Lively to step up the arrests," Rutland said without emotion.

"No!" Hussein replied sharply. "He is incompetent. I want him eliminated. Put Marla in charge. She has the zeal we need. Lively is not to be trusted anymore; he is greedy and out for himself. He hates the Christians, but only because they opposed his decadent group. We must have someone who hates them as much as I do . . . just because they exist.

"I want all the military leaders who are not in the Society purged immediately, too. If we are to rule, we must have absolute control. I will not make the same mistakes that others have made throughout history. We will prepare the way for the coming of the Great Leader."

"But I thought you were the Leader!" Rutland said in one of his rare emotional outbursts.

"You have earned the right to know, my comrade. I am the forerunner for our Great Leader. He cannot take his rightful place as long as the Christians remain. Even they know that. They believe it is their destiny to be removed by what they call 'the rapture.' I intend to remove them by annihilation.

"The Leader has revealed to me that Elder is the key to our plans in America. He has the ability to unite all the Christians. Without him they have no leader. Flush him out. Start killing the Christians until he surrenders!" Hussein ordered Rutland.

In another building several blocks away from the White House, a separate meeting was in progress, one that clearly had General Louis Gorman, chairman of the joint chiefs of staff, shaken.

"Are you sure of this, Colonel?" General Gorman asked as he shook his head. "This seems too incredible to believe—the U.S. military with traitors in its ranks."

General Louis Gorman had been a career Army officer for more than thirty years. When the depression of the nineties began, he knew the country was in for some hard times. His grandparents had lived through the 1930s depression and, as a boy growing up in New York, he had often heard them talk about it. They had warned him that the country was on a crash course with another depression.

What worried Louis Gorman was that the nation no longer had the character to accept economic depression. People were more dependent on the government, and he knew firsthand that the United States government was rotten to its core.

Several times he had heard rumors of a secret society operating within the government. Now he had proof that it was also operating within the military. Someone had sent his aide, Colonel Anderson, copies of secret memos directing a coup to take place in the top levels of the military. It even named the senior officers who would take charge. The name of General Louis Gorman was not on the list. Nor were those of most of his associates. The names were those of career "yes men" who followed the path of the current administration like lap dogs.

Normally, General Gorman might have written off such notions as the wild speculations of frustrated soldiers who had had their budgets cut too much, except that what he saw pointed to such an organization. And the climate of the country was ripe for takeover. *Good God*, he thought. *Just look what they're doing to the Christians in the name of justice.* Even several thousand service people had been arrested. Thus far, all of his objections had been to no avail. Hundreds of thousands of people had simply vanished. Now he knew why. "These camps, Colonel, where are they?" he asked.

The other senior military officers gathered in the room were equally shocked at what they had heard so far. They were career soldiers who had fought for their country's freedoms. They had assumed the government's campaign was against terrorists too. Now they realized they had been sucked in by the media, just like the rest of the country.

"The information pinpoints three of the camps, sir. They are marked on the map. At present there is one in Arizona and two in California. Other data indicates at least twenty additional camps are being readied, but no details have been given."

"You're sure about this?"

"Yes, sir," the Intelligence officer replied. "I went over the Israeli satellite photographs myself. There is no doubt about it. These are recently constructed camps; each camp has about one hundred thousand people interned."

The murmur went throughout the room. "A hundred thousand!" Another brigadier general said, "How can that be?"

"We believe that nearly two million people have been arrested so far, sir. Therefore, there will have to be many more camps. We think each camp could handle nearly a half million people eventually."

"Five hundred thousand people!" General Gorman said in disbelief. He knew his aide was a very thorough man who would not make wild statements without having the facts to back them up. "What could the ultimate purpose be?" the general asked. But inside he had a sickening feeling that he already knew the answer.

"I think there is another discovery that will help answer that question, sir," Colonel Anderson said, struggling to keep his professional objectivity. He had seen the photos and read the reports someone had sent him, and he still had a hard time believing it was true. It was so bizarre he questioned if the whole thing had been fabricated. But the facts were conclusive.

"Sir, the Israelis sent us data from their Bios satellite."

"Bios?" the general said quizzically. "Isn't that their weather satellite?"

"That's what our intelligence had been led to believe, sir. But now the Israelis have revealed the true nature of Bios. It is a radiation detection satellite that has been systematically mapping the location of every nuclear weapon in our country."

"What?" General Abbott, commander of the Air Force, growled. "You mean they have the capability to detect all of our nuclear devices?"

"I'm afraid so, sir," the red-faced major with Colonel Anderson said. "Even our nuclear subs. They are at least ten years ahead of us in this technology."

"Why those sneaky . . . ," General Gorman said admiringly.

"Sir, their satellite shows a nuclear device stored at the Arizona camp. About ten kilos," the colonel said grimly.

"A ten-kilo device at an internment camp . . . for what purpose?" the general asked of his aide. But even as he spoke the words he guessed the truth.

"Sir, the only logical conclusion we can draw is that the device is there to eliminate the camp," the colonel replied.

The tremor that went through the room of top military officers was genuine shock. The colonel flashed the satellite detector pattern on the screen, which displayed the most current distributions of nuclear devices under their commands. Flashing arrows indicated new locations; the most recent was centered in the Arizona desert. Every man present knew there were no nuclear storage facilities in that area.

The general stood and watched the screen for several minutes before he spoke. "There can be no doubt about the intentions of our government's leaders. A ten-kiloton device would turn this camp into nuclear dust. There would be no trace of anyone retained there."

"But, Lou, how would anyone in the government think they could get away with that, even if they had control of the weapon?" General Abbott asked in disbelief. "I would send the Eighth Air Force to bomb Washington if that happened."

"I believe you, Stub, and I suspect our government leaders do too. They must also believe that I would send the Eighth Army, if I had to. So there's only one logical conclusion, isn't there?"

General Robert "Stub" Abbott just sat looking at his long-time friend. There was just one logical conclusion: They would all have to be removed before the device was used!

"Gentlemen, I would say that we are in extreme jeopardy at this time," General Gorman said coolly. "The people who are capable of doing this to their own countrymen must not be allowed to get control of the United States military."

In the back of the room, a solitary figure was listening to the conversation intently. *I must tell Rutland as quickly as possible,* he thought as he heard the senior officers' discussion.

"Gentlemen, I would like to have a list of secure officers who can be trusted, as soon as possible," General Gorman said. "I don't have to tell you that both time and secrecy are critical. We will schedule another meeting as soon as the information is available. I suggest we keep a low profile in the meantime."

"How will we convince those under us that we're not paranoid or trying to take over the government ourselves?" General Abbott asked.

"I guess we'll find out what kind of leaders we really are, Stub," Gorman said grimly. Then he added, "I don't know if I would believe it myself."

Rutland carried out Hussein's orders to have Fred Lively removed as attorney general. President Alton issued the executive order and within a day Marla West had assumed the position of acting attorney general, just as Lively had several months earlier.

Even before he knew what was happening, Fred Lively found himself barred from access to the White House. "You can't do this," Lively screamed into the phone at Rutland. "I'll go to the press."

"If you do, you will find it is your last press conference," Rutland said unemotionally. "Or perhaps you would like to tell the Leader how you feel."

Lively felt the chill of death upon him. He quickly said, "No, I'll do what you say. I'm here to help."

Marla West was thrilled to be appointed as attorney general by President Alton. Her loyalties to Fred Lively lasted only until Rutland told her the Leader had selected her to head the purge of the Christians.

The last time anyone saw Fred Lively alive was when he left his apartment to meet with members of the NCLU. The official statement was that he had been drinking, and his car ran off the road. The state police found Lively, still in his car in the Potomac River, just above the dam. It was almost exactly where the terrorists' car had been recovered.

The scene in Atlanta was typical of hundreds of other cities throughout the country. Armed secret service agents loyal to the administration were kicking in the doors of homes of anyone suspected of harboring terrorists. Under the guise of martial law, the agents were given complete authority to arrest and detain anyone. America had become a police state. As more and more people were arrested on the vaguest of suspicions, there were fewer places for the Christians to hide. For the Jews, there were none.

In an abandoned bank building on the outskirts of Atlanta, John Elder was in a meeting with several of the CRC leaders. Data-Net had almost made banks obsolete, since the system handled all transactions and arranged all credit.

Elder was explaining the plan to organize safe houses all across the country and then begin an underground newspaper to publish and distribute information about the Society. Shepperd had been tremendously helpful in securing more recruits from inside Washington, and they were beginning to piece together conclusive proof of the Society's existence and its planned takeover of America.

Jeff Wells was back at the farmhouse working diligently to keep the funds flowing for Elder's groups.

He's the old Jeff, Karen thought.

She hadn't realized how depressed he had been over the misuse of his talents. Now that he had a goal again he was enthusiastic and totally absorbed.

Jeff had discovered the authorization codes for President Alton's transportation of the detainees to the various camps. With one stroke of his keyboard, he fouled up the codes so that no movement would be possible for several days. The trains that were needed in Atlanta were diverted to central Arkansas; those scheduled for Chicago were sent to New Hampshire, and so on. Jeff couldn't help but chuckle to himself when he thought about Rutland's reaction to this mess. Dr. Loo would not be on his most favorite person list, he knew.

It made Karen feel good to see how excited Jeff was. Before she went back to work on the underground newspaper, she bent over and kissed the back of his neck. Jeff stopped typing and took her hand. He kissed the palm of her hand gently. "The world will be a better place for our children," he promised her.

"I hope you're right," Karen replied, choking back her tears. *It all seems pretty pathetic right now,* she thought. *A handful of people against the government. Any mistake could get us all captured.*

On the first floor of the abandoned bank building, Bill Frost heard a commotion outside and glanced out through the dusty blinds into the street. What he saw chilled his heart. In the street, police in full combat gear were piling out of five cars. Someone had tipped the police about their meeting.

"The police are outside!" Frost shouted to the group. "We've got to go. Now!"

Shepperd acted instinctively, gathering the papers spread out on the well-worn conference table. He knew the documents must not fall into the hands of the police. They contained the details for developing the safe houses. Shepperd, accustomed to thinking about contingencies, had directed Elder to draft his notes on rice paper, much as the CIA and KGB did back in the twentieth century. He took out his butane lighter and struck the igniter. Once the flame was strong, he touched it to the rice paper. The results were immediate and spectacular: the paper literally evaporated into smoke.

"How many policemen are there?" Shepperd shouted to Frost as the last of the documents were incinerated.

"About thirty!" Frost shouted back frantically. *Dear God*, he prayed, *don't let us have come so far just to lose it all now. Help us.*

"They're taking no chances," Shepperd said to Elder as they exited the room. "Let's hope they don't know you're here." Once in the hallway, Shepperd said calmly to the men with him, "Above all else we've got to keep John from the police. We won't ever have the chance to rescue him again if they get him."

"Don't worry about me," Elder said just as calmly. "Try to get away yourselves."

"Very noble, Pastor," Bill Frost answered, trying to get his heart rate a little more under control. "But you really are the key to our organization. You have to get away."

"You can't sacrifice . . ." Elder was saying when Shepperd cut him short.

"Listen, we're just wasting time talking. I intend to get us all out. Follow me!" Shepperd ordered. He knew the police would cover the front and back exits before they entered the building. He also knew they would use the stairs. As far as anyone knew, the elevators were not working. Actually, only one elevator was working. Shepperd had hot wired it by tapping into the main power system. He stepped into the elevator, followed by the others. As soon as the doors closed he jerked the control box open and snipped the indicator wire with a small pair of pliers from his pocket.

"Now they won't see the elevator moving," he told his small group of conspirators. He waited almost five minutes before doing anything. No one in the group said anything during the interminable wait. They all knew that their safety rested with Shepperd, and they trusted his judgment.

Only John Elder spoke. "I suggest we use the time we have to pray," Elder said with a calm that reassured the group. Then he led them in a prayer, asking that God would see fit to give them mercy. They could hear the crashing sounds below their level as the police stormed the building, kicking in doors to offices in the lower floors. Shepperd punched the down button and prayed the old elevator would not be too noisy as it descended. He stopped it at the front entrance level.

"But this is where the police cars are!" Frost exclaimed.

"Exactly," Shepperd replied. "We need transportation, don't we?" The elevator stopped and Shepperd stepped out. He pulled his gun from its holster and waved it as a sign for the group to go before him. With a puzzled look, they obeyed.

As Shepperd exited the building, a startled young policeman stared at them. Shepperd had his FBI badge out and flashed it at the policeman.

"Load these prisoners in the van," he commanded.

"What . . . ," the young policeman stammered.

"Just load them in the van, will you?" Shepperd commanded again in his most authoritative tone. "There are more suspects around in back."

The confused policeman opened the rear of the van and the group stepped inside.

"Thanks" Shepperd said. "There will be more coming, so stand by." With that he stepped into the driver's seat of the van.

"Wait a minute," the officer said, in total confusion. "Who are you?"

"Shepperd, FBI. I'm a part of the anti-terrorist squad. We called in the report. Thanks for your help."

"You're welcome . . . ," the young man stuttered as he tried to decide what to do.

Before the officer could think about what was happening, Shepperd started the van and shifted into gear. He was gone in a second, leaving the policeman to sort it out.

By the time the assault teams came out of the empty building, Shepperd and the others had changed to the cars they had left several blocks away. Milling around nearby was a group of tough-looking youths, eyeing the parked cars. Shepperd walked over and handed the keys to one of the young men and said, "Take the van; it's yours. No strings attached." He chuckled as the confused group of would-be car thieves piled into the van and roared off in the opposite direction. "That should keep the police busy for a while," he said as he watched the van disappear.

Word was filtering back to Rutland from across the country that the level of public support the Alton administration had enjoyed in the past was rapidly declining. Citizens were having their doors smashed in by government agents who often used excessive force—all on the basis of frivolous accusations by their neighbors. The net result was that less than 5 percent of the assaults yielded any trace of the missing Christians or Jews. Disgruntled and unemployed citizens were using the system to wreak havoc on anyone who was better off than they were.

Rutland secretly asked his contact at Insta-pol to take a public opinion sample directed at the recent crackdowns. The results were alarming. The original support level of almost 80 percent had eroded down to less than 50 percent.

Now this latest thing with Elder in Atlanta, he thought silently. When word that the police had let Elder slip through their fingers reached Hussein, he had gone crazy. He ranted for nearly ten minutes about having the officers eliminated. He even went so far as to suggest a nuclear strike on Atlanta to eliminate Elder. Rutland wondered if the man he had revered and vowed to serve with his life was becoming mentally unstable. *Was this the affliction that defeated Adolf Hitler?* he wondered. Both men had made brilliant moves in the early stages, only to destroy their successes by irrational actions later.

Rutland had another piece of disturbing news from his informant on General Abbott's staff. The joint chiefs were aware of the camps and knew about the atomic device that would be used to destroy the camp in Arizona as a test. Now that the military was alerted, he knew they would have to move quickly or risk facing well-armed and disciplined foes within the military. Stopping them wouldn't be like rounding up the Christian "sheep."

Rutland was torn between telling Hussein or dealing with the generals himself. Normally he would have gone directly to the Leader, but he was concerned that an overt act against the military leaders would spark a revolt in the Armed Services. They were nowhere near ready to face that tiger yet. *It is better not to tell the Leader,* he decided. *When the group meets again, we will arrest the traitors.*

He knew he would need evidence, real or contrived, to convince the public. He would call Marla West; her agents would be needed if Gorman and his group were to be rounded up.

His concentration was interrupted by the electronic beep of his private line. "Mr. Rutland, we have a problem with Data-Net," Dr. Loo said as he studied the printout before him.

"What is it?" Rutland growled into the phone.

"I would suggest you come down immediately," Loo responded coolly. "It is critical."

Rutland slammed the door to his office so hard when he left that his receptionist jumped, knocking the telephone off of the desk. She knew he was headed to the basement area and would be gone several minutes at a minimum. She hurried into his vacated office and carefully exchanged his pen set with an identical set containing a sensitive listening device. She tried to be as careful as possible not to leave any sign that she had been there. She was terrified of Rutland, but the information she had received the day before convinced her she had to help the group opposing the administration. Her sister and brother-in-law had been arrested and taken to who knows where, just because they had been hiding the daughter of a friend in their home.

"What is it?" Rutland shouted at Loo, as he stormed into his office.

Loo did not even seem to notice Rutland's manner. "We have a problem," he replied unemotionally. "Look at this." He shoved a large pile of printouts toward Rutland.

Rutland shoved them back angrily. "Just tell me the bottom line! What's wrong?"

Loo shuffled the papers into neat stacks before he answered. "Apparently something in one of the subroutines has been altered. The trains scheduled to pick up the detainees have been re-routed to remote locations around the country."

"What!" Rutland shouted. He knew the effect this information would have on Hussein. "Can you straighten it out?"

"Yes," Loo replied without further comment.

Rutland was now highly agitated. "How long?"

"A day, perhaps; two at the most. But it will take another several days to re-route the trains to their original destinations."

Rutland knew that the temporary detention centers must be overflowing by now. Without the trains they would have to stop the arrests or risk attracting the media's attention. "Do it!" Rutland commanded as he got up to leave. He was beginning to hate the Asian scientist who seemed indifferent to their problems.

Just as Rutland was about to walk out, Dr. Loo said, "You have an even bigger problem, Mr. Rutland."

"What now?" Rutland growled at Loo, who still had his back to him.

"These errors are the result of Mr. Wells' actions."

"What?!?" Rutland snapped, stopping where he was. "That's impossible. Wells is dead. He died in a plane crash."

"He is the only person capable of making changes to the operating system. I can only make minor changes to his system. It is true genius," Loo said admiringly. "I still do not fully understand its interactive nature. It is almost human in its ability to re-program itself."

"You must be wrong!" Rutland argued, his frustrations obvious. "How do you know it's not just a flaw in your program?"

"Because I personally routed another train to one of the original locations. The system then selectively re-routed it to the most remote location possible. No, Mr. Rutland, this is not a system failure; it is a deliberate attempt to slow your detention down."

Rutland felt like his head was going to explode. *How could Wells be alive? It had to be Shepperd! He must have done a double switch if Wells wasn't on that plane they shot down. That stupid Lively!* he thought to himself. *If he weren't dead, I'd have him killed!*

"What can you do to keep Wells out of the system?" he asked the much smaller man. Dr. Loo was not intimidated by Rutland's implied threat.

"Nothing," he answered. "Absolutely nothing. That young man is the Michelangelo of computers. If he wants into the system, he can get in. Apparently he has built-in access codes that allow him to address the compiler directly. I really would like to know how he did it. The system never logs him in or out, and the system clock never shows his use time."

"Can we turn the system off?" Rutland asked in frustration.

"Yes, if you're willing to shut down the U.S. and European economies. We are totally committed to Data-Net for all transactions, including Mr. Wells' unauthorized expenditures."

Rutland stormed out of Loo's office and headed directly to his own office, where he made the call to Hussein. The secretary said he was in a meeting with President Alton. Rutland didn't even bother to buzz the president's office. He just walked over and announced to her secretary that he was going in. The flustered secretary was buzzing the president when Rutland opened the door.

"What is the meaning of this?" Hussein demanded as Rutland entered.

"I'm sorry, sir, but we have serious problems, and I knew you and the president would want to know immediately."

Hussein had never seen Rutland shaken by anything. He knew it must indeed be serious if he would interrupt their meeting. "Speak," he said more softly.

"Wells is still alive. He has entered the system and re-routed all of our trains."

"How is this possible?" Hussein screamed in a voice that was somehow not his own. "You said Wells was killed on the plane."

"Apparently Shepperd tricked our men into believing he was on that plane. Dr. Loo is positive that Wells is using the Data-Net system even now."

"Shut the system down!" Hussein commanded Rutland. "He will wreck our plans."

"If we do that, sir, we will collapse the economies of our friends and make ourselves the laughing stock of the world."

"Of course you are correct," Hussein replied as he glanced at Kathy Alton. She sat quietly as she heard Rutland's comments. What Hussein didn't know was that Kathy Alton was reinforcing her calm with increasing doses of a white powder.

"What is your suggestion?" Hussein asked.

Rutland was somewhat surprised by the question. He was used to making decisions, but not when Hussein was around. Then he followed orders only.

"I believe they are hiding in the Atlanta area," Rutland said emphatically. "That is where the police last saw Elder and Shepperd. We can reasonably assume that Wells is somewhere in that vicinity also. I suggest that we pull several thousand of our best agents into the area and search every house if we have to. We have no idea what Wells has in mind for Data-Net. I suspect he already has found a way to defeat our new ID system."

"Is that possible?" Hussein asked sharply. "I thought Dr. Loo said it was undefeatable." Only Hussein himself knew that the next step in the ID system was the inclusion of another number into the code. This number would be given only to those who swore allegiance to the Great Leader. Eventually all others would be prohibited from the system. Then, and only then, would the system be complete.

"Dr. Loo says Wells is capable of defeating it. Wells programmed in codes that allow him access to the main program from outside."

"Your suggestion is excellent," Hussein said, without visible emotion. "See that it is done."

"I would like to oversee the search myself, if you will allow me."

"Another excellent suggestion. Have the document drawn up, and the president will authorize it."

Kathy Alton acknowledged the "suggestion" by a nod of her head.

COUNTERATTACK

Jeff Wells was hunched over his portable terminal, busily working inside the Data-Net program, establishing lines of credit for the five or six million families that John Elder estimated had been purged from the system. He checked his credit accumulator and found that it had developed a $20-billion surplus already. "Boy, it would be fun to spend that much money," Jeff said teasingly to Karen. "The Congress had to be pretty creative to spend that much every day, huh?"

"A senator from the 1970s once commented, 'A billion here, a billion there, and you're talking about some real money.' Are you sure all these transfers won't be traceable?" she asked as she saw the account files being assembled.

"Positive," he said, grinning. "My program is kind of like an Indian who walks backwards and brushes away his tracks behind him."

"Just be sure you don't bump into a bear while you're walking backwards," she said as she hugged him.

"Hello. What's this?" Jeff said as his screen flashed.

"What *is* that?" Karen asked, as she too noticed the flashing symbol.

"I put in a special feature a couple of days ago. I wanted to keep track of our friends at the White House, so I flagged their accounts to flash whenever they were used. President Alton's account was just opened."

"There's nothing unusual about that," Karen commented as Jeff punched the keys. "She probably has to pay bills like everyone else."

"Except that her account was accessed from Cal Rutland's terminal," he said as the file began to print out. "He has been authorized to use a Defense Department jet tomorrow. Let's see where he's heading." Wells punched up the access code for Andrews Air Force Base and checked the flight plan schedule. "Here it is. The flight plan is from Washington to Atlanta."

Karen looked puzzled. "Rutland is coming to Atlanta? I wonder why?"

"I don't know," Jeff responded. "But we'd better let Shepperd know."

Karen went out to find the agent who was working with Elder, planning trips to other cities. "Don, you'd better come and take a look. Jeff has found something peculiar."

Wells quickly filled the agent in on what he had found. "Could be a normal business trip," Shepperd said, "but of course I don't believe it for a minute. If Rutland, Hussein's main man, is leaving Washington, it's serious business. And since we're near Atlanta, I suspect we're part of it. Can you dig up anything else, Jeff?"

"I'll try," Jeff responded, calling up the other White House access codes. "Look at this!" Wells shouted as the file appeared.

"What is all that?" Shepperd asked as the file filled the screen and scrolled past.

"These are all transactions made through the attorney general's account today. They're airline reservations, from all over the country."

"Check the destinations," Shepperd said hurriedly. The hair was tingling on the back of his neck. Something was definitely up.

Jeff instructed the program to verify destinations of the tickets purchased. The first twenty to fill the screen told the whole story: Atlanta, Georgia.

"They're bringing in agents from around the country," Shepperd warned. "They're going to do a house-to-house search for us! Eventually they'll pick up our trail. We need to warn the others and then clear out—fast!"

"Just a minute," Jeff said calmly. "We've been on the run since the beginning. If we move, I may have a problem finding another mechanical phone relay system."

"The next closest one is in Mississippi," Shepperd said.

"And what about the risk of moving all of our people and supplies so quickly?" Elder asked as he walked into the room from the porch, where he had been listening.

"What choice do we have?" Shepperd growled. "These are professionals. They will eventually locate this place."

"Why don't we scatter the troops?" Jeff said with a smirk on his face.

"What are you up to now?" Karen asked Jeff, who was grinning like a Cheshire cat.

"One thing about a totally cash-less system," Jeff said as he typed in more instructions, "is that it can work for either side. And we're on the controlling side now." He continued to type for several minutes before he halted.

"I have just canceled all their reservations," he said triumphantly. "I also invalidated all the codes in the attorney general's office. Basically the government is locked out of Data-Net."

"For how long?" Shepperd asked.

"It will probably take Dr. Loo and his team a day or two to figure out how to overcome the problem. I also instructed the system to override all flights to Atlanta. As of tomorrow at 4:00 A.M. the city of Atlanta has been removed from all flight reservations computers around the country. Oh yes, also at 6:00 A.M. the main computer at the Atlanta airport will shut down, wiping all of its memory banks when it does. The airport will be closed for a couple of days."

"I'm glad you're on our side now," Shepperd said with a whistle.

"I always was," Jeff said, smiling. "I just didn't know which side was which for a while."

Jeff Wells knew that he had a lot more in common with the people he was now helping than he did with any others he had been around. John Elder reminded him of his own father, who had always professed to being a Christian. In Jeff's mind, it was a settled issue. Just as he had decided that fraternities were not for him, he decided that Christianity was.

"That will give us at least two days to relocate," Shepperd explained to the group. "I suggest we start packing. We'll move out two vehicles at a time, starting tomorrow morning. We'll relocate to the base in Mississippi. Jeff, you and Karen will go in one van. John, you and four of the others will go in another. We'll have clean vehicles ready along the way, if necessary."

"I just wish I could see the look on those agents' faces when they try to fly out tomorrow," Jeff said, snorting. "And all those flights that were re-routed to accommodate them will be in limbo when the ticket agents discover that Atlanta is no longer on their computers."

The whole group laughed as they envisioned the chaos that would greet the government agents the next morning.

"We need to get word to our people in Atlanta to move out as quickly as possible too," Elder said to Shepperd. "They will bear the brunt for us otherwise."

"Already in progress, Pastor," Jeff commented. "I instructed the central AT&T office in Chicago to call all of our safe houses and leave the coded message we agreed on."

"Obviously the system will then wipe its feet as it leaves. Right?" Shepperd asked.

"Right," Jeff responded as he smiled at Karen. "And they will be toll-free calls, courtesy of Data-Net."

"Jeff, can you change the records of anyone using the system?" Shepperd asked as he sat down in the chair next to Wells.

"Sure," Jeff said. "You name it and I can do it while I'm inside the compiler."

"Can you give all the users a deficit balance in their accounts?"

"Sure," he said. Suddenly he caught on to Shepperd's idea. "I can even have the government garnish their wages for the deficiencies and attach their properties."

"Do it!" Shepperd exclaimed. "I think it's time we began taking the battle to the enemy. By the time we get set up in Mississippi the average American ought to be pretty fed up with the new system."

The next day was a tangle of confusion throughout the entire country. The FBI agents who arrived at the airports expecting to pick up their tickets to Atlanta discovered that, not only did they not have tickets, there were no scheduled flights to Atlanta—ever!

One of the agents was Carl Tooms, now little more than a prison guard since being banished to Arizona. When he had been sent to that God-forsaken part of the world, he had thought he would be in charge. Instead, he was now working for a woman from the attorney general's office.

It wouldn't be so bad if I was in charge, he thought. *There are some good-lookin' women in the camp*. But he and the other men were under orders to leave them alone now. Other screwy orders had started coming in: The prisoners were to get more food; families were to be allowed to live together; and worst of all, they were strictly off limits to all government personnel. *We might as well be running a Sunday school*, Tooms thought disgustedly.

In the beginning, camp policy had been Tooms' cup of tea. If one of the prisoners got himself killed, the guards just hauled him out in the middle of the night and buried him quietly. It had a great effect on the others; they lived in fear of the camp guards. But now, even some of the guards were protecting the prisoners. "It makes me sick," Tooms had said at least a hundred times to anyone who would listen.

Eventually he had come to blame all his problems on Donald Shepperd. *If Shepperd hadn't raised such a stink about that broad in Chicago, I wouldn't be here*, he thought angrily. He had even heard rumors that Shepperd had turned traitor and was now working with the terrorists. When the call came in for agents to go to Atlanta, Tooms had volunteered. This would be his one chance to redeem himself and also pay Shepperd back. Maybe he could even get his own camp. The very thought of being in control of a camp excited him.

The next day he was up early; he wanted to be one of the first to Atlanta. He had heard that Rutland might even be coming to Atlanta. *The others might fear him*, Tooms thought, *but he sounds like my kind of guy*. Tooms parked his car in the airport parking lot and made his way toward the terminal building. He checked his bags at the curb after saying a few select words to the sky cap, who tried to insist there were no flights to Atlanta. "You just put them on that conveyer," Tooms shouted at the older man, "and mark them 'Atlanta.'"

"Let him try to find his own bags then," the sky cap muttered under his breath as Tooms stormed away swearing.

"What do you mean you don't have my reservation?" Tooms snarled at the ticket agent in the Tucson Airport. "I'm a government official. I have to get to Atlanta today."

"I'm sorry, sir, but our records don't show your reservations."

Swearing loudly, Tooms said, "Then get me on the next available flight to Atlanta."

"I'm sorry," the frustrated ticket agent said, "but we don't have any flights to Atlanta."

"What do you mean, you don't have any flights to Atlanta? You mean they're all booked?"

"No, sir," the frustrated agent replied. "Atlanta does not show on our destination schedule."

"What?" Tooms shouted, his red face revealing his highly elevated blood pressure. "Atlanta doesn't show on your schedule? Atlanta is the hub of the entire East Coast. Thousands of flights go through there every day."

"I am sorry, sir," she said more forcefully. "I can only tell you what the computer tells me. There are no flights into Atlanta today. If you will leave your number, we'll have someone call you when flights are resumed."

Tooms offered a few more four-letter words and then headed off to find a phone to call the Atlanta director and apprise him of the situation. When he found the phones, there were lines waiting to use them. With no flights into Atlanta, he knew there had to be thousands of stranded passengers. He shoved his way to the front and flashed his credentials at a very frustrated woman who was trying to call her company in New York.

"I need to use that phone," he commanded as the man in front of her hung up.

"You and a hundred other people," she said angrily. "Just wait your turn."

"Listen, lady. This is government business. Step aside." With that he shoved her aside roughly.

Still fuming, she responded, "If you're with the government, then you're part of the problem. Idiot!"

Data-Net ID scanners had been installed at the entrance to every phone station. Verification of proper ID was required before any transaction could be completed, including long distance calls. Tooms ran his hand past the magnetic scanner before he placed his special government access card in the scanner's card reader. As soon as the ID card was scanned, the alarm sounded. He and all the others standing there were startled by the sound.

"Somebody grab him," the angry woman screamed. "He's a terrorist or something."

With that, several men pressed forward. Tooms reached inside his jacket for his gun and then realized he didn't have it. Even government agents were prohibited from carrying firearms aboard planes. He had packed it in the suitcase he had checked earlier.

The crowd seized him and held him down until a security guard, who had seen the commotion and heard the alarm, took him away in handcuffs. Tooms was shouting a broad variety of obscenities as he was shoved into the airport security van.

This scene, in differing degrees, was being replayed all across the country as agents attempting to reach their contacts in Atlanta triggered Data-Net alarms in the airports. Eventually a few did get through to the Justice Department Enforcement Agency in Atlanta by using their own ID, rather than the special card issued by the Justice Department.

In Atlanta, Cal Rutland was just landing aboard the Defense Department's small jet plane at Dobbins Air Force Base. The pilot taxied the plane around to the private runway and braked to a stop. As Rutland exited the plane, he saw an ashen Paul Crimmins, head of the Justice Department Enforcement Agency in Atlanta, approaching. From the look on the man's face, he knew something was wrong.

"What is it?" Rutland asked, his eyes narrowed so much he looked for all the world like a snake about to strike.

"None of our agents have made it to Atlanta, sir," the shaken agent said hesitantly. He had heard rumors of Rutland's power and his ruthlessness, and he had no desire to find out if all the rumors were fact.

"What do you mean, no agents have made it? Why?" Rutland roared in total fury.

"We're not sure, sir," Crimmins replied cautiously. "Somehow there has been a foul-up in the Data-Net system, and no flights can be booked into Atlanta. A few hours ago the Atlanta airport was shut down indefinitely because of a total computer failure. We don't know when the system will be operational again."

"Wells!" Rutland spat out. "He's using the system against us. Get your men to rent cars and drive to Atlanta," he commanded the trembling agent. "Do it now; they know we are after them!"

Crimmins paused a few seconds, trying to find a way to tell Rutland the rest. "We have another problem, sir."

"What?" Rutland asked as he squared off in front of the agent. He was so furious Crimmins thought he was going to strike him.

"The agents who tried to use their Justice Department billing codes have been arrested. Somehow the system identified them as terrorists. We're having very little success in getting them released so far."

"Wells!" Rutland swore as they headed into the hangar. He knew the group they sought would be long gone by the time they could clear up the mess with Data-Net. The whole exercise was a washout. Hussein would be furious.

"Have them refuel the plane!" Rutland ordered the agent. "I'll be returning to Washington immediately."

"What about our agents, sir?"

"I'll have the system straightened out in a couple of days," Rutland snarled. "Have them resume their duties where they are."

Within three days, the entire team from Atlanta began reassembling in Dentville, Mississippi, on a farm owned by a family member of one of the team. The security team had been briefed and all the necessary auxiliary power was in place.

"How did it go?" Shepperd asked as the semi-truck rolled to a stop in front of the enormous old cotton barn.

"We had a few anxious moments along the way at some roadblocks," Elder said, "but your documents were perfect. Where are Jeff and the others?"

"They're already inside setting up. We tweaked the dragon's nose a little the last few days. Now we need to get down to some serious planning."

As the group assembled, there was a definite air of optimism. For months they had seen the enemy as infallible, but now they realized the Society could be bested. And without violence. Shepperd had struggled with that issue for weeks; then John Elder had laid it to rest once and for all.

"The Lord said, 'Pray for your enemies, and do good to them. For in doing so you will heap burning coals on their heads.' That must be our position," Elder told Shepperd after a heated debate over using guerrilla tactics. "Neither I nor any member of the CRC will be a party to murder, no matter what the justification," Elder said. "This battle is not just against human greed. It is a struggle against powers and principalities. Literally, it is the timeless struggle by Satan and his forces against God and His forces. We will not win by armed conflict; not this battle."

"Do you have any objection to using confusion and frustration to keep them off guard then, Pastor?" Shepperd asked.

"None at all," Elder responded cheerfully. "We'll turn their neat little world upside-down."

Plans were made for Elder to meet with key CRC leaders around the country and prepare for the underground newspaper to begin publication. It was agreed that the paper, to be called "Truth," would be published weekly in at least six areas. Facts about the Society would be presented that could easily be verified by most Americans. Initially no mention of the plot against the Christians and Jews would be broached.

"If we can undermine the credibility of the leadership and pierce the veil of secrecy, the organization will fall," Elder said time and time again.

"The most important weapon we have is prayer," Elder told his second group of leaders. "You must organize your people into prayer groups that will maintain a twenty-four-hour-a-day vigil. We would like to think that our plans and ideas will win this battle; they will not! Until God's people pray without ceasing, the enemy will have the upper hand."

Throughout America the Christians, the Jews, and those who aided them began to organize into help and prayer groups. Within three weeks, nearly one hundred thousand Christians were on their knees in prayer at all times of the day, every day. Elder could feel the power of God's people growing stronger every day. So could Hussein.

"It is happening!" Hussein screamed at Rutland. "He is organizing them against us even now!"

"Wells?" Rutland asked, confused. Since the fiasco in Atlanta, Rutland realized he must be careful about using Data-Net. It was as if Wells could read his mail.

When he first realized that Wells had access to the White House computers, he had almost panicked. *Hunt's letter!* He had searched his personal files to see if any trace of his treachery remained. As soon as he confirmed that he had wiped out all traces of the transfers, he felt relief, but then he went a step further. He wiped out all records and memos sent to any member of the Society. He was certain there was no traceable link back to him.

"No, not Wells, you fool!" Hussein said angrily. He had become increasingly abusive since the Atlanta fiasco; he even began to doubt Rutland's loyalty.

"Elder is organizing the Christians against us. If we don't stop them, they will undermine all our plans," he railed. Hussein could feel his inner strength waning. Instead of drawing from the power inside, he was sensing pangs of fear—no, terror. The very emotions he had used to control those around him were now beginning to control him.

"But the Christians are still in hiding," Rutland explained calmly. "The police have orders to arrest them on sight, and our searches ferret out several hundred a day. We have nearly two million in the camps now."

"Fool!" Hussein screamed. "They are giving themselves up so they can organize the camps!"

Hussein was right. One of Elder's plans called for many of the lower-echelon leaders to allow themselves to be caught and sent to the camps, where they organized the people into help and prayer groups. Only the women and children were spared the rigors of internment. Tens of thousands of Christians volunteered to be arrested even though the brutality continued in camps run by men like Tooms. Christians were beaten and abused by the guards; many gave up their lives, but still the volunteers came.

The networks were forbidden to publish any of the most recent Insta-pol surveys. Support for the administration had dropped to less than 20 percent. Support for Data-Net had dropped to nearly zero. Most Americans never knew from day to day if they could buy what they needed or not. Those who had their properties attached by the government for account delinquencies, or their wages garnished, were fit to be tied. The merchants who used Data-Net sometimes feared for their lives when the system rejected a customer, which it often did.

Wells continued the harassment by disrupting the system periodically. For periods of up to four hours during peak usage the system would shut down totally. At other times the system alarms would go off for no apparent reason. Frequently the computers would signal the printers to spool paper, leaving a tangled mess at every Data-Net station.

The administration could not blame the errors on their source—Wells—for fear of undermining confidence in the integrity of the system itself. Now Wells and Shepperd were toying with a new idea: use Data-Net to strip the government of its operating capital. The cash flow from Data-Net's fees and government drug sales were rapidly making it possible for the government to resume normal operations, including more handouts to the public.

"If the average American begins getting his daily fix of government money, he will be back in Hussein's camp," Shepperd said.

Donald Shepperd had found a new purpose in life. When he had first discovered the plot against Christians, he had gotten involved out of a strong sense of justice. But now that he had lived and eaten with them for several months he had new feelings: He really loved them. It was the first time he could remember having any strong ties since his wife had died, nearly twelve years previously.

Shepperd observed John Elder closely and found him to be a man of unquestionable integrity, but he had something that went beyond just integrity: He had peace in the midst of chaos. Shepperd had commented to Elder several times that he wished he had that kind of assurance, but he couldn't piece it together in his mind. Elder had told him it was God calling him, but he couldn't accept that either. He had done too many wrong things in his life to believe that God, if there really was a God, would want him on His team. *No, God is just a fuzzy warm feeling that happens when you're around good people like these*, he told himself. One of the things he particularly liked about John Elder was that he didn't push his religion on anyone. He would defend his convictions without compromise and he and Shepperd had some heated debates over basic issues like abortion and crack babies. Once the debates were over, though, Elder always treated him as a trusted friend and ally. More and more Shepperd found himself agreeing, rather than disagreeing, with Elder.

"Jeff, I need you to schedule more food and supplies for the camps," Shepperd said. *It is unbelievable what Wells can do with a computer*, Shepperd marveled to himself. He could re-route trains, transfer supplies, even shift credits at will. *That must be driving the powers in Washington nuts*, he mused. *They can't keep him out, and they can't shut the system down.*

"Already done," Jeff said cheerfully as he put the final touches on a new set of instructions. "I also cut orders to assign some of the pastor's people to guard duty at the camps."

"How in the world did you do that?" Shepperd asked in amazement again.

"Oh, it was sim . . ." Jeff stopped, thinking of Karen's comment. Then he added, "I found the file where the guards are assigned and rotated. So I substituted the numbers of some of the pastor's people for other guards. Then I transferred the old guards to some remote cities. I couldn't do too many without arousing suspicion, but I could get twenty in this rotation. I'll do a few each time."

"What if they get caught?" Shepperd asked. He knew what their fate would be: execution.

"It's almost impossible," Jeff answered. "The assignments are made by random selection from the pool of camp guards. Then they are kept away from any population centers to ensure they don't divulge what they're doing. No one person knows who they are. Not since Fred Lively died.

"I have also begun the transfer of assets from the government's accounts," Wells said enthusiastically. "It won't be but a few weeks at most and the administration is going to start bouncing some checks."

"What did you do with the credits?" Shepperd asked as he slapped Wells on the shoulder affectionately.

"Oh, I put a 'little here' and a 'little there,'" Jeff quipped. Then he looked over at Karen, who raised her eyebrow slightly.

"He sent $100 billion to Israel," she said. "They need it to rebuild."

"And I transferred $400 billion to California to use in caring for the people displaced by the quake.

"I plan to send $100 billion or so to the Coast Guard to use in shutting down the drug traffic, if we can get the new drug bill killed," Jeff said.

"That will be a while yet," Elder commented as he entered the room.

"John, you're back," Shepperd said cheerfully to the man who had become a very good friend.

"Yes, I met with the CRC leaders in Georgia, Alabama, and Tennessee. We've just released our first edition of the "Truth" newspaper. Jeff, your program worked perfectly. The transmission through Westar Six fed the data to our printing facilities in six areas simultaneously."

"You used a satellite to transmit an underground newspaper?" Shepperd asked incredulously.

"Yeah, it was a lot easier than carrying them across the country. Now we can call it the 'overhead' newspaper, I guess," Jeff quipped.

The whole group groaned at his bad pun.

"What if it's traced?" Shepperd, the eternal pessimist, asked.

"Jeff used one of the military channels on the Westar satellite and put it through a scrambler," Elder said.

"A scrambler! Where did our groups get scramblers?"

"Procured them through the Government Accounting Office," Wells said, grinning.

"I shouldn't have asked," Shepperd said with a fake groan. "Are you sure you weren't a crook before we met?"

In Washington, Wells' access to Data-Net was causing chaos at every level. Rutland knew they needed some successes or more of the bureaucrats would change sides. He decided that in spite of the risks they would have to move on the military. With the might of the military under their control, the fence riders would fall in line quickly.

Several weeks earlier when General Gorman had met with his most trusted peers, they had scheduled another meeting, at which time the other general officers were to bring a list of the staff they knew to be loyal.

Armed with this information, Rutland had alerted Marla West to ready her agents. "This is our opportunity to purge the military. That list is invaluable. Have the room monitored, and prepare our senior military people to take command. We will make Gorman and his conspirators appear to be traitors who are attempting a coup of the government."

The secretary listening to the device hidden in Rutland's office immediately notified her contact, who quickly passed the word to the next contact, and ultimately to Shepperd. When Shepperd heard the details, he knew it would be their best chance to make contact with the loyal element of the military. He had to risk it.

Wells tapped into the Pentagon's phone trunk. He placed a call to General Gorman's private hot line.

General Gorman was startled when the phone rang. His hot line was reserved for "situations" only. "Yes!" he said sharply into the mouthpiece, assuming it would be a junior officer. "What is the problem?"

"General Gorman, this is a friend. Go to scrambler two, please."

"Who is this?" Gorman shouted. But Shepperd had already switched on the scrambler Jeff had appropriated earlier. He didn't want to take a chance that Gorman's phone was bugged. Even though he knew the room was "swept clean" every day, passive "bugs" could go undetected, as their own surveillance proved.

Gorman switched his scrambler to code two. No one but the other joint chiefs had that particular code, but he knew it wasn't one of them. "This is General Gorman. Who am I speaking with?" he asked coarsely in his best commander's voice.

"You don't know me, General, but I know of you. My name is Donald Shepperd. I am an FBI agent, or rather I was until the takeover of our government by Hussein and his Society."

"Hussein? Amir Hussein, the president's emissary to the Middle East?" Gorman asked. Suddenly it clicked in his mind. *Of course, that explained the use of nuclear weapons against Israel without Admiral Benton's knowledge.*

"The very same," Shepperd said. "He knows about your recent meeting with members of the general staff. You and the others are in grave danger."

"I don't know what you're talking about," Gorman snapped, suddenly very wary.

"You had a spy in your group, General. I wish I could tell you more, but we don't know who it is at this time. General, we're the ones who sent your aide the information on the camps. Most of it came from the Mossad. A few of their people are working with us."

"I understand," the general said as he relaxed. "Thank you, Mr. Shepperd. I'll handle it from this point."

"General, is there anything you can do?"

"I'll have to deal with first things first," Gorman said. "First we'll deal with the infiltrators. How can I get in contact with you?"

"You can't, General. But just leave a note in your Pentagon message box addressed to me. We read your computer mail regularly."

"But how can you. . . ." The line had gone dead.

General Gorman called in his aide, Major Brian Philmore. "I want you to hand-carry some messages," he told Philmore, the son of a long-time colleague from the academy.

The message read: "Most urgent we meet immediately. Same place, Wednesday, 0700."

"Be sure you hand-carry this to General Abbott. No one else is to see it."

"Yes, sir," the youthful-looking major said. "I'll do it."

That next Wednesday morning the conspirators met to discuss the information that Shepperd had provided.

General Gorman began, "Gentlemen, I don't have to tell you that our nation faces a grave danger from within our government. This Society is a cancer that has taken root in the very heart of the present administration. It has been nearly a year since the Congress was last convened, and there appears to be no move to re-establish a constitutional republic. I believe we have no alternative but to use our combined military power to force the Alton administration to reconvene the Congress and expose this plot to destroy democracy. Do you have your lists of field-grade officers that we know to be loyal to our cause?"

General Abbott spoke up, "We do, General. And we have already established the initial steps to secure the government."

Marla West had moved her team into position several hours before the meeting was scheduled to begin. The room was monitored with the latest sound-powered micro-detectors that were virtually undetectable. The receivers were set up in one of the rooms nearby. Two eight-track laser recorders would pick up every sound.

The agent in charge of the equipment listened intently as the general spoke. After nearly ten minutes he turned to Marla West and asked, "Do you have enough?"

"Yes," she said ecstatically. "With a little selective editing, this tape should make the evening news and get several generals shot.

"Be sure you get that list," she warned the agents preparing to assault the room. "With it we can purge the traitors from the military."

As quietly as possible, the ten agents moved down the hallway; they were so intent on their mission no one seemed to notice that there was no guard at the door. The inexperienced Marla West noticed it but simply thought to herself, *Stupid, over-confident fools!* Seconds later, the agents burst into the room where the meeting was taking place.

"You're all under arrest!" the first agent shouted as he leveled his automatic weapon at the officers.

"What is the charge?" General Gorman asked calmly, still seated. He had spent three years in a prison camp in Iraq during the Middle East war. He was not a man to spook easily.

"Treason!" the agent shouted again. "Now stand up and put your hands on your heads!"

The commanders and their adjutants stood obediently as the agents checked them for weapons.

"They're clean," the agent said into the small transmitter he was holding.

At that moment, Marla West stormed into the room. Sarcastically she said, "It looks like you and your good ole boys have stepped in it, doesn't it, General?"

"Perhaps," Gorman replied. "But you don't honestly expect to get away with arresting the commanding officers of the Army, Navy, and the Air Force do you?"

"Absolutely, General," West said laughingly. "With a little editing of our tapes of this meeting, you'll make headlines until the day you're all shot. And we'll have that list of your conspirators." She turned to Major Brian Philmore, motioned for him to take the sheets from General Gorman, and said, "If you don't mind, Major, you can hand that list to me now."

"Brian! You're a part of this madness, too?" the general said disgustedly. "You're a disgrace to that uniform and to your country."

"He's on the right side, General," West said mockingly. "You are a traitor!"

"It's you and your Society that are the traitors," Gorman said bitterly. "You don't really expect the American public to swallow your line, do you?"

Marla smiled as she looked down at the lists in her hand. "They will believe what the media tell them. And the media will believe what we feed them. They're bigger idiots than you are, General."

Looking at the sheets of paper Philmore had taken from Gorman, Marla frowned and then snarled at the general, "What is this?"

"Just what it says," Gorman answered, smiling. "You might want to read it for the benefit of your commandos here."

The big agent who had led the raid snatched the papers out of West's hands. "What the . . . ??" he exclaimed.

"Surprise!" the general responded as he quoted what he had written on the sheets surrendered to Philmore. "Smile, you're on Candid Camera."

With that, several Army assault troops stepped through the door brandishing automatic weapons. The sergeant leading them leveled his assault rifle and said, "If just one of you twitches a muscle, my men will cut you in half!"

"He really means it too," the general said casually. "You see, he has a sister locked up in one of your camps."

The secret service agents carefully laid their weapons down. They were woefully out-manned and out-gunned, and they knew it.

"You won't get away with this," Marla West screamed as she was handcuffed. "I'm the attorney general."

"Yes, and I'm the commanding general, so I outrank you," Gorman said with a big grin across his face. "Sergeant, I would rather appreciate it if you could keep these people out of sight for awhile. At least until we clean some of their friends out of our business."

"It would be my pleasure, General. You just say the word and they will be permanently out of circulation."

By the look on the angry sergeant's face, none of the secret service had any doubt that he was serious—deadly serious.

"I hope that won't be necessary, Sergeant. Not if our friends don't give you any trouble."

Marla was still screaming obscenities as they hauled the group away. Gorman saw the medic accompanying the soldiers inject her with a powerful sedative. She slumped over almost immediately.

ESCAPE

Rutland was afraid for the first time in his life. He had always assumed the Society would win, and he would be a part of it. Now it seemed that every plan they made went wrong. He had no idea what had happened to Marla West and the men who went to arrest Gorman. They had simply disappeared. Not even the FBI could get a lead on where they were being held. All he knew was that Gorman and the others were still free and constantly surrounded by elite combat troops. Even worse, one by one the top-level military officers committed to the Society were disappearing. The others would panic very soon if the Society couldn't come up with a solution.

Hussein was mad with rage.

"I am surrounded by incompetents," he screamed at Rutland and President Alton. "Everything will be lost if we lose control of the military. You must order the FBI to arrest General Gorman. With him gone, the others will collapse."

"That is not possible," Kathy Alton explained for the third time. She was frightened too, but she knew that Hussein was irrational in his demands. She simply could not command control of the Armed Forces. They would follow their leaders' commands, not hers. They had made that very clear.

"If we press the issue, the Army will revolt against us," she said calmly. "At least now we don't have them against us."

"We have the bombs!" Hussein ranted. "Are the bombs in place yet?"

"No, sir," Rutland said as he looked at Alton. "Only one is. We were going to test its effect before installing the others."

"Put them in!" Hussein shouted. "We will use them to force the Army to serve us. If they refuse, we will annihilate the camps." Hussein could feel the momentum shifting away from him. It was as if the dark lord had already accepted failure. *No!* a voice from inside him shrieked. *We cannot fail! The prince of darkness will torment us both forever, just as he has the others who have failed.*

Hussein knew that he was going insane. The voices that had guided him so clearly in the past now filled his mind with unbearable sounds. The fear they released inside him made him frantic. He could not fail! He must not! The abyss awaited those who failed.

"We can't annihilate the camps . . . ," President Alton started to say.

"You can, and you will!" Hussein screamed at her. "If you don't you will die too. Move the bombs to the camps immediately. The Christians will die and everything will be back as it was."

The next morning as he tried to get out of bed, Jason Franklin felt his weakness return. Franklin never slept late, but this morning he rose earlier than normal. He had a pain in his stomach that would not subside. As the morning passed, the pain grew more intense. He panicked when he realized what it was—the cancer again! Even as he thought about it the pain grew worse. He reached for the phone to call Hussein.

"Yes, who is it?" Hussein screamed into the phone that rang in his study. He hadn't slept for more than three days now; he feared closing his eyes. Each time he did the demons closed in on him, taunting him.

"You will burn in Hell," the demons cried out to him. "You thought the master would save you, but he will find another. You will burn!"

"No! Help me, Master," Hussein shouted as he blinked his eyes open when the phone rang.

"It is Mr. Franklin, sir," the guard who kept constant watch over his room said fearfully. "He says he needs to talk with you."

"Tell him no!" Hussein screamed. "I cannot help him. I will not help him!" With that, Hussein slammed the phone down. His piercing black eyes were sunk back in their sockets. They swept from side to side in a constant search for something, anything that would help relieve the madness that welled up inside. The guard heard him scream as he pressed his hands to his eyes. He was ranting, "Help me, Master. Please!"

Jason Franklin could hear Hussein's wailing over the phone even through the door to the guard's room. He hardly heard the guard say, "I'm sorry, Mr. Franklin. The Leader is unable to talk with you right now."

As Franklin dropped the phone to the floor, the pain was so intense that he gasped. He collapsed on the bed, where he sat for several minutes, trying to get some strength back. Then he reached into the side table drawer beside his bed and took out the small automatic he always kept close by. He ratcheted a cartridge into the chamber and pressed the gun to his temple.

The housekeeper would find him when she arrived later that morning. Jason Franklin realized the eternal error he had made long before that. As he passed through the long dark corridor that met him the instant after he pulled the trigger, the demons were swirling around him. "Another one for us," they screeched as they raked him with their claws.

Franklin screamed as the pain hit him. *But I'm dead*, he thought. *You can't feel anything when you're dead.*

He screamed again as the next demon raced by, ripping open his imagined flesh. "The pain," Franklin moaned. "It's worse than before."

At the new CRC headquarters in Dentville, Mississippi, the plans to launch a propaganda assault on the Society were going well. The third issue of "Truth" newspaper was in circulation and the Data-Net system was in chaos.

Jeff Wells was pleased with himself. The transfer of credits from the government had virtually stopped President Alton's ability to fund the anti-Christian campaign. Many of the government agents in the field had their credit cut off and had not been paid for several weeks. They were experiencing firsthand what the Christians had experienced earlier: It is very hard to live in a cash-less society without credit. Most had already taken to robbing merchants at gun point to get needed supplies. As a result, the police were treating the agents like criminals, too.

The underground network for Christians, which John Elder had organized, was working so well that it was virtually impossible to locate them. When the police attempted to dispatch teams to suspected safe houses, the messages were intercepted and warnings sent to the CRC members. All the police found when they arrived were copies of the underground "Truth" newspaper.

The police departments that were particularly aggressive in pursuing Christians suddenly found their credit cut off—personally and corporately. Wells had even been able to scramble the phone lines between Washington and the rest of the country so that messages often had to be sent by couriers, who were sometimes stranded in distant parts of the country without credit. As more of the "Truth" newspapers made their way into the public's hands, the anti-Society movement picked up momentum. Often, reluctant police officers simply refused to arrest the Christians they were able to find.

Jeff was putting the finishing touches on a new program to cut off funds to the abortion centers and organ banks when suddenly Shepperd rushed into the room. "Jeff, we have an emergency!" he said. "General Gorman has learned that Hussein ordered bombs installed at the other camps. He's planning to use them to blackmail the generals. He may be crazy enough to use them. We'll need to launch Project Truth as soon as possible. Are you ready?"

"I will be in a few more days," Wells said.

Shepperd had conceived a plan to make public all the information his men had assembled on the Society.

When the first underground newspaper had been published with facts about the Society and its roots in the government, the media had tried to discredit it, but as more and more information became available, several major newspapers began to pick up the articles. Try as they might, Rutland and his secret service could not locate even one of the twenty presses now printing nearly fifty million copies of the "Truth" newspaper each week. Since financing was no problem, thanks to Wells' Data-Net contacts, the paper was available nearly everywhere. Shepperd's plan required the support of a major television network. At this point, however, he didn't have one.

At Data-Net headquarters Dr. Loo was pondering what to do about Jeff Wells. Loo was a man without any real allegiance to the Society. He delighted in infuriating Cal Rutland when he reported Wells' interference in the system. To Kim Loo, the matching of wits with Jeff Wells was no more than a chess game.

I really wish I could have worked with Wells, Loo thought to himself. *He is a genius when it comes to computers.*

Loo had been trying unsuccessfully to set traps to detect how and when Wells entered the main computer. To date, his efforts had yielded him absolutely nothing. It was as if Wells was a phantom. The system logged no use of his time. It showed no use of the telephone network. And even when Loo knew that Wells was active in the compiler, the system showed no trace of his access.

There is no sense in getting frustrated about this, Loo told himself. *Wells is simply better than I am at what he does. He has designed a system that I thought was impossible with our present technology, and now he has created a computer program that leaves no sign that it even exists—brilliant. Together we could tap into any computer system in the world. With very little effort we could become the richest men in the world!*

For the last several weeks, catching Wells had become an obsession to Dr. Loo. But he was no closer than when he started. *It is like a two-year-old child playing chess with a grand master,* Loo admitted to himself. *Wells' capabilities are so far beyond my own that he thinks in another dimension. I will never trap him.*

Suddenly Loo had another thought. *What about Dr. Eison? Would Wells be careless enough to allow his girlfriend's father to have access to the system? Yes, he probably would,* he thought as he suddenly got excited, *because Wells' single weakness is caring about others around him. He is sentimental; therefore he is vulnerable.*

Loo thought about calling Rutland, but then he decided against it. Rutland was far too emotional about Wells. He might want to take over the plan that Loo had in mind, and Loo wasn't about to allow that to happen. Once he had a solid lead on Wells' whereabouts he would negotiate a 'reasonable' fee with Rutland for the information.

Immediately Dr. Loo contacted his long-time friend in the drug business, Ku Chow Li.

"Li, this is Kim Loo," he said as the other man answered the phone call. "I need your help."

"I assume this is something other than a social call, Dr. Loo," the head of the Chinese drug traffic in San Francisco replied coolly. "Things have not been going well for me since your cash-less system went into operation."

"I understand," Loo said amiably. "Even I have been reduced to working for the government. But I can assure you this will be very profitable to both of us. Do you have something to write with?"

"Yes, go on," the other man said as he shifted his position so that he could write on the tablet by his desk.

"I need a tap placed on Dr. William Eison's telephone."

"Who is this Dr. Eison?" Li asked.

"He is a scientist at the Livermore laboratory."

"It will be very difficult to tap a line at the research facility," Li said, stating what he knew was the obvious.

"You will be well compensated when I get the information I seek," Loo said. "I need a record of all Dr. Eison's calls to a particular number somewhere in the south—a number he will call very seldom, so there must be no mistakes."

"Old friend," Li said smoothly, "you know I don't make mistakes. In my business you rarely get more than one. I will arrange what you ask. You will hear from me again when I have the information."

As Loo hung up the phone, he was feeling more positive than he had in weeks. He knew that Dr. Eison had to be the one who warned Wells. Although he had no proof, he needed none. It would have taken a computer expert to understand Wells' logic enough to get into the system. Loo knew that Dr. Eison had that ability. He had seen more than once that Eison was his own equal; few others were even close enough to consider.

In another room in the basement of the White House, the FBI agent monitoring Dr. Loo's phone lines called Cal Rutland's office.

Rutland's secretary buzzed him to say that agent Grimes was on the phone. "Rutland here," he said, irritated by the interruption. "What do you want?"

"Mr. Rutland, I'm on duty, monitoring the White House lines. I was instructed to call you immediately if anything unusual happened."

Suddenly Rutland was alert. "Yes, what is it?" he said more pleasantly.

"Dr. Loo just placed a call to San Francisco where he talked with a Ku Chow Li. He made arrangements for a Dr. Eison's telephone to be tapped at a government laboratory. I thought you would want to know."

"Yes, thank you." Rutland beamed as he hung up. *Loo's on to something*, he thought to himself. He called the FBI headquarters. When the receptionist answered he said, "Put me through to Randall."

Without hesitation she punched the FBI director's private intercom line. She knew better than to tell Rutland that he was in conference. Her boss might run the bureau, but it was clear that Rutland ran him.

"I want you to put two of your best agents on someone by the name of Li in San Francisco. I believe his first name is Ku. I have the telephone number; you can get his address from the files."

"Do you mean Ku Chow Li?" Randall asked.

"I don't know who he is," Rutland said, showing his irritation. "Find out!"

"If it's Ku Chow Li, I know who he is," Randall said. "Ku Chow is the head of the Chinese Mafia in Chinatown. He ran the drugs there until Data-Net shut him down."

"Ah, that makes sense," Rutland muttered, more to himself than to Randall. "Just put a close watch on him, including phone taps. But don't let him know. This is important. Don't screw it up!"

Hussein will be pleased, Rutland thought as he hung up. *I'll hand him Wells' head on a platter*. That prospect brought a smile to his face.

At Livermore Bill Eison was wrestling with his indecision. He knew Jeff and Karen were still alive, because Jeff had left him a note in the Data-Net file. Then several weeks later, Karen had left him a new telephone number. The area code looked to be in southern Mississippi. He desperately wanted to communicate with his daughter, but he feared using the Data-Net link, lest he somehow tip off their enemies.

But finally he couldn't stand it any longer. *Karen is my only family in the world*, he rationalized to himself. *I have to know she is all right.* He dialed the number through his computer modem. When he heard the telltale tone signaling a computer hookup, he knew he had access to Data-Net. He left a simple message: "How are you Karen? I love you. Dad." Then he punched in the number Karen had given him. Data-Net would automatically dial that number and transmit his message. The phone hook-up would be no more than ten seconds; then Jeff's program would remove all traces of his call. He quickly shut down the terminal link and exited the routine.

In the main AT&T terminal building, Robert Hawn recorded the call made from the Livermore facility, just as he had been instructed by Li. He pocketed the small paper tape that contained the numbers for that day, including one to the Data-Net computer in Washington. Later that evening he met Li in a bar and handed the tape over to him. In return, Li gave the telephone engineer a small package of white powder.

As Dr. Loo sorted through the calls made from the government facility, he scanned the files into the main computer. He had programmed into the machine all known locations and phone numbers for other facilities that regularly interfaced with Data-Net. It was a simple process to sort out the common calls from the uncommon.

Within seconds the computer had sorted through the files and matched most of the numbers. Only three numbers failed to match that day. Since each call made from the facility carried an ID code matching it to the phone number selected, a seldom-used number was easily matched to the time Dr. Eison placed his call.

Ah, Dr. Loo thought as the printer spewed out the single number that matched all of his criteria. *A phone hook-up was made to area code B-601. That is in southern Mississippi. I believe we have located Mr. Wells, or more correctly, Miss Eison.*

Although he hated to do so, Dr. Loo had to use the Data-Net system to isolate the phone number down to a precise location. He called the locator routine and typed in the area code and phone number.

The Data-Net system records every phone call made to any modem in the country, Dr. Loo said mentally as he punched in the instructions to initiate the search routine. *The trace file contains a record of every electronic telephone terminal used to transmit the signal. It is a simple matter to trace any call from its origin to destination, thanks to Wells' creative brain.*

The printer in the central office where Dr. Loo was working came alive. It sounded a single burst of data as the trace information printed out.

As he reviewed the data, Dr. Loo muttered, "Wells is smarter than even I have given him credit for. He has found one of the old mechanical telephone systems from which he enters the system."

No wonder I haven't been able to trap him, he thought. *The old relays take several seconds to provide the trace information. In the meantime he simply instructs the system to ignore his entry. Clever, but not clever enough, thanks to Dr. Eison. I can't locate the exact spot where he is hiding, but perhaps Rutland can.*

Unknown to Dr. Loo, Cal Rutland had already issued the order to have the telephone engineer picked up and interrogated. He quickly provided an additional copy of the report that had been transmitted to Dr. Loo. Within ten minutes, Rutland had instructed Randall to have Dr. Loo arrested.

Dr. Loo was just finishing his analysis when the two agents came through the door. Whirling as he heard the door open, he said, "Who are you, and what do you want here?"

"Dr. Kim Loo, you are under arrest," the agent in charge said with authority.

"Under arrest!" Loo shouted. "What is the charge?"

"I was directed to arrest you," the agent responded without elaboration. "You will have to ask the director."

Rutland! Loo said to himself as he felt a chill. The agents proceeded to handcuff him.

"Wait, you fools!" Loo commanded while they were handcuffing him. "I need to shut down the terminal I am using." Loo knew that Wells might have a means of monitoring his search program.

"You'll have to take that up with the director," the agent said as he shoved Loo toward the door. "My orders are to arrest you—nothing else."

Loo was shouting obscenities as the agents hauled him toward the waiting elevator, where they shoved him inside. Once they reached the office level and the doors opened, Loo saw Rutland standing in the hallway.

"You fool!" Loo shouted at Rutland. "I found Wells. Now he may be warned."

The normally placid Rutland felt a small tinge of panic within. But he hid it as he answered, "You have been trying to deal with Wells. I have a copy of the phone report you received. You were going to sell us out."

"You pathetic fool," Loo replied. "Wells doesn't need my help. I was trying to locate his headquarters so that you can shut him down.

Now if he discovers the program I was running you'll never find him again."

Somewhere inside, Cal Rutland knew Dr. Loo was speaking the truth. For the first time in his life Rutland had made an error in judgment about someone's character. His confidence faded for the first time also.

"Let him go!" Rutland snapped at the agents.

"I'm sorry, sir," the agent in charge responded timidly. "I take my orders from the director."

"Take those handcuffs off him," Rutland snarled as his eyes narrowed and his face turned dark. He knew he had only one chance that Loo might be able to give him Wells' location before Wells discovered the trap.

The agent started to object again but the anger on Rutland's face stopped him. He knew, as they all did, that Randall was a flunkie for the White House. Rutland was in charge, not Randall. He stepped behind Dr. Loo and unsnapped the cuffs.

Loo rubbed his wrists. "I must get back to the computer center. Perhaps Wells has not used the system yet." With that he stepped back into the elevator, with Rutland close behind.

In Mississippi, Karen Eison had been working on an update to Jeff's program to shut down the government's funds. The channel into Data-Net had been left open by Jeff before he went off to get some rest. At Agent Shepperd's insistence, only Jeff knew the codes to enter the Data-Net system. Shepperd knew the risk of only one person knowing the codes, but he figured that if Wells was captured or killed, their operation was over anyway. He didn't want other people trying to activate the system and perhaps tipping off the authorities to their location.

As Karen sat down at the computer console to reassemble her program, she noticed the mixture of symbols on the screen. "Daddy!" she shouted as she recognized the jumbled mess as being the same data she had seen when she heard from him before. She hurried to get Jeff. Even though he was resting, she knew he would be glad to assemble the message for her.

She leaned over the cot and said softly, "Jeff, Daddy has sent us another message. I need your help."

Jeff had heard her come into the room. He hadn't been able to sleep, but he didn't need much sleep. Mostly he just needed to let his mind relax. When he heard what Karen said, he quickly sat up in bed and said, "Your father sent a message. How?"

"Through the Data-Net channel he used before, I think," Karen answered "Why? Is something wrong?"

"Probably not," Jeff said calmly. *No sense in getting Karen upset,* he thought. But inside, his heart was doing flip flops. He always closed the loop into the system when he dialed it, but someone calling from the outside would leave a traceable series of codes. Dr. Loo just might be sharp enough to trace their location.

Jeff hurried to the terminal, sat down at the console, and typed in several commands. He never had been a great typist, but his large fingers literally flew across the keyboard as he searched all the Data-Net files for any indication that a trace had been run. When he found what he hoped would *not* be there, his head dropped. The duplicate file showed a trace had been run and, in fact, was still open. He did what he could to scramble the results, but he knew that Dr. Loo would already have his information. He didn't understand why Loo would leave the trace routine activated, but he wasn't about to wait around to find out. He closed the Data-Net channel to their location and instructed the system to make one more output. The printer beside him burped only once before shutting down.

"Is something wrong?" Karen asked when she saw the despondent look on Jeff's face.

"No, nothing," he said as he retrieved the printout. "I'm just a little tired, I guess. Here's the message from your father. He sends his love and wants to know if you're okay."

Karen accepted the printout with a smile, but inside she knew something was troubling Jeff. He wasn't very good at hiding his feelings.

Jeff *was* troubled. Both Donald Shepperd and Pastor Elder were away meeting with members of the CRC. He wasn't sure what to do.

At Data-Net headquarters in Washington, a fuming Dr. Loo hurried into the computer room. He sat down at his terminal and began to search the system files for any indication that Wells had discovered his search routine.

Relieved, Loo sat back in his chair. "It doesn't appear that Wells has been in the system," he said to Rutland. "However, he has a capacity to cloak his actions that is beyond anything I have ever seen. I would suggest that you move quickly."

After learning the location of the suspected headquarters, Rutland called Hussein to inform him.

As Rutland outlined the details of what Loo had been able to uncover Hussein said, "Splendid, my friend. You have done well. Now we will put a stop to this rebellion."

Rutland wondered what Hussein would do if he knew about the search file being open so long on Loo's terminal. *Well, there is nothing that can be done about it now,* he told himself. *The task is to kill Wells before they can relocate again.*

"We can't use Data-Net to schedule any of our people," Rutland told Hussein. "Wells would intercept the activities and warn his people."

"How will you handle it?" Hussein asked, his eyes flashing with the hate seething inside of him. He wanted Wells dead, along with Elder and the others. He had erred by not having Elder killed when he had the chance, but he would not make the same mistake twice.

Rutland had already devised a plan. After the incident in Atlanta, he would not try to draw in outside agents to attack Wells and the others. He would use four agents from New Orleans to locate and destroy the camp. Loo didn't have the exact location but it wouldn't be hard to find. There was no way they could operate a camp housing several dozen people without leaving some telltale signs.

Rutland called the detainment center in New Orleans to talk with Ralph Butcher, the area director for the secret service. The secretary could hardly believe it was really Rutland who was calling. "I'll get him for you, sir," she said, her voice shaking slightly. Talking to Rutland was almost like talking to the president.

"Yes, sir," Butcher said as he tried to get his breath. He had literally leaped up the two flights from the detention area below. It was chaos, as it had been for weeks. The orders he had been receiving from Washington were a jumbled mess. Often the arrest orders were drawn up for the wrong people. Just yesterday he had sent men out to arrest the four-year-old daughter of a local official—as a terrorist no less! He was rapidly losing the confidence of his own people.

"I want you to handle a very important job for me," Rutland said as politely as his authoritative manner would allow. "It's crucial to the president and to the country."

Butcher, a minor official in the State Department until a couple of years before, was flattered. *Do something for President Alton! I didn't even think she knew I existed.* In reality, she didn't.

Rutland outlined the plan, without telling Butcher who the people at the camp really were. "I want everyone there killed," he said emphatically. "No one is to escape!" He wished he could handle the job himself, but Wells had him isolated in Washington. But that would be over as soon as Wells was eliminated.

"Listen carefully," Rutland continued. "You must not use government vehicles or access Data-Net for anything until this is completed."

"How will we get to this camp then?" Butcher asked. He clearly wasn't the most skilled agent in the world, and he thought only as he had been trained to think in the State Department: The government is the great provider of all needs.

"Steal a car! And steal whatever you need on the way. But do not use Data-Net. Do you understand me?"

"Yes, sir," Butcher replied, though clearly he did not understand. He thought terrorists were the ones who stole stuff—not government agents.

"Call me as soon as it's over," Rutland commanded as he hung up. *Idiots,* he muttered. *The whole government is full of idiots!*

In spite of Butcher's seemingly weak personality, he had one redeeming characteristic: the ability to select capable men. It was why he was tolerated by his superiors. Using that talent, he quickly selected four totally qualified agents for the task. Butcher knew they were ruthless . . . but intelligent. They would locate the terrorists and stamp out the vermin.

The men he selected were well qualified indeed. All had been drug dealers, recruited by the government for terrorist roundup after drugs had been legalized. They were all anxious to get off of the detention detail. It was menial work that had little or no prospects for profit. To these four, profits were all that mattered. They used their roles as government agents to maximum advantage. They had no respect for Butcher, but at least he knew enough to let them alone.

They narrowed in on the area to be searched, based on the information provided by Dr. Loo. They were confident they would be able to locate the camp once they got close enough.

Their first move was to steal a car from a nearby community, which they did with no difficulty. Armed with several automatic weapons, they knew they would have no trouble securing what they needed from citizens along the way. The leader, Andy Mowr, said to the others, "Maybe we can make this trip entertaining as well as profitable."

The team left New Orleans, driving toward the town of Dentville, Mississippi. The locator map they had showed Dentville to be closest to the area Dr. Loo had identified. They were glad to be back in their chosen profession: looting.

The four had been able to supplement their incomes by dealing in some of the new drugs. But Data-Net made it difficult to convert the drugs to cash, so they had started robbing locals for whatever they needed. But the pickings hadn't really been that good lately.

"Who do you think these people are?" one of the agents asked Mowr.

"Who knows?" Mowr replied. "And who cares? From what Butcher said, they must have a pretty good racket goin'. We'll just help ourselves to whatever they have. Once we're done, they won't have any need for it. Besides, dead men won't say nothin'."

"You think there will be some women there?"

"I wouldn't be surprised boys, so watch where you shoot. We wouldn't want to hurt no ladies, would we?"

The others laughed coarsely. Under Mowr's direction, they had been raping and killing around New Orleans. Their technique was simple; they used their credentials to force their way into homes and then looted them at will. They left no witnesses behind to identify them, including women and children. But the local authorities were beginning to close in. Only two nights ago they had almost been trapped in a home they were looting. One of the neighbors had seen them enter the home and had heard the screams from inside. The police arrived only moments after they left.

"By the time we get back, the heat'll be off and we'll be able to start havin' fun again," Mowr said, snorting at his own sick humor.

They had been traveling about two hours when the agent driving said, "We're runnin' low on gas. We'll have to stop soon."

"Find us a good out-of-the way place," Mowr said. "We'll use our credit cards."

"I thought Butcher said not to use our cards."

"I mean our 'thirty-calibre' cards," Mowr said, laughing like a snorting pig.

The others laughed too. They always did what Mowr said. They were afraid of him. He seemed to have no humanity; he got real pleasure out of hurting people.

Pulling off the interstate, the driver followed a narrow rural road into a small farming town. "There's just one station here," he said to Mowr.

"That's all we need," Mowr growled, as he armed his automatic weapon. "Pull in."

As the car rolled to a stop, an old man came out of the run-down building. "You need gas?" he asked nonchalantly.

"Naw, we came in here for lunch," Mowr replied in his typically sarcastic manner.

"I don't cotton much to smart alecks, mister," the unintimidated man retorted. "If you're a comedian, you missed your turn. This is a gas station."

The others in the car started to snicker, but one glance at Mowr's face told them that would be the wrong thing to do. The last thing the station owner saw was the muzzle of Mowr's automatic poking out the window. Mowr pulled the trigger and sent a hail of bullets ripping through the startled old man.

Mowr had not wanted to kill the man before they had their gas. There was always the chance that someone would hear the shots and come to investigate. *Well, that'll be their tough luck*, Mowr thought darkly. *The old hick deserved what he got.* "Get out and fill the tank," Mowr ordered one of the agents in the back seat.

He lost no time doing as instructed and began pumping the gas. He had barely begun when someone came out of a store down the street, staring in their direction. He called out, "What happened? I thought I heard shots."

Mowr cut him down where he stood. He slumped to the dusty street just as his wife came out of the store. She began to scream when she saw her husband fall to the ground.

Mowr leveled his weapon and pulled the trigger again. The woman died instantly as she fell across her husband's lifeless body.

"Too bad," Mowr said without emotion. "She wasn't bad lookin'."

In the other stores several people were peering out their windows. They were shocked at the drama unfolding before them. In the rural community of Compton, most of the problems confronting the nation had passed them by. They had seen the Christians and Jews hauled off by government agents, but they assumed they were terrorists. They had never seen anyone killed—certainly not their own friends.

Mowr knew what had to be done. The little town was dead from the time the agents entered it. There could be no witnesses. "Fan out," he instructed the other two men, who were still in the car. "Kill 'em all."

With that, he began spraying the store windows with his weapon. As the glass shattered, screams of terror could be heard. Those who tried to flee were cut down in the streets. Those who begged for mercy were shot where they stood. In less than three minutes, the carnage was finished. Twenty-three law-abiding citizens had learned, the hard way, that their rights could be violated too.

The killing was like a narcotic to Mowr. He searched every building, looking for someone still alive that he could kill. When he was sure there were no witnesses left alive, he went back to the car.

"Are you finished?" he growled at the agent pumping the gas.

"Yes," he replied, numbed by the thought of what had just happened.

"Then shut the pump off, stupid," Mowr said, as the gas poured out of the open tank.

The other man quickly shut down the pump and replaced the gas cap. The four men piled into the car and roared away toward the interstate again.

In the back room of the hardware store, a small figure opened the trap door to the cellar where she had been taking inventory of the canning supplies. When she heard the shots, she had opened the door only enough to see outside. What she saw frightened her so badly she had slammed the door shut and cowered in the cellar. That reflex had saved her life. Now she exited to find her mother and father both lying dead on the floor of their little store. She almost fainted at the sight. The hatred that took over gave her the strength to overcome her anguish. She had seen the car as it had pulled up to the gas station across the street. She had noticed it because they seldom saw strangers in town. She tried to recall as much detail as her racing mind would allow. She knew it was a white car, a Chevrolet, with four men inside.

She reached the phone and called the county sheriff's office. Even the automated Data-Net phones had not reached her little town yet. The call was routed through Jackson where the transaction was recorded for Data-Net billing.

"Sheriff's office," the phone dispatcher answered.

"This is Melissa Graves in Compton," the young woman said sobbing. "Someone has just murdered everyone in town! I was hiding, or I would have been killed too. Please, you've got to come. It's awful!"

"Calm down now, and tell me exactly what happened," the dispatcher said in a manner she used to calm distraught callers.

Melissa told the entire story, including a brief description of the car involved. The dispatcher, who would normally not issue an alert until an officer had investigated, sensed Melissa was telling the truth. She instantly sent out an all-points bulletin to the state police. At the same time, she dispatched a local deputy to the town.

At the CRC headquarters in Dentville, Jeff was pondering what to do. He was totally comfortable working with computers, but when it came to planning for an attack, he was at a loss. *Should he evacuate the camp?* he wondered. *And if he did where would they go?* That was Shepperd's or Pastor Elder's responsibility, but he had the nagging feeling that if he did nothing they were in real trouble.

Come on Jeff, he told himself. *Use your intelligence.* No sooner had he thought it than he had an idea. *What would Rutland do if he knew where we are located? He sure couldn't get out of Washington in time himself—not with me watching his every move, or more correctly, his every transaction.*

Transactions, Jeff said silently. *Rutland would need to contact someone close to find the camp. New Orleans was the closest city of any size.* Even as he was thinking, he activated the Data-Net link. As his fingers flew across the keyboard, he initiated a search for any phone calls made from the White House to New Orleans. Immediately the system responded: a call had been made from the president's office to a number in New Orleans. He searched the matching file for an address. He found it and cross matched that address to known government facilities. They matched. Rutland, or someone, had called New Orleans almost immediately after Dr. Loo's trace had been initiated.

Going on a hunch, Jeff searched the New Orlean's police files for reports of stolen vehicles, believing that any agents assigned to locate the CRC headquarters would not take the chance of being tracked through a government vehicle. There were hundreds of stolen car reports in New Orleans, but only one that coincided with the time and location he was interested in: a white 1999 Chevrolet.

Jeff set up a routine to search for subsequent police reports involving any vehicles matching that description. There was just one. A white Chevrolet carrying four men was involved in a multiple homicide in a small town in Mississippi, about two hundred miles from New Orleans—on a direct line with the CRC's headquarters. Coincidence? *Well, maybe,* Jeff thought to himself. *But on such coincidences, wars have been won or lost.* He had to decide what to do, in a hurry.

Mowr and his team of cutthroats continued on in a direct line toward Dentville, Mississippi. "Shouldn't we ditch this car?" the driver asked Mowr. "What if someone spotted us back there?"

"Don't be stupid," Mowr growled. "There was nobody back there left to spot us. We've got nearly a full tank of gas left. I'm not dumpin' this car now."

The others knew they were violating the cardinal rule of an assault mission: They had committed a crime and continued on in the same vehicle. By now there would be a stolen car report out too. But they did what Mowr ordered; they knew he wouldn't hesitate to do to them what he had done to the people of Compton.

Jeff decided what he had to do. He patched into the Mississippi State Patrol emergency network. He knew it was a risk; it left him vulnerable to a trace within Data-Net as long as the link was open. If Dr. Loo was monitoring, it was possible to identify the source. But it was a risk he had to run. If the attack on Compton was the work of an assault team, the CRC camp was in grave danger. The agents could be closing in even now.

Jeff sent an all-points bulletin to Highway Patrol stations from Compton to Dentville, giving the description of the stolen vehicle and the four men. Jeff was laying out all his cards. If the team was not headed in a straight line to Dentville, he had just diverted all the Highway Patrol units in southern Mississippi to the wrong place.

At the Mississippi Highway Patrol stations, the bulletin had just

been received, notifying all units to take up positions along the interstate and all main roads between Compton and Dentville. The all-
points bulletin said the men in the car were armed and should be
considered extremely dangerous.

Mowr ordered the driver to pull off the interstate and find a back
road into Dentville. It was nothing he could put his finger on, but
somehow he knew the police were alerted to them. He had made his
living most of his life by obeying his instincts; he wouldn't ignore them
now. Mowr was a man without conscience. He felt nothing for the
people he had killed, including those in Compton. They were just in
the wrong place at the wrong time. To Mowr, the only life that counted
was his.

"We're gettin' close," Mowr said to the others. "I can smell it. Pull
into that farm. We need some information."

Mowr knew only one way to do anything: brute force. He intended to grab one of the locals, find out what he could about any
unusual activity in the area, kill the hostage, and attack the target he
had been assigned. He knew they had to be close, but his information
only narrowed the search area to a few square miles.

Jeff called all the men in his camp together and told them what he
knew, or at least suspected, about the assault team headed their way.
Once the highway patrol had been alerted, all they could do was wait
until something happened.

The former FBI agents working with the CRC had their orders
from Shepperd: they were to take no chances if attacked. Although
Shepperd had agreed to Elder's decision not to attack government
forces, he did not interpret that to mean they could not defend themselves. His agents were armed at all times. In this emergency, they
went into their hidden cache of weapons and brought out some bigger
artillery. If the assault team hit their compound, they would not find
them as passive as most of the people they confronted.

"What the . . ." the startled driver said as he pulled onto the dirt
road leading to the farm. There was a large tree blocking most of the
road.

Suddenly alert, Mowr's eyes darted back and forth looking for any
signs of a trap. He had set enough traps himself to be wary of anything
out of the ordinary.

"It looks like it blew down in the last couple of days," the driver
said, as he looked closer at the pine tree laying across the road. He felt
relieved. His nerves were on edge since the thing in Compton. They
should have dumped the car already; that much he knew.

"See if you can get around it," Mowr ordered, even as he armed
his weapon. Everything looked normal, except for the tree. It was pos-

sible that whoever lived on the farm simply lacked the equipment to move it.

The driver eased the car onto the shoulder of the road. Even as he did so, several armed men watched from their well-concealed positions in the corn field. As the car swung around the tree, the driver saw a large silver-colored cylindrical tank, hitched to a tractor, directly in his path. He swerved to the right to avoid hitting it. Suddenly the ground gave way beneath the car's tires, and it lurched to one side as the frame bottomed out in the ditch.

Mowr let out a string of obscenities at the driver. He couldn't know that just such a mishap had been designed into the old road. "Get out and see how bad it is," Mowr ordered the others. He sat in the car with his weapon out of sight . . . but ready.

As the three men stepped out of the car, someone shouted from the field, "Lay down your weapons and put your hands over your heads. You're surrounded."

By pure chance, Mowr had found the compound he was looking for. But instead of catching them by surprise, thanks to Jeff's warning, they were ready.

The startled agents dropped their weapons shouting, "Don't shoot. We're government agents . . ."

"Shut up you fools," Mowr snapped. He raised his weapon to spray the field where the shout had come from.

When the ex-FBI agent saw the barrel of the automatic weapon peek over the car windowsill, he reacted instinctively. The LAARS rocket he was aiming was armed and ready. He squeezed the trigger gently and the solid motor rocket roared into action. It covered the distance to the car in less than a second, even before Mowr could fire a single round. The explosion of the rocket and the silver cylinder obliterated the car and the men who had been riding in it.

The fireball was visible from a mile away. A highway patrolman positioned at one of the county road blocks saw the fireball as it erupted. "What the . . ." he said aloud. He had never seen anything like that in his life. The sound reached him a few seconds later with a deafening roar. He fired up his engine and raced in the direction of the explosion.

When the patrolman arrived at the farm, only a solitary figure was visible. One of the ex-FBI agents dressed in coveralls was standing by the entrance road.

"What happened?" the startled patrolman asked as he saw the burning wreck.

"Some fools in a white car drove into the propane tank I had hitched to my tractor," the agent said in a Mississippi drawl. "Had guns stickin' out of every window. I guess they were gonna rob the place. Serves 'em right I guess. Besides, we don't have much to steal."

"You're very lucky," the patrolman said. "These are probably the killers we've been looking for. They killed twenty-three people in Compton. Wiped out most of the town. I'll get some of our forensic people out here to verify who they are. Just don't touch anything."

"You betcha," the agent said casually as the patrolman called in on his mobile phone. *It's a good thing we had that propane tank handy*, he thought silently. *It went up like a bomb when the LAARS hit it.*

The state police took pictures of the crash site and did a forensic analysis on the bodies. Satisfied that they were the men who attacked Compton, they removed the bodies and the demolished car.

Activity on the farm was slowed for several days until the area was cleared. Then Shepperd and Elder returned to the headquarters.

"We have to move quickly," Shepperd told the others the first evening they were back together. "It's only a matter of time until Rutland tries again. The next time it might not be a bunch of thugs. It could be the Army."

"I agree with Donald," Elder told the group. "It's time we pulled out all the stops. If we get caught, there will be no second chance."

In Washington, Cal Rutland knew his plan had failed. Butcher had taken off, and there was no word from the men he sent out. The CRC was getting bolder, and unless they were stopped immediately, the takeover could be in jeopardy.

THOMAS GALT

The largest media corporation in the world, the Galt Network, owned twenty newspapers, the World News Network, and the World Satellite Broadcasting System. The head of this conglomerate was Thomas Galt. Galt traveled throughout the world regularly checking on his empire. But when he was in America, he made his home in a small town just outside of Atlanta.

For years he had led the media assault against Christianity. When the government propaganda against Christians began, he gave maximum coverage to the stories. The liberal perspective of the other networks paled when compared to that of Galt's. He felt Christians were bigoted and tried to force their "Victorian" values on everyone else. Since Galt had lived a decadent lifestyle for most of his years, the attack on Christianity was his defense mechanism against the truth.

During the last year, however, Galt had begun to doubt his convictions about everything, including Christianity. He had often fought the Christians on abortion, the Crack Babies Bill, legalized drugs, and many other issues he personally believed in. His irritation over their absoluteness had motivated him to support any issue opposed by John Elder and his "mob," as he referred to them. But now, having observed the state of the world since all of his pet issues had been implemented, he knew he had been wrong. Clearly the legalization of drugs had spread their use throughout American society. Where the liberals had once been certain that the legalization of drugs would reduce crime, the exact opposite had happened. The former drug lords became legitimized businessmen, but youth gangs had taken over the illicit drug trade. The use of cheap substitutes that killed thousands of users every month became the new underground drug scene.

Once the Crack Babies Bill was passed and became law, it was assumed that humanity would benefit. Instead, a huge new business had been developed. Women on drugs were solicited to have children just so they could be processed for their organs. Wealthy clients, many of them his own friends, would place orders for mothers with compatible blood types to be artificially inseminated so that the organs of their offspring could be harvested. In their quest for eternal life, the wealthy were literally killing their own children.

Galt, now almost eighty, had built his company from a small advertising agency in Atlanta to a worldwide empire. In the process he had gone through several wives, lost his own children to drugs and alcohol, and lived a wretched, tormented life. He was simply tired of life and what was happening to Christians and Jews in America. The evidence was overwhelming that they were being persecuted, perhaps even murdered. He had been in the media business long enough that he didn't believe his own publicity. He knew the facts could be selectively skewed to make them appear any way the broadcaster desired. He also knew this latest information about the Society was true. He had been contacted more than a few times by influential men, including Jason Franklin, who wanted him to join a secret society. Several years back he had even attended one of their meetings. All that garbage about serving mankind and honoring the one they called the "Great Leader" reminded him of a college fraternity. The whole idea was ridiculous to him and he had told them so.

He had helped to spread the propaganda about Christian terrorists through his media empire, but he really was tired of it all. Death would be a relief. But in the back of his mind was a nagging doubt, planted there by his grandmother. She had been a devoted Christian and had often told him Bible stories when he was a child. Some of them he remembered even now, more than seventy years later— especially the one about the rich man and Lazarus. What if he was wrong? What if, instead of finding peace at death, he did go to a place of eternal torment?

He had gone through this argument with himself many times. There was no resolution to it. *Maybe it is just the addle-brained thinking of a senile old man,* he thought. He often thought about God. But, he reasoned, if he were God he would never allow someone like Thomas Galt into his kingdom. He had done too many things to too many people in his climb to the top. And he had even used his influence to help kill many of the people who followed God.

In one of those divine coincidences, Donald Shepperd called Thomas Galt just as he was seriously considering suicide. The boldest move the CRC group had ever made was about to take place and they needed the help of a major network. Since WNN was the biggest network Shepperd decided to contact Galt. The decision was made after Jeff searched the records and verified that Galt was not a member of the Society. He had never donated funds to any of their hundreds of front organizations, nor had he attended more than one of their leadership meetings. Wells had obtained Galt's private home number at his farm near Atlanta. All Shepperd could do was hope he was actually there.

When the phone rang the housekeeper answered, "May I help you?" She was accustomed to answering the private line without revealing any information.

"Yes. My name is Shepperd. I work with Pastor John Elder's organization. Ask Mr. Galt if he will talk with me for one minute. Tell him it's critical."

The long-time housekeeper was also accustomed to peculiar calls to one of the world's wealthiest and most eccentric men. She pressed the hold button and told Galt, "Sir, there is a Mr. Shepperd on the line. Says he works with Pastor Elder. He wants to talk with you. Says it's critical."

"Tell him I'm not here," Galt growled as he sipped his third brandy in the last hour. It didn't seem to help dull his conscience any more, he noted wearily.

"He ain't here," the housekeeper said with no conviction.

"Wait!" Shepperd said forcefully. Now at least he knew Galt was there. "Tell him I have information about the Society."

Punching the hold button, she repeated what Shepperd had told her. "He says he has information about the Society."

"I don't care . . ." Galt started to say. Then he stopped. "No, I'll talk to him."

The housekeeper carried the cordless phone over to where Galt was sitting and handed it to him.

"This is Galt. What do you want?"

"My name is Shepperd . . ."

Galt cut him off. "I know who you are. You're the FBI agent working with the terrorists."

"You know better than that, Galt. They're no more terrorists than Little Orphan Annie. We have information that will sink the Society once and for all, but we need your help."

"My help!" Galt almost choked on his drink. "We haven't exactly been allies, you know."

"If you're a real news man you'll want to hear the truth," Shepperd snapped. "If not, then God will use someone else." The comment even surprised Shepperd. He really did believe what John Elder had said recently. "If God is for us, who can stand against us?"

"Why should I help a bunch of idiots who are against everything progressive?" Galt said without any real conviction.

"Because you have seen the price Americans have paid for much of that progress," Shepperd responded. He could sense Galt's softening. He had hit a sensitive spot. He continued, "You and the others in the media have done these people a lot of harm. But I can tell you that not one of them bears you any malice. Now we want our country back, and you can help."

"How?" Galt asked.

"I'll send the instructions to your home today. After you have a chance to read them I'll contact you."

"No!" Galt said with an uncharacteristic sense of urgency. "I want to see this group of ragtag radicals you're involved with for myself."

That surprised Shepperd. He hadn't really expected Galt to get involved at all. Why would he want to check them out personally? Maybe he had a trap in mind.

"I can't do that," Shepperd said. "There is too much risk."

"For whom, Mr. Shepperd? You or me? If you won't comply, I want nothing to do with it."

Shepperd thought for a moment, then answered, "Okay, but it will have to be on my terms. I'll have someone pick you up at the MARTA station in Marietta at six o'clock this evening."

"I'll be there," Galt said as he hung up. *Now why did I do that?* he asked himself. *Maybe I am getting senile.*

Shepperd decided that they had to take a chance on Galt. They might be able to pull off the plan without him, but there was no certainty that any of the other media types would help either. He placed a call to his contact in Atlanta, filling him in on the details of the meeting with Galt.

At six o'clock that evening an old man got off the MARTA train and stood just inside the terminal. Several tough-looking youths were milling around outside the terminal, and there appeared to be no security guards on duty.

A man could get mugged in this place, Galt said to himself. He wished he had not made his bodyguard stay home, but he knew the presence of an armed guard would probably have scared off the people he was to meet. Now he wasn't so sure it had been a good idea.

Two of the young toughs entered the station and eyed him carefully. "What you doin' here, ol' man?" the smaller of the two asked.

"You talking to me?" Galt responded nonchalantly.

"Yeah, ol' man. Where's your wheelchair?"

"I left it with your babysitter," Galt said with the same grit that had put him on the top of the pile.

The youth turned red-faced, as his companion laughed. "It don't look like he knows who you are," the other teen-ager quipped.

"You shut up!" the smaller teen said through clenched teeth, adding a few more choice words. "I'm gonna cut you up, ol' man," he spat out as he clicked the switchblade open.

"If that's what you've got planned, you'd better bring a lunch, sonny," Galt said as he gripped his cane. "I took care of better men than you when I was twelve."

The youth took his position in front of Galt and started to swing the knife back and forth. Just then the turnstile doors swung and a large man stepped inside. "You can go now, guys," he said grinning. "He's alone."

The youths smiled back and slapped his hand as they exited. "Later, brother," said the knife-wielding youth as he passed the big man.

Galt sat down on the bench, his energy depleted.

"Sorry about that, Mr. Galt, but I had to know if you were really alone. I guess you are."

"Yes," Galt replied. "Though I had my doubts about the wisdom of it a few seconds ago. You're with Shepperd?"

"Yes, I'm Paul Brown," the man answered Galt as he shook his hand with a firm grip. "I'm really glad to meet you, Mr. Galt. We should get started; it's a long trip."

With Brown leading the way, Galt followed him to the waiting van. Once inside, another man ran a transmitter detector over his body.

"You gentlemen don't seem to trust anyone," Galt commented when the second man signaled that the sweep was negative.

"No, that's not true; we trust a great many people," Brown said. "I hope you'll be one of them."

Galt sat in silence as they drove away. In a few minutes they came to the old Peachtree-Dekalb Airport, which was all but abandoned except for a few private planes. As they approached one of the hangars, a sleek business jet was being tugged out.

"You mean we're going to fly?" Galt asked.

"Yes, sir," Brown answered. "We had to relocate a few months back. It seems the government didn't appreciate us."

"I heard about that," Galt responded. "A friend in Washington said you boys left our politicians a little red-faced." The story about the aborted bust in Atlanta had eventually spread throughout Washington, where there were few secrets. Rutland had seen to it that no news of the second attempt was ever known.

As the jet roared into the sky, Galt asked, "Do you mind telling me where we're going?"

"Sorry, sir, I can't do that. In fact, if you don't object, we'll pull the curtain shut. It would be better if you didn't know where we're located just now. No offense."

"None taken," Galt replied.

After making a wide sweep to the south, the pilot pointed the plane toward Dentville, Mississippi, where another landing strip was prepared for their arrival. Even if Galt was working with the government to pinpoint their new location, he would have a difficult time orienting himself. Twenty minutes later the plane slowed and began its approach into Dentville.

It touched down with hardly a bump and Galt said, "You have a good pilot."

"Yes, sir," Brown agreed. "He's an Air Force general."

After the plane rolled to a stop, General Abbott made his way back to the passenger compartment. "Welcome to . . ." then he paused, thought about it, and said, "Welcome to the real America, Mr. Galt. I'm Abbott."

"I know you by reputation, General. I understand you helped put a stop to a military takeover."

"Some in the administration might say I helped with a military takeover, Mr. Galt. Only time will judge."

Once they reached the waiting van, Thomas Galt found the curtains drawn again. "I see you're a cautious group of men," he said to General Abbott.

"You would be too, sir, if you had had the entire might of the United States government directed against you for as long as these people have."

"I suppose so," Galt agreed, "but it would seem they have given as well as they got."

"Not so, Mr. Galt. These people have had their constitutional rights denied, their families arrested, their properties confiscated, and their lives threatened. And you, sir, were part and parcel of their misery."

"We only reported the news as we saw it," Galt said without any conviction in his voice.

"No, Mr. Galt. You heard what you wanted to hear. Then you reported the news that would give you the highest ratings, not the truth. It would seem the founders of this nation did well in protecting the rights of a free press, but they never envisioned the abuse that it could lead to. The only crime that the Christians are guilty of is being courageous enough to stand up for their convictions. The only crime the Jews are guilty of is their parentage."

"There was evidence that the Christians organized terrorist squads," Galt countered. "They attacked the police when they couldn't force their way on the public."

"You don't believe that any more than I do, Galt," the general said angrily. "You'll see evidence that the Society staged the whole event, and the media bought into it—hook, line, and sinker, as the old saying goes."

Galt sat silently for the remainder of the trip. General Abbott could not have known the real impact of his words. They confirmed Galt's worst fears: he had allowed himself to be used to undermine the country that had given him so much. In his younger years he had been tough but fair. Now he was just greedy, and for what? Power? Wealth? What? *Maybe just greed itself*, he thought.

The van stopped at the farm serving as CRC headquarters where several men were waiting to greet the elderly Galt.

"Thank you for coming," a middle-aged man with a pleasant smile said, as he opened the van door.

"You're John Elder, aren't you?" Galt said. "I recognize your face from pictures."

"Yes, sir," Elder replied. "You certainly carried my photograph enough in your newspaper," he added, without any tone of bitterness. "Let me introduce you to my friends. I believe you already know Donald Shepperd."

"By voice only, I'm afraid," Galt said as he weakly extended his hand.

"And this is Jeff Wells . . . and his fiancée Karen Eison."

"Jeff, I know you by reputation," Galt said. "I understand you have been a real thorn in the side of the government."

"We do what we can," Jeff said with a sly grin on his face.

"We have some things to show you, Mr. Galt," Shepperd said. "And not a lot of time."

The next three hours were spent reviewing the data that had been collected about the Society and the role Society members played in the assassinations of the Supreme Court Justices, President Hunt, and a host of other government officials.

The evidence that it was the Society's infiltrators who initiated the violence against the police in the riots two years earlier was irrefutable. But the final straw for Galt was the evidence gathered through

Wells' snooping in the government's own records that the deception of the media had been planned, funded, and executed by members of the Society.

When Shepperd finished his barrage of information, the effect on Thomas Galt was exactly what he had hoped for. He was a man shaken in his basic convictions. "What do you want me to do?" Galt asked as his trembling hand tried to hold his pipe still enough to light it.

"We need to launch one final assault on the Society, and we need your help," Elder said. "We know if the government happened upon this camp and captured us, it would be only a matter of weeks until the emphasis would shift back to their side. Right now, Americans are fed up with the electronic system called Data-Net and, consequently, with the Alton administration. But that's only because Jeff is able to force errors into the system."

"And although we still control the military at this point, the administration might just win in a showdown. After all," General Abbott said as he reached over to light Galt's pipe, "the president is still the commander-in-chief. How well would the nation sleep knowing that Hussein had control of three thousand nuclear weapons?"

"What do you want from me?" Galt asked, trembling.

Jeff outlined the plan for Galt. When he was finished, Galt said, "If I didn't know what you people had already accomplished, I would say you were nuts. Are you sure you can do what you are proposing?"

"We have no choice," Abbott said angrily. "Hussein is certainly nobody's fool. He knows that we're able to watch his every step, thanks to Jeff here. He has something in the wings that none of us wants to risk. We can't afford to wait and see if he's crazy enough to do it." He then explained what they knew about Hussein's plans to obliterate the camps with nuclear bombs.

"You can't be serious," Galt said as he tried to imagine someone evil enough to destroy two million innocent people.

"Deadly serious," the general replied. "We must act quickly, and decisively."

"I'll help," Thomas Galt said with an excitement he hadn't felt in years. "You just be sure the other pieces are in place."

"Now let's talk about something important," John Elder said with a smile. "Mr. Galt, if you died today, do you know where you would spend eternity?"

Thomas Galt was sure he knew exactly where he would spend eternity, and it frightened him so much he couldn't sleep at night. His pride kept him from answering honestly. Instead he said, "I guess I'm not really sure."

John Elder spent the next hour discussing how Galt could be forgiven of his sins and could be certain he would spend eternity with Jesus Christ. It was not until Shepperd interrupted for the tenth time, saying they had to get Galt back to Atlanta to make the preparations, that the meeting broke up.

"I'll think about what you said," Galt said, shaking Elder's hand warmly. *There is a man who knows what he believes and is willing to die for it*, Galt thought as he headed back to the van. *I'm only willing to die to get away from the things I don't believe in.*

On the way back, Galt noticed that the curtains were not drawn. When he asked why, the driver said, "Pastor Elder said it would not be necessary." Galt was impressed more than he let on. Elder certainly was a man of his convictions.

A desperate meeting was taking place in the White House Oval Office, with three people in attendance: Amir Hussein, Kathy Alton, and Cal Rutland. The room had been swept clean with the most sophisticated electronic sensors in existence. Two miniature microphones had been detected in the room. One was concealed in the overhead light fixture. The other was truly ingenious. It was no larger than a penny and was actually planted in Kathy Alton's purse. Rutland knew the range of the small device had to be very limited, so he had the sweep extended to detect the base station. He was shocked to discover that his own secretary had hidden the transmitter in her desk. She was out sick or he would probably have shot her on the spot. What Rutland didn't know was that all the Christian sympathizers had been warned to get out of Washington.

"The room is clean," Rutland said to Hussein. He could see the insanity in Hussein clearly now. As more of the system had broken down over the last several weeks, Hussein's communications had digressed to fits of rage and wild rantings.

"We will not lose what we have gained!" Hussein railed at the two who represented his inner circle. Since the death of Jason Franklin and the disappearance of Marla West, the circle had grown much smaller. President Alton was still a true devotee. Rutland was still committed to the Society, but he had less and less confidence in Hussein. Rutland was a pragmatist. He knew the noose was tightening. Already Kim Lou had fled, leaving the Data-Net system in shambles. Rutland had not even told Hussein about that.

"We will move immediately on the plan," Hussein said as he paced around the room. "We have two thousand agents ready to go."

"Yes, sir," Alton agreed. "Since the agents are unable to use Data-Net to secure transportation, they will steal the vehicles they need."

At the mention of Data-Net, Hussein's face darkened. "We have them," he said in a hiss. "Wells is smart, but he is not infallible. Dr. Loo will make the system impenetrable. And with the bombs in place, the military will be forced to comply."

"Yes, sir," Alton agreed again. "The bombs will turn the tide for us."

Rutland thought he was going to be sick. The president agreed with anything Hussein said without question. He knew that at best they might round up transportation for two hundred men. How they would transfer three more bombs to the camps without the military intercepting them, nobody knew. With Wells in charge of the system and Gorman in charge of the spy satellites, they would know before the mob moved a hundred miles. Since Dr. Loo had fled, he knew they had virtually no access to Data-Net.

"I disagree, sir," Rutland said firmly. "It would be better to send a small group of agents into the area to secure the camps first." Rutland had already decided what he must do: flee to an area where Data-Net didn't control everything—perhaps Japan—but he would have to make his move before the whole country came down on them.

"You had your chance," President Alton said as she glared at Rutland, "and you blew it. We will crush the traitors while they sleep. We will not fail."

Rutland felt his face flush. He knew the plan was doomed. And with it his only hope of escaping. "You are an idiot!" Rutland shouted at Alton.

"Quiet!" Hussein commanded in a voice that was somehow not his own. His eyes mirrored his tormented soul. "I will decide what happens now," he shouted maniacally. "The first bomb will be exploded just as planned. We will also transport a bomb to Camp Two. This will give the military something to think about."

"The military won't stand idly by," Rutland said bluntly. He knew he was on thin ice with Hussein, but he was desperate to stall the plan. It was suicidal.

"Next we will attack the SAC base at Hanover," Hussein railed, now out of control again. "We will capture the bombers housed there and equip them with cruise missiles. Once we do that, the military must obey. If they do not, we will destroy their command centers with hydrogen bombs."

"But, sir . . ." Rutland started to say, but he stopped as he saw Hussein's eyes. There was a madness in them that told him the Leader was beyond reason. Hussein was living in a dream world created by his own insanity.

THE SOCIETY EXPOSED

At eight o'clock on the evening of September 12, 2003, Jeff Wells typed in the command for Data-Net to re-program all satellite demodulators to channel six on Westar Four, the channel operated by WNN.

Owner Thomas Galt had instructed the network chief to take the video feed from a laser-optic telephone line, also controlled by Wells. At exactly eight o'clock, all the networks and independent stations had their regular programming interrupted with a message from Thomas Galt, who had not made a public appearance in more than two decades.

In the message, prepared at the Mississippi camp, Galt addressed the nation: "My fellow Americans, we have interrupted this regularly scheduled program to bring you a message of vital importance. As you know, the government of the United States is in turmoil. But what you may not know is that there is a secret Society operating within our government that has initiated and sustained this turmoil for the purpose of taking over our country."

At the White House, Cal Rutland's phone rang. When he picked it up, it was President Alton, who asked frantically, "Are you watching television?"

"No," Rutland replied. "I rarely watch television."

"Well, you'd better turn it on right now. Thomas Galt of WNN is talking about the Society."

"What!!" Rutland shouted as he reached for the channel selector.

"The message is being broadcast on every channel in the country. Someone has tapped into the main distribution system and re-programmed it." The president added soberly, "It would appear that our time has run out."

"It has to be Wells again," Rutland blurted out. "We should have killed him when . . ."

"Watch what you say," Alton warned. "We're probably all being monitored."

Rutland turned his attention to the television. Galt was saying: "The messages you will hear were taped from actual conversations within the White House. I trust it will be as clear to you as it was to me earlier that we have been the willing dupes of an evil group of power-hungry people determined to control this nation."

The sound track being aired carried conversations between President Alton and Amir Hussein regarding the elimination of all Christians and Jews. The nation heard the discussions and plots to kill the secretary of defense, as well as the actual instructions from Hussein to Cal Rutland to eliminate Fred Lively, the acting attorney general. The video image showed photographs of Hussein, Alton, Rutland, and several other members of the Society together.

Then suddenly the discussions shifted to the detention camps and the conversation between Hussein and Rutland on the use of nuclear bombs to eliminate all evidence of their existence. Superimposed on the screen were satellite photographs of the camps, along with photographs from within the camps, obviously taken by someone with a hidden camera. Interspersed were recordings from within the camps themselves of guards cursing at the inmates and the obvious sounds of people being beaten. In the background the cries of women and the screams of children could be heard clearly.

The effect is perfect. Rutland thought somberly. *Not too dramatic, but very convincing. They have done a good job.*

The final scenes were the video tapes of the shooting of President Hunt while the original transcript of the speech he was planning to deliver was read over the air. But even more incriminating was the replay of the taped conversation between Cal Rutland and Jason Franklin in which Rutland was giving the details of how the Hunt assassination would be carried out. His final comments were that one of the plants in the CRC would do the assassination so there would be no link back to the Society.

Rutland sat mesmerized by the presentation. He realized that many of their most secret conversations had been monitored and recorded. The group watching them had not even tried to warn those who were to be eliminated. They were content to wait and bide their time, knowing that when the nation was ready they would present their evidence. He also knew the timing was perfect. The country was fed up with the cash-less system and fed up with chaos. The very methods the Society had used to cause the disruption in the economy were now allied against them.

Only Donald Shepperd and a select few others would ever know that most of the information came from monitoring by the Mossad. For years they had tapped the phones in the White House and planted a variety of listening devices throughout the executive offices. For obvious reasons, they did not wish the information to become public.

Cal Rutland took out the .357 revolver he always carried and laid it on the desk. Then he took out the bottle of vodka that he seldom touched, poured himself a large swallow, and put the gun to his head. His last thought was, *I wonder what eternity will be like.*

The report from the large-caliber weapon rang throughout the nearly empty White House. In her quarters, President Alton jumped when she heard it. She knew immediately that it was Rutland. *I wish I had the courage to kill myself,* Kathy Alton thought as she sniffed the white poison that had become a part of her daily routine. At first she had told herself she only needed it when her nerves were jangled. Then it seemed that they were jangled more all the time, so she used the white powder more frequently.

"I wonder what they will do with me?" she said idly as the drug began to take effect. "I don't think they would execute a president." *That means Grant will be president,* she thought lazily as the drug made her mind float. "Well, who cares," she said out loud. "One day we will rule the world. If not now, then later." She decided she should take a good hot bath. She ran the tub full of warm water and stepped into it. It felt so good. She just needed to relax. As she slumped down in the tub, she passed out from the combined effects of the drug and the warm water. The maid would find her when she came in to turn down the sheets on the president's bed.

In his study, Amir Hussein was unaware of the events that were taking place around him. He had just been thinking about how he would exact punishment on his enemies. Suddenly he was gripped with a fear unlike any that he had ever known. It was as if the power that he had used so often on others was now being directed against him. It was so overwhelming that he thought he would faint. He fell to his knees praying, "Lord, don't abandon me now. We are so close to winning. Your kingdom will be established."

In his mind, Hussein heard just the whisper of an evil he had never faced before.

"You have failed me, just like all the others," the voice said. "I will have to start all over again. You will be tormented until eternity ends," the voice hissed.

"But, Lord, I have served you with my life," Hussein heard himself say as he groveled on the floor in agony.

"Your life!" the voice said with the sharpness of a cobra's strike. "Your life means nothing. Do you hear? You could have had riches and honor when I ruled, but now you will see how I reward those who fail me."

Hussein felt his throat constricting. He was unable to breathe. "No, No!" he screamed with his last breath. "I don't want to die!" The next instant Amir Hussein felt his soul being pulled down into a dark abyss. He was frightened beyond all control. All he could do was scream, but no sound came out as he fell into the blackness.

The next day Vice President Grant announced that President Alton had suffered a fatal accident while taking a bath and had drowned. The Chief Justice of the Supreme Court immediately swore Grant in as president. The official ceremonies would take place at an appropriate time after President Alton's burial.

President Grant announced that effective immediately all citizens who had been arrested under the Alton administration would be granted their freedom and the full protection of the Constitution. He also recalled the Congress and announced that elections would be held for the presidency the following November.

He further announced that a full investigation would be conducted into the activities of the group known as the Society and the role they had played in the attempted takeover of the government.

"The government and military leaders who participated in the unlawful arrest and detention of American citizens will be prosecuted to the full extent of the law," he promised. The word went out that some of the lower-echelon people would be granted amnesty in exchange for information on the Society. The president let it be known that the decision to prosecute or not would be based on full cooperation with the investigation.

Suddenly there was a deluge of people who confessed to being duped by the Society and who asked for amnesty from the Grant administration. In his first official act, President Grant issued a proclamation stating that members of the group known as the Society would not be considered for amnesty unless and until they resigned any government or military positions they held. Nearly three thousand men and women resigned and requested amnesty, or at least consideration for a lesser crime than treason.

Jeff Wells was appointed by President Grant to oversee the dismantling of the Data-Net system as soon as feasible. An independent committee of non-politicians was appointed to design a system to help re-stabilize the American currency and economy.

The single greatest proponent of media reform was Thomas Galt. He set up a foundation to oversee his vast empire and became a crusader for the cause of Christianity. According to his own testimony, he now knew that the only hope for mankind was a total surrender to Jesus Christ as Savior.

"The intent of man's heart is evil," Galt shared on his prime time program called "Face the Truth." "It is only through the power of God's Son that we can change that heart."

His open testimony helped to spark the greatest revival of Christianity the world had ever seen. Nearly forty million Americans, according to the WNN Insta-pol, confessed their sins and accepted Christ as their Savior.

As John Elder told Galt, when he was remarking about this phenomenon, "It was bound to be, Tom. We had a hundred thousand Christians praying every day—at least half of them for you alone."

When the detention camps were opened, it was found that nearly two hundred thousand men, women, and children had died of starvation, neglect, or abuse before Jeff had been able to divert food and clothing to them. A memorial was established in Washington to honor these who had fallen in the defense of their faith. When the NCLU protested this violation of separation of church and state, the response, according to Insta-pol, was that nearly 90 percent of all Americans supported the government's position. As Thomas Galt so aptly said, "A nation without God is a nation without a conscience." The NCLU quickly withdrew their opposition as their funding dropped to a record low in the wake of the revival.

After the camps were closed, and the survivors were sent home, Donald Shepperd went to Chicago to check on the Cofers. He located Mary Cofer and the children back in their home, trying to get their lives back together. Her husband, Bob, had been killed while trying to escape from one of the camps. Through Shepperd's efforts, Bob Cofer became the symbol of the nation's conscience.

"We thought such things could not happen here," Shepperd said to Thomas Galt on "Face the Truth." "Instead, what Americans discovered is that the only difference between us and the Nazis or the Communists is opportunity. Man is inherently evil and needs redemption. Jesus Christ became that Redeemer."

John Elder found that his wife, Julia, was well and in good spirits. She had been secreted from one CRC camp to another for nearly a year. The other Christians had protected her identity so that she could not be used as a hostage against her husband.

Jeff and Karen were married in a simple ceremony, if there is such a thing, in the White House gardens.

What no one would know for another fifty years was that at the moment of Amir Hussein's death, another was chosen to prepare the world for the final conflict that would eventually pit the people of God against the forces of Satan.

"The one thing that we can be certain of," John Elder said to his congregation the first Sunday he spoke from the pulpit of his new church, "is that people have short memories. We weren't the generation to see the ascension of the Antichrist. But one day he will ascend, and that generation will not escape the persecution. Perhaps God in His infinite wisdom has given us a second chance. Let us pray that we will not waste it."

ABOUT THE AUTHOR

Larry Burkett is the founder and president of a nonprofit organization dedicated to teaching principles of managing money. Larry has degrees in marketing and finance and for several years served as a manager in the space program at Cape Canaveral, Florida, as well as vice president of an electronics manufacturing firm.

He hosts a daily radio program heard on over 1,000 stations and has written more than 15 books, including the best sellers, *Your Finances in Changing Times, Business by the Book , Debt-Free Living,* and *The Coming Economic Earthquake.* Larry and his wife, Judy, currently reside in Gainesville, Georgia. They have four grown children and six grandchildren.